Dread Spring

Elizabeth F. Shearly

ISBN (paperback): 9781738890040

ISBN (ebook): 9781738890033

For more information, visit www.elizabethshearly.ca

Editor: Maggie Morris, The Indie Editor

This is a work of fiction. The story and characters are strictly products of the author's imagination, and any resemblance to real people, living or dead, is unintentional and entirely coincidental.

Content Notes

Kidnapping, domestic abuse, pregnancy, death of family member, occasional use of obscenities, gunshot wound.

Please see the book's web page at www.elizabethshearly.ca for detailed content notes.

Dedication

I wrote and set *Dread Spring* on the unceded land of the Omàmìwininìwag (Algonquin), Anishinabewaki ᐊᓂᔑᓈᐯᐏ ᐧᐊᑭ, and Kanien'kehá:ka (Mohawk). I am a settler here. Colonial place names are commonly used in the region, and I have used them throughout this book. Please see the full Land Acknowledgement at the back of the book for more information and recommendations of post-apocalyptic sci-fi books by Indigenous authors from the region.

Chapter One

Log: The City, Richard A. Phillips, Deputy ECM, 13 May 20—

Glitch discovered in the City's town control mechanism. Towns' range greatly reduced. Currently exploring remedies.

A chirp and trill broke the morning silence, and a finger of dread curled in Chloe's gut. Outside, the little robin landed and hopped across the bare yard, carefully avoiding the last little patch of snow that hadn't yet melted. The excuses were wearing thin—testing the soil couldn't be delayed forever. The grandfather clock in the corner of the dining room ticked over and struck seven a.m.

While snow had glistened on the ground and the bare branches had rattled in the frigid wind, pretending winter would never end had been easy. Pretending their food stores would never run dry had been easy. None of them were genuinely fooled, not even the kids.

"Look! A robin!" said Terry as he popped through the doorway from the kitchen. He ran to the window to get a better look.

"That means it's spring," said Connor, trudging in after him. He would know best of any of the kids what spring meant for the farm. He sat across from Chloe with his back to the window and crossed his arms.

"Yup, spring is right around the corner," said Chloe.

Vishesh stepped into the dining room, carrying a couple of steaming mugs. He must have heard their chatter, because he raised his eyebrows at Chloe as he laid a mug on the table in front of her. Vishesh's tea wasn't caffeinated, but having a hot drink in the morning was better than nothing. Chloe took a sip and winced. Very slightly better than nothing. The dandelion root was always more bitter than she expected.

"Can I help with the testing?" said Connor.

"Nah, don't worry about it," said Chloe. "Vishesh and I have it covered. Besides, don't you have a book report to work on?"

"He does," said Sheila as she swept in from the kitchen, carrying breakfast. Flora dodged in after her and joined Terry at the window.

"Sheila won't mind if I do it next week," said Connor.

"Yes, she will, and she's sitting right there," said Chloe.

Connor rolled his eyes, snatched his breakfast off the table, and slouched out of the room. Teenagers. His stomped retreat rattled their dishes and echoed up the stairs. If he wasn't careful, he'd wake up Monty.

Vishesh sat across from Chloe. "To the table, littles," he said.

As always, they scampered to obey him. Flora climbed up beside Chloe, and Terry plunked himself between Vishesh and Sheila on the other side. Monty's chair sat blessedly empty at the head of the table. And at the foot . . . Chloe swallowed down the pang that Gloria's empty chair sent to her heart. She couldn't get Gloria back any more than she could all the other folks they had lost, but with some work, and probably a lot of luck, she could keep everyone else she loved alive a little bit longer.

***

Chloe straightened up and handed the last soil core from their vegetable patch to Vishesh. She brushed her dirty hands onto her jeans and squinted at the expanse of mud and crispy stalks from last year's crops. Beyond their field, the skeletons of last year's wildflower meadows stretched on over the hill. Before armageddon, they'd all been cornfields, or soybeans, or canola or whatever mono-crop the farmers were growing in the good old days.

"I think we should get a couple cores from over there, too," she said, gesturing to the meadows.

"Thinking of expanding the veggie patch this year?" said Vishesh.

"No, just for a baseline," said Chloe.

The wind picked up, and Chloe pulled her hat down more firmly over her ears. The uneven soil crumbled under her boots as she crossed to the nearest meadow, just thawed enough to take the spring cores. The dry stalks from the previous summer's weeds turned to dust as she pushed through them to get at the ground. She punched the sample collection tube into the earth, capped it, and pulled up a chunk of soil. She batted the yellowed stalks away from her head, but they tangled in her hair and hat as she straightened.

Vishesh took one look at her and smiled thinly. "I hope this core was worth it. Some of those burrs are never coming out."

"Just take the core, would you?" Chloe tossed it to him and whipped off her hat. "Dammit, this one's my favourite," she said. She tried to pick all the tiny bits of weed out of the wool, but they broke into tinier pieces that were even more impossible to remove.

"What will this core tell us that we don't already know?" said Vishesh.

"It'll give us an idea of whether our treatments are doing anything. There's no point in keeping them up if they aren't reducing soil contamination," said Chloe. She jammed her hat back on her now tousled head, weeds and all.

Vishesh nodded and slid the core into the casing with the others. The morning mist had given way to a sunny blue sky, though the breeze still chilled Chloe's neck. She pulled her collar more tightly against it.

The soil testing kits had been developed just after armageddon, when no one really knew how much fallout they would get here. Their little farm was an ocean away from armageddon's nukes, but then again, radioactive isotopes from Chernobyl had been found here too, back in the day. Back when everyone had thought Chernobyl was a big deal.

Chloe and Vishesh crunched back across the field to the shed they'd turned into a testing centre, a refuge from the kids where no one would mess with their samples while the tests were running. A thin stream of smoke already puffed from the chimney; good thing Vishesh had thought to light the stove before they'd gone out for the soil cores. Being able to feel their fingers would make it easier to set up the tests. They'd start with a screening first, and then test the ones that turned pink with contamination for a more detailed idea of the exact contamination level they were dealing with. Anything that wasn't pink would be safe to plant in for sure; no more testing needed. They'd run out of testing kits if they didn't screen the samples first. Where would they even get more kits now that the rare travelling merchants had disappeared completely?

Vishesh added the screening solution to the first sample, and it bloomed pink already. Chloe caught her breath. Maybe that was the one from the meadow? Vishesh added the solution across the row of cores, and one by one, they all turned bright pink to match the first. Chloe sagged against the workbench. They both stared at the cores in frozen silence, waiting the requisite five minutes, more out of habit than necessity.

"All the same," said Vishesh, finally.

"Yup," said Chloe. "The same as the untreated one."

"Yup."

Chloe pinched the bridge of her nose. The treatments were doing nothing. All that work, all that well water, they'd poured into the vegetable patch, for nothing.

"We still have to run the tests," said Vishesh. "Just because the treatments aren't making a difference doesn't mean . . ."

"Doesn't mean we're all going to get radiation poisoning and die if we eat food from the field," said Chloe.

"Yeah," said Vishesh. "We'll run a few tests and make sure."

Chloe left him to it; every second she spent staring at the bright-pink samples, the panic in her chest threatened to claw its way out. The chilly air helped a little.

Sheila stuck her head out the back door and scanned the yard. Her sharp gaze zeroed in on Chloe. Too late to duck back into the shed and avoid her responsibilities in favour of her spiralling thoughts.

"Chloe! There you are!" Sheila called. Shrieks and snatches of little voices singing escaped out the door as she held it open.

"Yup, here I am," said Chloe.

"Can you fix the well? Not getting any water up here," said Sheila and slammed the door again.

Chloe turned back to the shed. You'd think by now Sheila would know Vishesh was the handy one around here, not her. Chloe glanced at the upstairs windows, and Monty stared down at her. He didn't even try to hide his spying anymore.

***

Vishesh finished setting up the tests. He stepped out of the shed and shut the door firmly behind him. The morning sun glinted off the greenhouse roof and caressed the little seedlings cozy inside. They would need an uncontaminated garden to grow in soon.

Chloe frowned as she watched the house and jumped when Vishesh touched her shoulder.

"What's up?" he said.

"Nothing," she said and shook herself. "Sorry, there is something. The well's broken again."

A jolt of anxiety shot through Vishesh's chest. How was she so calm about the source of their survival being out of commission? Maybe she just trusted him to fix it. So he would, as he always did.

"I'll take care of it," he said. "Worried about the soil?"

"Obviously. Why do you ask?"

"You just seem spacey, that's all," said Vishesh.

"Taking a moment to avoid the hordes," said Chloe, but she smiled. It was always total chaos in their farmhouse, but it reminded them all that there was still life on Earth, even after armageddon. They wouldn't have chosen to live here if they didn't enjoy it on some level, even if Chloe would never admit it.

"Go have some lunch," said Vishesh. "Those tests won't be complete until after dinner. We can meet back and check them then." And give each other moral support for the worst-case scenario. Chloe had summed it up nicely: soil too radioactive to grow their food. They die. Which would happen a whole lot quicker if he didn't get the well fixed.

Vishesh used the outside door to the cellar to avoid the hordes himself. Getting slowed down by the kids descending on him would just make this repair drag on than it needed to. Assuming he could pull it off at all. He ducked under the low door frame and took a moment to let his eyes adjust to the dim cellar. He hunched over to keep from bashing his head on the joists, the ductwork, and the pipes running from the well across the house and turned off the breaker for the well pump.

They'd used well water for their intervention because it was the only water they could count on to be clean. Unfortunately, their strategy had also caused extra wear on the well pump. Sure enough, one of the belts had snapped and needed to be replaced. Vishesh rummaged in their spare parts pile, scavenged from the surrounding houses over the years. They'd taken apart what felt like a million appliances, pumps, panels, anything they could get their hands on, scrounging the parts they could use. Back when the travelling merchants from the corporations stopped by regularly, they hadn't been as reliant on scrounging.

The belt Vishesh needed was at the bottom of the pile, of course, but it was in decent condition. Their last one. Some parts were like this: guaranteed to wear out eventually, like a ticking clock in the back of Vishesh's mind. A clock running down alarmingly fast. And with no replacement, what would they do when time was up? Even Monty wouldn't be able to live in denial then. They had minors to take care of; they couldn't only think of the lifestyle they wanted. Chloe was right about that.

Vishesh made the repair and flicked the breaker on, and the pump immediately hummed to life. *Good*, at least for now.

As soon as Vishesh came up the stairs into the hall, he smiled.

"No, you can't give her the remote, but keep the batteries, Connor. Put those back in," said Chloe from the other room. She had set up a media centre with a hard drive they'd found a couple years back, so they could watch TV, as long as they only did it during daylight hours when the solar panels were providing extra power.

"I said it's her turn with the *remote*, not the *batteries*."

"It's the spirit of the agreement that matters, Connor. *Put them back in.*"

Vishesh left his boots in the entryway and hung up his jacket. Chloe said she was bad with kids, but you'd never know it to listen to her. Connor grumbled something, but complied, judging by the clicking of the battery cover back into place along with Flora's raspberry.

Vishesh poked his head into the kitchen. Sheila stood at the sink, scrubbing something and humming to herself.

"Water should be back," he said, and she turned, giving him a soft smile.

"I heard it come on," she said and sighed. "Best sound in the world."

"You can say that again," said Vishesh. "Need any help?"

"You're sweet, but I'm enjoying having the kitchen to myself," said Sheila.

Vishesh grabbed an apple for his lunch and joined the others in the living room.

Connor slumped back on the couch with his arms crossed over his chest while Flora flicked around on the TV. Chloe sat between them, mending a hole in the knee of a pair of Terry's jeans. Terry was playing dress-up with the clothes from the mending basket, almost all of it much too big for him.

Vishesh almost ducked out of the room when Flora put on the episode of *My Little Pony* where Fluttershy finds her backbone. Everyone in the house could recite it from memory, line for line, at this point. But plenty more mending waited in the pile of summer clothes at Chloe's feet, so Vishesh grabbed a torn shirt from the basket and sat by the window instead. With spring breathing down their necks, this might be some of the last downtime they'd have for a while. The winter days were short and sleepy, but in summer they did the work that sustained them all year long.

Chapter Two

Log: The City, Richard A. Phillips, Deputy ECM, 13
May 20—

ECM consulted concerning town range glitch. Range
reduction approved by ECM; no glitch present.
Townrunners indifferent to restriction; no support
for my position above the resident level. No immediately apparent recourse to reverse ECM's decision.

C hloe leaned back in her dining room chair and sighed. Flora
wiggled next to her, but at least her bum connected with her
chair seat. Terry fiddled with something under the table, but at least
he was keeping his constant stream of noise to a soft hum.

"I need help carrying," Sheila called from the kitchen. Connor
rolled his eyes and tilted his chair back onto two legs, daring Chloe to
make him go. She sighed. It would take less energy to just do it herself.

"I'll get it," said Vishesh and put his hand on her shoulder to keep
Chloe in her seat.

"You always get it," said Chloe quietly, and he just smiled at her.
Chloe's stomach churned; she couldn't help that she didn't feel the

same way about Vishesh that he felt about her, and she didn't want to take advantage of his feelings to make him do all the work, even though he didn't seem to mind. He was already gone into the kitchen before she could insist.

Something tiny rolled across the table and into Flora's lap. She squawked and scrambled up to stand on her seat.

"Oh no, Flo, absolutely no standing on your chair," she said.

Flora wobbled dangerously, and Chloe grabbed her arm to steady her. "But Terry—"

"Terry wasn't standing on his chair when he flicked that at you," said Chloe and tugged Flo gently back down to her bum.

"So he can throw stuff?" said Flora and scowled up at Chloe.

"Standing on your chair is dangerous. Throwing stuff is just rude. Still unacceptable," she said, cutting Flora's protests off and raising her eyebrows at Terry.

"I'm not sorry," said Terry. "Flo was looking at me."

Chloe heaved a sigh but left it there. Trying to settle fights in this house just gave her a headache. Thankfully, Sheila and Vishesh were back with the food, and they served everyone, including Monty's empty place at the table. Connor glanced at the empty chair, then away. There was a reason he always sat near the foot of the table with Sheila and Vishesh.

The kids' bickering cut off with thumping footsteps on the stairs. Terry picked at his plate with his fingers, and Vishesh nudged him gently and shook his head. That kid had no survival instincts. Everyone watched the hallway, still and silent, until Monty loomed in the doorway and glanced around the table.

"You didn't have to wait for me," he said and plunked himself down at the head. He dug into his food, and everyone else silently followed suit.

If Chloe hadn't been watching for it, she would have missed the chickpea that sailed across the table and landed by Flora's plate. Flora's wide-eyed gaze jumped to Terry, and her eyes filled with tears. Chloe put a hand on her knee under the table, willing her to pull herself together, but she was only three, and the youngest.

When she started to sob, Monty's perpetual glare landed on her.

"What's her problem?" he said.

"I'll handle it," said Chloe and gathered the little one onto her lap.

"Food not good enough for her?" said Monty.

"I said, I'll handle it," said Chloe and pulled the little shaking body in closer to her chest, but Flora just sobbed harder.

"A good smack would handle it much better. It'd stop that racket anyway," said Monty into his plate, as if he wasn't even talking to them.

Chloe ground her teeth. It was a good thing Monty mostly stayed away from the kids. If he ever laid a finger on one of them—

Vishesh shot her a warning look across the table. She must be making her murder face. She retreated to the living room, Flora in her arms. They rocked together in the rocking chair by the windows, the sunset casting a glow over the room. Flora's sobs slowed, and finally, she was quiet. Chloe kept rocking, just held the warm little body to herself, letting Flora listen to her steady heartbeat.

"Did I get you in trouble?" Flora whispered.

"No, baby," Chloe whispered back. "I can't get in trouble. I'm a grown-up. I got you. You're safe with me." She almost believed it, too.

Once Monty had retreated upstairs, Chloe brought Flora back to the table, and they finished up their cold dinners. Vishesh and Terry stayed to keep them company, and Terry almost made Flo spurt water out her nose when he did his grumbly bear impression. It wasn't an intentional impression of Monty, but it would not be good to let him see it. Chloe pulled Terry aside after dinner.

"Don't do your grumbly bear for Monty, okay?" she said.

Vishesh passed her on his way to the hall and gestured out to the shed. She nodded and turned back to Terry.

"Why not?"

"Trust me, Terry," said Chloe and held his gaze until he nodded and looked away. "I'll be back at bedtime." She squeezed his shoulder.

"Whatever," said Terry and slouched into the living room.

Chloe shook her head. Connor was a bad influence on the littler kids, but telling him that would only encourage him.

Chloe laced up her boots and pulled on her hat. Now that the sun was low, she could probably use a coat over her sweater; the wind tended to pick up around sunset. Once she had her coat on, Chloe dawdled across the yard to the shed, the light from its windows guiding her over the uneven ground. She crammed her hands in her pockets, but the wind still nipped at her face. Once she slipped inside the shed, Chloe sighed at the warmth and the distinctive earthy smell that filled the small space.

Vishesh stood at their workbench, assessing the results. All she had to do was ask for the damage, but she fiddled with the door, making sure it was closed tightly behind her. Chloe pulled off her hat and crammed it in her coat pocket. She couldn't delay anymore and approached the bench.

Chloe stood by Vishesh and knit her brow as she surveyed the results. She didn't have all the numbers memorized, just the thresholds, but these figures were way outside the safe range. *Way* outside. They couldn't eat anything grown in that soil, not even for one season, not if they wanted to keep living out the rest of their lives. And the kids still had long lives to live out, if they could manage to keep their radiation doses low enough.

"I think I'm reading this wrong," said Chloe.

Vishesh shook his head. "You're not."

"I must be," said Chloe. Her throat was closing. Something was trying to claw its way up through her chest and out her mouth. "I must be."

Vishesh didn't answer, but he put his arm around her. They had their stores, what was left from the winter, anyway. It would last them . . . six weeks maybe? If the adults didn't eat too much. They'd planned to plant their first crops this week, but there was no point now.

"We're going to have to get help," said Chloe. What else could they do? They needed clean soil and their method of achieving it hadn't actually achieved anything.

"You know that won't fly with Monty," said Vishesh.

"It doesn't matter," said Chloe.

"It *does* matter. We founded our household on the principle—"

"I don't give a flying fuck! I'm not going to let Monty kill us all because he's too stubborn to ask for help. What has he even done besides complain about the way *we* do all the damn work around here?"

"Chloe," said Vishesh. He took her by the shoulders and locked eyes with her. "Don't do anything stupid."

She took a deep breath. It would be Sheila and Connor and the other kids that would bear the fallout of a confrontation between her and Monty.

"We have to try," said Chloe. She gestured at the tests. "We can't use this."

"I know," said Vishesh. "Let's just present the facts."

"You're right," said Chloe. "He'll see reason. We tried to take care of it without involving the towns, but there's literally no way to do it." Monty wouldn't see reason, and Vishesh's wavering smile said that he also knew she was lying. This was going to be really unpleasant.

"Let's get the kids to bed," said Vishesh.

Chloe nodded. They'd call a meeting after the kids were asleep. Connor might still be listening, but Chloe would try her very best not to yell loud enough for him to hear, this time.

***

When Chloe was snuggled up with Flora in bed reading like this, the pool of light from her lamp encompassed their entire world. The two of them could sink into the book and forget whatever else existed outside of it. Chloe regretfully finished reading Flora a chapter and kissed her goodnight. She closed the door to their room firmly; it wasn't good for the kids to hear them argue. She poked her head into Connor's room.

"You good?" she said.

"Yeah," said Connor and put his book down. "Are you?"

If he was old enough to ask the question, he was old enough to hear the answer. He didn't need the burden of too much detail. Even after armageddon, thirteen counted as a kid.

"Yeah, I'll handle it."

"Like you did at dinner?" said Connor. He wasn't accusing her, not quite.

Chloe took a deep breath. This wasn't about her, not personal. "We have some stuff to figure out. We'll let you know when there's something to tell."

Connor scowled. "Once you've made all the decisions without me."

Chloe stepped inside and closed the door behind her. So much for a quick check-in. "I know you don't want to hear this, but you're still a kid. And I know you don't think of it as a burden, but trust me, once you're an adult, you'll be glad you had a couple more years before you had to deal with survival stuff."

"What if I can help?" said Connor.

Chloe smiled softly. "If you can help, I'll let you know. I promise."

Connor shrugged and picked up his book again. Chloe sighed, showed herself out, and shut Connor's door. He could probably still hear them through the door if they yelled, but maybe he wouldn't be able to pick out the words. Chloe had promised Gloria that she would take care of her son, and that included sheltering him as long as she could, despite the fact that he didn't want to be sheltered.

Vishesh and Sheila already sat in the living room, Vishesh mending a pair of jeans and Sheila picking out the seams of a ragged shirt and winding the thread onto an old bobbin to make new clothes for the kids.

"We're going to need to have a meeting tonight," said Chloe from the doorway and crossed her arms over her chest.

Sheila nodded and put her work down on the couch. "I'll get him."

Once they were alone, Vishesh caught her eye. "When in doubt, just imagine what Gloria would do," he said quietly.

Chloe heaved a sigh and shook her head. "I know." *Just keep it together this time.*

Footsteps thumped on the stairs, and Chloe crossed the living room to hover by the fireplace. Maybe the warmth from the fire would soothe her pounding heart. As Vishesh tidied his mending, and Monty stomped through the doorway and enthroned himself in his wing-back chair on the other side of the fireplace. Sheila shut the French doors to the hallway and perched on the couch again, back to picking away at the old shirt.

"What's all the fuss about?" said Monty, glaring at Chloe.

She refused to glare back. "I called this meeting to discuss the state of the vegetable patch." She tried to keep her voice as neutral and professional as possible.

"Why? What's wrong with it?" Monty demanded.

"We took soil samples this morning and ran volatility tests this afternoon," said Chloe. "We obtained the results, and it's clear that the patch is no longer viable for growing food."

"What horseshit is she on about?" said Monty, glaring at Vishesh.

Chloe clamped her mouth shut until her jaw ached. How could Vishesh stay so calm? He shrugged.

"The numbers don't lie. Any food produced on the land we tested will severely harm anyone that consumes it. If not right away, then over time," said Vishesh.

"Then test more land," said Monty. "What? Did you only test the one field we've been using? Why the hell do we have this whole farm if we're only going to use one patch?"

Chloe pressed her lips together and took a deep breath. It was a mistake.

"Got something to say, miss scientist? I see you over there, looking down your nose at me."

"Monty, honey, I'm sure they're doing their best," Sheila cut in. "They don't have your farming experience. I'm sure they just need you to explain how to do it right."

"Don't want to admit you don't know something?" said Monty. His smile made Chloe sick to her stomach. "It's not a weakness to ask for help. Go ahead."

Just get through this. Play the part. Fighting will only make things worse. Connor's scowling face popped into Chloe's head. She couldn't let him hear her fighting with Monty. She had to set a good example and work together, compromise.

"Absolutely," she said, keeping the sarcasm from her voice by imagining that she was talking to Gloria instead of Monty. "Which fields would be best to take samples from?"

Monty rolled his eyes in his *Lord give me strength* gesture. "All of them! How else do you expect to find the safe areas?"

Even ignoring the fact that they didn't have nearly enough tests to run them on every field on the property, it would take days, maybe weeks, and they didn't have nearly that long to figure something out. Not to mention that if they found a field that was suitable, they'd have to clear it and somehow get clean water there to irrigate it.

Chloe nodded and tried to look thoughtful instead of murderous as she turned to stare into the fire. It had always been hopeless. Monty was so deep in denial, he would never ask the towns for help. He was sure they could take care of it on their own, despite all evidence to the contrary.

"Shall we vote, then?" said Sheila.

"Vote?" said Chloe, frowning at her.

"Of course," said Sheila. "In the spring we always vote on whether to contact the towns. It's in the articles." She smiled softly at Chloe, as if she was sharing a secret.

"Yes, let's," said Vishesh. "All in favour."

Chloe and Vishesh said *aye* in unison.

"All against," said Vishesh.

Monty and Sheila voted as expected.

"It's a tie," said Sheila.

"So let's break it," said Monty. "Get Connor down here. He's old enough to vote."

"What—" said Chloe, but Vishesh cut her off.

"There's nothing in the articles about getting a tie-breaking vote from an underage person," he said.

"We have to break the tie somehow. We all know Gloria would have been on my side," said Monty.

Chloe realized too late that her mouth was hanging open and snapped it shut. Not only would Gloria not have been on his side, she would have chewed him out for trying to use her *son* as a pawn to get his way. Chloe had to get out of here before she did something she'd regret. She glanced frantically at Vishesh, but he looked just as shocked as she felt.

"We won't do anything for now," said Sheila. "Let's all sleep on it and talk again soon." She put her sewing away and yawned. "Come on to bed, honey." She held out her hand for Monty and he took it, letting her lead him back upstairs. Because he had gotten his way. No decision *was* a decision to do nothing, which was what he wanted.

Vishesh sighed out the breath he'd been holding and put his face in his hands. "That went better than I was expecting," he said, his voice muffled.

"Yeah, at least we didn't yell and wake the kids." The kids who would starve if they didn't do something. "Fuck," said Chloe under her breath. "We can't just sit here and do nothing."

"No, we can't," said Vishesh and leaned back in the chair, closing his eyes. "Sheila was right about one thing. We should sleep on it."

"Probably," said Chloe. "My nightmares are going to be unbearable tonight."

"See you at three a.m. when neither of us can stand them anymore," said Vishesh and got up and stretched. He'd always had the wiry kind of strength that Chloe admired, but ever since they had met back in undergrad it had been obvious to her that they'd never be more than friends. Vishesh always seemed to second-guess himself and defer to her. God, she missed Gloria's quiet confidence.

"Sure," said Chloe, "I'll meet you in the kitchen at three." Sadly, that wasn't uncommon these days. They'd had all winter to stew about whether or not the field would be viable, but having their answer wasn't actually comforting, in the end. They would have to join another settlement, move closer to the City, get better access to the towns.

"Hey," said Vishesh and bumped her shoulder with his. "Think about it in the morning. We'll figure it out."

He was right. *Don't think too far ahead. Next, get some sleep. Just focus on that.*

"Yeah, goodnight," said Chloe. She banked the fire while Vishesh's footsteps padded up the stairs and across the hall to the room he shared with Terry. Maybe she should sleep on the couch. No use bothering Flora with her inevitable tossing and turning. Sleeping in her clothes ruined the entire next day, though. Chloe sighed and followed Vishesh up the stairs to toss and turn in her own bed.

***

Thank you, mouthed Vishesh to Chloe and slipped out the back door. Monty was stirring upstairs, and the kids were getting restless. Sheila had clearly needed backup, but what with the four hours of sleep Vishesh had had last night, he was in no shape to help her. Not that Chloe had slept more. But she'd waved him emphatically out the door, and he hadn't had the energy to refuse. The absence of any caffeine-laden beverage really got to him on days like this.

The frosty grass crunched under his boots, leaving a dark trail in his wake as he crossed to the shed. The birds sang their hearts out, and the air was so still that his puffs of breath floated gently away behind him as he walked.

The meeting last night had confirmed it: they couldn't wait for Monty to agree, even if there had been a chance in hell of changing his mind. There was a much better chance that he'd come up with some loophole in the foundational articles to ensure that he always got his way from now on. He had a guaranteed vote from Sheila until the end of time, so all he had to do was put some weird tie-breaking rule into effect and Vishesh and Chloe would lose any power they'd once thought they had.

When Gloria was alive, they'd at least had a voice of reason, someone Monty had pretended to respect. Now that she was gone . . .

Vishesh pushed into the shed and shut the door. A damp chill crawled up his spine, and he bent and lit the tiny stove in the corner. The basket of kindling by the stove was starting to dwindle. Maybe he could talk Flora into collecting some more with him once it wasn't quite so chilly out. He rubbed his hands together; he'd need full feeling in his fingers. He pulled the kindling basket into the middle of the room and emptied it, piling the kindling neatly beside the basket, until a glint of metal sparkled through the branches. Once only a handful of twigs was left, he grabbed the receiver from the very bottom and took it to the workbench.

Monty was fully aware that they had a receiver, but if he decided he wanted to prevent them from communicating with the towns for good, all he'd have to do was knock out this one irreplaceable fragile piece of equipment. Better to make it a little hard for him to find, just in case.

Vishesh cranked the charging handle a couple of times and held his breath as he switched the receiver on. It hummed to life, and he let his breath out. This thing had been shut off in a kindling basket for three years, since they'd last used it. Vishesh tapped out a message and hit Send:

Decontamination request, next available slot. Coordinates to come upon reply.

He blew on his hands as he waited for a response. The tiny stove cut the chill, but it was by no means warm yet. It would be fine if they didn't get a reply right away. Vishesh glanced over to the receiver even though he knew there hadn't been a reply yet. Monty never came in here, but Vishesh still nearly jumped out of his skin when a squirrel pattered across the roof. If Monty found out what he was doing . . .

The receiver chimed, and Vishesh hunched over the tiny screen.

Undeliverable. Recipient address unavailable.

What? That wasn't possible. The receivers were tuned to the closest town. The addresses never changed. The only way the recipient would be unavailable was if the town had switched off their receiver, but why would a town cut themselves off from the rest of the world like that? Vishesh swallowed hard. Unless it wasn't by choice.

Chapter Three

Log: Town Kappa, Richard A. Phillips, Townrunner, 14 May 20—

Personnel assembled, and decommissioned Town Kappa appropriated. Working relationship with ECM untenable. Priority: Repair faulty Town Kappa hydroponics garden, ASAP. Backup rations sufficient for six weeks at current personnel level.

C hloe levered herself out of her chair at the dining room table and staggered to the entryway. The only perk to getting up at three a.m. was that she and Vishesh had time to talk privately. The floors in the old farmhouse were creaky enough that they would hear anyone coming long before their hushed voices could be overheard. If Vishesh had followed their plan, a town was on the way. She'd check in at the shed after the seedlings in the greenhouse were watered. The spring decontamination schedules would be packed, and they would need to get the town here as soon as possible so they could get those seedlings in the ground.

Connor silently followed Chloe to the hall and put on his boots alongside her. They didn't speak until they were in the greenhouse with the door slid shut behind them. They had put the greenhouse together right at the beginning from windows they'd stripped from nearby houses, along with a sliding door. The soil in here was protected from the rain, and they watered it using well water to keep everything decontaminated. The rows of seedlings were almost ready to be moved outside; they would never be able to keep this many plants alive in the tiny greenhouse, not to mention they would never fit. But it would be better to keep them small in here than to move them out into contaminated soil and guarantee a crop too compromised to eat.

"So what happened? I didn't hear any yelling," said Connor, still focused on the squash seedlings he was watering.

"No decision was made," said Chloe.

"You didn't call a vote?" said Connor.

Chloe wanted to lie to him. The kid had been through enough. "Sheila did."

"Stalemate," said Connor. "I told you I would come and help. You know I'd vote for your side."

"That's the problem, kiddo," said Chloe. Connor thought there were sides: hers and Monty's. There was just one side: the side of the farm. Or that's how it used to be. She couldn't tell Connor that Monty had suggested that he participate in the vote. He had no idea how miserable Monty would make him when he took her "side" as he'd said.

"You want me to vote for Monty?" said Connor.

"The fact that you're saying it that way is the problem," said Chloe. "Voting was never supposed to be a popularity contest." It was meant to be an official record of decisions, nothing more. Everything was supposed to be discussed and decided before a vote ever took place.

They were supposed to be working together toward a common purpose. It would be so easy to blame Monty for the way things had changed, as Connor clearly did. Who could blame the kid? He only knew about what he saw in front of him. Since Gloria had passed, she and Vishesh had been putting less and less effort into compromising with Monty.

"I–I know I can't do what Mum did," said Connor. He still wasn't looking at her, but determination shone in the kid's eyes. "I don't understand why you all like Monty so much that you'd let him ruin your lives."

It was Chloe's turn to look away. They didn't have anywhere else to go. But of course, that wasn't quite true, was it? There were always other settlements, or even the towns. Theirs was hardly the only farm. They could move closer to the City, somewhere more accessible to the towns. But the kids loved Sheila too much to leave her behind, and she would never agree to leave without Monty. Finally, Chloe sighed.

"It's complicated, kiddo. I know, adults are always using that as an excuse not to answer questions," she said. "We're working on it, okay?"

"Fine, whatever," said Connor and shrugged in the way that meant he would leave it because she wanted him to, not because she'd changed his mind.

Everything else that Connor probably wanted to say to her floated through Chloe's mind. He was right: the little kids were suffering; they would starve if they didn't do something; Monty was essentially dead weight, because he never did any work around the farm.

"Head on back to the house when you're done," said Chloe and brushed the soil off her hands. How had it gotten under her nails? She'd been using a watering can for heaven's sake.

"Cutting out early and leaving the kid to do the work?" said Connor.

"I have some work of my own in the shed," said Chloe.

Their eyes met, and Connor nodded. Chloe wrapped her arm around his shoulders and squeezed him to her side. He was as tall as her. Damn, he was growing fast.

The cool breeze hit Chloe as she stepped out of the greenhouse. She crossed the wide yard to the shed, and the smell of dirt drifted in the air. The murmur of snowmelt running through the ditch down by the driveway was far more cheerful than radioactive runoff had any right to be.

Chloe paused to brush some tree debris off Gloria's gravestone on her way by. Leaving would also mean leaving Gloria's grave behind.

"Why'd you have to go and die?" Chloe muttered. Without any antibiotics, they hadn't been able to do anything for her, and Monty had withheld his permission to hunt some down until it was already too late. Chloe would not make the same mistake again, even if it meant leaving their farm. She was not going to lose any more of her family.

Chloe slipped into the shed. The kindling basket was uncomfortably empty, and the gleam of the receiver showed through the handful of sticks arranged on top of it. No wonder Vishesh had taken Flora out for some more this morning. Chloe dug the receiver out and unfolded the note from Vishesh tucked in beside it.

What a strange error message. He'd made it clear that the receiver required her attention, by pointing her vaguely to the shed at breakfast, but with Monty hanging around, he couldn't be any more specific. The receiver wasn't intended to communicate with just anyone, it was more like a walkie-talkie: agree on a frequency beforehand and then coordinate your calls between the two parties. If Iota wasn't responding, they had no choice but to contact a third party. That's where Chloe came in.

Chloe plunked her laptop on the workbench and swiped the dust off with her sleeve. She hooked the receiver up to it and started poking around. She wouldn't have long before someone asked where she was, someone like Monty. Connor could try to cover for her, but it wasn't his job to get in the middle, despite how much he might want to.

Jackpot! Unused code for the towns. It was the same structure as the receiver's code, but instead of pointing to a town as the confluence point, it pointed to the City. Lucky didn't even begin to cover it. Chloe quickly activated the unused bits and updated the receiver.

Town Iota not responding to decontamination request. Please respond ASAP.

The City must have had someone watching for messages constantly, because the receiver chimed in moments.

Confirmed, Town Iota AWOL. Identify yourself.

Uh oh. She wasn't supposed to be on this channel. If she admitted to being a small farm, they would brush her off. But she couldn't lie. She just needed a town to decontaminate their field. That was it.

Individual in need of decontamination assistance. Coordinates attached.

Chloe rubbed her palms on her jeans as she waited for a response. What was the point in trying not to look desperate? They *were* desperate. She sent a follow-up:

Please send town at next available opportunity.

Still nothing. There was no way they hadn't received her transmissions. Fingers crossed they were trying to figure out the nearest town's schedule. Chloe glanced out the window and tapped her foot. *Come on!* She tried again:

Children present at settlement requiring decontamination.

If she had to beg to get food for the little ones, she would do it on her hands and knees. Finally, the chime, and then:

Settlement outside City range. No town to be dispatched. City out.

Fuck! Chloe pounded the workbench with her fist, and her chest crumpled in on itself, shoving out a wracking sob. Chloe fought down the urge to smash the receiver onto the floor of the shed and watch it burst into a thousand pieces. They still needed it whether the City rejected them or not. It was their only link to anyone who might be able to help them. Her shuddering breath served to clear her head. She wiped her eyes with the back of her hand and turned to her laptop. She set the receiver back to normal and scribbled an update to Vishesh's note.

She stashed both back in the kindling basket, took a few deep breaths, and ran a hand through her short hair. The last thing she needed was for Monty to comment on her bedraggled appearance. She stepped out of the shed. Vishesh and Flora were crossing the vegetable patch on their way to the shed to drop off their haul of kindling, and Chloe waved and met them halfway across the yard.

"I noticed the basket was getting empty," she said, raising her eyebrows at Vishesh. "Thanks for collecting all that, you two."

"Here," said Flora, holding out her tiny pile of sticks.

"I'll take that," said Vishesh. "You go with Chloe. I'll put away the kindling." He nodded to Chloe and took the little bundle from Flora. Maybe he would have some idea of how to contact another town.

"Hold my hand!" said Flora and grabbed Chloe's hand, hauling her across the yard toward the house. Contacting another town was the only way to get the help their lives depended on.

***

Chloe didn't get a chance to talk to Vishesh alone, but when he came in for lunch, his face was drawn. He clearly hadn't thought of anything else, either.

Maybe if they bothered the City enough? Every day? Maybe more than that? As often as they could? It wouldn't be that hard to set up a bot to message their coordinates to the City at intervals—

"That's wrong, Chloe," said Connor. "That's actually an *L*, Flo."

Chloe shook herself. She was supposed to be doing letters with Flora, but she'd let her mouth run on autopilot. Her eyes met Vishesh's across the room where he was doing math with Terry. *Just focus on this moment.* They would get through this.

"Sorry, Flo. I'm back," she said. "What are you supposed to be doing, Connor?"

"Sheila wants me to write a book report or something?" said Connor.

"Then I guess you'd better write it or something," said Chloe.

"I would be if you knew your letters," he said, and by some miracle, the kid was smiling.

"Maybe Flora can teach me," said Chloe.

Flo looked up at her, wide eyed. That little one had the innocent look absolutely down. "Okay," she said. "Here's your letter, Chloe." She pointed to *C*.

Goosebumps rose on Chloe's arms. Monty filled the doorway, his eyes burning into her, a piece of paper crumpled in his fist.

Sheila popped her head in from the kitchen. "Recess, kids!" she said. They didn't need to be told twice and hustled into the hallway. Sheila followed them out and closed the French doors, leaving her and Vishesh alone with a simmering Monty.

He didn't move, didn't speak. He was waiting for Chloe to stammer and try to explain, maybe even to beg his forgiveness for going behind his back. Chloe crossed her arms over her chest and sat back on the couch. Two could play at that game.

Vishesh fidgeted by the window, but he followed her lead. Monty considered her the ringleader, considered Vishesh beneath his notice unless he was using him to needle Chloe.

"Well? What do you have to say for yourself?" said Monty, finally. He tossed the crumpled paper on the coffee table in front of Chloe.

"I could ask you the same thing," said Chloe.

"I'm not the one who *begged* for help from the City itself, broke all the rules, and made us all look like backwoods trash," said Monty dismissively. "I'm not the one with anything to justify. Clearly, you haven't read our foundational articles if you think this was acceptable on any level."

Clearly you haven't read them if you think sitting up in your room all day spying on those of us—including the kids—doing the real work is acceptable. But Chloe couldn't bring herself to say it. She took a deep breath and swallowed her anger.

"To plot behind my back when we all *agreed* not to do anything yet," said Monty. "Voting is a privilege, you know, Chloe, not a right."

The bottom dropped out of Chloe's stomach, and she planted her hands on the couch to keep from tilting over. Monty was floating the idea of taking away her voting rights? He really thought he had the authority to do that to her, to any of them? The articles made it clear that they were all equals: no one person had any more power than the others. What did Monty expect her to do? Agree with him?

"That's bullshit, Monty, and you know it," said Chloe, but her voice came out strained. The gleam in Monty's eyes intensified.

"When was the last time you read through the articles?" he said. It had been a while. They were locked in a cabinet. Chloe couldn't fight down the panic this time. What was stopping Monty from rewriting them? Changing them? How would any of them know what he'd done? He'd taken them down; they were in his handwriting. If he'd rewritten them . . . "That's what I thought. You don't have a clue what's in the articles. I do. So when I tell you that voting is a privilege, you better believe it."

To Monty, this was a power struggle, and he'd almost sucked her in. But this wasn't about power over the farm; this was about keeping them all alive. Taking care of the kids.

"Fine, Monty. What do you want from me?"

"Want from you? I don't want anything from you," said Monty. "As long as you stick to what we all agreed on in the foundational articles of this settlement. As long as you don't break your word. We all *signed* the articles after all."

He wasn't going to make this easy. All he wanted was to be right, to crush her under his boot.

"You read that," said Chloe and gestured to the note. "You know there's no help coming. What do you propose?"

"I already told you what to do," said Monty. "Find some uncontaminated land to plant on, and get to planting."

"You know we don't have the resources to do that," said Chloe.

"Then *find* the resources," said Monty. "What were you doing when I came in? Just sitting around with the kids?"

And what were you doing, besides snooping around in the shed?

"We already tested enough samples to know that there isn't any uncontaminated land around. We need a town to process our field," said Chloe. "That's the reality, Monty."

"Oh, that's the reality, is it? Too lazy to find what we need yourself? Going to beg others to come save you?"

Chloe got slowly to her feet. Monty was big, tall, and condescending. But she was right. There was only one way to handle this.

"Yes," she said. "I'm going to get the help we need to save our *lives*. Even if that means begging for it. If you read that note, you'll know that Town Iota is not responding, not to us or the City. We need to track them down and see what's up with them. Bring them back here if we can." She brushed past him and opened the French doors. Chloe paused and bit back the scathing comments that flooded her mind all of a sudden. *Go ahead and play king of the farm. Keep your pathetic games away from my kids. Get off your ass and start doing some actual work around here.* Every one of them would just make things worse, for her certainly, but for everyone else as well. Standing up to Monty was one thing, antagonizing him unnecessarily was something else.

Vishesh followed her out into the yard, where the screams and yells of the kids playing floated on the breeze. As long as they were safe and healthy, nothing else mattered. Vishesh fell into step with her as they crossed to the shed. The two of them needed somewhere they could talk without scaring the kids.

Chloe opened the shed door and paused. Dented plastic, shattered glass, and bits of circuit board covered the floor.

"The receiver," whispered Vishesh.

Chloe turned just in time to see Monty in the kitchen doorway, a cold grin on his face. He didn't want them to contact anyone, and now their only line to the towns was gone.

***

Leaving the kids alone with Monty was not Vishesh's first choice. With any luck, finding Town Iota wouldn't take long, but still. That tyrant could do a lot of damage in a short amount of time. On the other hand, he wasn't going to let Chloe go on this wild goose chase alone.

The last signal from Town Iota had come from just inside the City's professed range. Which was bullshit because their farm itself had been well inside the range a few years ago when they'd founded the place. It would have been very bad planning to establish a settlement out of range of the towns.

Sheila popped her head into the living room. "Can you come watch the stove, Vishesh?" she said.

"Sure thing," said Vishesh and followed her back into the kitchen.

"I hear you're taking a trip," said Sheila, eyes carefully fixed on the turnip she was peeling.

"That's right," said Vishesh. The stew simmered on the stove, but it didn't require babysitting. Sheila had used it as an excuse to get him in here to talk to her.

"Monty say yes to it?" said Sheila.

Vishesh sighed. "It's not always up to Monty."

Sheila shrugged and chopped the turnip in half, then into smaller pieces.

"He's not always the easiest man to live with," she said.

Vishesh chuckled and shook his head, but Sheila looked serious.

"Chloe's always stirring up trouble," said Sheila. "You don't have to go along with her all the time, you know."

"Stirring up trouble isn't how I'd put it," said Vishesh. *Trying to keep them all alive* was more accurate.

Sheila shrugged again. "Doesn't know how to keep the peace. That's the same thing."

"Was there something you wanted to talk to me about, Sheila?" said Vishesh, an edge of annoyance he could no longer mask creeping into his voice.

"Don't forget who brought us here," she said. "We wouldn't have this farm if it wasn't for Monty."

Not technically inaccurate but completely irrelevant as far as Vishesh was concerned. The farm would have been driven into the ground years ago if it hadn't been for Gloria and Chloe. Even Sheila did more to take care of the place and their family than Monty did.

"It can be hard to change your view of someone, even if the person has changed," said Vishesh. "Monty used to be—"

Sheila slammed the knife onto the counter. "I know what you think of me, Vishesh." She turned hard eyes to him. More battle scars lurked behind those eyes than he remembered. "I don't need your opinion on my husband, or your pity." She scraped the chunks of turnip into the stew pot, and Vishesh considered himself dismissed.

Sheila had called him in there just to try to get him on her and Monty's side? To get him to team up with them against Chloe? When Sheila knew that Chloe was in the right? He'd never understand her.

Clearly, the kids were fine alone in the living room, so he put on his boots, stepped into the waning light, and stomped out to the shed. Chloe was out there, which would normally have been a deterrent, but with the battle lines clearly drawn between them all, any need for secrecy had evaporated.

Vishesh hustled across the yard. He hadn't bothered to put on his coat, and the wind bit through his sweater now that the sun was low.

Chloe hunched over her laptop on the workbench when he slipped in and shut the door behind him. She glanced up.

"Marked Iota's coordinates on the map," said Chloe.

"Is it nearby?" said Vishesh. He came up behind her and looked at the map over her shoulder.

"Just a few kilometres away," said Chloe. "If we leave in the morning, it shouldn't take too long to get there. A few hours at most."

"Nice," said Vishesh. "I just got a pep talk from Sheila."

"Oh yeah? What was it about?"

"She said I don't have to follow your every opinion like a sheep, essentially," said Vishesh.

Chloe rolled her eyes. "Like she's one to talk."

"Yeah," said Vishesh. That look in Sheila's eyes flashed into his mind again. "I dunno."

"What do you mean?" said Chloe, frowning.

He shrugged. "I always thought that too, but maybe there's more to her."

"I'll believe that when I see it," said Chloe.

At the end of the day, was he really so different from Sheila? How often did he question Chloe's plans?

"You really think this is best?" he said.

"What?"

"Trying to track down Town Iota?"

"What else can we do?"

"We could try to rebuild the receiver or try to get in touch with another settlement," said Vishesh, but he refused to meet her eyes. Sheila had shaken him more than he cared to admit.

"We could. But what if Iota is in trouble?" said Chloe.

"Because we're in a position to help them?" said Vishesh. "We could get in touch with nearby settlements."

"All the nearby settlements we knew about are gone, Vishesh," said Chloe. "Our best bet is to check out Town Iota. Who knows, maybe someone from the City will be checking on them, too."

"But what if—"

"Look, if you don't want to come, you can stay here," said Chloe, her hands on her hips. "I've told you what I'm doing, and you're welcome to join me."

Vishesh just nodded. No way was he letting her go alone. There was a reason Town Iota had stopped responding, and he wanted to be there to find out what it was.

Chapter Four

Log: Town Kappa, Richard A. Phillips, Townrunner,
15 May 20—

Message intercepted en route to the City. Settlement in need of decontamination. Personnel capable of altering access permissions to bypass towns likely to have insight into hydroponics. Decontamination patterns take precedence. Will investigate coordinates provided and locate individual ASAP.

C hloe and Vishesh kept accidentally banging elbows as they trudged in for dinner, but neither of them apologized. They took off their boots in silence. Chloe hadn't meant to make it awkward between them, but she wanted to be clear: her plan was not up for debate. She delayed hanging up her coat to let Vishesh get out of her way and then followed him through to the dining room. Everyone else already sat around the table, silently eating. A bowl of stew languished at her empty place, and another at Vishesh's. She glanced at the grandfather clock in the corner: ten after five. They'd been sitting down to dinner at five thirty ever since the day they'd founded this place.

"Thanks for finally joining us," said Monty. He glanced up from his bowl, daring Chloe to argue with him.

She slipped into her place and took a bite of stew. Cold. Of course it was. She kept her gaze fixed on her food and focused on eating. Monty seemed content to watch her choke down her cold stew and not bait her anymore, which was a mercy. She couldn't risk pissing him off so close to leaving the kids alone with him and Sheila.

"Connor, tell me about your plans for running this place. I know Chloe thinks you're too young to have a valid opinion, but I want to hear it," said Monty.

Chloe's stomach clenched. Connor frowned, glancing between her and Monty, who waited attentively for Connor to respond. Was it not enough that Monty insisted on baiting her? Vishesh's level-headed nature made him a less worthwhile target. Connor was a kid, a teenager at that. What could Monty hope to gain from needling him?

Monty had even phrased it in such a way that if Chloe stepped in, it would only confirm what he'd said: that Chloe didn't want to know what Connor thought. Chloe swallowed and went back to her food. There was nothing she could do besides keep herself calm. She would talk to Connor after. *Just get through the meal with everyone in one piece if at all possible.* She had left the table with Flora the night before, so getting up and walking away again tonight was not an option.

"I'd call in the towns," said Connor, glaring at Monty. How could Connor not know that this was exactly the response Monty was looking for? The gleam in Monty's eyes practically shouted that to Chloe. She glanced at Sheila, probably the only one who could intervene now, but she placidly ate her stew, eyes fixed on her bowl, seemingly oblivious to the volatility of the dinner table.

"Would you now? Even though there hasn't been a vote?" said Monty.

"There's no alternative," said Connor.

"Isn't there?" said Monty and smiled indulgently, as if he were a teacher using the Socratic method on a student instead of a cat toying with a defenceless little mouse.

"The towns were built to decontaminate the environment," said Connor. "We haven't found a way to do it ourselves, so we need them."

"Perhaps," said Monty. "Wouldn't it bother you to be so dependent on a system that doesn't care about us at all?"

Connor looked puzzled. "I never thought of that."

"Don't you think we should be self-sufficient? Not calling others in to clean up after us like babies?" said Monty. He didn't wait for Connor's answer. He knew Connor didn't have one. "I don't like to be treated like a helpless kid. I like to take care of myself." He shrugged.

Connor glared at his bowl, then glanced at Chloe, still frowning.

Thankfully, dinner was almost over, and Monty disappeared back upstairs immediately after he finished eating. Sure, it left them to clean up and wash the dishes, but better that than have him hanging around making the kids nervous.

Chloe cleared the table, and Vishesh washed the dishes while Sheila took Flo and Terry into the living room to read a story. Connor silently helped dry the dishes and put them away. He was tall enough now to reach the high shelves.

"I can take over drying, Connor, if you want," said Chloe when the table was cleared.

"I'm good," he said and glared at her.

Chloe sighed, but she nodded and retreated to the living room. She was trying to be nice, but he heard anything she said distorted through the lens that Monty had built at dinner. Trying to take over meant that she didn't trust him to do it or thought he was too young to handle it.

Even a kid like Connor, who knew Monty was a jerk, was still swayed by his words.

Chloe finally got a chance to talk to him alone once the other kids were in bed. She'd read Flora her bedtime story, as usual, and she popped her head into Connor's room. He lay on his bed reading and didn't look up from his book. Chloe knocked belatedly, went inside, and closed the door.

Chloe put her hands in her pockets, and then clasped them behind her, and then moved them to her hips, then let them hang awkwardly at her sides. She took a deep breath. Why did she feel like a grade five making a speech in front of the whole class?

"Aren't you supposed to wait until I tell you to come into my room?" said Connor.

"Um, yes, I did say I would do that," said Chloe. Why was she so nervous talking to Connor? It was almost as if she were talking to Monty through him somehow. The thought made her sick. She had to do something. She took another deep breath. "I don't think you're too young to have an opinion."

"Yeah, okay," said Connor, glancing up from his book just long enough to roll his eyes at her.

"You don't have to believe me," said Chloe. "I just need you to hear it from me. I value your opinion. And no matter what Monty says, asking for help when you don't have the answer or the capacity to do something yourself doesn't make you a baby or a child or helpless."

"Whatever," said Connor.

"Being self-sufficient, or independent, or whatever, isn't the pinnacle we should all strive for," said Chloe. "The fact is, people always need each other."

"God, you think I don't know that?" said Connor and slammed his book onto his night table. "I don't care what Monty says!"

"What?" said Chloe. "Why are you mad at me then?"

"You're leaving! You're going to leave me, all of us, with that jerk. You're going to find the town and you and Vishesh will join them. Why would you want to come back here and fight with Monty and starve and die of radiation poisoning with us when you could live in a town and have perpetual clean food and water and nice people to see every day?"

"Whoa," said Chloe, holding up her hands. Chloe took a second to reassess the situation. "Okay, one, I'm not—we're not—leaving you. We're going to find help and bring them back here. Two, there are lots of reasons for me to come back. I'm still teaching Flo her letters, for one thing. And who would read her bedtime story if I was gone? Connor, I would never want to leave you guys." *You're like my kids.* But she couldn't say that, not to Connor, not so soon after he'd lost his real mom. Instead, she sighed. "Three, who would want to live in a town? Always on the move, eating gross hydroponic food, being ordered around all the time." The pain behind Connor's anger was obvious now, and so was the fear in his big brown eyes. Just like Gloria's, at the end.

"You promise you'll come back?" he said.

Looking down at him there on his bed, eyes downcast, hands clasped in his lap, he was just a skinny kid who'd lost too many people in his barely thirteen years on this planet.

Chloe knelt in front of him and took his hands. The contrast between her olive-skinned fingers and his brown ones was just another reminder that she wasn't Gloria.

"Yes, I promise I'll come back," she said and squeezed his hands. "In fact, I need you to keep something for me. I'll bring it by in the morning before we leave."

"What is it?" said Connor, warily meeting her gaze.

"My collection," said Chloe, and Connor's eyes went wide.

"You want me to take care of your collection?" he said.

"Yes, I know it'll be safe with you, and when I come back, you can return it to me."

"Are you sure? What if I lose it?" said Connor.

Chloe laughed. "How will you lose it?"

"Okay, fine," said Connor. "But I'm still mad at you for leaving. Don't think you can bribe me like this."

"Fair enough. I do want someone trustworthy to watch my stuff while I'm gone, though," said Chloe. Who knew what Monty would decide to mess with these days?

Connor nodded sagely and let Chloe wrap her arms around him and hold him close.

"Be home for dinner tomorrow," said Connor.

"For sure," said Chloe.

Connor picked up his book again, and Chloe retreated and closed his door as she left.

***

Chloe's breath puffed out in the still morning air, cut through only by chirping birds welcoming the sunrise.

"What happens if we can't find Iota?" said Vishesh. Last season's weeds crunched under their feet. There had been no real need to clear the long driveway last summer, or even the summer before that. They had no car and nowhere to go. And since no independent LunaCorp merchants came this far out anymore, what use was a driveway?

"Without a receiver, we can't call another town. So we die of radiation poisoning," said Chloe. What did Vishesh want her to say? She hitched her laptop bag up on her shoulder.

They paused when they reached the highway. Scores from the towns marred the smooth roadway because they used to pass this way so often, their legs digging into the soft pavement in summer for decontamination and cracking the brittle asphalt in winter when they brought the Gobi merchants around. It was more pothole than pavement. Still, the highway led to Town Iota's supposed location, and it would be easier to follow the flat road than to try to cut across hilly fields and fences.

The wind picked up when the sun was well and truly above the horizon. The trees set a little back from the road didn't provide much shelter. Vishesh spotted a big rock under the trees, which they used as a seat. Chloe pulled the map out of his pack and took a seat next to him. The cold from the rock seeped through her coat and chilled her bum as she pinpointed their location on the map. They were still going the right way, as long as Iota hadn't moved in the interim.

They each took a drink of water, and then packed everything back up, and climbed the embankment back to the road.

"I can take a turn with the pack if you want," said Chloe.

"No, that's okay," said Vishesh. "You've got your laptop."

She wasn't about to argue it. They still had two hours of walking ahead of them even to get to the town. If they were going to get home before dark, they wouldn't have long to establish what was happening to Town Iota and beg help from them. Maybe promising Connor that she'd be home for dinner had been too ambitious. They couldn't leave the kids overnight though. No, they had to get there and back today.

Chloe unzipped her coat. The sun coupled with the pace they were setting was enough to make the chill breeze pleasant. They still hadn't seen another living soul. Not that they'd expected to. Why would anyone be out here?

After another hour, Chloe called a halt to double-check they were going the right way. There was no sense in rabbiting off in the wrong direction. Again, she ran her finger over the map to the road they followed.

"What's up?" said Vishesh and took a swig from their water.

"The town should be there," said Chloe and pointed a little way down the road. No hint of Iota was evident from here, but maybe when they got closer?

"So what do we do?" said Vishesh.

Chloe sighed. If they went to the last known location and there was no sign of it, they could still make it back to the farm. They would have lost a day, but nothing more.

"We go here," said Chloe and poked the spot they'd marked on the map. "What else can we do?"

"And if they're gone?" said Vishesh.

"We go home," said Chloe.

"And then?" said Vishesh.

"If you have a better suggestion, go ahead," said Chloe, shaking out the map. She folded it roughly.

Vishesh put the map away, and they headed back to the highway.

***

It never got easier for Vishesh to go into one of the old villages, the ones that stayed put, from before armageddon. The building that stood at the mark on their map used to be a motel, a row of identical doors and windows set in a long low building. The parking lot in front was cracked, and a sapling sprouted from the gutter, between the curb and the asphalt. One of its bare branches was growing into the eaves. They walked past the once-fenced-in pool, filled now with a layer of dirt and leaves, last season's weeds a lattice of crispy grey bones in its depths. All in all, no sign of Town Iota.

Vishesh shuddered, and he focused on the road in front of them. The back of his neck prickled, and he glanced furtively over his shoulder, half-expecting to see a face in one of the motel's windows, but it was still and silent but for the whistling of the wind. Even the birds were quiet now, probably the time of day. Maybe they also avoided the ruins of old villages.

A glint of sunlight drew Vishesh's eye, and a grey SUV turned onto the highway ahead of them, going in the opposite direction. Vishesh and Chloe both froze. Had cars always been so loud? They stayed frozen as it hummed past, not even slowing down. It wasn't possible that the driver hadn't noticed them; people of any kind were rare and people leaving their settlement rarer still. So why were folks driving? Where was there to go?

They stared after the car for a few long minutes. Chloe pored over the map, but a distant rumble caught Vishesh's attention, and another car came into view and roared past them, a hatchback this time. He caught a glimpse of passengers and the trunk filled to the top, but they whipped by so fast it was hard to be sure.

"Could they be coming from Iota?" said Chloe.

"Maybe," said Vishesh. "Do we want to find out?"

"Yes, obviously," said Chloe.

It wasn't obvious to him. No one good still had a working car, and he was reluctant to get any closer to them than they already were. But Chloe seemed determined, and he wasn't going to let her go alone. She set off the way the car had come, and Vishesh followed.

Chapter Five

Log: In transit, Richard A. Phillips, Townrunner, 16 May 20—

Coordinates yielded a settlement not populated by requisite personnel. Residents less than forthcoming; Town Iota most likely candidate for their whereabouts. Currently en route to Iota's last known location.

A total of four cars passed them before Iota came into view. The town was collapsed on the ground, its legs buckled beneath it, having crashed through a farmhouse, leaving only two walls and half the roof intact. Town Iota was as tall and wide as the house and three times as long. The sun glinted off its metal top, and the front sparkled with shattered glass, most likely from the impact with the farmhouse. Huge faded lettering down the length of it and a stylized palm tree logo branded the hulk: *GOBI*. The wreck seemed deserted, but where else would the cars have come from? Vishesh grasped Chloe's arm.

"What?" she snapped.

"Aren't you even a bit concerned that there are people in there?" said Vishesh.

"I hope there are," said Chloe. "That's what we're looking for, isn't it?" Chloe shook off his hand.

"We're not looking for just anyone," said Vishesh. His low voice was almost a whisper.

"Yes, we pretty much are," said Chloe. "Hello?" she called and ignored Vishesh's wince. She strode around the back of the town to the grubby steel ramp; the big back doors hung wide open, but the darkness inside hid anyone who might have been lurking within.

Chloe had never been inside a town before, just watched them from the outside while they worked. The processing apparatus on the bottom munched up the soil and spat it out decontaminated. She'd sometimes seen faces at the windows, those inside just as curious about her as she was about them, but she'd only ever spoken to a handful of town residents, usually a designated couple of go-betweens for the settlements.

Chloe hesitated at the bottom of the ramp, unsure whether she wanted to know what was inside. If there had been an accident, there could be carnage that she didn't want to see. On the other hand, there could be survivors who needed help. Not that she would be able to do much. But who else was there?

The second step up the ramp was easier than the first and the third easier than that. Vishesh scampered up after her and glanced around like a mouse on the kitchen floor when she flicked on the light at four a.m. Chloe smirked.

"Afraid of something?" she said.

"Yes, most definitely," said Vishesh.

"What?" said Chloe.

Vishesh shook his head. "I don't know," he said. "It's just creepy, eh?"

Chloe shrugged and stepped into the town itself. The smell of oil and machinery brought her back years to a time when such things had been commonplace. Getting on a train, walking past a gas station, wandering downtown window shopping. She waited for her eyes to adjust to the darkness.

Anything that had been here in the loading dock was gone; the place was empty. Dull metal tapped under her feet as she made for one of two open doorways through which she glimpsed corridors running the length of the town's long body. She hadn't noticed from the outside that the windows had all been removed, leaving the long hallway open to the air. A row of doorways lined the inside of the corridor, gaping into unlit rooms. Chloe ducked her head into what looked like mechanical maintenance, a medical center, and a lab. When these things had been thrown together, in the wake of armageddon, there hadn't been time for aesthetics. Now cold bare metal was too familiar for Gobi to overhaul their original design.

She climbed the stairs at the end of the hallway to the town's bridge. The floor listed at a slight angle because of the way the town sat, half-inside the farmhouse. Vishesh still tagged along behind her, and at least he'd stopped nagging.

The bridge rested in the shadow of the farmhouse, and it took Chloe a minute to notice that someone was there, sitting in the driver's chair, in fact. They stared at each other, the shock on the man's face surely mirrored on her own. Chloe's voice came out as a croak, and she cleared her throat.

"Are you the townrunner?" she said.

He shook his head. "Are you a town resident?" he said.

"No," said Chloe. "We're from a nearby settlement."

Vishesh elbowed her.

"Your friend doesn't trust me," said the man and grinned, making his boyish face look a little mischievous.

"Seems that way," said Chloe and smiled back. "We need our fields decontaminated, but it doesn't look like Iota is in any shape to help us. I wonder where all the residents went. Do you know?"

"Sorry," said the man and shrugged. "I'm in the same boat. Looking for a town to help my people out."

"I'm Chloe." Chloe stuck out her hand.

"Aaron, pleased to meet you," said the man and shook Chloe's hand.

"This is Vishesh," said Chloe, pointing over her shoulder to where Vishesh loitered near the door, his arms crossed over his chest.

"Pleasure to meet both of you," said Aaron. "I'm not used to meeting new people."

Chloe laughed. "You can say that again. We haven't even been off our farm in years."

"Yeah, leaving was weird for me, too," said Aaron. "But I guess I can't stay here."

Chloe's stomach growled. "Do you have any food?"

"No, I didn't bring any," said Aaron.

"We'll share. Come have lunch with us," she said and beckoned Vishesh.

He approached reluctantly, and the three of them unfolded seats from the back wall and sat down to a little meal in the wrecked bridge of the wrecked town.

***

Chloe sat back. The food had left her stomach grumbling. It hadn't even been enough for just herself and Vishesh, but eating in front of someone without offering them food seemed wrong, so she'd shared. With some food in her, her mind started to wander again.

"How will we find another town?" said Chloe. She glanced around the dark bridge. The windows were shattered and the ceiling partly caved in. The town's receiver should be here somewhere. Maybe there was a way for towns to contact each other baked into them. At the very least, they could contact the City and let them know that Iota was out of commission and abandoned. Chloe crouched in front of the driver's seat, under the steering wheel, and wrenched open the dashboard. The scuffed panel came away too easily. Someone else had already opened it up. All the town's guts seemed to be here, including Iota's receiver. Unfortunately, unlike theirs, the instruments on the town needed power to work. "Come look at this," said Chloe over her shoulder, and Vishesh slouched over beside her and bent to peer at the dashboard.

He shook his head. "Totally mangled," he said. "Someone's been in here, but they didn't have a clue what they were doing."

"Might be some useful parts, though," said Chloe.

"You and your collection," said Vishesh and straightened. "Do we really have time for this?"

"All this receiver needs is power," said Chloe. "Besides, when will we get another chance to raid a town?"

"That's what I thought, too," said Aaron.

"Oh yeah?" said Chloe. "Did you have a look around already?"

"For sure," said Aaron. "Other people already took the solar panels and most of the glass. I found a few things they missed, but it was mostly picked over by the time I got here."

Chloe unplugged the receiver and fished a screwdriver out of her laptop bag. "I wonder how long it's been like this."

"And why the radio signal was coming from somewhere else yesterday," said Vishesh, back to lounging with his arms across his chest, watching Aaron.

Chloe shrugged. "Probably within the margin of error," she said.

"Seems like you two know your stuff," said Aaron.

"It's not normally such a useful skill," said Chloe. "For me, at least." She pointed to Vishesh. "He's the handy one."

"That so?" said Aaron.

"Yup, he's the one who can fix things. I'm more likely to break anything not soldered to a circuit board."

"Don't oversell my skills," said Vishesh through clenched teeth. He glared at Chloe, and she frowned back at him.

"Don't sell yourself short," she said.

"Sounds like you two make quite the team," said Aaron. "No wonder you came running to the town's aid."

"It's not like that," said Chloe. "Not exactly. We need help from them, like I said. Aha!" She pulled out the receiver and motioned Vishesh over with the pack. "Keep this little puppy safe for me," she said. "Let's go search the rest of this place. I bet there are tons of little gems just waiting to be found."

"You go," said Vishesh. "I'll rest here." He still watched Aaron warily.

Chloe shrugged. She didn't need Vishesh to help her pick over the rest of this place. She went back the way they'd come and ducked into the medical centre first.

As it turned out, there wasn't much more to salvage from the town. The solar panels and the windows were not the only valuables that had been taken. All of the medical equipment was gone, along with everything from the hydroponic garden that wasn't nailed down and a decent amount that was. Whoever had raided this place knew what they were looking for and didn't hesitate to take it.

Chloe found the kitchen next to the hydroponic garden, near the back. She methodically checked every cupboard and drawer, plus the pantry. Any scrap from here would be worth taking. Evidently, whoever had raided this place knew that, too. The only useful appliance left was the fridge, which was built right into the metal bulkhead.

Chloe paused to look out into the open hallway on this side. The wind whistled through the empty window frames. Vishesh was not totally wrong that Aaron being here was slightly suspicious. If the cars they'd seen really had come from here, then chances were he had been here at the same time. Had he hidden from the raiders? Had he waited for them to leave before coming to check the place out? Both were questions worth asking. The people who had dissected this town had known exactly where to look and exactly what to take. The quarters were practically untouched, as was the lounge. It was as if the raiders had had a schematic of the place and just hit the high points: food, medicine, solar panels, and glass.

Chloe wandered back to the lab and rooted through the drawers. There were a few soil tests in a bottom drawer and some interesting equipment in a lower cupboard. She pulled out an optical microscope and plunked it on the lab bench. She brushed off the dust. The kids would have a good time with this, especially if she could find any glass slides hiding in here somewhere.

She opened all the upper cabinets on the hunt for slides and covers, and she hit the jackpot. A cardboard box of seed envelopes. *Seed-verts by LunaCorp* was printed in bright-green letters across the box, and the original branded LunaCorp tape still sealed the top. Chloe breathed out slowly. There had been rumours that these were in development but never any hard proof. Seeds that would grow in contaminated soil but wouldn't take up the radioactive elements into the edible parts of the plant. With Seed-verts, they wouldn't need to worry about the condition of their soil. They wouldn't ever need decontamination help again. They could let the rain water their fields, maybe even keep animals someday, if they could get any.

Where had this town gotten Seed-verts? Why were they keeping them in the back of a cupboard instead of distributing them to the settlements?

***

Once Chloe had wandered away, the two men watched each other warily. Vishesh hadn't tried to hide his suspicion, but Aaron didn't seem perturbed by it.

"I'm telling the truth, you know," said Aaron.

"I never said you're not," said Vishesh.

"But you think I'm lying," said Aaron.

Vishesh shrugged.

"I'm from a settlement, like you. I just want to help my people." Aaron paced to the sliver of window with a view past the crumbled farmhouse wall and looked out, his back to Vishesh. Aaron's blond hair was a little uneven, but not in the *buzz cut that's been growing out* way that their family sported, more in a trendy *two-hundred-dollar feathered cut* kind of way. And he must have product in it. No one could get such perfectly tousled waves otherwise. "We wouldn't live long without the towns."

"Let me guess," said Vishesh. "Suddenly, your settlement is outside their range."

Aaron turned and pierced him with a look. He nodded, slowly. "They refused to help you?"

"That's right. Not sure what they have to gain by it. They weren't much for conversation," said Vishesh.

"Are you going to leave your settlement? Move?"

Vishesh sighed. This was exactly the kind of question he didn't want to answer. He was very aware that Aaron hadn't supplied any information about himself, besides saying he was just like them, the likelihood of which was vanishingly small. He and Chloe had put in a lot of work to get here, and they had fairly uncommon skills.

"Are you going to move yours?" said Vishesh.

Aaron quirked an eyebrow and then laughed. "Not a chance in hell," he said.

Vishesh scowled at him, but Aaron seemed unfazed.

"We have a good setup," he said. "We're not going to find that anywhere else."

"Even if you can't feed your people?" said Vishesh.

"We'll make it work," said Aaron. "How many of you are there at your farm?"

Vishesh frowned again and Aaron held up a hand.

"I only ask because my settlement is fairly large. You'd be welcome to join us."

"I don't think so," said Vishesh. "Thanks anyway."

"The offer stands, if you change your mind."

"If you're so much like us, how come you can invite an unspecified number of people to join you on a whim? Aren't your fields contaminated too? Isn't that why you're looking for a town?"

"I never said I'm in exactly the same position. Still, I would like to help if I can," said Aaron.

That was strikingly similar to what Chloe had said. She had wanted to come here, not only to get help from the town, but to see if they could help Iota in turn. Even though they had nothing, she still wanted to help. Maybe that was what Aaron meant as well. If they joined forces, maybe they could solve their common problem. Though there was still the question of how Aaron happened to be here.

"Did you see any cars when you got here?" said Vishesh.

"Cars?"

"Yeah, we saw a bunch of cars coming from this town. That's how we found it: we followed them," said Vishesh.

"What kind of person would have cars?" said Aaron and turned back to the window.

"That's what I wondered as well," said Vishesh. After a moment, he continued, "You didn't answer my question."

"I would think the people who raided this place must have had cars. Solar panels and sheet glass are hard to move, impossible on foot," said Aaron. He turned back to Vishesh, suddenly earnest. "I know you don't trust me, Vishesh, understandably so, but don't you think the world would be a little better if we all trusted each other a little more?"

"Honestly, no, I don't," said Vishesh and took a step away from Aaron. "I haven't forgotten the early days after armageddon, and I'm not likely to. The people who have my trust earned it. If you want it, you'll have to earn it too, show me you're trustworthy."

"Whoa, intense, Vishesh," said Chloe from the doorway. "I'm flattered, though." She carried a big cardboard box through the doorway and plunked it on the driver's seat.

"What did you find?" said Aaron. He crossed quickly to the box and peered inside. "Seeds?"

"Yup, seeds," said Chloe and turned to Vishesh. "You know the ones they were developing—allegedly developing—a couple years ago?"

The radiation-resistant seeds. But they had never been successfully made. Admittedly, their farm had not been in contact with the wider world for years. Was it possible that the legendary seeds had been developed in the interim? That would mean no more need for towns; they would be set for life.

"I remember," said Vishesh. He locked eyes with Chloe.

"That's them," she said.

Aaron glanced between them, clearly only half following their conversation but piecing it together by the second.

"Seed-verts," said Vishesh, more to kill time than anything. "Clever. Like sieverts."

Would Aaron kill them for these seeds, to save his own settlement? Why had Chloe brought them here where he could see them? They could easily have left and come back for them once Aaron had gone.

Vishesh groaned. "You *want* to share them." Chloe must have brought them here on purpose to share with Aaron.

"We all need them," she said.

"Maybe too much," said Vishesh and raised his eyebrows.

"Have a little faith in humanity, Vishesh," said Chloe. She turned to Aaron. "These seeds will grow in any soil, contaminated or not. They'll grow good food that you can eat, regardless."

Aaron's completely blank face while he took in the information sent a shiver crawling up Vishesh's spine. No surprise? No joy? Nothing?

"We're willing to share them with you," said Vishesh. "We're trusting that you'll share them with us, too."

Aaron's gaze flicked to him and then back to Chloe. "You could have kept them for yourself, hidden them," said Aaron. "Why didn't you?"

"Unlike some people, I want to help others when I can," said Chloe.

"But you're starving. You said so," said Aaron.

"Yes, and so are you," said Chloe. "Even half of these seeds would mean my settlement is set. Why would I want to keep more than I can use when you need them, too?"

Vishesh ran a hand over his face. What if there was a drought or a flood and the seeds didn't sprout? What if animals dug them all up? What if they weren't able to save seeds from this season for next season? What if *those* seeds didn't sprout? What if they didn't produce as much as normal seeds? Of course it would be better to take them all! Impossible now that Chloe had made her naive offer.

"Fine, we'll split them fifty-fifty," said Aaron.

Why did it feel like Aaron was granting *them* a concession?

Chapter Six

Log: Town Iota's last known location, Richard A. Phillips, Townrunner, 16 May 20—

Town Iota no longer emitting locator signal; last known position will have to suffice as coordinates, supplemented by view from the air.

Chloe stowed their portion of the Seed-verts in Vishesh's pack and left the box for Aaron.

"You're sure you don't want to share the coordinates of your settlement with me?" said Aaron. "I'd like to be able to come check on you."

Chloe glanced at Vishesh's dour expression. "If I told you, I don't think Vishesh would ever speak to me again."

"You won't give us yours anyway, right?" said Vishesh.

Aaron laughed. "Touché."

Weird, that sounded like a helicopter. Chloe peered out the small smashed-in section of window. Yes, that was definitely a helicopter; the sound was unmistakable even after so long without hearing it.

"If you think people who have cars are bad news, what do you think of folks with helicopters?" said Aaron.

"There's no way we'll get out in time," said Chloe.

"Nowhere in here to hide where they can't find us either," said Vishesh.

"We'll face them," said Aaron. "If they're coming here at all." He stashed the box of Seed-verts in the busted dashboard and checked to see whether it was visible from the doorway. When he was satisfied, he settled back in the driver's seat, where he had been when Chloe and Vishesh entered.

"What else can we do?" Chloe asked Vishesh, and he shrugged.

"Seems like we face them," he said.

Chloe tapped her foot, her heart pounding in her chest. Vishesh strapped the pack firmly to his back and stood next to her. Good thing he'd insisted on coming with her. Facing this alone would be unbearable.

Sure enough, the helicopter landed nearby, kicking up dust, and three people stepped out and made their way slowly to the rear of the town. Two tall figures and a shorter one; two dressed in town uniforms and the third—was that a suit? Their words were unintelligible from so far away, though they didn't seem as if they were trying to be quiet. Only one set of footfalls sounded lightly up the steps to the bridge. They must have split up.

The suited man appeared in the doorway and paused. Grey eyes took them in from behind his glasses, the dark frames contrasting with his clean-shaven white face, his dark hair straight and neat. It was a nice suit, pinstriped and tailored to his slim build, but was it really practical for armageddon to wear something dry clean only? Suit man glanced over his shoulder and then put up his hands.

"We weren't expecting anyone to be left," he said.

"Thought your people already cleaned the place out?" said Aaron.

The man in the doorway glared at Aaron. "No," he said. His gaze wandered over the rest of the bridge and settled on Vishesh and then Chloe. Their eyes met, and Chloe had to keep from taking a step back. Did he think they'd wrecked the town? It was much more likely that *he* had done it. If none of the others were going to break the silence, she would. Only one way to sort this all out.

"I'm Chloe," she said. "This is Vishesh and Aaron." Both men glared at her when she gestured to them, and she shook her head. "A couple of distrustful, jumpy guys."

"Richard Phillips," said the man in the doorway. Also distrustful, but not in the least jumpy, from the look of him.

"Phillips?" said Aaron, raising an eyebrow.

"That's correct," said Richard. His gaze swept over Vishesh and Chloe, maybe expecting them to recognize the name as well. There were disadvantages to being out of touch for years at a time. Should they know who this person was?

"That tells me all I need to know," said Aaron. "We'll be lucky if this monster lets us go our separate ways in peace." Aaron crossed his legs and settled into his chair. "Right, Deputy?"

Chloe's stomach tightened. Not let them go? She'd promised Connor that she'd be home for dinner. And obviously the life-saving Seed-verts in Vishesh's pack needed to get back to their farm.

"Not any longer," said Richard and shook his head sharply.

"Oh no? Likely story," said Aaron and chuckled. "You're trying to convince me you've abdicated?"

"I see no value in convincing you of anything," said Richard. "I was told I might find a certain individual here."

"Why are you looking for them?" said Vishesh, and Richard's intense gaze snapped to him.

"I require a specific skill set," he said.

"What's the skill set?" said Chloe. Someone else looking for help on this smashed-up wreck of a town?

"Software development," said Richard.

Chloe took a breath to respond, and Vishesh elbowed her hard. Richard's gaze pierced her and choked the breath in her throat. She clearly didn't have to say anything: this man already knew that she was what he needed. The man that Aaron had said was unlikely to let them go, whom he'd called a monster. The chances of her being home for dinner were plummeting.

Footsteps tramped up the stairs behind Richard, and he stepped aside. The shorter person in town uniform came through the doorway.

"What have you been doing, sir?" she said. "Seems like you've scared these folks pretty bad."

Richard jerked his chin at Chloe. "That is the developer."

The woman looked Chloe up and down. "Hm, doesn't look like a town resident to me."

"I don't believe she is," said Richard.

"Can't appropriate her then, can we?" said the woman.

Richard sighed. "No, I am aware of that."

"Maybe tell her next time, then?" said the woman. "I'm Brianna. You are?"

"Chloe," said Richard.

"I wasn't asking you, sir."

"I'm Chloe," she said.

"What does that mean, *can't appropriate*?" said Vishesh.

"Town residents can be moved between towns on orders. You're not town residents, so he"—she jerked her thumb over her shoulder at Richard—"can't order you around."

"Theoretically," said Aaron.

Brianna's dark eyes narrowed as she turned to Aaron. "And who's this piece of work?" she said.

"That's funny coming from you," he said. "I'm Aaron."

Brianna shrugged. "Okay, sir," she said and turned back to the door, "I'm out. This circus is on you. We'll wait for you outside, hopefully with Chloe." She gave Chloe a final nod and tromped back down the steps, her footfalls fading along the hallway.

"As Brianna stated," said Richard, "you have no obligation to follow my orders. I would, however, ask that you allow me the opportunity to convince you. I will install myself in the lounge, and I would appreciate if you would join me." He held up his slim hands again. "Perhaps we can come to an arrangement." He nodded to Vishesh, then more stiffly to Aaron, and left the bridge.

"Remind me why we left the farm, Vishesh?" said Chloe. Why had they left their safe little haven for this world that they knew was full of backstabbing jerks all trying to get ahead?

"Survival," said Vishesh and patted his pack. For themselves and for the kids.

Right. Just get through this and get home with the Seed-verts.

***

Chloe took a deep breath and entered the lounge. Richard sat in an armchair, scrolling through a phone. The light glinted off his glasses as he looked up, and for an instant, Chloe could have been in another time, meeting a friend for coffee or for a business meeting, back before the world fell apart. She wiped her palms on her thighs and took a seat opposite him.

Vishesh followed her in and leaned against the wall near the corridor, his arms crossed over his chest.

"Thank you for joining me," said Richard, tucking his phone away.

Chloe shrugged. "Make your pitch. We're on the clock."

"Of course. I run a town not far from here, Town Kappa. As I'm sure you know, recently, settlements' food supplies have dwindled. As a result, we've found ourselves short of rations," said Richard.

"I thought towns grew their own food hydroponically," said Vishesh.

"Just so, very astute," said Richard. "Normally, you would be right. Unfortunately, Town Kappa's hydroponic garden is nonfunctional and we are unable to use it to its full potential."

"Nonfunctional how? What makes you think I can help?" said Chloe.

Richard shrugged. "We're not entirely sure. The computers are not working. That's all anyone can tell me."

"So you need me," said Chloe. Town Kappa didn't even have staff who could identify the problem, let alone solve it.

"The City won't help you?" said Vishesh.

For the first time, Richard hesitated. "Our relationship with the City is tense. We object to the range reductions they have imposed. They believe we should follow orders."

Those very range reductions were keeping any towns from coming to their farm and probably many more settlements like theirs. They had the Seed-verts now, but that only helped their little farm. If they could keep Town Kappa running, maybe Richard and his people would find a way to fight the City and get help to those other little farms as well. If Chloe said no, if she refused to go along with Richard's request, their own farm would be fine, assuming the Seed-verts worked as intended. The residents of the other small farms, however, would starve or die of radiation poisoning with no towns to periodically decontaminate their soil.

"Of course I'll help," said Chloe.

"Chloe!" said Vishesh. He slid to his knees in front of her and snatched her hand. "You can't seriously be going along with this guy? You heard what Aaron called him: a monster. Do you really think he's trustworthy?"

Chloe shook her head. "Anyone can be trustworthy if you give them a chance, Vishesh. Besides, how could I stand to look at myself in the mirror if I left whole settlements to starve because I was too afraid to help them?"

"Fine, help them. But don't go with him to his town," said Vishesh. "Please." He must have been expecting her to brush Richard off. He must have thought that she was meeting with Richard just to get him off their backs so they could retreat to their little farm and hide away from the world again.

When armageddon had taken hold, Chloe had never in a million years thought that her skills would be useful again, let alone save lives. As far as she had been concerned, she had a weird archaic education that was maybe good for entertainment but no longer of practical value. But here was Richard, telling her that he could use her skills to save actual lives, today. How could she pass up that chance?

That being said, going with Richard to his town was a terrible idea. There was no doubt about that. He would never let her leave if her skills were so valuable to him. He'd conscript her as a town resident, and then he'd order her around like Brianna and the rest of his people. She turned to Richard.

"I'll help you," she said. "How could I not?"

"Thank you very much," said Richard. "Town Kappa is not far from here, as I said."

"But Vishesh is right," Chloe continued. "No way am I coming with you to your town."

"I'm afraid I'm not following you," said Richard, his eyes narrowing.

"Your phone," said Chloe. "I'll do old-school remote tech support with your best programmer."

"Fine," said Richard. His face cleared back to nearly expressionless. "Come with me."

"Come where?" said Vishesh.

"The helicopter, of course," said Richard. "I can't get you in touch with anyone from here. The helicopter is connected to the radio network, but my phone isn't."

Chloe stood and locked eyes with Vishesh. He gripped her hand as if he wanted to physically hold her back. She couldn't pass up a chance like this, to help so many people in a way that maybe no one else could.

"I'll spend an hour or so coaching someone through the fix," she said, still holding Vishesh's gaze. "We'll be home for dinner. I promised, and I'll keep it."

Vishesh shook his head. "I really hope you're right," he said. "I can keep an eye on you from here." He nodded to the open corridor. If that helped him cope, Chloe wasn't going to refuse.

"Excellent," said Richard. "Shall we?" He gestured to the hallway for Chloe to go first.

She trudged down the corridor, through to the loading dock and down the ramp again. Richard fell into step with her silently as they descended the ramp. He nodded at Brianna as they passed her, and the three of them approached the helicopter. The other uniformed resident was already sitting in the cockpit, and she also gave them a nod as they came level with her.

Brianna climbed in first and helped Chloe up after her, then Richard climbed in behind her. Chloe perched on the edge of one of the seats. Brianna sorted out the headsets and handed one to Chloe. As she adjusted it on her head, Richard shut the door. He took a headset as well, then buckled himself into his seat. Brianna punched a few buttons on the radio, and static came through Chloe's headset.

"Hello?" she said.

"You better buckle in," said Brianna over the headset.

"What? Why?" said Chloe, but she already had a sinking feeling in her stomach.

The cacophony of the helicopter blade spinning up drowned out Brianna's response, and Chloe fell back into her seat as the whole cabin lurched and tilted. She scrambled to buckle herself in and glared at Richard. He was leaning back in his chair with his eyes closed. Brianna adjusted the sound settings and tried again.

"Never been in a helicopter before?" said Brianna and grinned at her.

"Never been kidnapped before," said Chloe, not taking her eyes from Richard. His total lack of reaction was infuriating. He could at least have the decency to show a little remorse.

"Wait, you didn't agree to come?" said Brianna, frowning. "What the fuck, sir?"

Richard's eyes snapped open at that. "It's done," he said, glaring back at Brianna.

"What makes you think she'll help us now that we *kidnapped her*?"

"She'll help," said Richard, and his intense gaze flicked to Chloe.

Chloe didn't want to admit it, but he was right.

"I might help," she said. "But I'm not helping *you*. And I'm not doing it for free."

"Understood," said Richard. He raised his eyebrows at Brianna and then turned his back on them. Chloe stared out the helicopter window as well. The land flashed below: mostly fields, tangled with years of bracken, divided by gouged and pitted roads, every single one taking her farther from Connor and the rest of her family. She was never going to be able to keep her promise.

***

Vishesh gripped the edge of the window frame painfully tight as the helicopter drifted slowly away and out of sight. The silence rang in his ears, and he pried his fingers loose from the window ledge.

"See?" said Aaron around the big Seed-vert box in his arms. He shook his head. "Monster."

Vishesh let his breath out in a sigh. "How did you know who he was?"

"Phillips," said Aaron. "They run the City. He can say he's not one of them all he wants, but actions speak louder than words, right?" He waved in the direction the helicopter had disappeared.

A distant rumble had Vishesh's heart leaping, but it plummeted again when two cars came into view: a grey SUV and a hatchback. The ones they'd followed to find this place.

"For fuck's sake," said Vishesh. "I can't deal with more jerks right now."

"Don't worry," said Aaron. "They're with me."

Vishesh rubbed his hands over his face. "So I was right," he said. "You're the one who stripped this town."

"That's right," said Aaron and grinned at him. "We did a pretty good job. I can't believe we missed these seeds. Never found anything half as good in the labs before. They must be a new thing."

"You've stripped towns before?" said Vishesh and immediately felt silly. Clearly they'd stripped towns before. He and Chloe had been sure of that the second they saw this place. It had been expertly ransacked.

"Are you coming?" said Aaron.

"Where?" said Vishesh.

"To the cars. No point in staying here."

"Why would I get in a car with you?"

"I'll give you a ride home," said Aaron, a smile playing around his mouth.

"We've already been through this. I'm not telling you where our settlement is."

"You sure? There's a reason you and Chloe were so anxious to be home. You said yourselves that without the Seed-verts you're carrying all your people will die. Let me come see your setup. I wasn't lying that I have a settlement not too far from here. Maybe we can help each other out."

"And you would help us why?"

"As I said, I'd never have found these seeds if it wasn't for Chloe. Anyway, you might find it's nice to have an ally now that Chloe's gone. Don't you think?"

Shit. Chloe was gone. Monty would win every single vote by default. They had one less adult to help run the place. Even with these Seed-verts, he wouldn't be able to do all the work necessary to turn them into crops by himself. He couldn't afford to refuse help, even from someone like Aaron, who was clearly taking advantage of his vulnerable position.

This was going to end badly. If there had been any other choice, Vishesh would have taken it. But he couldn't go back to the farm without Chloe and expect everything to just work out.

"Fine," said Vishesh. "Let's get out of here."

Aaron followed him out of the carcass of Town Iota to the cars.

Chapter Seven

Log: En route to Town Kappa, Richard A. Phillips, Townrunner, 16 May 20—

Requisite personnel acquired (C). Town Iota located; evidence suggests expert sabotage. All Town Iota residents MIA.

"There's Town Kappa," said Brianna. She'd been blessedly silent during the short helicopter ride and had seemed determined not to meet Chloe's eyes.

Town Kappa hovered in the middle of a field below them and crawled slowly across, churning the earth as it went, decontaminating the soil so that edible food could be grown. Town Kappa was identical to Town Iota, if a little more weatherbeaten: long and narrow with propulsion legs down each side, like a giant mechanical centipede. *GOBI* and the palm tree were too faint to make out down the side. At least Town Kappa was still responding to decontamination calls. After the City had refused Chloe's decontamination request, it had called into question whether any towns were responding at all.

They landed on a helipad on top of the town, and Richard finally turned to her. He took off his headset, and Chloe followed suit.

"Would you like the tour, or shall I show you directly to the hydroponics facility?" he said.

Chloe stifled a bitter laugh. "You're so sure I'll still help you, now that you've kidnapped me?"

"You said you would help and I believe you'll keep your word," said Richard. His gaze unnerved her, and she glanced at Brianna, who quickly wiped the desperate look off her face.

Chloe sighed. "You know I will," she said. "Even though I didn't actually agree to this. Once I've had the tour, we'll talk terms."

"I thought the terms were already clear," said Richard.

"You didn't keep your end of the deal, so we'll have to *renegotiate*," said Chloe.

"Fine," said Richard and popped open the door, letting in the grinding and rumbling of the town processing the soil. "The town is not extensive, so time to decide on your terms is limited."

From the roof, Town Kappa seemed plenty big. The breeze whipped around them, and the smell of turned earth floated up and mixed with the mechanical smells of the hulk. The Ottawa River glinted in the sunlight with the Gatineau Hills looming behind, no more than blue outlines in the distance. It had been a long time since Chloe had seen so far. A figure in the house's yard watched Kappa's progress across their fields. There were likely even more folks inside who were ecstatic to have the town here to decontaminate their land, as Chloe would have been, back home at their farm.

Chloe followed Richard down into the loading dock and turned, only to find that she was alone; Brianna had not followed her. She and Richard strode up one of the long corridors running the length of the town. Aside from being intact and the constant hum of the machinery under their feet, it was pretty much the same as Iota. Richard waved vaguely at each room as they passed but didn't pause to let Chloe get a good look at anything. The other inhabitants ducked into doorways to let them by and eyed Chloe curiously, but they didn't speak to Richard or to her.

"Here's the lab," said Richard, waving at an open doorway.

Chloe craned her neck as they passed. Maybe she would get a chance to run in and check the cupboards for more Seed-verts the towns might be hoarding. A woman in a lab coat was running a soil test, but Richard was already climbing the steps to the bridge, and Chloe didn't have time to linger.

Chloe caught her breath as she climbed up to the bridge. The pink-and-gold sunset filled the windshield, the fields and the meadows beyond striped with the long shadows of the trees that lined the road. The scene shifted as the town turned, and the spell was broken. Chloe steadied herself on a handrail. Dinner time, and she wasn't home. She'd broken her promise to Connor; being kidnapped wasn't an excuse, not to a kid. Vishesh had better have made it home to tell them what had happened. Chloe shuddered, imagining what Monty would say when he found out what she'd done.

"Shall we continue?" said Richard.

Chloe nodded and followed him down the steps on the other side of the bridge. Richard resumed his cursory tour and pointed out the lounge, the kitchen, and finally, the hydroponic garden. He had been right: they'd arrived at the hydroponic garden before Chloe had settled on her terms.

Brianna poked at one of the empty hydroponic racks. She jumped when they entered and glanced back and forth between them.

"Stay," said Richard. "Once we've established the terms, you will outline what we need from Chloe."

"Yes, sir," said Brianna. She crossed to the doorway and stood with her back to them, her hands clasped behind her.

"You better not expect me to call you *sir*," said Chloe.

Richard's eyes flashed. "Not unless you want to."

No way in hell was Chloe ever going to do that. She just shook her head at him.

"To business," said Richard. "Name your terms."

If this were a negotiation, she would ask for more than she thought she could get. But there didn't seem to be much point in negotiating with someone willing to kidnap to get his way.

"Why should I bother? All evidence would suggest that you're just going to do whatever you want regardless of any terms we decide on."

"I keep my word," said Richard. "I never promised to leave you at Town Iota."

"Fine," snapped Chloe. "When you have your precious hydroponics running, bring your town and decontaminate my settlement."

"Coordinates?" said Richard.

Chloe gave them.

Richard scowled and pulled out his phone. He tapped a few times and then shook his head. "It's outside our range."

"Are you serious? You're not even willing to go outside your range in exchange for not starving? You sound just like the City."

Chloe recoiled as Richard's face twisted into a grimace. He prowled away down one of the long garden rows, and then stalked back and sighed, his features smooth again.

"The range limits of the towns are controlled remotely from the City. If I could circumvent the restrictions, believe me, I would," said Richard. A shadow passed behind his eyes.

So much for asking for more than she needed. He couldn't even give her the lowest possible demand she could make. She sighed.

"Just take me home when all this is done, then."

"That's all?" Richard watched her quizzically.

"What else can you even give me?" said Chloe. She wandered to the back of the garden, past the vertical racks of empty growing stations.

Richard and Brianna's quiet conversation in the doorway was unintelligible from back here. Whatever. The worst Richard could do was refuse to take her home, which, let's face it, he probably would either way. He'd already said her skill set was rare, and if they needed it for the hydroponics, how long until they needed it for one more thing, and then another? She'd fix the hydroponics regardless. What else was she supposed to do now?

***

"I brought you some dinner," said Brianna.

Chloe squinted at the console. She'd found a stack of dusty manuals in a high cupboard at the back of the garden, and she had two of them spread across her lap with a third perched on the edge of the console.

"You know what?" she muttered. "It might be easier to rebuild this from the ground up instead of following the manuals. It'll take me just as long to decipher all this as it will to develop my own algorithms."

Brianna peered over her shoulder. "You understand those?"

"Evidently," said Chloe. "Why else would I have them here crushing my legs?"

"Okay, obviously, it's time for dinner, smart-ass," said Brianna and slapped a dish of food on top of the manuals in Chloe's lap.

Chloe glared at her, but Brianna glared right back and then pulled up a chair to sit beside Chloe at the console.

"For what it's worth, I didn't know about the kidnapping thing," said Brianna, not meeting Chloe's eyes. "Neither did Dorothy. The pilot. We thought he'd convinced you to come with us."

"Then I guess your conscience is clear," said Chloe. She really tried to keep the sarcasm out of her voice.

"We need food," said Brianna. "Badly."

These people were not starving to death, and Chloe would know. Those first few years after armageddon . . . She shook her head to clear the flood of images.

"So do we," she said, instead. She took a deep breath and then kept eating. After a quiet moment: "There are kids at my farm."

Brianna looked up. "Kids?" Her face brightened with something like hope.

"Not mine—not biologically, I mean. They're mostly strays we picked up over the years." Except Connor. Gloria had chosen their farm. She'd thought he'd be safe there, and while she was alive, he had been. And while Chloe had been there. But she wasn't there now.

"We don't see many kids in the towns," said Brianna. She leaned a little closer to Chloe and spoke quietly. "But I'm pregnant."

"That's still a thing that can happen?" said Chloe before she could filter the words. At least she managed to keep her shudder at bay.

"Apparently," said Brianna, and her laughter filled even the darkest corners of the empty room.

"I mean, congratulations," said Chloe, grimacing.

"That's okay," said Brianna. "I guess I managed to avoid getting completely irradiated. Dorothy likes to joke that it's going to be a radioactive mutant baby, but we got a gene sequence done back before we left the City, and it seems completely normal." She poked her tummy. "Don't you, little sproutling?"

"You left the City that recently?" said Chloe. "Richard seems really touchy about it."

"Yeah, you should have seen him when those range restrictions went into effect," said Brianna and put on a stiff affect. "Mother, what you have done is reprehensible. I will not be party to such an egregious overstep of power."

"Mother?" said Chloe.

Brianna froze with a bite halfway to her mouth and then slowly lowered her fork. She cleared her throat. "Richard Phillips? You didn't already know who he is?" said Brianna.

Chloe shrugged. Aaron had said something about Richard being a monster, but she wasn't going to repeat that to Brianna, who clearly worshipped him.

"He was supposed to take over the City from his parents," said Brianna. "But he left. Now he's just a townrunner."

Chloe rolled her eyes. "Playing at being a townrunner until he makes up with his mommy and goes back to the City." Everything made so much more sense now.

Brianna laughed. "You don't know Xander very well—I mean Richard. Don't call him that." She looked as if she'd accidentally swallowed a gobstopper. "Don't tell him I told you that name, either."

"Why not?" said Chloe, and she couldn't help chuckling.

"We've known each other since we were kids. It's not something he wants spread around," said Brianna.

"You know I hate the guy, right? Telling me that just encourages me to spread it around." But the thought made her uncomfortable. Betraying something so personal seemed wrong, even after what he'd done.

Brianna shook her head slowly. "No, it doesn't. You're not a jerk."

"I wish I were a jerk. I'd be at home right now with the kids," said Chloe. *Standing between the kids and Monty* was what she really meant.

"Yes, probably," said Brianna. "But then you'd have to live life as a jerk."

"Thanks for dinner," said Chloe and bent back over the console.

Brianna took Chloe's empty plate and stacked it on top of her own.

"I am so glad to be done with morning sickness," said Brianna. "I'll come back and check on you later. You'll need to sleep at some point. There are quarters for you upstairs." She held up her hand. "I know, I know, the sooner you get done here, the sooner you can get home. You'll probably find you work better after a good sleep, so it'll even out."

"I established the opposite in grad school," said Chloe. She didn't look up again, and Brianna left.

***

Vishesh clutched the handle on the inside of his door. His stomach churned, whether from motion sickness or from what he was about to do. He and Aaron sat silently in the back seat of the SUV.

"This it?" said the driver, glancing at him in the rear-view mirror. The entrance to the farm's driveway was just visible through the long shadows.

Vishesh nodded, and the SUV turned slowly into the lane, crunching the skeletons of weeds that choked it. It had only taken about twenty minutes to drive back the way he and Chloe had walked for hours this morning. Vishesh's pack rested heavily in his lap, since he'd declined Aaron's offer to put it in the trunk. Not that it would make a difference. Aaron was not just here to drop Vishesh off; the hatchback following them up the drive was evidence enough of that.

Nothing stirred in the still yard or silent house as their headlights flashed over it. Vishesh got out of the SUV and slung his pack over his shoulder. The hatchback pulled in beside them and parked. Vishesh waved at the empty upstairs windows. Maybe someone was looking out that he couldn't see; more than likely, the kids were curious if they weren't already in bed. Aaron followed him toward the front porch, but Vishesh waved him back. Even if Aaron insisted on coming in, Vishesh wanted to talk to everyone first.

Vishesh poked his head in the door. "Hello?" he called in a low voice.

Sheila crept down the stairs. "Shh," she said. "I just got Flora down. She didn't want to sleep without Chloe."

Guilt squeezed Vishesh's heart.

"Where is Chloe?" said Sheila. She glanced past him out the front window, and her eyes narrowed. "What have you done?" she hissed.

"I didn't have a choice," said Vishesh. "We weren't the only ones looking for Town Iota, not by a long shot."

"Chloe?"

"Not with them," said Vishesh. "Another scavenger got her."

Sheila didn't have to say, *This is why I voted against involving outsiders.* "Serves Chloe right. She wanted to go find other people, and this is what other people do. At least *she* didn't lead them straight back to us." Sheila glared, her hands in fists at her sides. "I'll get Monty. You better invite them in."

Vishesh sighed, flung his pack onto the living room floor, and stepped back outside. He beckoned to Aaron, who spoke in a low voice to the large figure standing next to him and then sauntered toward the house.

"Be quiet," said Vishesh as Aaron passed. "The kids are in bed."

"Kids?" said Aaron, and he paused.

"Yeah, so don't wake them up," Vishesh said and waved Aaron toward the living room.

Monty already lounged in his usual wingback chair in the dim corner by the fireplace, and Sheila settled herself on the couch with her mending as they entered. The pool of lamplight highlighted her rhythmic stitches. Vishesh took his seat by the window, and Aaron stood in the centre of the room. No one offered him a seat.

"Got a lot of guys out there," said Monty and gestured with his chin.

Aaron smiled. "We wanted to make sure Vishesh got home safely. I didn't want you to lose any more folks."

"Chloe," said Monty. He managed to pack derision, sadness, and affection into that one word.

"I tried to tell her not to trust that townrunner," said Aaron and shrugged. "She wouldn't listen."

Monty was nodding. "That's Chloe, all right. You're not a townrunner yourself?"

Aaron laughed. "Definitely not. I'm just an honest settlement leader, like you." Aaron leaned against the mantelpiece, turning his back on Vishesh to face Monty squarely. "I couldn't see much of your farm on the way in, but from what I saw, it's a nice little place."

Monty looked pleased, but he shrugged. "It's not much, but it's gotten us through a few years so far. Keeps us independent."

"Seems like your biggest problem is rogue subordinates," said Aaron.

"I try to keep them in line, but that's a big job, even for me," said Monty and laughed.

"I don't get to talk to other settlement leaders too often. Maybe you can help me with a problem I've been having," said Aaron. *Here we go.*

"Of course," said Monty. "Happy to help other leaders learn the ropes."

"How do you have power?" He gestured to Sheila, who hadn't even looked up, her needle glinting as she sewed. "I noticed your solar panels, but it's dark."

"Excellent question!" said Monty, and Vishesh shuddered at the condescending look on his face. "We salvaged some batteries a while back. Not much, mind you, but enough to run a light or two and keep the water and fridge running overnight."

"Of course," said Aaron. "Seems so obvious now that you've said it."

"The best ideas always do," said Monty.

Aaron was good. If he'd gone with praising Monty's intelligence or calling him a genius for such a dead simple idea, Monty would immediately have been thrown into suspicious mode. Aaron had done this before, probably many times.

"I doubt I'll be able to return the favour, but is there anything you're wrestling with at the moment? I can do my best to lend a hand," said Aaron.

"As you said, mostly insubordination," said Monty. "Vishesh here and Chloe, who you met, have this idea that we need to decontaminate the soil in our fields. I've told them so many times that we don't need the towns, but they won't listen. Maybe you'll have better luck."

"That's a hard one," said Aaron. "Chloe, at least, was a tough nut to crack." He turned to Vishesh. "I don't know of a way to deconta-minate the soil without the towns, I admit." He pretended to ponder for a moment. "Though, we do have plenty of resources at our settle-ment." He turned back to Monty. "Hear me out," he said, holding up his hand despite the fact that Monty hadn't made to interrupt him. "What if we joined our settlements together? I'm sure we would be stronger if we combined our resources, and with your expertise, we could build something even bigger and better than either of us have right now."

Vishesh could practically see Monty weighing the options in his head. No matter what he might say, he ultimately knew that they couldn't survive here, not with the state of their soil. Vishesh glanced at his pack. All he had to do was tell Monty about the Seed-verts and Monty would refuse Aaron's offer. But Vishesh hesitated.

Chloe was gone, probably for good. If they didn't go with Aaron, if they stayed here, the three of them and the kids, what would happen? They'd try to get by with the Seed-verts, Monty would win every vote, and Vishesh would be the only thing standing between Monty and the kids. Vishesh swallowed and glanced at Sheila. She had finally looked up, and she watched Monty, who only had eyes for Aaron and the vision he had spun. Vishesh couldn't count on Sheila to side with him, not if it meant standing firm against Monty. Vishesh kept his mouth shut.

"I like the way you think," said Monty. "Damn, we were never introduced." He flung a glare at Vishesh. "Name's Monty," he said and stuck out his hand.

"Aaron." They shook hands. "Pleased to meet you."

"You're welcome to spend the night, Aaron," said Monty. "We'll talk more in the morning."

"Yes, I think sleeping on this proposition would be wise," said Sheila, her usual soft lilt replaced by a hard edge to her voice. She tossed her mending on the couch and glared at Monty, who followed her, almost meekly, from the room.

Once they were gone, Aaron deflated against the mantelpiece. Vishesh stood and slung his pack over one shoulder again.

"You can sleep on the couch. Your guys will have to make do with the cars," he said.

Aaron turned to him. "You'll be better off with me."

Vishesh shrugged. He'd come to the same conclusion. But he'd be damned if he was going to admit that to this prick.

"I can't help but notice you didn't mention the Seed-verts," said Aaron. "Those would let Monty avoid the towns' assistance for the foreseeable future." His eyes danced as if he were in on a joke.

"Probably," said Vishesh.

"Ah, well," said Aaron. "Whether I understand your reasons or not, as long as you're on my side, we'll get along fine. Goodnight!"

Vishesh shut the French doors and padded upstairs. On Aaron's side? Did he always have to be on someone else's side? Why couldn't anyone be on his side for a change, even himself?

Chapter Eight

Log: Town Kappa, Richard A. Phillips, Townrunner, 16 May 20—

C rebuilding hydroponics garden. Potential to extend town range as well. Likely no other personnel available who can do so. Utmost effort to be extended to obtain deactivation of range restrictions.

C hloe paced up and down one of the rows of hydroponic racks.

"There's more space in the hallway, if you want," said Brianna from the doorway. "Everyone else is asleep."

"You're not," said Chloe.

"Nope, but I'm on my way there," said Brianna. "Just wanted to waste some time telling you where your quarters are. It's okay, I got the message. You're not going to sleep until this is done. Anything you need before I go?"

"Not unless you can get my laptop connected to the town network. The interface on this console is brutal," said Chloe.

"I can't, but Richard can do it," said Brianna.

"But he's asleep?" said Chloe.

"This might surprise you, but I don't actually keep tabs on the guy twenty-four seven," said Brianna.

"I can look for him," said Chloe. "I'll see you in the morning."

Brianna's footsteps retreated down the hallway, echoed up the stairs, and faded away. The silence rang in Chloe's ears. The town wasn't running anymore. Everyone probably really was asleep, and they trusted her to wander free. She might not get another chance to check for those Seed-verts.

Chloe stuck her head into the hallway and crept to the loading dock, across to the opposite side of the town, and through the doorway into the other hallway. She ducked into the first doorway and then tiptoed to the next. On second thought, it would probably be better *not* to sneak like a creep through the halls. Brianna had told her she was free to leave the hydroponic garden. If she got caught darting from one doorway to the next, it would raise a lot more questions than if she was just wandering down the hall. She took a deep breath and relaxed, trailing one hand along the long windowsill as she went.

The silence of the dim hallway reminded her of the farm, when she couldn't sleep and got up at three a.m. She wasn't alone; people sleeping nearby always made some kind of noise that her subconscious picked up on, even if she couldn't hear them on a conscious level. Her farmhouse probably felt just like this right now, her family tucked safely away for the night.

The lab was the last door before the steps up to the bridge. They seemed to leave the doors open in this town. Chloe flicked on the light and squinted as her eyes adjusted. She had found the Seed-verts at the top of one of the back cupboards in Town Iota. She couldn't help looking over her shoulder as she crossed the lab, but no one watched from the doorway. The cupboard door creaked as she opened it and she froze, but still, no one appeared. She scanned the shelves before her. Empty.

Not empty, of course. Soil test kits and lab equipment she wasn't familiar with, all the usual stuff. No Seed-verts, though. Maybe Richard's falling out with the City meant they hadn't provided Kappa with any, or maybe Richard had already given them out. Chloe sighed and closed the cupboard door, silently this time. She flicked the light off on her way out, and leaned on the windowsill to stargaze while waiting for her eyes to adjust to the dim light in the hallway.

"Find what you were looking for?"

Chloe jumped and stifled a scream. "Jesus Christ, Richard," she said, clutching her chest.

He stood at the top of the steps up to the bridge, his hands in his pockets. He didn't seem angry, but he was so hard to read. "Did you?"

"Did I what?" said Chloe, wearily.

"Find what you were looking for," said Richard, slowly.

"No," said Chloe.

"Are you going to tell me what it was?" said Richard.

Chloe sighed. Was there any point in hiding it? If a plot to conceal the Seed-verts did exist, he wasn't in on it.

"I —" Richard swallowed. "I don't expect you to trust me." He came down and stood beside her, and they looked across the dark landscape together, the hills in the distance merely shadows that blocked the bright stars scattered over the heavens.

"Good," said Chloe. "I don't trust you." A jerk acknowledging her feelings toward him. How novel.

A tiny blinking light tracked across the sky. Satellites still orbited up there, going about their business, maybe looking down on the meat-sacks below with pity.

"I figured your people would be working all night. There are tons of farms to decontaminate, right?" said Chloe.

"The settlement inhabitants like to keep an eye on us while we work," said Richard. "That, along with the reduced number of settlements under our jurisdiction due to the range restrictions means that there is no benefit to night shifts."

Those range restrictions again. How did the City implement those? They must have remote control over the town's propulsion based on their GPS location or something. It made sense that the City would be able to coordinate where each town was allowed to go; there was no sense in having their ranges overlap, not to mention coordination between cities. If there were still any other cities running, out there somewhere.

"Can you hook up my laptop with network access?" said Chloe. "It would make writing this hydroponics program you want much easier."

"Yes," said Richard. "I'll leave the login in the garden for you." He turned, and Chloe almost called him back to tell him about the Seed-verts, but she changed her mind at the last minute and let him go.

***

Chloe hung around, watching the stars, and ate the last of the dried apple she'd had crammed in her pocket from home until she was sure Richard would be finished. True to his word, exactly what she needed was in the hydroponic garden when she got back there: access to a profile set up for her. She made quick work of creating her new program with the algorithm she'd already mapped out and transferred it over to the terminal. She tested everything on one of the racks and even got in a few hours of sleep in her chair once it was done.

"Chloe?" said Brianna and shook her shoulder. "Did you get it working?"

Chloe snorted and pried her eyes open. Three vertebrae popped, and a muscle in her shoulder seized as she stretched out her back. Ten years ago in school, her body had fared much better after pulling an all-nighter in her desk chair.

"Yup," said Chloe. "I tested it on one of the racks last night, but it should be good for all of them. I'll implement it as soon as you or Richard give the okay."

"You could have slept in a real bed, you know," said Brianna.

"If I'd done that, you wouldn't have woken me up," said Chloe. "I need to get home."

"Let's have breakfast, and we can talk about that," said Brianna. "I have an idea."

Brianna refused to tell her any more until they'd grabbed trays of food from the kitchen pass-through window and sat down in the lounge next door with their food. A few other residents milled around or chatted together. Chloe hadn't seen any kids since she'd arrived at Town Kappa, but that wasn't surprising. As soon as armageddon hit, most folks had sent their kids away somewhere closer to the equator, where the longer growing season meant that they stood a chance of getting adequately fed.

"Richard suspects that there's a way around the range restrictions," said Brianna. "As you might have gathered, we don't have any residents up to deciphering whether it's even possible, let alone getting it done. But you?"

Chloe shrugged. "As long as the source code's accessible from our end, I can take a look."

"If you can do it, that means we can go to your farm. Decontaminate your soil. Whether the City approves it or not," said Brianna.

"Yes, you *could*," said Chloe. "What are the chances that Richard would agree, though? I've already done what he wanted. Why would he bother?"

"You really don't trust him," said Brianna.

Chloe fixed her with a deep side-eyed stare.

"Of course you don't," Brianna continued. "Why would you? He's not usually so . . . kidnappy. He's just desperate to take care of us, after we've all sacrificed so much for him."

"I appreciate your defending me, Brianna, but it's really not necessary," said Richard, and both Chloe and Brianna jumped.

"Of course not, sir," said Brianna. "I was attempting to convince Chloe to help us circumvent the range limits."

"After she completes the hydroponic repairs, of course," said Richard.

"They're done," said Chloe. "Just need approval from one of you to implement them across all the racks."

Richard turned back to Brianna. "Did you succeed in convincing her to do us one more favour?" said Richard.

Brianna glanced at Chloe, who sighed.

"I'll work on it on the way to my farm. And if I get it done, you decontaminate my settlement when we get there," said Chloe.

"Agreed," said Richard. "After the currently scheduled pattern is complete."

The floor vibrated, and the town rumbled to life around them. The scenery moved past the window, slowly at first, but gradually sped up.

"It's that time of year," said Brianna. "We'd work through the night if Richard let us."

Chloe gave Richard a significant stare. Maybe his insistence on giving his residents nights off had less to do with pros and cons and more to do with giving them rest. Chloe smiled in spite of herself.

"Make sure you provide Chloe with anything she needs," said Richard. "If you'll excuse me, I'd like to inspect your work on the hydroponics and get them up and running ASAP." He nodded to Brianna and strode from the lounge.

"Does he ever rest?" said Chloe.

"Not that I've seen," said Brianna.

"What about you? How did you get stuck babysitting me?" said Chloe.

"I'm the deputy townrunner. I take care of whatever is most important for the town. At the moment, that's you," said Brianna.

Chloe rubbed her hands on her jeans. She'd agreed to help in the first place because it would make a difference to so many lives. Somewhere along the line, what with the kidnapping, the larger goal had been subsumed by her anger toward Richard and morphed into hostility toward all of the town residents.

Town Kappa sped along what must once have been a highway, trees and old hydro poles flashing past the window. In open spaces, towns could get going fast.

"Wouldn't going to my settlement put you wildly off schedule? I'm sure the town has tons of other decontaminations to do," said Chloe.

"Probably," said Brianna. "Getting out from under the City's thumb is more important. Richard does the prioritizing. I just follow orders." She grinned at Chloe. "Mostly. If I don't agree with them, I also mouth off to my superior."

"I noticed," said Chloe. "Richard doesn't seem to be the type to put up with that."

"I told you, we've been friends since we were kids," said Brianna. "Plus, he knows I'm usually right."

"I'd started to notice that, too," said Chloe with a smile. She took a deep breath. "Time to get to work on this range restriction."

"Head on up to the bridge. I'll clean up our dishes and meet you there. The driver should be able to point you toward the hookup for your laptop."

"I can help clean up," said Chloe.

"Nope," said Brianna. "Your time is way too valuable to spend doing dishes, especially since we only have you for a short while longer, judging by how fast you rebuilt that hydroponics disaster." She snatched their dishes and disappeared into the hallway.

Chloe swallowed the lump in her throat. Monty's attitude had gotten to her much more than she'd wanted to admit to herself. These people valued her abilities, and she was able to give them something that they really needed. A pang of guilt bubbled up through Chloe's chest as she grabbed her laptop and trudged toward the bridge, running her hand along the handrail below the window for balance. She'd been away from the farm overnight. Connor was never going to forgive her. She couldn't waste time imagining a life among these folks, making a real difference. She could never abandon her family, her kids.

Chloe yawned as she climbed up to the bridge, and she tried to stifle it.

"Up all night?" said the driver and poked her head around to glance at Chloe. Dorothy, Brianna had called her, the helicopter pilot with monolid eyes and short black hair from the day before.

"Almost," said Chloe. She gripped one of the handrails by the door and watched the landscape whip toward them and then get eaten up under the town's many legs.

"Fair enough," said Dorothy. She gestured with her head; her hands busy at the wheel of the town. "Hookup's over there."

"Thanks," said Chloe.

How was Dorothy able to control the town at this speed? Chloe barely saw a turn coming before the town was banking into it, likely gouging a rut in the road with its many sharp legs. Chloe tore her eyes from the windshield and staggered across the bridge to the spot Dorothy had pointed out and set up the laptop to mess with the town's source code.

***

The blankets cocooned Vishesh into a snug bundle, and he didn't want to move and risk letting in a blast of chilly air. Flora and Terry were probably trying to be quiet, but their whispering was pretty much as loud as regular voices. Vishesh rolled over.

"He's awake! Can I jump on him now?" said Flora.

"Yes, you may," said Terry. Where they had gotten the idea that Terry could make rules for Flo was a mystery.

"No, you may not," said Vishesh, his voice gravelly. "I'm getting up, wee folk." He opened his eyes. Two little faces poked over the edge of the bed, watching him.

"You came back," said Terry.

"I said I would," said Vishesh.

"Chloe's back, too," said Flora.

Vishesh's heart leaped, before he remembered he was talking to a three-year-old.

"I don't think so," he said. "But we can check." The two little ones trailed him into the hallway. He crouched and spoke seriously. "We have a visitor this morning. He's . . . Aaron," said Vishesh. Calling him a friend seemed a little disingenuous, and calling him an ally probably wouldn't make sense to these two.

Connor poked his head out of his room and scowled at them. "Some stranger, but not Chloe?" he said.

"Yeah," said Vishesh. "We can talk about it after breakfast."

"I'm not having breakfast with a stranger," said Connor.

"Me neither," said Terry.

Vishesh sighed. "You two go get dressed. I'm going to chat with Connor for a few minutes."

Flora and Terry disappeared into their rooms, a chorus of banging drawers cut off a second later when Vishesh straightened, followed Connor into his room, and shut the door.

"Chloe wanted to come back," he said. "She wanted to keep her promise."

"Oh yeah? What was so important that she couldn't?"

Connor was a mature kid, but still a kid. Telling him that she'd been kidnapped might be too much, but anything less might suggest that Chloe had disappeared on purpose.

"We ran across some folks who needed her help, and she agreed to help them," said Vishesh.

"She thinks they're more important than us? *We* need her help," said Connor.

"I know we do," said Vishesh. "I don't have to tell you that things don't always turn out the way we plan them. Downstairs, there's someone who's convinced Monty to consider leaving this settlement entirely."

"Leaving? How will Chloe find us if we leave?" said Connor.

"I'm not sure," said Vishesh. "But he's right that we can't stay here. Our little family . . . we can't survive just us anymore. Especially without Chloe."

"And we have to take care of the kids," said Connor and nodded sharply.

"Not to mention the rest of us," said Vishesh.

Connor looked at him askance.

"It's not healthy for us to be so isolated. In a few years, what will you do? When I was a teenager, I went off to university. Hanging around here taking care of the little kids, you'd never get to be your own person. If we join a larger settlement, there might be other folks your age. Maybe even a real school, a larger community for us to be a part of."

"I don't care about those other people. I just want Chloe to come with us," said Connor. He looked down and blinked hard.

"We'll find her," said Vishesh. "We'll find a way to let her know where we've gone, at least." He was telling the truth. He had to be telling the truth. He would miss Chloe just as much as Connor would.

"Okay," said Connor and wiped his tears away impatiently. "Breakfast."

"Breakfast," said Vishesh. "Let's get the kids downstairs."

They all followed Vishesh down the stairs. Flora peered into the living room, trying to get a glimpse of the stranger, but the French doors were closed. Either he wasn't up yet, or he'd already gone outside, because Vishesh didn't see him, and Flora made no sign that she had.

Sheila already had the kitchen humming along making breakfast, and she turned when they all came in the room.

"Good morning everyone," she said, beaming around at the kids. "Yes, Flora, I know you slept all alone last night, I'm very proud of you. Terry, don't eat that, it's not cooked yet. Connor, can you stir the oatmeal, please? Terry, don't go in there, our guest is still trying to sleep. Flora, I'm already making breakfast, don't get the granola out."

Vishesh took Terry's hand and led him away from the door into the living room, Sheila's words having had no discernible effect on him. Vishesh ignored Terry's grumbling and they looked out the dining room window together. The heavy clouds threatened a downpour before too long.

Sheila had enough to deal with without taking time out to talk to him, but it sure seemed as if she was giving him the silent treatment. A larger community would definitely be good for all of them.

Heavy footsteps on the stairs silenced the chatter from the kitchen, and Terry watched the hallway. After Monty turned the corner, the French doors creaked open, and he disappeared into the living room. Murmured voices and a few chuckles reached them, and then Monty came through into the dining room, and light footsteps retreated up the stairs to the bathroom.

"What're you staring at?" said Monty, scowling around the table.

"Nothing, dear," called Sheila. "Everyone head to the table. Connor, help carry."

Monty scraped his chair across the floor and dropped into it, and Terry followed suit. Flora looked up at Vishesh, wide eyed.

"Come on, Flo," he said and put out his hand to her. She shook her head and glanced at her chair; her tiny frown threatened to dissolve into full-scale bawling. The only free seat for Aaron was Chloe's, right next to Flora. Vishesh desperately wanted to suggest they let the kids eat in the kitchen, but Monty glowered at him, and he couldn't bring himself to do it.

Connor spoke up from the kitchen doorway, carrying in the pot of porridge. "I'll switch with you, Flo. Take my spot."

Flora nodded and scampered around the table to climb up beside Vishesh, and Sheila followed her around to her usual spot. Great, now a preteen was braver than him. Aaron appeared in the doorway, and Vishesh gestured to Chloe's empty chair. Monty spooned porridge into his bowl and didn't look up.

Once the whole family and Aaron were settled around the table, Sheila was the one to break the silence.

"So, Aaron, where are you from?" she said. It seemed like a question from another time. It *was* a question from another time.

"I run a settlement just across the river," said Aaron, which was more information than Vishesh had been able to get out of him in an entire day. Sheila was going to be the hardest to convince, and it seemed Aaron could tell.

"In the hills?" said Sheila.

"That's right," said Aaron. "They're well protected."

"Not much farmland up there," grunted Monty.

"We have a good amount of infrastructure. We get by," said Aaron, and he smiled at Sheila. The scrape of spoons in bowls grated on Vishesh, but he wasn't about to speak up.

"Are there kids there?" said Terry.

"Not many, I'm afraid," said Aaron. "You'd be one of the oldest."

Terry grinned. "The oldest? I'm almost youngest here. Can we go?" said Terry. He turned to Monty, pleading with his eyes.

"I don't see why not. Sheila?" said Monty.

Sheila clenched her jaw, her face blank. Vishesh couldn't believe Monty would stoop to doing this in front of the kids where Sheila wouldn't fight him, even if she wanted to for once.

"We'll talk about it later," she said, not taking her eyes from Monty.

"Unfortunately, there's very little time. I have to be getting home," said Aaron. Maybe he could tell he wasn't going to convince Sheila;

maybe he just thought teaming up with Monty was the best long-term plan. Sheila glanced at him and then stared at her bowl. She wasn't eating, just pushing the food around.

Chloe's absence was a weight on Vishesh's shoulders. He should stop this. Teaming up with Aaron was not in the best interests of their family. And yet, having Monty jerk them all around with impunity wasn't, either. Chloe had trusted Aaron; she'd thought joining forces with his settlement was a good idea, that going it alone was unsustainable for their little family. Vishesh swallowed hard.

"We'll have to vote before you leave, then," he said.

Sheila's glare flicked to him. She set her jaw and jerked a nod. "I don't think a formal vote is necessary in this case," she said.

"I beg to differ, dear," said Monty. "The voting process is merely a formality, but we must have a record of such an important decision. All in favour of relocating our farm to Aaron's settlement, say *aye*."

"Aye," said Vishesh. He refused to look at Connor, but the kid's stare was burning a hole in his head.

"Aye," said Monty. "It's settled. No need to vote, my sweet." Monty's smile twisted. "Unless you'd like to do so. For the record."

"No." Sheila's gaze snapped to Monty. "No thanks. I think the decision is plain enough already."

"Excellent," said Aaron. "I'll inform my men, and we can get this place ready for your big move!" He pushed back from the table and strode out the front door, slamming it behind him.

"I'll need to get to packing the kitchen," said Sheila and slid her chair out as well. She retreated through the kitchen doorway, leaving the rest of them to stew in the awkward silence, broken only by the shouting and banging that drifted in from outside.

***

Connor finished his letter to Chloe and slipped outside. A few drops of rain tapped out a beat on the greenhouse roof and dotted the dirt path he followed to his mum's grave, sheltered under the big tree. The elements had faded the words painted on the gravestone, but Connor knew them by heart. *Gloria. Loving mother, taken too soon.*

"Hey, Mum," Connor whispered. "We're leaving." He sniffed and blinked at the tears that blurred the familiar stone. "We'll probably never come back. Now that Chloe's gone, I don't know what's going to happen."

Chloe had wanted to go for help when his mum got sick. She'd said there was medicine that could have cured her. But Monty had resisted for long enough that his mum had died, sooner than any of them expected.

A leaf crunched behind him and Connor turned.

Aaron stopped short. "Mind if I join you?" he said.

His guys crawled over the roof of their farmhouse and used their tools to dismantle the solar panels and lower them down to the cars.

"Whatever," said Connor.

Aaron stepped up beside him and bowed his head. "Do you want to tell me about Gloria?" he said.

"My mum," said Connor. "She died. Now she's gone. Just like everyone else."

"I'm sorry," said Aaron.

Connor shrugged. It wasn't Aaron's fault. It wasn't even Aaron's fault that Chloe was gone.

"At my settlement," said Aaron, "we keep families together."

"I thought that about us, too," said Connor. He gestured to the gravestone. The drops of rain painted it darker grey, almost black.

"I have more resources. *We* will have more," said Aaron. "We'll be able to make a real difference to your family's life."

"And Chloe?"

"Of course, she'll be welcome to join you, if she's able."

"What do you mean, *able*?"

"Aaron hesitated. "The person she went with . . . might not let her go. She didn't exactly agree to leave with him in the first place."

"He abducted her," said Connor.

"I don't know if I'd go that far," said Aaron.

Vishesh had said she'd agreed to help. Having adults constantly lie to him and pretend it was for his own good was getting old.

"Let's get out of the rain," said Aaron.

The downpour beat hard enough to penetrate the cover of the tree now.

"I think the cars are packed. You ready to go?" said Aaron.

No. He would never be ready to leave his mum behind. "Yeah," he said. Throwing a tantrum like a baby wouldn't change anything. Might as well face this head-on.

Aaron nodded, and Connor followed him across the mushy grass to the cars and got in out of the deluge.

Chapter Nine

Log: Town Kappa, Richard A. Phillips, Townrunner,
17 May 20—

Hydroponics functional and several personnel ramping up production. C exploring range restrictions and possibility of circumventing same. B implementing decontamination schedule for settlements within current range, subject to change.

C hloe hunched over her laptop. It wouldn't go far from the dashboard and still stay connected to the town hookup. She stretched and her back popped in three places. Yawning, she shook out her hands.

"This should be possible," said Chloe, rubbing the bridge of her nose.

"Oh yeah?" said Dorothy, her eyes still on the road.

Chloe had actually been talking to herself, since Dorothy didn't seem too into conversation and they were alone on the bridge, but having someone to bounce her ideas off was sometimes helpful, so she went with it.

"Yes, I have everything I need, at least I thought I did. I keep getting a fatal error, and obviously, I don't want to implement anything that could crash the whole town," said Chloe.

"You could do that?" said Dorothy.

"Theoretically, yes," said Chloe. "I don't know if the town would let me. I'd hope that it wouldn't . . . " Chloe lurched forward and caught herself on the wide dashboard as the town slowed to a stop and then halted with a jerk.

Dorothy sat back in her chair and crossed her arms over her chest. "Better get cracking," she said.

"Why?"

"We're at the edge of the restricted range," said Dorothy.

"Um, why?" said Chloe. "There are plenty of settlements inside the current range."

"I don't make the rules, princess," said Dorothy and jerked her head toward the doorway.

Richard leaned on the doorframe, his arms crossed over his chest as well, watching her. He raised his eyebrows at her and she returned the look.

"The agreement was that I take you home once the hydroponics were implemented," said Richard. "They're implemented, so I'm fulfilling my end of the deal."

Chloe glowered at Richard. What was his angle? He wasn't really going to let her go, was he? He'd been so obsessed with her *skill set*. "Don't you want the range restriction cracked?" she said.

He shrugged. "If it's beyond your capacity, we'll take a transport to your settlement," said Richard. "I did agree, however, to try my utmost to decontaminate your field. That includes doing everything in my power to circumvent the range restrictions, which currently involves you working on the problem."

"How long do I have?" said Chloe resolutely. *Beyond her capacity*.

"How long do you need?" said Richard.

She'd already been away overnight and missed breakfast. She'd be home for lunch. But to show up at the farm with a town . . .

"How long will it take us to drive there?" said Chloe.

"Half an hour," said Dorothy.

"Give me another hour to crack this. If I haven't gotten anywhere by then, take me home," said Chloe.

"Acceptable," said Richard. He nodded as though he'd done what he came here for, turned on his heel, and stepped lightly down the stairs off the bridge.

Chloe shook her head. Something wasn't right about this. He kidnaps her and then lets her go home, just like that? Way too easy. Either way, the range was not going to unrestrict itself. Chloe bent over the laptop again, her neck screaming in protest.

"Why doesn't this have a wireless mode or something?" Chloe grumbled. Wireless mode. That was it! She turned to Dorothy. "Is there any reason you'd want to keep your connection with the City intact?"

Dorothy shrugged. "We never contact them, and the City never moves, so no location necessary."

"I'll take that as a no," said Chloe, and she couldn't keep the smile from lighting up her face. "I found a dark mode in the unused code for the town. It's probably just something one of the original creators was playing with, but it looks like it works like an offline setting."

"Honey, I have no idea what you're talking about," said Dorothy. "Just let me know when it's safe to drive."

"So you know back in the day when software would go online to check for updates and people used to get around it using offline mode?

It's like that," said Chloe. She moved a bit of code around, activated the weird dark mode snippet she'd found, and then tested it.

"I do not," said Dorothy. "Sounds like knocking out a security camera so you can sneak through undetected."

Chloe took her eyes off the log to look askance at Dorothy. "Something like that," she said.

"You done? You stopped typing," said Dorothy. "Looks like the computer is hacking itself."

"We'll find out as soon as this is validated," said Chloe. The success message flashed up on the screen. "Yes!" Chloe tried to implement it again and got the same error. "No. Crap." What was she doing wrong?

At the end of her hour, Chloe still hadn't figured it out, but she also didn't want to leave this problem behind and never get to take a crack at it again. Chances were she'd wake up in the middle of the night with the answer within a week.

"Time's up," said Brianna.

Chloe put her head in her hands. "I'm so close." When had Brianna even gotten here?

"Sorry, Chloe," said Brianna. "We can't wait here any longer. We have a decontamination schedule as long as my arm. Unless you want to stay and keep working . . ."

Chloe shook her head. Getting to the bottom of this error could take days.

"Richard's waiting for you in a transport in the loading dock." Brianna turned to Dorothy. "Were you helping?" She smiled and bent to kiss her.

"Nope," said Dorothy. "Hindering, if anything. You know I can't do computers."

"I'm sure you were excellent moral support, love," said Brianna.

Chloe sighed. "Crap. I hate leaving a problem just sitting there." Chloe replayed their conversation in her head. "Yes, Dorothy, you were excellent moral support. Thanks."

Chloe packed up her laptop, and Brianna hugged her as she passed. Chloe's mind was still tangled with the code she'd been deciphering. "I have the code on my laptop," she said. "If I figure it out, I'll call." Except their receiver was smashed. But with any luck, Vishesh would be at the farm with their salvage. "It'll look like it's coming from Town Iota."

"I won't ask. Thanks for doing the hydroponics," said Brianna, her hand resting protectively on her belly. "Baby Dot needs their nutrients."

"I thought we weren't calling them that anymore," said Dorothy, but she couldn't hide her smile.

Chloe smiled as well, finally coming back to earth. "All the best with ... Baby Dot," she said. "It was nice spending time with someone other than my family." And she was a little surprised to realize it was true.

***

The moment Chloe and Richard were clear, the town turned around and headed back toward the settlements within their range.

"They're not waiting for you?" said Chloe. She'd assumed that he would be a terrible driver, that Dorothy chauffeured him everywhere. He seemed fine, though, if anything, very experienced at dodging potholes.

"Certainly not," said Richard. "I have all night to apprehend them, worst-case scenario."

"They don't need you to run the place?" said Chloe.

Richard raised his eyebrow at her. "You did meet Brianna, didn't you?"

Chloe shrugged. She had thought he'd be one of those guys who assumed nothing would work in his absence and then be shocked when things actually ran more smoothly instead. Chloe kept her eyes on the horizon to head off the queasiness pooling in her belly. She'd never been carsick back in the day, but her stomach seemed to have forgotten how to handle this speed of movement in the intervening years. Or maybe being alone with Richard was making her nervous. He *was* a good driver.

"The driveway's coming up on your right," said Chloe, and Richard slowed down.

The weeds that had tormented her and Vishesh on their way out had been flattened and ground into dust, and the long driveway was rutted and churned to mud. Chloe's heart pounded, even though she was fairly sure she knew what they were going to find. Richard didn't comment on the state of the driveway; maybe he thought it was always like this. He stopped near the house and put the SUV in park. Chloe popped her seatbelt and cracked open her door. She took a deep breath. Even if they weren't there, she'd find some clue and track them down.

Chloe hopped down from the black SUV and slammed the door behind her. The mud squished under her boots, churned up by what had clearly been a fleet of vehicles. Richard followed her across the yard, and when she stopped, he stopped alongside her. Frogs chirped in the silence, and the wind ruffled Chloe's hair. She jammed her hands into her pockets and set her jaw.

"It appears to have been stripped," said Richard.

Chloe glared at him. *Thanks, Captain Obvious.* The solar panels had been removed none too gently: shingles littered the muddy yard, and a gaping bare patch of chipboard marred the roof. Two of the big front window frames gaped, having had the panes popped expertly from them, and the front doorframe drew Chloe in like a black hole, the door itself nowhere in evidence.

Decontaminating their fields would be pointless now: wherever her family had gone, they weren't planning on coming back.

Chloe reflexively wiped her boots on the doormat before stepping over the empty threshold. The couch was gone, along with the TV and the appliances. They must have had a team of people cleaning this place out. Which meant that Monty had agreed to let *someone* help. Goddamn Monty! He'd refused to even entertain the idea of seeking help any time Chloe had proposed it, but coming from someone like Aaron he'd clearly jumped at the chance.

At the top of the stairs, something drew her to Connor's room, and she poked her head in. Sure enough, there was her collection, tucked under his desk, a note sitting on top. Her things seemed to be intact, not that they were particularly useful, even to Chloe. It might as well be a museum collection at this point, but she couldn't seem to let it go. It had taken her long enough to build that leaving it behind would be a permanent loss. And Connor had left it behind. He didn't expect her to find them.

"Have you read the contents of the note?" said Richard.

Chloe jumped and took a deep breath. "Not yet," she replied and pulled the drawstring on her pack tight. She straightened, and opened the note, read through it, and then tucked it carefully in her pocket. "Fucking Monty," she said under her breath and slung the pack onto her back.

"And Monty is . . . ?" said Richard and stepped back to let her pass.

Chloe made short work of her own room; they'd left a bunch of clothes she'd be happy to have, but whoever had cleaned the place out had taken the rest.

Richard stood at the top of the stairs, arms crossed across his chest, and stared her down.

"Who is Monty?" he said again.

"Douchebag who wouldn't call for help," said Chloe and pushed past Richard. "I guess he changed his mind. I hope Vishesh was here when he did at least. Anything you want to strip from this place?"

Richard followed her down the stairs. "Everything worth taking seems to have already been taken."

"Might be worth looking at the well and the sump pump. Some of those parts are hard to come by and maybe got missed," said Chloe. Nothing else sprang to mind, so she dumped her pack at the top of the stairs and continued down to the cellar. She threw the cellar door wide so that she would have a shaft of light to see by and snorted. So much for the valuable parts being missed. The entire sump pump was gone, and the well had been taken apart and raided.

"They were very proficient at stripping a settlement," said Richard, hunched over behind her in the low cellar.

"Same thing at Town Iota. Aaron's been busy," said Chloe. She climbed out the cellar door, took a quick look around the greenhouse (lost cause), and made for the shed.

Chloe paused at Gloria's grave. The rain from the morning had given way to a chill wind, and Chloe shivered. Gloria had known they'd someday need to leave their safe little bubble, but they'd all thought they had more time before they'd have to face it. One goddamned infection, and now Gloria never would.

The shed proved just as fruitless as the rest of Chloe's search, and she stomped back through the kitchen door and banged it shut behind her. Richard leaned back against the counter and watched her half-heartedly search the kitchen cupboards.

"What's your survival plan? This place is no longer viable," said Richard.

"Hm, I don't know," she said and slammed a cupboard. "Since all of this is your fault, I think it's only fair that you take me in."

"That's acceptable," said Richard. "Town Kappa can make use of you."

"*Make use of* me, yup that sounds about right," said Chloe. The cupboards were empty. No food was left here, nothing left here at all. She glared across the kitchen at Richard.

"I expect that you have conditions," said Richard, infuriatingly placid.

Chloe shrugged. "I'm not really in a position to make demands. I don't come with you, I starve or die of radiation poisoning, maybe both at once."

"Come with me, then. Help me," said Richard. He leaned forward, his gaze burning into her. "I didn't just mean that the town can use you, I meant *I* can use you."

Chloe's stomach leaped, and she stepped forward. Richard was attractive, despite the suit and the manipulation. She shook her head. He couldn't mean he wanted a physical relationship with her; he'd never even hinted at that.

"Your skills are not exactly common anymore, Chloe," he said.

Ah, her skill set, of course. Her obsolete skill set that was suddenly so essential that his town couldn't live without it. Being able to program again had its own allure, even if she did have to deal with Richard. If she could crack the range restriction, she could make a real difference, maybe even pass it around the other towns . . .

"Fine, but I'm not doing it for you," said Chloe.

"I wouldn't dream you'd ever do anything for me," said Richard.

Wait, was he making a joke? Chloe frowned at his completely impassive face.

"And I have conditions," she said. "Don't look so satisfied with yourself, I would have had conditions anyway."

"Of course," said Richard. "State them."

"I don't take orders from you," said Chloe. *Keep to the essentials here.* Richard would twist any agreement they made to his benefit. He couldn't seem to help it. "If we find my people"—Chloe gestured around at the house—"we get in touch and make sure they're okay."

"Done," said Richard. "Let's go."

Chloe's chest tightened. He'd agreed to that way too easily, which could only mean bad things for her.

As they crossed the muddy yard again, Chloe shaded her eyes from the evening sun and looked out over the empty vegetable patch. That's what had started this whole thing, when she and Vishesh had tested that field, right there, and found out there was nothing they could do on their own. Joining with Richard, breaking the range restrictions, was the best way of finding her family again.

Chloe swung her pack into the backseat of the SUV and climbed in the passenger side. Richard turned the SUV around, and Chloe watched in the side mirror as the farmhouse disappeared for the last time behind her.

***

Vishesh couldn't tear his eyes from the road ahead of them, in some places visibly crumbling. The highway crossed a bridge over open water, and Vishesh held his breath. They turned onto a smaller road and followed the Gatineau River northeast. The neighbourhood to their right would have been a normal suburb back in the day, probably with a little school and a corner store. The sign for a Chinese restaurant flashed past, not yet weathered away.

The river rushed by on the other side, high in its banks from the snowmelt coming down from the hills. What would normally be rapids was a placid surface, though the occasional branch being carried along showed how swift-flowing the water really was.

By the time they passed the Lucky Luke sign on their left, Vishesh had a suspicion where they were going, which was confirmed as the entire convoy slowed and turned into a rutted lane by the Farmer's Rapids generating station. Monty was right that arable land was scarce up here, but with enough power and the hydroponic gardens they'd likely stolen from towns, Aaron might have been telling the truth when he said they got by okay.

A couple of warehouses with big windows across the front greeted them, along with a few reassuringly well-dressed and well-fed folks. A short white woman with bright-red lipstick stepped forward to greet Sheila when she descended unsteadily from the SUV in front of Vishesh's. The two of them conferred while Vishesh got Terry unbuckled, and they both climbed down to the pavement. Sheila glared at Vishesh, clearly not having forgiven him for this entire situation. The other woman held out her hand.

"Hi, I'm Portia," she said with a customer-service smile. "You must be Vishesh."

"That's right," he responded, and they shook hands.

Sheila opened the back door of the SUV.

"I see you have some little ones. We should get them squared away first."

"We're staying together," said Sheila. She gathered Flora in her arms, the little girl's face snuggled into her neck.

"Of course!" said Portia and turned to Vishesh. "Will you be joining them?"

He frowned at her and gripped Terry's hand tighter. "I'm staying with them."

Portia's gaze drifted to Sheila to double-check, and she nodded, reluctantly. Portia shrugged. "We'll find space for all of you, then."

Terry clung to Vishesh's hand and stared wide-eyed at the strangers that milled about, pretending they weren't watching him with just as much interest.

"I thought Aaron said there are other kids here," said Vishesh.

"There are," said Portia. "These folks don't see them too often."

Alarm bells sounded in the back of Vishesh's mind, but he pushed them away. He'd made this choice, and there was no going back.

Aaron and Monty strode around the SUV side by side, Connor in their wake, staring at the ground.

"Let me show you around, Monty," Aaron was saying. "You can meet back up with your family after you get the tour."

"As long as Vishesh is confident he can get everything sorted out," said Monty, giving him a pointed look.

"I'll stay with the family," said Vishesh.

Connor jammed his hands in his pockets and scowled at the ground.

"Maybe Connor can come with us?" said Aaron. "I'm sure he'd be interested in how this place works."

"What do you think, kid? Chloe's not here to baby you, so you ready to join the grown-ups?" said Monty.

Connor glanced at Vishesh.

"We'll still be here when you get back," said Vishesh, quietly. His heart broke to have Connor's well-being entrusted to two snakes who didn't have his best interests at heart, but they would at least keep him safe. Vishesh also wanted Connor to be able to relay the tour back to him, since he'd declined to go himself. He tamped down his guilt and smiled at Connor.

Connor stood up a little straighter and took his place on the other side of Aaron. The three of them retreated toward the generating station. Vishesh turned back to Portia, who also watched them go, a strange look on her face. She glanced at him.

"He'll be okay," she said. "Aaron values his people, and you're his people now."

Vishesh nodded. "Lead the way to our quarters."

Portia laughed. "You sound like you're expecting a barracks. We have a nice row of houses."

Vishesh took one more look over his shoulder, but the others were out of sight. He squeezed Terry's small hand gently in his and followed Portia down a muddy footpath. Sheila trudged beside them, still carrying Flora.

"When can I expect you to forgive me?" Vishesh murmured to her.

"When we can be sure what you've gotten us into," said Sheila. "Maybe not even then."

Houses, clean food, power, maybe even a community. Vishesh, for once, let himself hope for the best. There was something odd about the way Portia had talked about the children, but otherwise, this place seemed well thought out. Maybe once they'd settled in, they could even get a message to Chloe, let her know where they'd gone. Vishesh's heart clenched. Even if she did know, it was likely she wouldn't be free to come and join them. She had been kidnapped, after all.

Chapter Ten

Log: Town Kappa, Richard A. Phillips, Townrunner,
18 May 20—

C acquired as permanent personnel. Tasked with circumventing range restrictions. Scheduled decontaminations being carried out by B. Hydroponic repairs
progressing well. Distress call received from the City.
No reply planned.

C hloe finally had a build of dark mode that wasn't throwing
up any errors, and she'd integrated it into the town's infrastructure. She set the whole thing to compile so she could make sure
everything was playing nicely together. It would probably take hours,
so no point in sitting here waiting for it. She wandered from the bridge
up to the living quarters that Brianna had shown her to last night
when they had gotten back. Thankfully, Brianna hadn't asked her any
questions; she'd probably guessed what Chloe and Richard had found
at the abandoned farm.

Chloe closed her door, lay back on her bunk, and stared out the
tiny skylight at the painfully blue spring sky. She pulled Connor's

note from her pocket. His handwriting was just like Gloria's, whether intentionally or because she was the one who had taught him to write. Chloe swallowed the lump in her throat as she read the short letter again.

Dear Chloe,

You weren't back for dinner like you said and you're still not back now. I guess that means you don't care about your collection. If you come back looking for it, I guess you'll be glad it's still here where you left it.

Monty wants us to go with this guy Aaron. If he knows where, he hasn't told the rest of us. Vishesh says you running away wasn't your fault. I hope you helped those people you wanted to stay and help.

Connor

Chloe tucked the note back in her pocket and stared out the skylight again. Where did Connor learn to be so passive-aggressive? Were teenagers naturally like this, or had the dynamic at the farm been worse than Chloe thought?

Richard could probably help her to find her family, but he had no motivation to do so. She would have to do it herself if she ever wanted to see them again.

A knock on her door startled Chloe upright.

"Yes?" she called. Who would be knocking on her door? The only people she knew were Richard, Brianna, and Dorothy.

"Got any plans for lunch?" said Dorothy through the door.

Chloe opened it. "I thought you'd be busy."

"Nah, I don't drive the decontamination patterns. I go too fast and wreck the fields," said Dorothy, almost smiling.

"Brianna asked you to keep an eye on me, right?" said Chloe. She stepped out and shut her door.

Dorothy shook her head. "We've all lost people. Most of us have lost everyone."

Chloe followed her down the stairs, past the bustling kitchen, where they grabbed their meals, to the lounge. Dorothy pointed across the room to two empty seats behind a table of laughing residents, and Chloe followed her there.

"I thought I'd lost everyone back in the day, but new people managed to worm their way into my heart and now it's happened all over again," said Chloe.

"Yeah," said Dorothy. She bumped Chloe with her shoulder. "Best not to sit alone in a locked room, eh?"

Chloe sighed sheepishly. "I guess you're right," she said.

"How's knocking out the City's metaphorical security cameras going?"

"I'm not sure yet," said Chloe. "I think it's going well."

"Taking a break before getting it done?" said Dorothy, conversationally. There was no rush now that Chloe was here for . . . well, forever.

"Not exactly. The code is compiling. It'll probably take a few hours. Then I just have to test it, then hopefully implement it, if there aren't any errors," said Chloe.

"Hours? You must have a high suspense tolerance," said Dorothy. She either had no sense of humour or an excellent sense of humour.

"Is this what the towns normally do? Just go from settlement to settlement, running decontamination patterns?" said Chloe.

"In the spring, yeah," said Dorothy. "We've only been doing this for a little while."

"And before that?" said Chloe.

Dorothy grinned wolfishly. "Nope, not a chance, princess," she said. "Weasel information out of Brianna."

"She told you . . . that she told me . . . what she told me?" said Chloe, grinning back.

"Yes, she did," said Dorothy, suddenly serious. "Don't spread it around. Richard is . . ."—*scary, violent, unpredictable*—"more vulnerable than you think."

Chloe raised her eyebrows. "It wouldn't make him angry?"

Dorothy shrugged. "I don't know if anything would. If he was, he wouldn't show it. Not the way you're thinking."

"Kidnapping, yes, violence, no?" said Chloe bitterly.

"He does what he has to to keep us alive. Now that includes you."

"And you all are just fine with the kidnapping?" said Chloe. "If you'd known I wasn't coming willingly, would you still have gone along with it?"

"Would you call him out for saving your life? The life of your partner?" said Dorothy. "Your kid?"

"I — " Chloe shut her mouth. That had been the exact choice Dorothy had been called upon to make. Brianna and Baby Dot, who no doubt wouldn't develop properly if Brianna didn't get the nutrition they needed. Chloe would have been relieved to find her family still hanging around the farm, but on some level she was glad they had gotten out of there. As long as they were somewhere better, hopefully not totally dominated by Monty . . .

"That's what I thought," said Dorothy. She gripped Chloe's shoulder. "We'll look for your family, too. Crack those range restrictions, and we'll search for them properly."

Chloe didn't mention that turning on her dark mode would probably also knock out their network access and maybe communications, but it wouldn't be permanent; as long as they were within the prescribed range they'd be able to turn it off again. She nodded.

"Thanks for dragging me out of my room," she said.

"No problem," said Dorothy. "Brianna said something about a bug with the hydroponics. But I figured you hadn't eaten."

"Sorry, has Brianna been waiting for me this whole time?" said Chloe.

"Yeah, she would have wanted you to eat first, too," said Dorothy. "I'll take your tray!" she called after Chloe as she hurried from the lounge, trying not to jostle too many residents as she went.

***

Without farm chores and kids to care for, Chloe was at a total loss. Squashing the hydroponics bug took next to no time, and her check on the compiling code showed it would take a few hours more. With nothing else to do, she sat on the bridge with her laptop, poking around on the network. Was it possible that Aaron had accidentally taken something from a town that could be tracked to his settlement? Maybe a car or a part of a town?

Kappa ground to a halt for the night and when the driver said a terse goodnight to Chloe, she jumped and looked around. The windows showed her own face and her laptop screen reflected back at her. Yikes, she still hadn't eaten dinner. The sun was below the horizon, its last rays just streaking up the sky, turning the low clouds bright pink and orange. Maybe she could still scrounge something to eat.

Chloe left the laptop to keep compiling her code and wandered through the emptying hallway to the kitchen. The window was shut for the evening, no trays of food left on the counter. If Brianna and Dorothy hadn't been babying her, she might just starve.

"Miss dinner?" said Richard as he came up behind her. His hair was rumpled, and he had doffed his suit jacket.

"Yeah," said Chloe and sighed.

"Me too," said Richard. "Come on in. We can cook something. The kitchen's always open to all residents."

"You don't mean you want me to cook for you, do you?" said Chloe. His appearance was unsettling enough without having him stare at her while she tried to cook whatever she could scrounge up into a meal. She shut the door behind them.

Richard chuckled. "As a townrunner, I would be within my rights to order you to cook for me. I explicitly stated *we* can cook something, and that is my intention." Richard rolled up the sleeves of his dress shirt and rummaged around in the big fridge. He laid a couple of wizened zucchinis on the countertop and added a brick of tempeh. "Behold, our feast."

"Oh dear," said Chloe. She rooted in the pantry and came up with soy sauce, hot sauce, and a couple of potatoes. Back in the day, she would have added something more savoury, but it was impossible to get spices at their latitude and meat was practically nonexistent. Bioaccumulation rendered pretty much any animal product besides honey too labour-intensive to keep decontaminated.

Richard sliced the tempeh while Chloe washed the zucchini and then passed it to Richard to slice while she made the sauce. The kitchen here was bigger than the one at the farmhouse, which was to be expected, considering they had to feed about thirty residents here in the town. It gave Chloe plenty of room to leave space between her and Richard. She *wasn't* admiring his hands as he sliced, just his technique. Obviously.

When he finished the prep, Richard washed his hands and added a splash of oil to heat in a wok on the induction burner. He ran a hand through his hair. Okay, fine, she had to ask.

"I don't know you very well," said Chloe, "but you seem pretty worried about something."

Richard sighed. "My distress is not your concern," he said. "It's my responsibility to sort out town affairs."

"I see why Brianna mouths off to you," said Chloe.

Richard's mouth quirked up. "Is that so?"

"Especially if you always pull this *I must shoulder the burden alone* crap."

"I don't consider it to be *crap*. A leader's role is to unburden his subordinates so that they are free to optimize the efficiency of their own tasks."

"My code is compiling, so no tasks to optimize here," said Chloe. She popped herself up onto the countertop and tapped her heels on the cupboard door below.

Richard shook his head and dumped the tempeh into the hot pan. The sizzling would drown out anything more that Chloe tried to say. Which was definitely the point. Chloe's throat went dry as Richard stir-fried their food, using economical movements. Must be his technique again. The excellent technique of his exposed forearms. Richard scooped the cooked food into bowls and put one on the counter next to Chloe. He stood across from her and held his bowl with one hand so he could eat with the other.

"It seems the City is asking us for help. Asking me for help, I should say," said Richard, staring into his food.

"Your parents?" said Chloe.

Richard's sharp eyes locked onto hers, and he nodded.

"You're in a fight with them," said Chloe. What she wouldn't give to have parents left to fight with.

"It's more complicated than that, but yes, I suppose," said Richard.

"Did you say you'd help?" said Chloe.

"I don't plan to answer them," said Richard.

"Do you know what they need help with?" said Chloe. "Maybe it's important."

"I don't know the exact details, no. It's likely to be important, yes. They have many capable staff members. I'm certain they can handle it."

"But what if—"

"I'm sorry if I led you to believe that I was seeking advice. I appreciate you listening to my problems," said Richard.

The cooking had given the impression of a thoughtful and caring person, but it turned out Richard was the same cold jerk he'd been since he kidnapped her.

"I should go check my code to see if it's compiled," said Chloe. She grabbed his empty bowl and took it to the sink. "And I'm sure you have tons of important tasks to attend to. I'll clean up." She busied herself at the sink and didn't look up as he hesitated, one hand on the doorknob. In the end, he left without a word.

Chloe was getting too comfortable here. Richard had kidnapped her, and the others had gone along with it. She couldn't afford to make friends, to settle in here. One, her family was waiting for her out there somewhere. Two, anyone she got close to could be ripped away at any moment. She dried her hands and pulled out Connor's note again. No, she did not need to lose anyone else.

***

Vishesh had not been expecting Aaron to show up on their doorstep during breakfast.

"Want a cup of tea?" said Vishesh. He stepped aside to let Aaron into the house. The rest of the family sat around the kitchen table. There was no dining room in their new house, but the kitchen was more than large enough to contain them all.

"You have tea?" said Aaron.

"Not *tea* tea," said Vishesh. "Just steeped fennel, mint leaves, and dandelion root."

"I'll pass," said Aaron with a grimace. "I came to ask you on a tour of the settlement, if you're interested. You missed out when you arrived."

Connor hadn't had a chance to relate any of the tour to Vishesh since the past day and a half had been a whirlwind of unpacking and meeting other folks around the settlement, including a handful of other children.

"Sure," said Vishesh. He called goodbye to the family and grabbed his coat from the hall closet. He stuffed his hands in his pockets. Since armageddon, the moodiness of March had been moved forward to May, only more so. The wind today was biting, which was probably why there was no one out milling around. Aaron fell into step beside him, and together they crossed to the generating station. The hum of the overhead wires running across the road set Vishesh's teeth on edge, but it meant they had power, and plenty of it.

Aaron let them into the station through a door on the side of the dam, and the splash of the turbines drowned out the annoying hum. The generating station seemed to be running along smoothly, though plenty of what Aaron called to him over the ever-present noise went over Vishesh's head.

They toured the hydroponic garden next. Aaron led the way through the vertical racks of kale, green beans, tomatoes, soybeans, and blueberries. Vishesh brushed his thumb over a worn Gobi palm tree on the end of one rack. So they *were* from the towns.

"Have you hooked in the garden from Town Iota yet?" said Vishesh, casually.

"Not yet," said Aaron. "We're still working on it." Strange, he didn't seem ashamed to admit that he was the one who'd raided Town Iota. How he'd known that the town was crashed and vulnerable was the open question. "The Iota engineers are making progress. Slow progress, but progress nonetheless." So there *had* been town residents present when Aaron had first arrived at Town Iota. Why would they have agreed to come here to his settlement instead of hailing another town or the City for help?

They passed through a heavy door and across a covered patio to another low building.

"This is where I spend most of my time," said Aaron, gesturing Vishesh through the doorway. "The nerve centre of the settlement."

An empty desk at one end of the room overlooked a sea of cubicles. Where had they scrounged cubicles from? Vishesh peeked over the dividers at the handful of people hunched over keyboards. It was like an office from back in the day.

"My office is back there," said Aaron, gesturing to the corner of the space. The corner office. The population of nearby settlements was half-starved, and this guy had a corner office. The cognitive dissonance short-circuited Vishesh's brain. A young man in town uniform approached Aaron.

"Sir, you wanted me to check in when I"—he glanced at Vishesh—"completed my task."

"Excellent work," said Aaron. "Wait for me in my office." The young man retreated. "An engineer from Town Iota. He's doing really well here so far."

What happened to the folks who didn't *do well* here? Vishesh didn't want to know the answer to that.

"So you *appropriated* all the town residents then?" said Vishesh.

Aaron shrugged. "Where else were they going to go once the town was wrecked?"

Vishesh nodded, as if he were agreeing, but in his experience, no town resident would choose to live in a settlement or vice versa. Over the past few years, everyone had chosen a side and dug in their heels, in some cases literally. The chances were vanishingly small that a whole town suddenly agreed to drive away with some random dirt-folk who claimed to be a settlement leader.

He followed Aaron back out into the wind, the clouds now spitting on them as they crossed back to Vishesh's new house.

"Make a list of your skills, no matter how minor, and we'll help you fit in here," said Aaron. "Wouldn't want you to just sit around bored." He tossed a smile over his shoulder at Vishesh, and Vishesh tried to return it. So that was it, then? He'd traded a life where he had to, practically single-handedly, run the whole farm for an empty existence of being a cog in a machine, likely discarded if he didn't have any "value" to bring to the settlement? This was the whole reason he'd refused to join a town. He and Chloe both had refused to be ordered around ever again. Looked like that was about to change.

Chapter Eleven

Log: Town Kappa, Richard A. Phillips, Townrunner,
19 May 20—

C successfully circumvented range restriction, uti-
lizing what will hereinafter be referred to as "dark
mode." Hydroponics online and fully functional.
Decontamination proceeding apace (supervisor B),
priority given to settlements outside of the official
town range. In case of the eventuality that dark mode
fails, decontamination of neglected settlements must
be maximized.

C hloe followed Brianna across the muddy yard, so like the one
at her old farmhouse. A wizened old man greeted them with a
shotgun and a scowl.

"Why are there two of you?" he said.

"I'm glad you asked," said Brianna. "Chloe, you want to explain
yourself?"

Chloe glared at Brianna and then turned to the old man. "I'm recently from a settlement myself, and I wanted to make sure you have everything you need. Clean water, electricity."

"We have a cistern to collect rainwater, and we don't need power," said the old man. "Just get on with the fields. I don't have all day." He clutched his gun a little tighter, and Chloe recoiled.

Brianna smacked her shoulder. "Chloe here's not been with the town long, as I'm sure you can tell. Point me toward the fields, and I'll get the town running a pattern for you."

The old man gave Chloe one last suspicious glare and then stepped toward Brianna to establish the decontamination area. Rainwater? Didn't they know that they were poisoning themselves with rainwater? Groundwater was the only safe drinking water source due to the limited bedrock aquifer recharge rates in the area's silty soil. All the Seed-verts in the world wouldn't keep folks from irradiating themselves with water from a cistern. Chloe rubbed her palms on her jeans, suddenly aware of the windows of the farmhouse looking down at her. An impulse to get out of here swept over her, along with the awareness that the man before her and anyone else living here were likely slowly dying of cancer as they spoke.

Brianna was right, though. Telling them that wouldn't do any good. If they weren't using well water already, there was likely no way for them to get it. Either they had no well or it was long-since defunct. The only reason the well at Chloe's old farmhouse had been functional was that she and Vishesh—mostly Vishesh—had known what to raid from surrounding houses and known how to repair their machinery with it.

The old man actually shook Brianna's hand, and Brianna grabbed Chloe's arm and towed her back to the loading dock, up the ramp, and waited until the ramp was shut to burst out laughing.

"There's nothing funny about people slowly dying of radiation poisoning," said Chloe.

Brianna sobered and sighed. "You're right," she said. Brianna plodded across the loading dock to the hallway. "You think most folks at little settlements like these have power?" She paused to quirk her eyebrow at Chloe. "Did you see any solar panels?"

"I guess not," said Chloe and followed in Brianna's wake.

Brianna shook her head. "The receivers they use to call us are usually the highest tech these folks have access to. When the towns carried Gobi reps, there might have been something we could do for them—if they were desperate enough. But now?" Brianna shook her head and stomped up the steps to the bridge where she passed along the decontamination pattern info to the driver, then cocked her head at Chloe. "That means you had power at your farm?"

"Yeah," said Chloe. "Vishesh and I scrounged up a bunch of panels." Chloe tried to swallow the lump in her throat. Their life had by no means been perfect, but in retrospect, their quiet little farm existence had been paradise compared to the alternatives that these settlements had to face. Or being separated like this.

"We'll find your family," said Brianna.

Chloe shrugged, unable to speak without risking a sob crawling up her throat.

"Let's go to the lounge since our work is done for the day," said Brianna.

Chloe cleared her throat. "That's all you have to do today? I thought you had a whole bunch of responsibility around here."

"Some days more than others," said Brianna and beckoned her off the bridge.

They settled in the lounge, side by side on a loveseat. They watched the farmhouse go by, then trees, then the farmhouse, back and forth as the town ran a pattern across the field. The vibrating hum of the decontamination mechanism was starting to feel soothing rather than grating.

"Did Richard tell you about the communication from the City?" said Chloe.

Brianna frowned. "He did not," she said. A couple of town residents passed in the hallway. "What was it about?"

"He said they were asking for help," said Chloe.

"They would," said Brianna and rolled her eyes.

"What do you mean?"

"Anything to get Richard to talk to them."

"But what if the City really needs help?"

"Why would they approach their estranged son with his ragtag team of deserters if they really needed help?"

"Search me," said Chloe. "I'd just hate to be wrong and suddenly have something happen to the City. No City, no network. No network, no communications with the settlements at all."

"When you put it that way . . ." said Brianna.

"Trust me, I have no love for the City. They're the ones who put my settlement out of range and started this whole thing. Maybe one day, we can find a way to keep the towns running without the City's oversight, but for the time being, it's essential to the structure of the decontamination apparatus as we know it."

"Fine, fine. I'll get in touch with the City and see what's up. But if Richard asks, I'm blaming you."

"We'll have to do it while we're stopped," said Chloe. "If you want to use the network, you'll have to deactivate dark mode, and as soon as dark mode is deactivated, the range restrictions will come back into effect, and we'll lose locomotion control. My fix is a workaround, not a real solution."

"Maybe you should get to work on the real solution, then," said Brianna.

"I've been thinking about it," said Chloe. "It would involve cutting the City out as the routing system for the network. It would take cooperation from the other towns, though. What are the chances of that happening?"

Brianna chuckled darkly. "Zero," she said. "Town Kappa is the only anti-City town. All the other townrunners were chosen for their loyalty to the City. And by that I mean the Phillips family. Don't look so excited—they don't consider Richard a Phillips since he left."

"It doesn't make sense for them to want to be under the City's control. Wouldn't they rather be autonomous?" said Chloe.

"You really are new around here," said Brianna. "The City gave them their power, and the City can take it away. You and Richard might be all *burn the system down*, but people like you two are few and far between."

"What about you?" said Chloe.

"Me?" said Brianna, taken aback. "I never really thought about it. I want a better world for my kid, whatever that looks like."

"Yeah," said Chloe. "Me too."

***

Chloe looked up from her lunch in the lounge when a Town Kappa resident made a beeline for her. She recognized the person, but she didn't know their name. True, she'd only been here a few days, but still, she hadn't put any effort into getting to know these people, maybe because part of her assumed she would be leaving them behind soon. And another part of her didn't want to get attached.

"You're wanted on the bridge," said the resident.

"Okay, I'll be there . . ." Chloe trailed off as the resident turned their back and walked away. It was fine that they didn't care about her. She didn't want them to, anyway.

She tidied her lunch tray and headed to the bridge. Dorothy nodded to her from the driver's seat, but Brianna ignored her, staring fixedly out the windshield. They were on the road again, heading to the next of an endless series of settlements.

Brianna turned to her, as serious as Chloe had ever seen her. "Chloe," she said. "I'm assigning you temporarily to the City."

"I'm sorry, what?" said Chloe. Brianna could do that? Chloe was a town resident now, but she'd made a deal with Richard not to order her around.

"Care to rephrase that, resident?" said Brianna, regarding her coolly.

"Not really," said Chloe. "What did the City have to say about the distress call?"

"That's an excellent question," said Richard. He stood in the doorway to the bridge, and when Brianna turned to him, he shut the door slowly. "Deputy, the other door, please. Dorothy, stop the town."

Chloe clutched a handrail as the town slowed and then jerked to a stop. Brianna scampered for the other doorway.

"Now, let's discuss this, shall we?" said Richard.

Chloe's chest tightened, despite the calm, even friendly, tone of Richard's voice. Dorothy had said he didn't get angry, at least not loudly or violently. This must be what she'd meant. Brianna stood next to Chloe, her hands clasped behind her back, seemingly at ease.

"Deputy, it seems you have acted without proper authorization," Richard continued. "Reassigning personnel is well within your rights.

However, corresponding with the City is not within a deputy's purview, as I'm certain you are aware."

"Yes, sir," said Brianna.

"I'm sure you are also aware that it is not necessary for a townrunner to allow a deputy an opportunity to explain their actions, an opportunity I am currently affording you."

"Yes, sir," said Brianna.

"Please, enlighten me, Deputy."

"I considered your judgement to be compromised with regards to the City, sir. I couldn't allow your personal feelings to jeopardize the integrity of the town network, particularly when we have a unique resource at our disposal, exactly what the City requires at the moment." Hearing herself described as a *resource* made Chloe's stomach churn.

"I wanted to help the City," she said. "As I told Brianna, I don't agree with what they're doing, but the risks of leaving them to fall apart are too great to ignore."

Richard turned to her slowly and raised his eyebrows. He didn't take his eyes off her as he spoke to Brianna. "Deputy, it seems we have an insubordination problem beyond just your actions." He turned to Brianna and smiled. "I think I may have found a solution. The two of you seem determined to count your loyalty to the City over your loyalty to this town and to me. It seems only right to transfer both of you to the City, for the time being."

"Yes, sir," said Brianna.

"There," said Richard, turning back to Chloe. "You have what you want. Dorothy, please transport the former deputy and Chloe to the City and return here."

"Yes, sir," said Dorothy, her voice hard. She didn't have anything to say about Richard vindictively separating her from her partner? Neither Brianna nor Dorothy spoke up.

"According to our deal, you can't order me around, *sir*," said Chloe.

Richard smiled. "I haven't done anything of the kind, resident," he said. "Our agreement said nothing about Brianna whatsoever."

"Seriously, Richard, is it really necessary to—" Chloe began, but Dorothy cut her off.

"I'll take care of it, sir."

Richard turned on his heel and left the bridge, the open door gaping behind him.

"What the hell?" said Chloe, rounding on Dorothy. "You didn't even want to fight for your partner? Why do you two let him push you around like that?"

Brianna cocked her head at Chloe. "We all knew this was going to happen," she said, as if Chloe was dense. "Going behind the town-runner's back? He could have done much worse to us."

"How is this town rebellious if you still just unthinkingly follow the townrunner's orders? See, this is why Vishesh and I refused to join a town."

"And how did that work out for you?" said Dorothy.

"It was working *fine* until the City—" said Chloe.

Brianna sighed. "Let's just get to the City and solve their stupid problem so we can come home."

"Richard will let you come back?" said Chloe.

"You think he would let his parents have me?" Brianna snorted. "You think he'd let them have *you*? He didn't even want them to know about you."

"Then why—?"

"Brianna will look after you," said Dorothy.

"I don't need looking after," said Chloe.

Dorothy shook her head, and Brianna rolled her eyes.

"After what you just did with Richard here, Brianna will have to stick with you twenty-four seven to keep you out of trouble at the City."

"Yup," said Brianna. "You only think Richard is bad because you haven't met his mom."

"Yet," said Dorothy.

"With any luck, I can keep her away," said Brianna.

"Don't count on luck," said Dorothy and held Brianna close. "Richard wants her back—in one piece."

***

Vishesh caught Monty in the hallway. He'd been talking to Sheila, and he was on his way out.

"Hey, Monty," said Vishesh. "You wouldn't have any idea where our TV and things got to, would you?"

Monty glared at him. "Why would I? I have enough to do without chasing after whatever junk you've misplaced," said Monty, heading for the door.

"But I want to watch it!" said Flora from the living room, and then she wailed. The media centre Chloe had put together for them at the old farmhouse hadn't made it to their new place. On purpose, Vishesh had no doubt. Not having to watch Flora's favourite episode over and over anymore was a relief, but that would be preferable to the screaming. So many changes all at once, plus Chloe disappearing, was obviously too much for the little kid, and Terry and Connor had just been hiding it better, so far.

Sheila held Flora in her arms and rocked her slowly in the rocking chair, letting her get all her feelings out.

"I'm going to talk to Aaron," said Vishesh. "There are a few other things of ours missing. Maybe he knows where they ended up."

"Can I come with you?" said Connor. He closed his book but kept a finger in it to mark his page.

"Sure, kid," said Vishesh.

Connor grinned and tossed his book on the table. He brushed past Vishesh on his way to get his boots and coat on.

Sheila still wasn't speaking to Vishesh, but she deigned to nod at him. He returned it and followed Connor out the door.

"Let's see if he's in his office," said Vishesh.

Connor crammed his hands in his pockets, and he nodded, staring at the ground. The house was noisy, and Connor always had his nose in a book; they still hadn't discussed their new settlement. "What was your favourite part of the tour Aaron took you on?"

"He has a bunch of computers," said Connor. "Maybe I can learn to code."

Like Chloe.

"Sounds like a good idea. There's got to be a programmer here somewhere, and Aaron mentioned something about a school a while back. Maybe you could have classes."

"You think so?" said Connor, and his face lit up.

"Can't hurt to ask," said Vishesh, shrugging. He unzipped his coat. The day had turned warm and sunny since this morning. They crossed the deserted yard to the back door of Aaron's office building.

No one answered Vishesh's knock, so he pushed the door open. Heads popped up from the cubicles and then ducked back down when they saw him. Vishesh led Connor across the open space. Today, a big man with dark-brown skin sat behind the desk overlooking the cubicles, and his gaze tracked them as they reached Aaron's door, which stood ajar.

Knocking on someone's office door was surreal, but that's what Vishesh did. Aaron looked up from his desk.

"Come on in," he said. "Shut the door behind you. I've been meaning to talk to the two of you."

"Me?" said Connor. He ambled in after Vishesh and shut the door, as Aaron had asked.

"Of course!" said Aaron. "I'm sure you've noticed how highly we value kids in our community." He beamed at Connor in a way that made Vishesh's shoulders tense toward his ears.

It was worse when Connor smiled shyly back. He should have taken Connor under his wing more since his mother's death. Gloria had entrusted his care to Chloe, but now that she was gone as well, Connor was completely rudderless, searching for someone to look up to. And Aaron was very easy to look up to.

"We actually came here looking for some of our things," said Vishesh.

Connor looked adorably crestfallen at how easily he'd been distracted from their mission to get Flora her show.

"I'll see what I can do. Send me a list, and if I can get them tracked down, I'll let you know," said Aaron. "Now, Connor. I have someone in mind to be your trainer."

"We had some thoughts as well," Vishesh cut in, but Aaron waved him away, and Connor didn't even glance at him.

"You do?" said Connor.

"Yes," said Aaron. "He used to be a nurse before armageddon, and now he's my head of security."

"Security?" said Vishesh. "We wanted someone with programming experience—"

The office door opened, and the man from the desk poked his head in.

"Aaron?" he said. "You wanted to see me?"

"Yes, Neil, I was just telling Connor about you," said Aaron, beaming back and forth between them as though Vishesh weren't there.

Connor, meanwhile, glanced at Neil and had to visibly keep from letting his mouth fall open in wonder. Having a role model who looked like him would be good for Connor, but something like jealousy was still bubbling in Vishesh's gut.

Neil was tall and broad, sure, but he had a steady look about him, maybe from his training as a nurse, as though nothing could throw him off balance. It didn't hurt that his muscles noticeably rippled beneath his T-shirt as he shut the door. Vishesh swallowed, in a suddenly dry throat. Was he jealous of Neil getting to spend time with Connor, or Connor getting to spend time with Neil?

"Hi, Connor, I'm Neil." He shook Connor's hand, and Vishesh had the sudden urge to smack it away. Chloe might have been the one that Gloria chose to look out for her son, but all of them felt some responsibility for him. They were the only parents he had, and Vishesh wasn't going to let this go without a fight.

"Hi, Neil," said Vishesh and held out his own hand. "I'm one of Connor's guardians. I assume you have experience working with children?"

"Vishesh!" said Connor. "I'm not a child."

"I ran first aid training for youth, back in the day," said Neil. He shook Vishesh's hand and then gripped his shoulder. "I'll take good care of your kid," he said quietly. His glance at Aaron was barely perceptible, but it gave Vishesh a modicum of faith that Connor would be safe with the man, since he seemed aware that Aaron was bad news.

"He needs a teacher, not a trainer," said Vishesh under his breath.

"Can I go with Neil now, Vishesh?" said Connor. "I don't have anything else to do." Sheila hadn't started the kids' schooling back up since the move. They had a lot to sort out, now that Chloe was gone.

"I think that's up to Neil," said Vishesh. "I'm sure he's very busy."

"True," said Neil and grinned at the kid. "But you can shadow me, maybe learn a thing or two?"

"Awesome," said Connor, and he almost succeeded at keeping the excitement out of his voice.

"Drop him at home before dinner," said Vishesh.

Neil nodded curtly and led Connor out the door. Vishesh couldn't tear his eyes away and stared at the closed door until Aaron cleared his throat.

"Vishesh," he said. "I hope I didn't overstep with that training thing."

Vishesh shook his head. "On the way over here, we were chatting about finding him a teacher. Security wasn't really what I had in mind. But first aid could be useful."

"I thought so, too," said Aaron. "Speaking of useful, I have a little problem that I'd like your help with."

Aaron led him to some kind of misaligned antenna, and Vishesh tuned it, no problem. Once he was finished, he belatedly thought to ask what it was for.

"It's a surprise," said Aaron and grinned.

The tension in Vishesh's shoulders crept up his neck to the back of his skull. Anything that made Aaron happy was bound to make someone else miserable.

Chapter Twelve

Log: Town Kappa, Richard A. Phillips, Townrunner, 19 May 20—

C and B departing imminently for City, to return ASAP. In the eventuality that they are not returned promptly, countermeasures may be necessary. In the interim, spring decontamination efforts proceed apace.

Brianna silently pointed out the City to Chloe from the air. The hillside covered in bracken sat at the top of a cliff, beside the river. Major's Hill Park. Chloe used to come here to watch the fireworks on Canada Day when she was little.

"I thought the City was like a big town. I didn't know it was a settlement," said Chloe.

Brianna shook her head. "It's not a settlement. It's just been sitting there so long it's overgrown. It has hover functionality and legs, too. Or so I've heard. I've never seen them, myself."

Chloe squinted down to the hummock and identified the body, legs, and solar panels of a huge town, curving all the way down the long hill. The City. Narrow footpaths wound between a patchwork of blue and orange tarps and coloured tents, filling the green-space around it. A knot of people sat around a fire pit up by the cliff, and another group played ball hockey at the bottom of the hill.

Their helicopter landed on a helipad nearby, and both Dorothy and Brianna hopped down from the helicopter, leaving Chloe to scramble after them. The two women stood at attention as two figures approached to greet them, and Chloe awkwardly tried to figure out what to do with her hands.

An older white woman, flanked by a man, came out to meet them. Her short hair, long dress, and the robe overtop of it rippled in the breeze. A man in a suit trailed her and stopped a pace behind. Three guesses who these folks were. Chloe braced herself for the authoritarian rulers Richard had fled from in disgust.

"Brianna, Dorothy," said the woman, nodding to each of them in turn. She looked Chloe up and down. "And you are?"

"Chloe," she said.

"The one who's going to solve our problem for us," said the woman. Her face thawed into a smile, and she shook Chloe's hand. "Welcome. I'm Isabelle Phillips. This is my husband, Laurence. I'm sure you've heard all about us from Richard. Don't believe a word of it." She laughed, sounding younger than her years, and tucked Chloe's hand into the crook of her arm. Chloe had no choice but to walk with her when she turned toward the City. "Have you ever been to the City before?"

"No, I came from a settlement," said Chloe, slightly dazed. This was Richard's terrifying mother?

"A settlement! Goodness! I'm sure you're excited to have returned to civilization, especially with your skills." She stopped talking as she led Chloe into the loading dock of the City, up the massive ramp. If

Isabelle hadn't had Chloe's hand pinned to her arm, Chloe would have reeled back. The cacophony of dozens of voices talking at once; the rainbow of colours in every corner; the glint of metal laid out for sale; mingling scents of foods Chloe couldn't even identify, she hadn't smelled them in so long, maybe even spices, crashed over her. Stalls filled every inch, cheek by jowl, in rows across the floor, and up on the walkways above them. "The Gobi merchants set up here when I prohibited riding the towns' coattails, and the LunaCorp ones moved in soon after," said Isabelle, gesturing to the room at large. "If there's anything you need, this is the place to buy it."

Isabelle took her straight to the back of the dock, to where elevator doors opened behind a forbidding guard. The elevator had been added after the fact, maybe salvaged from a nearby building. Isabelle must have noticed her dumbfounded expression, because she smiled again. "I got tired of climbing all those stairs. You know, the City is four stories tall." The uniformed town resident that stood with his back to the elevator doors stepped aside as Isabelle approached, and she ignored him as she entered, still half-dragging Chloe with her. The doors were closing and Brianna peeked around the guard's wide frame. Isabelle was separating them. Panic shot through her limbs, but Chloe took a breath. Isabelle seemed so nice. Richard was completely biased. Nothing bad was going to happen to her just because she was away from Brianna.

"I'll take you straight to the bridge. Something is interfering with our locomotion. Normally, that's not something we use, as you probably gathered," said Isabelle and laughed. "I see you have your own laptop with you, so you can get right to work. Don't worry, I don't expect you to solve it instantly. I'll show you your quarters on the way by—we'll pass them up here on the fourth floor." The elevator slowed to a stop, and the doors opened. Isabelle stepped out, still firmly pressing Chloe's hand to her arm. "Of course, you can take breaks whenever you want. The problem is somewhat urgent, but we want you in top form."

The windows in this hallway looked out over the snowmelt-swollen Ottawa River far below at the base of the cliff to the white-and-brown-patched hills on the other side. The City was safe up here on the cliff, but judging by the water level, settlements farther up- or downstream might be flooded. Chloe had always reassured herself that the City was taking care of things like that, making sure settlements didn't flood with contaminated water. But after her own experience asking the City for assistance, it seemed likely that no one was helping them.

"I called for help from my settlement and received a rebuff," said Chloe. "They said we were out of range."

"Oh dear," said Isabelle. "I'm not sure this is the place to have this discussion, nor do I have the proper time to devote to it at the moment. I'll get you set up on the bridge, and then, I'll tell you what, I'll meet you for dinner. We can talk about your little settlement all you like then, and I'll address any questions you might have about the City." She beamed as if she were excited to talk about the puny little farm Chloe was well aware she didn't give two shits about.

Nevertheless, Chloe found herself smiling back. It had been a long time since someone had taken her under their wing like this. "I'd like that," she found herself saying.

"Excellent! It's a date. I'll have someone come get you. I bet you'll lose track of time working on this problem of ours," she said, leaning forward conspiratorially. "I'll even make sure Laurence is out so we can talk privately."

"Thanks," said Chloe.

"Of course! I'm happy to do it," said Isabelle. "I have to run. See you later!" She turned on her heel and strode off the bridge, leaving Chloe a little disoriented in her wake. Even the bridge here was overwhelming, almost four times as large as the one on Town Kappa, with about a dozen uniformed people stationed at various dim screens around the place. A resident with a brittle smile showed her to a proper desk. Scratches and scuffs marred the metal surface, but at least she had some elbow room here.

Chloe pulled out the chair and set up her laptop on the desk, then plugged in the hookup and started working.

***

Chloe surfaced from her haze of code. In the back of her mind, something felt wrong. The bridge had gone silent. She looked up. Isabelle strode cheerfully toward her.

"Chloe! How's it going?"

"Not great, unfortunately. I'm having trouble pinning down the source of the interference." She scowled at the laptop screen again. "It's within the range that could be emitted by some kind of machinery, but I've been told that nothing new has been implemented recently. It could be a long process, narrowing it down."

"Any resources you need, they're yours. *After* you have some dinner and a rest," said Isabelle. She reached over Chloe and shut her laptop with a snap. Good thing Chloe hadn't gotten anywhere or Isabelle could have lost her hours of work. She rubbed her palms into her eyes.

"Poor Chloe," said Isabelle. "My son not treating you right? You seem tired." She leaned in close as Chloe got to her feet. "Or is he treating you *too* right?" She cocked an eyebrow.

Chloe frowned. "Nothing of the kind, Isabelle." What would shut down that line of questioning? "He's my superior officer, and he's been treating me like he does all his town residents: he takes care of his own."

"Mhm," said Isabelle. "Dinner is set up in my quarters."

A resident flattened himself against the wall as Isabelle swept Chloe off the bridge and through the first door in the hallway.

"Home sweet home," said Isabelle and motioned Chloe to the table that was already set for the two of them.

"This whole place is yours?" said Chloe. The suite probably had the same footprint as their old farmhouse. A curved window covered the entire front wall, the living room and dining room positioned to take in the view. Still, the comfortable couch faced a big TV and a faux fireplace. The wizened old man Chloe had talked to just this morning saying, *We don't need power*, flashed into her head.

Isabelle waved dismissively. "Laurence and I need somewhere to entertain our guests. I don't mean to be rude, but I'm famished. Would you mind terribly if we ate?"

"Sure," said Chloe.

"Excellent!" Isabelle took the seat at the head of the table, and Chloe sat to her left where she could look out the window at the view, still just visible in the fading light.

Chloe picked up her fork and paused. Meat. *Rack of lamb*, her mind dredged up from its depths. Her mouth watered, and Chloe swallowed. She glanced at Isabelle, who was not in the least fazed. She seemed sure of the provenance of the meat, as she cut a piece and popped it into her mouth without blinking. Chloe cut off a small piece, added mint sauce, and slid it into her mouth.

Her grandma's smiling face popped into her head. Some family holiday gathering played out in her mind's eye. Her cousins chatted in the background, and a loud laugh echoed from the other room. *Take your time,* her grandmother was saying, *I'll sit with you while you finish. I'm flattered that you're enjoying my food so much!*

"Haven't had meat in a while?" said Isabelle.

Chloe glanced at her, jolted back to reality. All those folks were dead. No point in dredging up old memories. They only led to one place.

"We have a reputable source. Mostly lamb and veal. It's easier to make sure they stay uncontaminated."

"Makes sense," said Chloe.

"You're a programmer?" said Isabelle.

"Computer scientist," said Chloe.

"Sounds much too prestigious to be hidden away at a settlement. I didn't think there were many computers hanging around those places," said Isabelle.

"There aren't," said Chloe.

"How did you end up at one?" said Isabelle. "I know the early days are fraught for many of us." Isabelle leaned forward to clasp her arm. "I understand if you don't want to talk about it."

"No, that's okay," said Chloe. "My friend Vishesh and I were offered positions on a town, but we chose to help build a settlement, get it up and running. Then we just . . . never left." It wasn't the entire truth, but Isabelle nodded.

"I understand," she said, gesturing at the City around them. "You dig in somewhere, build a life, and it's hard to uproot yourself, so to speak." Her lips pressed together as if suppressing a smile at her own wordplay.

"How did you become the manager of the whole region?" said Chloe. "There must have been some tough times in there."

"I was elected, of course," said Isabelle, a note of pride in her voice. "I've taken this region through hell, and I don't intend to give up any time soon. Richard's devotion to his people didn't come from nowhere—I taught him everything he knows about running a town." She sighed. "I'm glad he has good people with him. For a while there, I was afraid . . ." She glanced at Chloe, and then pasted on a smile. "Never mind," she said. "Everything is working out. I'm sure with time, he'll come back to us of his own accord."

Chloe was not at all sure of that, but she just nodded and took another bite.

"What kind of work—" Isabelle cut herself off as the floor vibrated beneath them and then shuddered. Their plates and glasses rattled. "Excuse me," said Isabelle, her face suddenly hard. She strode out the door without another word.

The floor lurched, and Chloe gripped the edge of the table. Their dishes slid a foot to the left, and then to the right. Chloe caught hers before it slid off the table, but Isabelle's crashed off the edge and shattered, scattering food and shards of glass and porcelain over her chair and the floor. Chloe used the table to steady herself as she dashed to the huge front window.

The City's headlights flickered on, dimmed by layers of dirt and greenery. Chloe pressed herself against the glass as the City lurched again, the familiar hum of a hover vibrating through the floor and window into her feet and fingertips.

The City had reawakened, and, judging by her reaction, unbeknownst to Isabelle.

***

Vishesh barely touched his dinner. Connor still wasn't home. They ate early because of the kids, that's why Neil seemed so late bringing him. It was barely six. Thankfully, Monty wasn't home to needle Vishesh about it, and he made it through dinner and dried the dishes while Sheila washed. If she had been talking to him, she probably would have chewed him out for letting Connor go off with a stranger.

The creak of the front door opening almost made Vishesh drop a glass. He set it on the counter and hurried into the hall.

"Finally," he said as Connor shouldered past him into the house. Nagging would have no effect on the teenager, so he didn't bother to try.

"Sorry," said Neil from the porch. "Maybe I can make it up to you? I bet you haven't been out for a drink in a long time."

Vishesh started to shake his head.

Neil pitched his voice a little lower. "I'd like to talk to you about Connor and . . . Aaron." He glanced at Sheila, who had poked her head into the hallway from the kitchen.

Vishesh sighed and nodded. "Let me get ready." He hung up his dishtowel, waved to Sheila, knowing he wouldn't get a response, and padded upstairs to get ready to go out, maybe put on some jeans without holes in them. Or at least holes that had already been mended.

He dragged on a pair of black jeans and looked himself up and down in the mirror. They would have to do; it's not as if he had an extensive wardrobe. What did it matter what he looked like, anyway? He was being silly.

Neil waited for him on the porch and looked him up and down when he came out the front door. Vishesh's face heated, but he returned the once-over. This godlike nurse slash security head could never be interested in him. Not in reality, but fantasizing about it was fun. Neil *had* asked him out for a drink. Vishesh smiled to himself as he followed Neil down the path toward the public buildings in the centre of their settlement.

"What's up?" said Neil. He must have caught the smile.

"Just thinking I haven't been asked out for drinks in years," said Vishesh and grinned.

Neil returned it. "I haven't asked anyone out in a long time, either." Neil laughed at his shocked look. "Yes, I have an ulterior motive, but I still have a few serious things I want to talk to you about. No harm mixing business and pleasure, right?"

Vishesh swallowed hard. First date nerves made his heart race. He shouldn't have clarified that this was a date.

"Hey," said Neil. He stopped Vishesh with a hand on his arm and turned to face him. "I'm sorry. I didn't mean to pressure you. Let's just focus on Connor."

Vishesh nodded and took a deep breath. He'd been into Chloe so long with no reciprocation, admiring someone and having them return the sentiment was jarring. "At least until I have a drink in me," he muttered, and Neil laughed.

"How long has it been since you've had alcohol? Do I need to worry about you?"

"Fair point, I'll pace myself," said Vishesh.

Neil nodded. "This is the only settlement I've ever seen with a brewery. Keeps us complacent." He murmured the last part, but Vishesh caught it. Aaron was too clever by half.

The light from the pub windows painted the ground in front of the big house and differentiated it from its dark neighbours. Neil sauntered up the driveway, Vishesh a pace behind him. Neil held the door, and Vishesh flinched back a step as the chatter from within hit him.

"Need a minute?" said Neil.

Vishesh shook his head. "No, I'm good. The kids are loud, but there are only three of them," he said. "Not used to quite so much noise anymore."

Neil grinned. "Half the settlement crams in here most nights."

Vishesh stepped inside. Every corner seemed to be packed with people. "Only half?" he said.

"Yeah, this is the nice bar," said Neil, a bitter edge to his voice.

Vishesh glanced at him quizzically, but Neil shook his head.

"Let's get settled," he said over the noise. He led Vishesh to the bar and procured their drinks, then they installed themselves in a back corner booth with Neil facing the entrance, beers in hand.

"How do you all grow uncontaminated grain?" said Vishesh, eyeing his glass.

"It's well filtered," said Neil and shrugged. "The beer is the least of your worries." Now that they were somewhat hidden, their voices covered by bar chatter, Neil was dead serious. "Aaron is trying to use Connor, like he uses me. He sees a big Black man and thinks *intimidating bodyguard*. Sure, I used to do kickboxing back in the day, but it was a hobby, a way to stay in shape. Remember when we all used to worry about gaining weight?" His smile was humourless. "That's all he sees about me, the parts he can use."

"You'd think being a nurse in the post-armageddon era would be far more valuable," said Vishesh. He had been worried about this, ever since Aaron had set his eye on Connor.

"Nah," said Neil. "Aaron doesn't care about keeping people alive. Maybe the kids. Otherwise, there are more where we came from."

"What?" Vishesh frowned. He couldn't mean that.

"You think he has enough uncontaminated food for all these people?" said Neil, raising his eyebrows. "And this is the *nice* bar."

"He feeds his people radioactive food?" said Vishesh. "Why doesn't anyone say anything?"

"It's not that simple," said Neil. "You saw Aaron's crew."

Ah. So that's how it is. "You'd think being slowly killed by radiation poisoning would make people care less about the repercussions of rebelling."

"Most of them don't know. He keeps people segregated into groups, feeds them different stories." Neil shrugged. "It's pretty simple to do, actually. No one wants to believe that they've been strung along. They're happy with the lies he feeds them."

Vishesh heaved a sigh. So he'd made a big mistake bringing his family here. He'd known it was a possibility. It hurt to have it confirmed.

"Hey," said Neil. He covered one of Vishesh's hands with his own on the table. "Don't beat yourself up. You want to help your family, join us."

"Us?" said Vishesh.

"The rebels," said Neil, and a ghost of a smile played across his face. "Aaron has bigger plans than just this settlement. Lucky for us, he's been harvesting the best brains from the towns to put them in motion. The kind of folks who only pretend to take his shit lying down." He gave Vishesh a significant glance, as if *he* was one of those folks.

"I don't know . . ." said Vishesh. What would happen to his family if he was found out to be a rebel? Neil had made it pretty clear that Aaron's crew would get involved at the merest hint of trouble.

"You don't have to answer now," he said. He fell silent as he tracked someone walking across the bar toward them, behind Vishesh.

Portia, in jeans and a cardigan, slid in next to Neil and eyed Vishesh warily.

"It's okay, Portia," said Neil.

"He's done it," she said and grabbed a drink from Neil's glass.

"Shit," said Neil. When she handed back his glass, he took a long drink as well.

"I don't know how he got the antenna aligned," she said. "We've all been misaligning it for a month."

The bottom dropped out of Vishesh's stomach. "I know how," he said and then took a drink of his own. "Shit, I'm sorry."

"It's not your fault," said Neil. His steady gaze centred Vishesh. "You didn't know."

Portia crossed her arms over her chest. "The new guy is messing up all our plans."

"Vishesh brought his family here to keep them safe," said Neil pointedly.

"Yeah, well, they sure aren't safe now," said Portia.

"What's Aaron doing?" said Vishesh.

"He's summoning the City," said Neil.

"Summoning?" said Vishesh.

"It's exactly what it sounds like. Barring interference I doubt they can muster, the City should be on its way here already," said Portia.

Chapter Thirteen

Log: Town Kappa, Richard A. Phillips, Townrunner, 19 May 20—

B has returned alone, leaving C at the City unaccompanied. Disciplinary action will be taken. Attempts have been made to contact the City, but no response has been forthcoming. Direct intervention appears to be required. I will depart personally ASAP.

C hloe didn't wait for Isabelle to come back. She staggered to the bridge, and the floor still shook under her feet as the City tried to free itself from years of debris and root systems. The market stalls, elevator, and fancy decor that Chloe had seen all pointed to there being far more weight in the City than it was designed for, probably far more people as well. But it might get off the ground anyway unless Isabelle's folks were able to prevent it.

Isabelle stood in the centre of the tense bridge with her feet braced and her hands clasped behind her back. Her sharp eyes darted to the driver.

"Take *back* control, or must I do it for you?" she barked.

"Yes, sir," said the driver.

Chloe slid into the desk and opened her laptop. This must have something to do with the interference she'd been studying; she'd isolated the signal, but before it had just been incomprehensible noise, hence her conclusion about mechanical interference. It wasn't noise anymore.

"I'll smash in the hover before I let someone hijack our City," snapped Isabelle.

"Wait!" said Chloe, and Isabelle's piercing gaze snapped to her. "I think I found the signal."

"Counteract it immediately," said Isabelle.

"It's not that simple, I can't just—"

"Make it that simple, resident," said Isabelle. "Otherwise, mechanical intervention will be undertaken."

"Okay, give me a minute," said Chloe.

"You have three minutes. Countdown please," said Isabelle, and a countdown appeared overlaid on the windshield.

"The minute was figurative," Chloe grumbled but tried to focus. The seconds ticking down out of the corner of her eye were in no way helpful.

It shouldn't be possible for someone to remotely control the *City*. Wasn't there any kind of security? Wait, this was based on the same technology she'd been studying for days on Town Kappa. She'd convinced their settlement receiver that she was a town and had the rights to contact the City, so why shouldn't someone be able to trick the City into thinking it was subordinate to them and should be under their control? But the trick was being pulled on the hijacker's end. Counteracting it might not be possible from here.

Short of smashing in the hover, how else would it be possible to stop the City from going . . . wherever the hijacker wanted it to go?

If she could put a similar dark mode in place to the one she'd given Town Kappa, they might blip off the hijacker's network. No time for that. A more mechanical approach would be necessary, but something reversible. Not smashing anything. She fished out her screwdriver.

Chloe shot up from her chair. The countdown was at fifty-eight seconds. The back of the driver's station was accessible, and Chloe tripped down a couple of steps and caught herself on the console. She ripped open the dash, and there it was. The machine controlling this entire giant City, at her fingertips. She didn't have time to mess around with it—she needed to locate one component in particular. She scanned the blinking lights and ran her screwdriver over each component in turn. That was probably it. She took a breath and located the cable connecting the little GPS receiver. The contact wiggled and then came loose in her hand. With any luck, now, even if the hijacker got them off the ground, there would be no way to remotely move the City, at least not reliably. She unscrewed all the screws affixing the GPS in turn and it finally came free.

"Chloe, report," said Isabelle sharply.

"I've removed the GPS receiver. It won't prevent the hijacker from engaging hover functionality, but it will stop them from steering the City or summoning it to their location."

Isabelle stared her down. "Good work, town resident. This will give us time to assess the situation. Emergency meeting in five minutes," she said. "Chloe, with me."

Chloe crammed the GPS receiver into her pocket and followed Isabelle back to her quarters. Isabelle took in the carnage of their meal at a glance, and her mouth tightened.

"Chloe, I have no doubt that you are loyal to Richard, like all of his other lap dogs, but you could do great work here in the City. I'd like you to consider staying here with us. We have a big problem on our hands," she said and gestured to the smashed dishes that covered the floor. As if to drive her point home, the floor lurched under their feet and then trembled.

Was Chloe loyal to Richard? He had proven that he was driven only by what he thought was best for his town. But he'd also taken her home. He was as good as his word. His exact word, to the letter and nothing more, but his word nonetheless. On the other hand, he'd also implied that Isabelle was some kind of despot, and she seemed like a really good leader, a good person, even.

"I'm not sure, Isabelle," said Chloe.

"You don't have to decide now," said Isabelle. "I have a meeting to run. Stay here. Eat. Relax. I'll be back." She stalked out, which left Chloe alone in the suite.

Chloe let out a breath. Richard had promised to help her check on her family if the opportunity ever arose. She'd never get that kind of promise from Isabelle. Even if Isabelle wanted to, the responsibilities of the City far outweighed anything a town had to contend with.

But living here would let Chloe fix things on a much broader scale than being a single town's resident. She'd have influence over the entire region, all the towns under this City, not just one. What if she could make all the towns more efficient and remove the need for Isabelle's range restrictions? Then again, it hadn't just been Richard who had warned her against Isabelle; Brianna and even Dorothy had thought Chloe was way out of her depth.

In Chloe's experience, there was only one surefire way to uncover someone's true character: say no to them. Picturing saying no to Isabelle made Chloe's skin prickle and dread pool in her gut. Even more reason to find out what she was dealing with up front, before she was bound to the woman as her subordinate.

***

Chloe had had no idea how long Isabelle was going to be, and she didn't want to get caught snooping through the suite, so she kept herself busy cleaning up the shattered dishes and then collapsed on the couch and pondered what she'd say to Isabelle when she got back.

A handful of magazines littered the floor, and Chloe picked them up and fanned them across the coffee table. She pulled one out to pass the time: the cover was a glossy photo of a smiling woman in a field, a town running a decontamination pattern in the background. *Oasis Magazine*, April 20— issue. Gobi had a corporate magazine? Yup, articles about town maintenance and dealing with settlements. A few issues of *Phases of LunaCorp* were mixed in with the *Oasis* back-issues as well. Were there references to Seed-verts in these?

She licked her finger, ready to start flipping pages in earnest, but the door to the suite slid aside. Chloe tossed the magazines back on the table and stood up from the couch. She took a deep breath and squared her shoulders.

"I see you've been thinking about my offer," said Isabelle with a smile.

"Yes," said Chloe and licked her lips nervously. "I have a few questions for you first."

"Please, allow me to get comfortable so that I can listen to you properly," said Isabelle. She settled herself on the couch that Chloe had recently vacated, leaving Chloe standing in the middle of the room, as if she were being interviewed. Or prosecuted. She cleared her throat.

"When I contacted the City, requesting help for my settlement, I was told that it was impossible to provide us with aid," said Chloe.

"My understanding is that your settlement is outside of the City's range," said Isabelle.

"The new, smaller range, yes," said Chloe.

"And how were you able to contact the City? Which town did you go through? Kappa?" said Isabelle.

Chloe's stomach clenched. She had the distinct impression that she wouldn't want to face the consequences for modifying the receiver. But a cursory look through the communication history would reveal anything she tried to hide now. Best to get it out in the open.

"I contacted the City myself," said Chloe, more defensively than she intended. "Town Kappa didn't have anything to do with it."

"And when you were told we would be unable to help you? What did you do next?" said Isabelle. When had this conversation morphed from Chloe grilling Isabelle to the other way around?

"I went in search of a town," said Chloe.

"And you expected this town to break the rules somehow and come to your aid? Do you know how many settlements are outside of the City's range? There is a reason that the range is restricted," said Isabelle.

"Do *you* know how many settlements you've left to rot with your range restrictions, Isabelle?" said Chloe.

The door slid open, and Richard stepped into the room, taking in the unfolding drama at a glance.

"Richard," said Isabelle and shot him a smile. "Welcome home!"

"I'm just passing through," he said stiffly.

"Of course," said Isabelle. "Please, sit down. This conversation affects you as well."

What the hell was Richard doing here? He'd flatly refused to consider even responding to the City's distress call, and now he was here in person? Richard shook his head and planted his feet where he was, by the door.

"No thanks," he said. "Please continue."

"You must have come so far, Richard. Won't you rest?" said Isabelle, patting the couch beside her.

"I'm perfectly comfortable here, Mother," said Richard. "Chloe, please continue."

Under Richard's hard gaze, the butterflies in her stomach settled. She turned back to Isabelle.

"So you admit that you've left many settlements, many *people*, to die of radioactive contamination by decreasing the towns' range," said Chloe. She continued before Isabelle could interrupt. "Do you also admit that you withheld potentially life-changing Seed-vert seeds from those settlements that you could have used to help offset the consequences of having abandoned them?"

Richard gasped. Isabelle's expression didn't change, though she drew herself up slightly.

"We encouraged all of the settlements that were in contact with the towns to migrate inside the new range limits, so the Seed-verts were superfluous," she said. "We gave them resources to do so, and the support of the current settlements close to the City. Opportunities were plentiful for the settlements that would have been required to move."

"It's interesting that you should say that," said Chloe. "I was a member of one of those settlements, and I never heard anything of the kind. Even when I contacted the City for help, no one mentioned anything about support for relocation."

"And would you have listened if they had?" said Isabelle. "From all of the settlements we did contact, only a handful agreed to move within the City's new limits."

"The dirt-folk are attached to their dirt patches," said Richard. "Right, Mother?"

"Richard! What a bigoted thing to say," said Isabelle.

Richard raised his eyebrows at Chloe. She had no doubt that he had gotten the phrase from his mother, as he claimed.

"Seed-vert seeds?" he said.

"Radiation-resistant seeds I found in Town Iota. The box wasn't even opened. Did you know?" said Chloe.

"No. I knew R&D was underway. I was not aware that distribution was imminent," said Richard. "The settlements also seem to be unaware of their existence. Presumably, they were never intended to be distributed. Are they in your possession?"

Isabelle tried to interject, but Chloe talked over her. "No, Vishesh and Aaron took them."

"I think this calls for a little town summit," said Richard.

"Richard, don't you dare!" said Isabelle. They both ignored her.

"Are you still engaged here, Chloe, or shall we return home?" said Richard.

The word *home* echoed through Chloe. Town Kappa was not home, not to her. Her family. Vishesh. Connor. Flora. None of them were there. Chloe sighed and nodded. Richard had promised to help her make sure her family was okay. She'd never get that kind of promise from Isabelle.

"I think I've thwarted whoever was trying to take control of the City," said Chloe. "I've at least given these folks enough time to hopefully sort out what they are going to do next."

Richard slid open the door and motioned Chloe to precede him through.

"Wait, Chloe, the Seed-verts—" said Isabelle, but the door slid shut behind Chloe and Richard before she could finish whatever honeyed words she was about to pour into Chloe's ear.

***

Vishesh still sat across from Neil and Portia in their booth at the pub, all of them nursing the possibly contaminated beer. Just like all the other knots of folks in booths scattered across the bar. Nothing to see here.

"He's going to take down Town Lambda next, tomorrow afternoon. It'll be at its nearest to our settlement, so most convenient to strip then," said Portia.

"Okay, you have to tell me how you know all this," said Vishesh. He couldn't handle it anymore. Portia knew too much, was too willing to share her information. How could she not be planted by Aaron's?

Portia stared him down. "I fuck Aaron. He likes to torture me by giving me information he knows I can't use."

Vishesh blinked back at her. "What makes you think it's accurate? And why wouldn't you be able to use it?"

"Oh, it's accurate," said Portia.

"Aaron can't imagine that we'd be working together with folks from the other side of the settlement," said Neil.

"He can't imagine that anyone would believe his little pet, either," said Portia.

"But you do?" said Vishesh to Neil.

Neil nodded. "Yeah, I do."

Vishesh shook his head. "I still don't get this division in the settlement," he said. "Why does everyone let Aaron get away with treating his people so badly?"

"It's more than one division," said Neil. "He plays one side against the other. Whatever sides he can invent. Not everyone falls for it, but most do. Human nature is hard to beat back."

Why was Neil bringing him in on this? What could he possibly contribute? He was just a post-doc geneticist who worked part-time in the campus machine shop. What use were his skills now? All he had of value was a pack full of Seed-verts and a random piece Chloe had ripped out of Town Iota.

Except it wasn't random. It was Town Iota's receiver.

"What if we could warn Town Lambda," said Vishesh.

"How would that help?" said Portia.

"It'd let the people get away, at least," said Neil. "Even if it wouldn't save their town. They could find refuge at a nearby settlement or find another town."

"Aaron . . . kills them?" said Vishesh.

"Either that or brings them here," said Neil.

"Not a huge difference for most folks," said Portia. "You haven't seen the other side."

"Why?" said Neil. "How would you warn them?"

"I'm not sure if I can yet," said Vishesh.

"If you can, it might put a wrench in Aaron's plans," said Portia.

"And it would put your family in danger," said Neil. He covered Vishesh's hand on the tabletop with his again. "Are you sure you're willing to do that?"

Vishesh heaved a breath. "I put them in danger just by bringing them here," he said. "They will be as long as Aaron is in charge."

Portia elbowed Neil. "Looks like you convinced him. Nicely done," she said.

"As long as you're sure," said Neil. "I won't ask you to help us unless you're comfortable with the stakes."

"I think comfortable is a bit of a stretch," said Vishesh. "But it's worth the risk."

"Remember you said that when shit hits the fan," said Portia. She drained her beer. "Time to get going."

"I'll walk you," said Neil. "Vishesh?"

"Yep," he said. A wave of lethargy swept over him as he stood.

Portia slid out of the booth and threaded her way through the still-crowded bar. Vishesh and Neil followed her to the door, weaving between tables and other patrons. The three of them walked in silence for a block or two. Portia bumped Neil with her shoulder. He didn't even weave sideways.

"Sorry I crashed your date," she said. "Next time, just tell me to fuck off." She grinned at the no-doubt embarrassed look on Vishesh's face, then waved and peeled off from the two men.

"Brat," said Neil under his breath.

"You live over this way as well?" said Vishesh.

Neil shrugged. "I figured I'd walk you home," he said. "Do you mind?"

A smile crept over Vishesh's face, in spite of himself. "Not at all," he said.

They sauntered in silence up the quiet street, frogs and crickets the only creatures calling out through the night. Vishesh stopped at the bottom of the path leading up to their porch. Neil raised his eyebrows.

"Don't want to be seen with me?" he said.

"Could anything embarrass a teenager more than accidentally seeing his guardian and his teacher . . ." He trailed off. He'd been about to say *kissing*.

"Yes?" said Neil and stepped in closer. He smiled down at Vishesh, who was suddenly unable to string two words together. "I really want you to finish that sentence," Neil breathed into his ear.

Vishesh swallowed hard. "Together?" he tried.

"Vague and noncommittal," said Neil, only a little bitterly. "I get it."

Vishesh stepped away from Neil's body so that he could see his face. "I really like you. It's hard for me to get into the feelings stuff right now. But maybe next time I can walk *you* home? You don't have a nosy teenager, not to mention Sheila, peering through your curtains, do you?"

Neil studied his face. "I do not," he said, still pensive. "But I want the feelings stuff, Vishesh." He shook his head. "I'm happy to wait until you're ready to get into it, but I really do want the *feelings stuff*."

Maybe once they were settled in here? Once they overthrew Aaron? Vishesh sighed. "There's never going to be a time when it's not complicated, is there?"

Neil laughed. "I wouldn't count on that, no," he said.

"I'll work on it, then," said Vishesh.

"See you tomorrow?" said Neil.

Vishesh nodded. Neil gave his arm a squeeze and sauntered away, then paused to wave back over his shoulder. Vishesh let out his breath slowly. Yes, he would need to untangle his head in short order. If he let it get in the way of something happening with Neil, he'd always regret it.

Vishesh quietly slipped inside, trying not to wake the kids. He thought guiltily of Sheila putting them all to bed on her own again, but this rebellion was more important than his occasional absence. Plus, Sheila still wasn't talking to him, so it's not as if it was making her hate him even more than she already did.

"Where've you been?" said a voice from the shadows.

Vishesh jumped out of his skin, and he sagged against the wall.

"Monty?" said Vishesh. "That's creepy. Turn on a light."

A lamp clicked on in the living room, revealing Monty, slumped in an armchair, watching him. He had a clear view to the street, and he would have seen Vishesh and Neil out there a few minutes earlier.

"I was out with a friend," he said, gesturing to the window and the walkway.

"I saw that," said Monty. Even in the dim light, Monty looked as if he'd aged ten years since they had moved here. All his ideas about being Aaron's second in command and ruling from behind the throne, so to speak, had been dashed instantly upon their arrival. He was struggling to find a place here, as they all were, but he was the one who Aaron had duped the most thoroughly. Sheila and Vishesh had at least had some idea of what they were walking into.

Vishesh had no doubt that Aaron would find a use for Monty's vicious streak, and he really didn't want to be around when that happened. "If that's all you needed," he said and retreated up the stairs before the older man could answer.

Chapter Fourteen

Log: The City, Richard A. Phillips, Kappa Townrunner, 19 May 20—

Chloe recovered from the City. We will proceed with all due haste to Town Kappa. It appears as though Seed-vert seeds are more reality than I realized. Further investigation required.

C hloe and Richard had driven in silence for a half hour. She'd followed Richard out of the City to his waiting car, where he laid his jacket flat in the back seat and motioned her to the passenger side. He ducked into the driver's seat and finally took a breath, loosened his tie, unbuttoned his collar and cuffs, and rolled up his sleeves. The City couldn't watch him here. But Chloe could. He'd run his hand through his impeccable hair, willing to let her see this less formal side of him. She'd missed his awkward solicitude. Or maybe she'd just missed . . . him?

The light from their high beams bounced along the surprisingly intact road, the electric car motor whisper quiet. Richard knew where he was going; he was likely retracing his drive to come and get her.

Exclusively to come and get her, even though he couldn't have known that she would end up going with him. If she hadn't had the ammo of the Seed-verts in her back pocket, she might even have found Isabelle convincing enough to make her agree to stay. Would Richard have tried to convince her, if he'd shown up and she'd refused to go with him? He'd been willing to take that chance, knowing he'd be forced to see Isabelle in the process.

Chloe had known that he had a strained relationship with his parents, but one moment really nagged at her.

"Your mom didn't call you Xander," she said.

"No," said Richard. He kept his gaze fixed on the road.

"When Brianna told me not to call you that, I figured it had something to do with your parents, your weird history with them."

"It doesn't."

"Oh, okay."

Chloe was hypnotized by the curves in the road. They popped into view and then immediately disappeared behind the car. Their car could have been standing still and moving the tiny slice of road around them, instead of the other way around. Here in their little bubble, they weren't resident and townrunner, they were just Chloe and Richard.

"Why did you come and get me? It's eating up a lot of energy," said Chloe and motioned to the battery display on the dashboard.

"You required transport," said Richard.

"You could have sent anyone," said Chloe.

Richard laughed, but it was grating, bitter. He shook his head. "You witnessed how deftly she disposed of Brianna, who had express orders to remain at your side. If you think anyone else would have made it into that suite, you're mistaken."

"Your father would have stopped them?"

"Simply one of a handful of City residents loyal to Isabelle," said Richard.

"Why did they let you by?"

"Several reasons," said Richard. Chloe expected him to continue, but he fell silent.

"You really didn't know about the Seed-verts?" said Chloe.

Richard sighed. "I owe you an apology. I'm very sorry for kidnapping you. I have no expectation that you will trust me when I say: no, I was not aware of the existence of the Seed-vert seeds. Perhaps in time, you'll understand why I acted as I did."

"Oh, I understand, Richard. I understand that you saw an opportunity to save your people, a one-in-a-million opportunity to avoid watching them starve to death, and so you took it. Just because I understand doesn't mean I forgive you, or that I agree with what you did." She let the words hang there between them, watched Richard's jaw working. Chloe turned away from him. The bushes at the side of the road whipped by into the darkness. "Maybe one day I'll trust you, Richard. I'm not ruling it out."

"You may call me Xander, when we're alone," said Richard. "If you wish." He stared straight ahead. The car slowed and then turned into a driveway. Town Kappa loomed out of the shadows. Richard pulled into the loading dock, bouncing them in their seats, and parked.

"I don't think that's—" Chloe began, and popped her door open. The cabin light flared.

"Please," said Richard. He turned to meet her gaze, something soft and vulnerable behind his eyes. "Call me Xander."

Something in the back seat caught her eye, and Chloe turned. Her pack. Her most valuable, irreplaceable possessions. Richard must have brought it in case she wanted to stay in the City. Her breath caught, and the name tumbled from her lips. "Xander."

Their lips met before Chloe could reengage her brain. Xander's mouth tasted crisp and clean, and his agile lips were soft against Chloe's.

They both pulled back, and the light in the car dimmed and went out, leaving only the lights from the garage. Strange shadows hid Xander's expression.

"My apologies, Chloe," said Richard. "I appreciate that you have returned to Town Kappa. A meeting will be scheduled in the morning to determine strategies for the town's future, and I would appreciate it if you would attend." He ducked out of the car, and he was gone.

Chloe took a deep breath and tilted her head back on the headrest. She hadn't kissed a guy in . . . god, since she was in grad school? The look in his eyes, though, when he'd asked, *begged*, her to call him by his informal name, the name only his best friends seemed to know. After knowing the guy only four days, it seemed silly to think they were that close. If he was manipulating her again, he was doing a really excellent job of it.

Chloe opened the car door and dragged herself up. She glanced into the backseat. Her collection sat there on the seat, just waiting for her to grab it. It meant everything that Richard had brought it to give back to her instead of keeping it to use as leverage against her.

Chloe slipped her hand in her pocket, and came up with the City's GPS receiver. *Whoops*. She'd forgotten to return it. Chloe tucked it into her pack and slung the whole thing over her shoulder.

The weight of everything that had happened on this long, long day seemed to settle in her bones all at once. She glanced up to the stairs leading to her quarters. If only Kappa had an elevator like at the City. No elevator, no guards. That had been the moment, in retrospect, that she had known she wasn't going to stay at the City. That last flash of Brianna's face as the elevator doors closed. Everything else had just been her logical side justifying her decision. The human brain was unsettling, not logical in the least.

***

Chloe knocked on Richard's door. It was after breakfast, not too early. She wouldn't be able to focus unless she talked to him about this. The door opened, and she pushed past him into his quarters.

"Okay, so I've been thinking about it, and we need to figure out how to function without the support of the City," said Chloe.

Xander made a sound from behind her and she held up her hand.

"What we need is a peer-to-peer network. No overlord controlling from afar, direct communication and consent to give control to another town upon request. No overrides, no range restrictions. Maybe we can dismantle the City's network and redistribute it . . . Yes, that's the way to get it done, but we'd need access to the servers to take them apart, obviously. Access Isabelle will never allow. But it *would* have the added bonus of removing control over the towns from the City, no matter who was controlling *it*."

"Chloe," said Xander, and she finally stopped to look at him. *Whoa*. He wore a T-shirt and PJ pants, his hair was rumpled, and he wasn't wearing his glasses. The lights were low, the shades drawn.

"Oh my god, I woke you up," said Chloe, stumbling for the door. "I'm so sorry, I just didn't think I'd be able to focus until—"

Xander caught her arms and looked into her face. "Just let me get my glasses. Sit."

"No, Xander, I . . ." Chloe trailed off, and Xander's eyes danced as she used his nickname.

"I'm not going to lose my mind and kiss you again," he said. "At least not over that." He gestured to the coffee table and two chairs in a corner of his quarters. "Sit."

Chloe sat. She rubbed her hands up and down her jeans in an attempt to alleviate her sweaty palms.

Xander sat across from her, one ankle on the opposite knee. "Okay, I'm ready. The City."

"Right, the City," said Chloe. What had she come here to talk about again? "Step one is redistribute the City's servers. Step two is pass them out to the towns. Give them autonomy."

Richard fixed his penetrating glare on her.

"You don't like my plan?" said Chloe.

"You presume that the current townrunners desire autonomy and that they would utilize it productively," he said. "I beg to differ."

"So install new townrunners," said Chloe.

"Who would select this new crop of townrunners?" said Richard and shook his head. "I admire your ambition, Chloe, but I believe beyond a doubt that central control is necessary for the network to function productively."

"With you at the head of this central control, no doubt?" said Chloe, a bitter smile twisting her lips.

"I have the experience necessary to successfully fill such a role, yes," said Richard.

"You're saying the system is good the way it is as long as you're the one running it?"

"I suppose I am, yes," said Richard.

"I'm not too ambitious, Richard," said Chloe. "You're not ambitious enough. If you think you're the benevolent exception to the corrupting influence of power, I'd hate to be the one to bring you back to reality."

"And reality is?" said Richard, his face gone completely blank now.

"You want power just as much as Aaron or Isabelle. You want to be able to make everyone do things your way, but if your way is so wonderful, why force people to adopt it? If they can see it's the best, wouldn't they leap at the chance?"

"An idealistic notion, to be sure," said Richard. "People make decisions with their emotions, not with logic and reason."

"Except for you," said Chloe.

Richard shook his head. "Even me," he said softly. He didn't elaborate, but something stirred behind his eyes. He cleared his throat. "As you might have guessed, the other townrunners don't trust me," said Xander. "They were chosen mostly for their loyalty to my parents. Let me think about it." Xander rubbed his face under his glasses.

"I'm really sorry I woke you up," said Chloe. "I'll go and let you sleep now."

"That's okay," said Xander. "Pretty well everyone is aware that I sleep at odd hours and refrains from disturbing me in my quarters, except for you."

"You knew it was me before you opened the door," said Chloe. It wasn't a question.

"I was fairly certain, yes," said Xander, and his eyes crinkled at the corners.

"And you let me in in your pyjamas," said Chloe.

Xander pretended to study his state of dress. "Looks that way." He went serious. "Chloe, you don't know many residents here, and after yesterday, it would be understandable if you want to talk to someone."

"After yesterday?" said Chloe.

"Encountering a settlement without clean water, being manipulated by Isabelle . . . my actions in the car," said Xander. "Despite my being a contributing factor to your potential turmoil, I want to be clear that you can speak to me about whatever is on your mind."

"Getting buy-in for this town network is on my mind, figuring out how to get the settlements clean water is on my mind," said Chloe. Anger rose in her chest and threatened to choke her.

"Chloe, all you've wanted since you came here is to return to your family—"

"Wrong, I want to help wherever I can," said Chloe. The last thing she wanted to think about right now was her family. With no leads on their location or even whether they were safe, she would drive herself to distraction wondering whether they were okay.

"We're going to get them back," said Xander softly. He took her hand from where she was practically rubbing a hole in her pants and squeezed it.

Xander's earnest face blurred through her tears, and he crouched next to her chair. He gathered her into his arms, and Chloe dissolved into sobs. Everything that had happened for the past week flooded over her, and her entire body shook with sorrow. She buried her face in Xander's shoulder and wrapped her arms around him. He didn't say anything, just pressed her to his chest and let her cry.

***

Vishesh waited until the kids were gone from the bedroom to show any signs of wakefulness. He needed privacy for what he was about to do. He silently padded to his pack and opened the top. He pulled out the Seed-verts and put them aside and then felt around for the receiver. He laid it on his lap.

Chloe had ripped this receiver out of Town Iota, but she'd done it carefully. If he could get it powered, it should be functional. He unplugged the bedside lamp from the wall and fished out his pocketknife. He cut and stripped the lamp cord, then did the same for the receiver's power supply. He twisted them together, one side and then the other. Getting his hands on electrical tape or wire connectors would have been hard to justify, especially since Aaron had watched Chloe extract this receiver.

Vishesh glanced at the bedroom door. Still shut, of course. He plugged in the lamp cord. The screen blinked on. The lack of burnt smell was an encouraging sign that his makeshift connections were good.

The nearest town to them should be Town Lambda, the one that Aaron was supposedly going to target next. Any transmission that was sent from this receiver could be intercepted; there was no such thing as a private line in the radio network. Checking in with Neil would be ideal, to see what exactly he should say, but there was no way to secretly get this receiver out of the house or surreptitiously show it to the others. He would have to do this himself. Once he turned the receiver off again, no one would be able to discover that *he* had sent the signal.

Fingers crossed that Town Lambda listened to his warning. He'd have to come up with something that they couldn't ignore, that they would believe without question. They didn't have much time to act, if Portia's information was correct, so he had to convey urgency. He couldn't risk a long conversation being intercepted, one or two messages, maximum, was all he had. That's assuming no one walked in on him right now. He tapped in a message, sent it, and prayed that it would reach the right town, that they would understand, that they would listen and act.

There was no answer, and Vishesh ran out of time. He clicked the receiver off, unplugged it, and buried it in his backpack again under the Seed-verts. He shoved the pack under his bed and got on with his day.

The sunny, gorgeous weather called to the whole family, so Vishesh distracted himself by taking the kids out to play. He and Sheila walked side by side, hands in their pockets, while the kids ran ahead to the open field that they used as a park. The few other littler kids from the neighbourhood slowly gathered as well, and Vishesh nodded to their guardians and made small talk about how fast they were all growing and how thankful they were to have a safe place to raise the little ones. Sheila still wasn't talking to him, but it was less obvious when there were other adults to make conversation with.

A series of engines rumbled from over the hill. In the distance, a convoy of cars and SUVs made their way down the lane and onto the road, turning in the direction where Town Lambda would likely be.

"Vishesh?" said Connor and touched his arm, and Vishesh jumped.

"Sorry, Connor, what is it?"

"Neil's here," he said. "Can I go?"

Vishesh waved to Neil, who was approaching across the muddy field. "Yup, you go ahead," said Vishesh. He caught Sheila glaring at him out of the corner of his eye. She hadn't had any say in Neil's appointment as Connor's mentor. As if Vishesh had.

By the time they headed home for lunch, Vishesh had his coat draped over his arm, and he was still sweating. He should have put on a T-shirt this morning. The breeze only cut the hot sun slightly, but Sheila still went straight to open the windows on their little house when they arrived.

Vishesh jogged up the stairs and burst into his bedroom. He froze. Seed packets littered the floor and the map hung off the side of the bed. His pack lay limp in the middle of the room. He glanced under the bed and into his pack to be sure, but he already knew he wouldn't find anything. The receiver was gone.

***

Portia stepped out of the shower and heard the front door open. She wrapped a silk robe around her body and sauntered into the living room as Aaron sank onto the leather couch, his head tilted back, his eyes closed. He could almost be a normal guy, getting home after a long day at work. Almost. His eyes opened, and he pierced her with a hard stare. In spite of herself, Portia's pulse quickened and her pussy tingled. That was the really twisted part about their relationship. Portia wasn't a good actor; in fact, she was a shit actor. She didn't need to pretend with Aaron because whatever perverse part of her controlled her arousal was totally into him, despite her better judgment.

Aaron waved her over, and Portia sank to her knees and crawled to him, his gaze still burning into her. She sat back on her heels.

"Next time, take the robe off first," he said in a low voice.

"I thought the tantalizing peeks would be better," said Portia and made a show of examining her own cleavage.

"Mmm, maybe," said Aaron. His cock bulged in his pants, but he didn't make a move to free it or to undress her.

Portia loosened the robe's belt and pushed it off her shoulders, the silk sliding over her skin and making her shiver. Her nipples tightened in the cool air, and knowing that Aaron's steely gaze was eating her up didn't hurt, either.

"We hit Lambda today," said Aaron conversationally. "You know what we found?" He wasn't looking for a response. "It was abandoned. They'd even stripped the solar panels and water purifiers from the town. Why do you think that would be?"

Portia glanced up. His face was still impassive, but he raised his eyebrows, waiting for her response.

"They knew you were coming."

"Very good, baby," said Aaron. "How could they possibly have known we were coming?"

"Someone warned them," said Portia.

"I bet you wish you could have warned them," said Aaron. "Come here."

Portia undid the belt the rest of the way and left the robe pooled on the floor as she settled between his knees. He grabbed her hand and pressed it to his fly, against his pulsing erection.

"Would you have warned them if you could have?" said Aaron.

"Yes . . . Sir," said Portia. Her breath caught on the word, as much as she hated giving Aaron its power. His cock jumped at it as well.

"Too bad there's no way for you to help them," said Aaron. A smile stole over his face.

That was true. She couldn't help them. None of the members of the rebellion had the infrastructure to contact a town.

"You're wondering who it was," said Aaron. "A loose cannon, not acclimated to living here yet. He will be dealt with." He shifted. "I think it's about time for my cock to be down your throat, don't you?"

Portia's whole body shuddered. Yes, she really agreed. She'd file any other information Aaron spilled away to think about later, as she always did. Now was not the time to try analyzing it, with her brain half-addled by his presence. Her near-perfect memory came in handy for that part.

Chapter Fifteen

Log: Town Kappa, Richard A. Phillips, Townrunner, 20 May 20—

Chloe related everything that occurred at the City during her stay there, as did Brianna. We have formulated a plan to decontaminate as many settlements outside of the City's restricted zone as possible. Some discreet inquiries into the prevalence of Seed-vert seeds among the towns have not borne fruit, and other towns have been less than cooperative. It seems that the seeds are a touchy subject among townrunners. More investigation is necessary. Town Lambda did not respond at all.

C hloe and Dorothy played checkers in the lounge.
"I'd have pegged the two of you for chess players," said Brianna. She stood over them and studied the board.

"My brain can barely handle this amount of strategy at the moment," said Chloe. She jumped her piece over Dorothy's and sat back.

"Since you have so much time on your hands, I'll put you to work," said Brianna. "Once this pattern is done, we'll pop out of dark mode and catch up on messages. I want you to review the communications sent to and from Town Lambda for the last twenty-four hours."

"Cassandra was hit?" said Dorothy. She gave Brianna a sharp look.

"Seems that way," said Brianna.

"Who's Cassandra?" said Chloe.

"The townrunner," said Dorothy. "She'd never go down without a fight."

"You knew her?" said Chloe.

"We know them all," said Dorothy.

"Cassandra we liked," said Brianna. She blinked back tears. "*Like*. We *like* her, because she's not dead."

The towns were just Greek letters, points on a map to Chloe. But to Brianna and the other residents, they were actual people, probably friends. Maybe even family.

"I'm sorry," said Chloe.

"Check the message log," said Brianna. "The rest of us are going to Lambda to investigate." She strode out of the lounge.

Dorothy nodded to Chloe and followed. Chloe tidied the checkers and wandered up to the bridge. The driver ignored her, as usual. Her laptop was hooked up, but she'd have to wait until dark mode was switched off to get into the message history for another town.

Once they'd ground to a halt and she'd regained access, the message they were looking for was obvious.

Richard and Brianna met her on the bridge when they got back from Lambda. Brianna scrolled through the message history Chloe displayed for them on her laptop.

"Here it is," said Chloe, prodding the screen.

Brianna and Richard gathered around to look over her shoulder.

Debilitating raid imminent. Evacuate personnel from Town Lambda ASAP. Remember Town Iota.

"That would do it," said Brianna.

"Someone warned them," said Chloe.

"Someone with accurate information regarding the target and timing of the raid," said Richard.

"So they're definitely premeditated," said Chloe.

Richard nodded.

"Did you find any survivors? Any clue to who did this?" said Chloe.

"Nope, still nothing," said Brianna.

"Our lead suspect is still Aaron," said Richard.

Aaron, who presumably had her family under his thumb, destroying towns and making all the residents disappear.

"No chance Isabelle could be doing this? Seems like she'd prefer it if the settlements didn't exist at all," said Chloe. "And if there are no towns, there are no settlements."

"Nah," said Brianna. "No settlements means no one to lord it over. She wants settlements—she just wants them firmly under her control."

"Hence keeping the Seed-verts under wraps," said Chloe. "I'll bet I can find out who sent this message. Maybe not a location, but a serial number or *something*." The answer she found after poking around in the metadata couldn't be right. "Something must be wrong with the metadata," she said. "It looks like the message came from Town Iota."

Richard stared out the windshield, hands clasped behind his back. Chloe glanced that way, but the road stretched away into a curve, a wetland just off the edge of it.

"What are you thinking?" she said.

"It must be Aaron," he said.

"And if it is?" said Chloe.

"He has your family." Richard finally turned to meet her gaze. His expression was so soft and sympathetic that it nearly made Chloe take a step back. Something clicked in her brain.

"Vishesh!" she said. "He had Town Iota's receiver. He could easily have hidden it from Aaron."

"You're saying he's the one who warned Town Lambda?" said Brianna.

"It's a possibility," said Chloe. Her stomach sank and then twisted in knots. "What would Aaron do to someone who betrayed him like that?" Neither Richard nor Brianna answered, and Chloe changed her mind and held up a hand. "Actually, I don't want to know."

"I suggest we focus our energy on locating Aaron's settlement. We will require an accurate location if we are to travel there and free Chloe's family," said Richard.

"What?" said Chloe. "You agreed to help me make sure my family was okay, not free them."

"It seems to me that they will not be safe until they are freed from Aaron's control," said Richard.

"Hell yes, let's do it," said Brianna.

Chloe couldn't even form a sentence, so much swirled through her head. Of course she wanted to chase Aaron down and stop him from doing this to any more towns; of course she wanted to find her family, but she had no more expected Richard's help than she had Isabelle's. Richard had proved when he kidnapped her that he only cared for his own people, above all else, and she found it hard to believe that he would put them in danger just to rescue her family.

"Wait," she said. She grabbed Richard's arm and turned him. "What's in it for you?"

Real pain flashed over Richard's face before he could hide it. Or maybe he wasn't trying to. "As I said, I don't expect that you'll ever trust me after I effectively kidnapped you, but you'll find I care about doing the right thing. If Aaron is allowed to continue debilitating and stripping towns, who will decontaminate the settlements? Do you expect he'll be kind enough to leave enough towns to work the land?"

"No, of course not," said Chloe, and to her surprise, her stomach sank a little further. Part of her had wanted him to say he was doing it for her, just for her and her family.

Richard—Xander chuckled. "And of course, a happy side-effect is that it might get me into your good graces." Then he winked—*winked*—at her. Chloe thought her eyes might bug right out of her head. He laughed aloud as he turned and left the bridge, Brianna at his heels.

Chloe shook her head. He was an enigma. As she turned back to her laptop, Chloe caught the driver's glare out of the corner of her eye, as though he was about to spring from his seat and strangle her. She did a double take, and his eyes were fixed on the road, placid as could be.

***

"You can do this," said Brianna, holding both Chloe's hands in hers and staring into her eyes. "We need the townrunners on board so they'll let you meddle with their towns' software. You have to make them feel like we're united, like they're part of a greater whole. That we can work together as a team to accomplish something."

Town Kappa sat unmoving on a highway, and Dorothy fidgeted in the driver's seat, probably anxious to get going again.

"Remind me again why you can't do this?" said Chloe.

"Everyone knows I'm loyal to Richard, and no one trusts Richard," said Brianna. "You're impartial."

"Isabelle didn't seem to think so," said Chloe, but Brianna ignored her.

"Talk about how Aaron took your kids, how he picked off the towns one by one. You can do this, Chloe."

Richard strode onto the bridge, barely gave Chloe a glance, and nodded to Dorothy. Eight empty frames immediately populated the windshield. The video feeds connected one after another, revealing folks who could only be the other townrunners. The display names just showed the town designations: alpha, epsilon, zeta, omicron, sigma, upsilon, rho, and psi. Only eight. More than twenty towns had been commissioned a few years ago when they had first been implemented. Had so many really been destroyed, or were these simply the only towns willing to listen to what they had to say?

Richard motioned for Chloe to step forward so that she'd be in the frame with him. "Good afternoon," said Richard. "Welcome to the town summit. Thanks very much for taking the time to speak with me—"

"Okay, Phillips," said an older white woman, labelled Epsilon. "Cut the bullshit. Do you have help for us or not?"

"Greene," said Richard. "There is nothing I would like more. Unfortunately, simply stating the solutions we have developed would be inadequate. It's important that you all understand how exactly they function, along with their limitations."

"I doubt any of us require a detailed explanation, as long as appropriate documentation is supplied," said a heavily made-up woman who was near Chloe's age, Town Omicron.

"Unfortunately, Eloise, no such documentation exists," said Richard, giving her a wry smile.

"Of course not," Eloise replied.

"I agree," said a young man who was visibly shaking, Town Zeta. "No point in telling us how the thing works. Have the engineers sort it out."

"I, for one, want to know what we're getting into before we let this upstart tamper with our towns," said a gruff man with a large grey beard, Town Alpha.

"Perfectly understandable, Chabot," Richard cut in. "As I was saying. I will provide a summary, and those interested can delve more deeply at their convenience. I hope that will prove satisfactory, Greene?" The Town Epsilon townrunner nodded stiffly, and Richard continued. "The system we have devised is called dark mode. It prevents the City from monitoring your location or applying range restrictions; however, when it is activated, it also renders all communications inoperative."

"That wasn't so hard, was it?" said Greene.

"As noted, I have omitted many pertinent details. If you feel you have enough information to allow my developer to apply the dark mode patch to your town, by all means, we can cut this meeting short and proceed."

"Remotely?" said a brown-skinned man whose gaze seemed to pierce them even through the video connection, Town Psi.

"Not at this time, Pierre," said Richard. "We are developing the capability to implement the patch remotely."

Developing what? If they hadn't been in a high-pressure call, Chloe would have shot Xander a searing glare. As it was, she just ground her teeth.

"Simply inform Town Kappa that you wish to proceed, and I will ensure the necessary personnel are transported to your town," Richard finished.

Four of the talking heads on the windshield spoke at once. It was unintelligible but certainly not positive feedback. Richard raised a hand to quiet them, and they eventually trailed off.

"I have no plans to implement the patch unless specifically authorized by the townrunner of each town," said Richard. "I encourage all of you to consider the implications of the recent hijack attempt on the City for your town and any alternative strategies you have access to. I have no doubt that in short order, the organization that tried to take control of the City will put in more of a concerted effort. You and I both know that many towns have been destroyed recently, and that the culprit has not been apprehended."

Richard turned to Chloe. The babble from the townrunners covered his quiet words. "You're up," he said. "This is our only chance."

Chloe nodded and stepped forward. "Townrunners," she said.

"Who are you?" snapped Town Epsilon.

"I'm Chloe Michaels," she said.

"Who are you, Chloe Michaels?" said Town Psi, his eyes still just as penetrating. "Why are you addressing us?"

"I'm the one who created dark mode," said Chloe. "I understand your reluctance to implement my patch, considering you don't seem to trust Richard. I want to make the case for using my creation, our only defence against the City hijacker at the moment. If we all go dark at once, it'll give us time to come up with a permanent defence against Aaron's, the hijacker's, control. I'm currently working on something—"

"Working on something is not enough, Chloe," said Town Sigma, a calm woman who had been completely silent so far. "You're clearly very competent, but as a scientist myself, I know that there is a large gap between hypothesis and implementation. Using your dark mode will paint a target on each and every town who does so. If we are seen to be resisting the City, I suspect the hijacker would not take kindly to it. No, I won't be risking my residents on a half-baked project."

"I know that if we work together as a team, we can get ahead of the hijacker, in case he does succeed in taking the City," said Chloe urgently.

"Miss, I see that you are desperate, but I think this is beyond your understanding," said Town Alpha.

Chloe tried to swallow down her rage, but it bubbled up and spilled out in words she never meant to say.

"Who the fuck are you to tell me what I understand? Aaron took my kids! My family! I have a way to stop him from taking everything from all of us, and you're not even willing to try? You refuse dark mode out of spite, just because you hate Richard, and you refuse to work together because you all want to protect your own interests." Brianna tried to grab her arm, but Chloe shook her off. "Richard was right. You're not worthy of being townrunners, none of you. It's obvious you got your positions from sucking up to Isabelle. Good luck sucking up to Aaron instead.

"What I was offering was your last hope. Enjoy ruling over towns that are taken down and scrapped for parts. Town Kappa won't be joining you, just so you know. We're not going to let the City push us around anymore."

"Please close the line," said Richard's mild voice.

The dumbfounded faces on the windshield blinked out. Chloe's rage pounded through her veins, then slowed, and dissipated.

"That wasn't quite what we discussed," said Brianna.

"Crap, I'm sorry," said Chloe. "When he said . . ." she trailed off, the rage choking her again for a second.

"I get it, being talked down to is shitty," said Brianna.

"Shitty enough that I wrecked our chances of saving the towns when Aaron takes over," said Chloe.

"We will make alternate plans," said Richard.

"By the way, Richard," said Chloe. "What was that about a remote patch?" Now she let the searing glare through.

"That's right. You had better do your utmost to implement it, don't you think?" He raised his eyebrows mildly. "Deputy, with me." He turned on his heel and left the bridge, and Brianna scampered after him.

Should she be angry that he had promised something she might not be able to deliver, or flattered that he had faith in her abilities? Either way, she better get to work.

***

Vishesh and Neil had gone through the same song and dance as the previous evening to get out to the bar together. Portia sat alone in their booth when they came in.

"Go sit. I'll get drinks," said Neil.

Vishesh nodded, still too overwhelmed by the noise to try to talk over it out here.

"I hear you did something foolish, new guy," said Portia as he took a seat opposite her.

"What do you mean?" said Vishesh. She had to be talking about the message to Lambda, but how could she know about it?

"You've done more than one foolish thing in the last twenty-four hours?" said Portia.

"What foolish thing?" said Neil and put their drinks on the table. He slid into the bench next to Vishesh.

"Remember last night when I said I might be able to contact Town Lambda?" Vishesh stared into his beer and wrapped his hands around the glass.

"I remember," said Neil.

"This morning, I figured out how to do it," said Vishesh.

"That's awesome, Vishesh," said Neil, but Vishesh shook his head.

"No, not really. Aaron already knows it was me. I wasn't sure until Portia just said so, but when I got home at lunch, my receiver was gone. So I figured it was only a matter of time."

Vishesh caught the tail end of a silent conversation between Neil and Portia. Portia rolled her eyes and huffed.

"Fuck. Fine, I'll help get him out," she said.

"Out?" said Vishesh. Out of trouble with Aaron?

"Out of the settlement," said Neil. "I know another place, across the river. They can hold their own against Aaron. You'd be safe there."

"And my family?" said Vishesh.

"Slow down, there," said Portia. "I never said I'd help with *that*."

"Portia's right," said Neil. "It would just be you. It'll be risky enough as it is."

They wanted him to run. To leave his family, after everything. And not just leave his family, leave them *here* with Aaron. With someone who could serve them contaminated food any second and they'd be none the wiser, someone who wanted to turn thoughtful, brilliant, compassionate Connor into what? A security officer?

"No," said Vishesh. "I'm not running."

"Either you run, or Aaron takes you," said Portia. "Does to you what he's done to us. To all of us. Eats you up and spits you out."

"Then I'll resist, like you two," said Vishesh.

Neil took his hand in both of his own. "That's sweet," he said. "You know we'd love to have you. But he'll use your family against you. Are you ready for that?"

"The only way I can help my family is to bring Aaron down. How can I do that from a safe settlement across the river? Besides, do you have any idea how miserable Sheila would make my life if I dragged all of them here and then abandoned them?"

"Isn't she already not speaking to you?" said Portia.

"Yeah, but it's only been four days," said Vishesh. He took a long drink and cradled his glass. "She's justified, anyway."

"The silent treatment takes way too much effort," said Portia. She drained her glass and thunked it on the table. "We should have a meeting soon."

"When?" said Neil.

"When Aaron takes the City in a couple days?" said Portia.

"Days?" said Vishesh. "What's he waiting for?"

"Beats me," said Portia. "I don't analyze the plans. I just pass them on."

"I'll spread the word. Meeting day after tomorrow. Something tells me we'll need it," said Neil.

Chapter Sixteen

Log: Town Kappa, Richard A. Phillips, Townrunner, 23 May 20—

Towns Gamma and Rho discovered downed, each further north along the river than the last. All we can do is hope that they are leading us to Aaron's settlement. No more word from the City; the other destroyed towns don't appear to have been warned. It seems likely that the whistleblower was apprehended directly after their message to Town Lambda. Survivors from Town Lambda have not been located as yet.

C hloe sat with Brianna in Xander's quarters. He stood in profile, looking out the windshield as the landscape inched past and then periodically wheeled in a decontamination pattern. With all the downed towns recently, more settlements needed processing than the towns could serve, even within the restricted range the City had implemented.

"We're the only town with dark mode. Don't the other townrunners realize that it's the only way to protect themselves from whatever Aaron is doing? Why wouldn't they want to implement it?" said Chloe.

"In brief," said Xander, "they don't trust me."

"Why not? You didn't kidnap them or anything, did you?" said Chloe.

"Very amusing. No, but I am my mother's son. They are fully cognizant that I will do and say whatever I think is necessary to get what I want. I have made no secret of the fact that I believe I should be in control of the City and, thus, the towns, that I would be a better ECM than my mother is. Any modification to their towns could come with some secret bid to control them."

"They'd prefer the unknown threat from Aaron to what they see as a certain threat from you," said Chloe.

"And that's why you shouldn't get a reputation as a manipulative jerk," said Brianna and poked her belly. "Let that be a lesson, Baby Dot. Manipulate in the shadows or not at all."

"It doesn't make sense," said Chloe. "Can't they see the other towns falling apart around them?"

"They would prefer to take their chances that they won't be next, that someone else will neutralize the threat before it affects them," said Xander.

Chloe put her face in her hands.

"I'll go get Dorothy to check messages. Maybe one of those stubborn jerks has changed their mind," said Brianna and the door hissed as it opened and then shut, leaving Chloe and Xander alone.

Chloe slid her hands through her hair, down her neck, and kneaded her solid muscles. If only she could fix up that crappy desk on the bridge, maybe they wouldn't be throbbing with pain.

"May I?" said Xander.

"Be my guest," said Chloe, waving at her shoulders. "It's your patch that killed my back over the last couple days."

Xander moved in close behind her and rubbed firmly at her knotted shoulders. "I very much appreciate it, Chloe," he said, his breath tickling over the back of her neck.

How was this the same guy who gave the townrunners an ultimatum? Who always held her infuriatingly to the exact letter of her word? Chloe's shoulders loosened. The man who had come to rescue her from Isabelle, who had taken her home to her farm when she'd asked. The one who hadn't stood for the City's callous range restrictions when none of the other townrunners were even willing to have the solution handed to them whole-cloth.

"I just don't get it," said Chloe.

"You can bend your brain as much as you like. Logic won't provide the answer to this. It isn't rational," said Xander. "They are afraid, they're paranoid, they're looking to the City for help, and the City is denying everything. Is it any wonder they won't accept help from a pariah like me?"

"I guess not," said Chloe. The time when she hadn't trusted Xander was a hazy memory now.

The town slowed and then jerked to a stop. They would have to in order to deactivate dark mode.

"Don't you have more important things to do?" said Chloe, not that she wanted him to stop working the knots out of her back. Or touching her.

"Not currently," said Xander.

A bang on the door made Chloe jump, and Xander's hands stilled.

"Perhaps I do," he said.

"It's Isabelle," said Brianna through the door.

Xander's hands disappeared from Chloe's back. She hauled herself to her feet and followed him to the door, which slid open.

"Tell her I'm not interested," said Richard.

Brianna's pale face brought Chloe up short.

"What does she want?" she said.

"It's a live call," said Brianna. "She must have been watching for Town Kappa to reappear."

Richard swore under his breath, grabbed his suit jacket off the back of a chair, and shrugged it on as he followed Brianna down to the bridge.

The chatter of the entire town of people reached them before they'd even descended the stairs. Clearly no one wanted to hear about this second-hand. The voices died away as Richard entered the bridge.

"Dorothy, accept the call," said Richard.

Dorothy flicked a few switches. Maybe they would discover that yet another town had stopped responding, or maybe the City had finally been hijacked.

Isabelle's face filled the windshield, larger than life.

"Townrunner," said Isabelle. "I require your immediate cooperation."

"Noted, ECM," said Richard. "What seems to be the problem?"

"Armed raiders are currently approaching the City," said Isabelle, much too calmly. "My understanding is that you have developed a method of circumventing City control. I would request that you deploy it in cooperation with the other townrunners immediately."

"I would, except that they all uniformly refused my offer when I extended it days ago," said Richard.

"They won't refuse my orders, and you damned well know it."

"Let's ask them, shall we?" said Richard. He spoke to Dorothy in a low voice, and the windshield went dark and then eight frames appeared, Isabelle in one. The six remaining townrunners appeared one by one until they were all present.

"The ECM has proposed that—" Richard cut off as the last frame was populated. Aaron smiled down at them.

"Good afternoon everyone!" he said. "Thank you so much for including me in this little chat. It's my first summit—you *do* call them *summits*, right?"

"If you aren't a townrunner, get off the call," said Isabelle.

"Rude!" said Aaron. "I'll forgive you this once, since I'm willing to bet you don't know who I am, but I think you might want to consider speaking to me with a touch more deference, since I'm the one who will soon be in control of this entire backwater region."

"I don't know who you think—" said Isabelle.

"That's enough. I just came on to address all you townrunners. If you even think about popping into Phillips' *dark mode*, I'll hunt you down anyway, and your lives and those of all your residents will be forfeit. Just wanted to give you fair warning. As a courtesy.

"I have to run, but Isabelle, I'll see you soon!"

His face blinked out. Chloe could hear herself breathing in the ringing silence, and then everyone spoke at once. Richard leaned forward and said something in Dorothy's ear, and the windshield went dark.

Isabelle's face reappeared, full-size. He hadn't engaged dark mode then.

"Are you out of your mind, Richard?" said Isabelle. "Sending out the patch? After what Aaron said?"

"Dark mode will buy them time," said Richard. "You yourself ordered me to implement the patch. We'll be in touch. Dorothy, if you please."

Isabelle's face blinked out, and the highway in front of the town reappeared.

Richard had unilaterally overridden the townrunners' wishes and patched dark mode onto all the towns, with full knowledge that Aaron would retaliate.

***

When Richard had asked Chloe to implement the patch remotely, she hadn't realized exactly what he had had in mind. She wouldn't have gone along with it if she'd known . . . would she? Maybe it had been naive of her to think that he would wait for the okay from each of the townrunners and send them the patch individually, knowing that Aaron was taking over the City as they stood here.

"Patch successfully broadcast, Sir," said Dorothy.

She projected a map of the region onto the windshield, and they watched each town blink out, one by one, as the patch did its work.

Chloe took a step forward and opened her mouth to chew Richard out, but Brianna grabbed her arm and spun her bodily around.

"Not now," she said in an undertone.

Chloe shook her hand off and rounded on her, but the look on Brianna's face stopped her in her tracks. Brianna was usually the first to critique Richard's actions, the first to tell him when he was over the line. This time, her face seemed frozen in a neutral rictus.

If Brianna wasn't going to do it, someone had to.

"Richard, implementing that patch without the towns' consent? Knowing full well they will pay the price from Aaron?" said Chloe.

Richard turned to her slowly. His face carefully neutral. The expression sent a shiver down Chloe's spine.

"It appears as though resident Chloe disagrees with my actions," said Richard.

Every eye on the bridge was trained on Chloe now, and none too kindly. Whatever. Did none of them have a shred of integrity?

"Damn right I do. You asked them if they wanted the patch. They said no. Aaron *threatened* them, and then you *forced* the patch on them. Did I leave anything out?"

"Perhaps the fact that you are my subordinate and thus unqualified to pass judgment on my actions?" said Richard, still disturbingly calm.

Chloe stifled a growl in the back of her throat and shouldered past some town residents to her laptop in the corner. If no one else would help her, she would take the patch back herself.

Brianna grabbed her shoulder. "What the fuck are you doing?" she hissed.

"I'm undoing the damage *your* townrunner has done," said Chloe.

"You can't—"

"Just watch me," said Chloe.

She shook Brianna's hand off. Turning dark mode off remotely would be pretty well impossible, since the whole point was to hide from the network, and the network was the only way to reach the other towns.

Fuck! This was what happened when you joined the goddamned towns. Her own work, twisted and used for the machinations of the powerful. She'd thought Xander was different, she'd thought he had integrity . . . but had she really? He wanted power just like the rest, and what good was power if you didn't wield it?

"Sir," said Dorothy.

Chloe glanced up. The map still covered the windshield, but . . . weird . . . a little dot appeared on the map. It had to be a town. Chloe could have sworn they'd all gone dark. *There!* Another one lit up. Richard shot her an icy glare.

"I didn't do anything," said Chloe, faintly.

"No," said Xander.

"Then what's going on? We've been using dark mode for days, and it's always been totally stable. I swear my patch was as well," said Chloe. Maybe it was a bug in the remote implementation? She had put it together fairly quickly. Not being able to test it properly had been killer.

"It's not the patch," said Brianna.

"They have elected not to remain in dark mode," said Richard.

"They've all turned it off," said Chloe.

All of Town Kappa stared at the screen as all six dots came back into view.

***

The knock on Vishesh's front door around lunchtime made him jump. He looked at Sheila, but she shrugged and nodded to the door.

Aaron himself stood on the porch, an umbrella folded at his side. Vishesh took a steadying breath and opened the door. He'd known this moment was coming, but that didn't soothe his pounding heart.

"Just the man I want to see," said Aaron and shot him a grin. "Get your coat and come with me. I have a problem, and I think you're just the one to help me with it."

Refusing was not an option. Vishesh did as Aaron said and found himself walking in step with him toward his office.

Aaron led him to a pair of cars idling outside the nerve centre, both flanked by two members of Aaron's crew. Aaron motioned Vishesh into the back seat of the SUV and slammed his door. Vishesh jumped as the other side door popped open and flinched as Aaron hopped in and clicked his seatbelt. Vishesh belted himself in as well, the motion both familiar and totally strange.

The SUV pulled out of the driveway and turned onto the main road.

"Your little warning worked, you'll be glad to know," said Aaron, smiling benignly across at him. "Not only that, but guess who else found your message?"

Who else could it be but Chloe? Vishesh didn't answer.

"Yes, that's right," said Aaron. "Chloe and Richard fucking Phillips."

"Together?" said Vishesh.

"Why, yes," said Aaron. "They seemed pretty close when I chatted with them earlier. I guess she must have decided to stay with him after all. It didn't look like she was a prisoner so much as an accomplice."

If Chloe was working with a town, she had a good reason. That didn't help the dread making Vishesh's heart pound. If she was working with a town, she had no other option. Or she'd given up on them.

"What was your call about?" said Vishesh.

"You don't need to worry about that. Doesn't seem like they got the message *I* was trying to send. Anyhow, I just wanted to update you on how your little stunt panned out. And of course, to offer you the opportunity to help me."

"Why would I help you? I know you've destroyed multiple towns," said Vishesh. *And poison your own people, and govern using fear.*

"Doesn't matter either way to me, whether you're in a cell or out and free helping the cause. I have others who can do the same things as you," said Aaron. "I suspect it will make a big difference to you, however."

"If I refuse, you'll toss me in a cell? And if I agree? Will you let me live as I have been, with my family?"

Aaron laughed. "You've got me there. I'd keep a close eye on you, of course. You and I both know you have a better chance of escape—of sabotaging my plans—if you come out and work for me than if you're rotting away in a cell."

Vishesh glared at him.

"I can be reasonable, you know. If you help me, I'll consider letting you see your little family again, okay? If you do a good job, that is. No more of this sneaking around trying to upset my plans." Aaron smiled genially. "Deal?"

Vishesh stared out the window. He hadn't been downtown in many years. They crossed a different bridge than they had on the way over, this one offering a direct view of Parliament. The view was surprisingly unchanged. Yes, the limestone buildings would eventually melt away in the acid rain, but the restoration efforts that had been recently completed before armageddon would keep them standing for many years yet.

Aaron was going to make him do something despicable if he agreed to help. Then again, he wasn't wrong. Better Vishesh work on something and sabotage it than someone else work on the same thing who wasn't so rebelliously inclined.

The road curved around a cliff face, and they turned into Major's Hill Park. Last he'd been here, the majority of the park had been a sweeping lawn, broken only by carefully manicured beds of tulips lining the network of pathways twisting through the shaped and pruned trees.

If he'd been dropped here without context, he wouldn't have realized it was the same place. A sea of tents and tarps led to a bracken-covered mound, and fissures the length of the mound indicated that it was the City, that it had been disturbed recently.

The driver cursed under his breath and drove steadily through the tent city, along a path of crushed tents and toppled two-by-fours that had clearly been broken not long ago—likely by one of Aaron's trucks. A hunched figure paused their digging through a crushed tent and scrambled off the makeshift road just in time to evade their SUV.

"Why bother?" said the driver under his breath. "They won't be here much longer, one way or another."

If the City hovered through here on its way out of the park, there was no telling how much of this tent city would be destroyed. The hover itself was minimally destructive, though the high air pressure might crush objects into the ground . . . and heaven help a person that got caught beneath it. Okay, it was minimally destructive *in theory*, but the propulsion mechanism, the multitude of sharp legs that found purchase by digging repeatedly into the ground and dragging backward, would obliterate any structures they encountered. Better hope Aaron didn't plan on moving the thing. Though his attempt to activate the hover function would suggest otherwise.

If Aaron ordered him to get it working again, would he be able to do it, knowing the destruction and loss of life it would directly cause, let alone indirectly? No, not a chance, even if it meant passing the burden on to someone else.

The driver pulled right into the loading dock and killed the engine.

"Here we are!" said Aaron and sprang from the SUV.

The loading dock was hardly recognizable as such. Every surface was covered by some kind of makeshift market stall arrangement, most of them abandoned. Aaron opened Vishesh's door for him personally, flanked by two of his people, and Vishesh climbed down.

"I've been waiting for your help with bated breath," said Aaron and slung an arm around his shoulders.

Vishesh instinctively hunched, allowing Aaron to lead him wherever he would.

"We're having a little problem with the hover function, and I suspect someone has tampered with the autopilot as well. I have a feeling you'll be able to get to the bottom of it for me, eh?" said Aaron.

"The hover?" said Vishesh.

"That's right," said Aaron. "The hover was working for a short period of time and then cut out."

Exactly what he'd been afraid of. Aaron wanted to use him to kill people. "I won't do it, Aaron," he said. He spoke quietly, but he knew Aaron heard him from the painful dig of his fingers into Vishesh's shoulder.

"I think you will," said Aaron.

"What makes you think that?" said Vishesh. They climbed the stairs to one of the long hallways that ran the length of the City, Aaron still propelling him along.

"You think you have nothing to lose? I can name a few things," said Aaron. "I hope you won't make me use my leverage against you, because I'd really rather not. I know how much you want to stay with your family. If you refuse me, you must know that would be off the table indefinitely."

"That's fine," said Vishesh. "I can live with not seeing them again. I can't live with the loss of life that would result from what you're asking of me."

They climbed the stairs to the bridge and paused in the doorway to survey the space. The man standing in the centre of the bridge turned and smiled at him. Monty.

"Finally," he said. "Get to work on that hover."

Vishesh shook his head. Monty had come up in the world since he'd spied on him through the front window in the dark. Ratting Vishesh out to Aaron must have earned him a huge pile of brownie points.

"It seems Vishesh's principles are getting the best of him today," said Aaron.

"Nonsense," said Monty. "He's easy to persuade. Just like Chloe. Threaten one of their precious children, and they hop to it before you can even snap your fingers."

Vishesh's pulse roared in his ears. "You're supposed to be those kids' guardian, and this is how you treat them? What would Sheila say?"

Aaron tsked. "He has a point, Monty. Your suggestion of threatening those children is quite beyond the pale." He turned Vishesh roughly to face him, his expression still placidly neutral. "I, however, have no such compunctions. After all, *I'm* not one of their guardians."

He didn't have to say any more. His threat could range anywhere from killing a kid outright to letting them die of radiation poisoning, or a paltry permanent maiming. The exact nature of the threat didn't matter; Vishesh could not countenance any of the children suffering. He hunched his shoulders again, and Aaron gave one a squeeze.

"There it is," he said and beamed at Vishesh. "I quite like when we all work in harmony. Let me or Monty know what you need. Hover first and then the autopilot."

***

Portia nursed her beer and waited for Neil to arrive at the bar. She had to tell him about Vishesh, even though imagining his reaction was making her sweat. Every time the door opened, Portia fought down a jolt of adrenalin, only to grumble to herself when some rando came in instead of Neil.

Portia finished off her last gulp of beer and headed for the bar, which is why she didn't even see Neil come in.

"Hey, stranger," he said from behind her, and Portia jumped a mile.

"Shit, don't do that," she said.

Neil immediately frowned. "What's wrong?"

"I'll tell you when I get my drink!" She tossed the last couple words toward the bartender, who waved her away.

"Go sit," said Neil. "I'll bring it to you."

Yes, doing this to Neil was going to be a bitch, but keeping it from him would be worse.

Portia slid back into her spot in their booth and interlaced her fingers. She took a deep breath and tried to find that place of stillness deep inside that she accessed when Aaron had her kneel at his feet while he worked. Her leg jiggled, and she frowned. Nope. Without him here, it wasn't going to happen. Mercifully, Neil was on his way back with the drinks.

"Okay, tell me. What's Aaron done now?" said Neil before he'd even settled across from her.

"Remember how Vishesh sent that message, and we were all waiting for Aaron to drop the hammer on him?"

"I remember," said Neil, and fear filled his eyes.

"Aaron took him to the City today," said Portia.

"Okay," said Neil. "That's it?"

Portia studied her hands in her lap. "No," she said. "He's using Vishesh's brats as leverage to make him get the City running again. I don't know the exact details, but Aaron is sure Vishesh won't want to do it."

"But he will if Aaron threatens those kids," said Neil.

Portia nodded, and guilt choked her. Which made no sense, because this wasn't her fault. She was just the messenger. "He walked into it," she snapped. "We offered to get him out."

Neil smiled softly at her. "I'm worried about him. too." Why was Neil so damn nice? He drew himself up. "I think it's finally time, Portia."

"What?" said Portia, and she couldn't keep the desperation out of her voice. "Over some guy you just met? Seriously?" Neil was abandoning her, just like that.

"Not only that," said Neil. "Vishesh has friends out there. Maybe together we can finally finish this once and for all."

Once and for all. Kill Aaron. Or at least drive him out. Portia blinked hard and resisted the urge to run away, leave Neil before he could walk out on her. Run back to Aaron, keep living her stable life where she was useful and hated herself. Without Aaron, what would she even be?

"You'll have to keep things running here until it's time," said Neil.

Portia didn't trust herself to speak, so she nodded instead.

"It'll be okay, you know. We'll get to the other side," said Neil. He tried to take her hand, but she snatched it away.

"Whatever, I know," she snapped. "Just run along after your boy toy. I'm more than capable of handling this place."

Neil scowled at her. *Finally*. "I don't appreciate you taking your issues out on me. I'll see you around." Neil left his half-empty glass on the table as he stalked out of the bar.

Portia drained her own glass and then reached across and slid Neil's to her side of the table.

Chapter Seventeen

Log: Town Kappa, Richard A. Phillips, Townrunner, 24 May 20—

Deputy Brianna and I have gone through the notes from the Kappa residents' meeting and it seems clear that this will require splitting our residents into two camps. We cannot force those who would stay safe to risk their lives to storm the City, and we can't forbid those unwilling to sit and do nothing from going to the aid of their fellows. Either would result in certain insurrection. We must hope that those who have taken over the City have met with some sort of resistance and that our window to plan a counteroffensive is not permanently shut.

C hloe jolted awake at the knock on the door to her quarters. She peeled her face off her laptop, which had gone to sleep, and stumbled to the door. She slid it open a crack and peered through at Brianna.

"Bad time?" said Brianna.

Chloe cleared her throat. "No, I just woke up. Why?"

"You have a keyboard imprint on your face," said Brianna.

Chloe rubbed at her cheek. "That's not why you're here."

"No, but I'm glad I came now," said Brianna. "What were you working on?"

"I was trying to increase the efficiency of the water purifiers, maybe enough that they can be run on one little solar panel."

Brianna's face lit up. "Did you succeed?"

"I don't remember, probably not," said Chloe. "Want to come find out with me?" She stepped aside so that Brianna could pass into the cramped space. Cramped or cozy, depending on the day.

Chloe woke up the laptop and frowned at the code she'd been building. It looked pretty solid, despite how distracted she'd been and how tired, evidently.

"What's the verdict?" said Brianna.

"Not done but could be soon," said Chloe, already formulating the next steps in her head.

"That's great, but not why I'm here," said Brianna.

"Of course," said Chloe. Brianna had woken her up for something.

"I know you're not a trained resident, and you don't understand the hierarchy here. You're bound to make some mistakes. The town-runner and I both get that," said Brianna.

Chloe's heart sank. This was an official visit from the deputy town-runner, telling her off for her behaviour.

"Richard really likes you, so he's willing to put up with a lot," Brianna continued. "But I need to warn you, Chloe, you have to step into line. Richard and I and even Dorothy might put up with you stomping all over the chain of command and our conventions, but you've already begun to make enemies among the other residents. You absolutely cannot contradict the townrunner in public. I hear what people are saying behind your back."

"I don't give much of a crap what people are saying behind my back," said Chloe. "If Richard doesn't like it, he should say something."

"This *is* him saying something, Chloe. This is how the towns operate."

"He told you to say this to me?"

"No, he doesn't have to—"

"Great, then, sounds like he actually doesn't care. It's no one else's business but his and mine," said Chloe.

Brianna huffed and chewed her lip. "You really don't care if people hate you?"

"Why should I?"

"You might need their help, or at least their cooperation, one day," said Brianna.

"I doubt it," said Chloe. "I've been getting along fine on my own for a long time. Besides, when it comes down to it, I don't need people to help because they like me or whatever."

"If you think so," said Brianna.

"If people undermine me out of spite, I don't need their help, anyway."

"I hope you're right," said Brianna. "I tried my best. You can't say I didn't warn you."

"Fair enough," said Chloe. The tension slowly ebbed from her body. Back in school, she'd pandered to everyone, trying to follow their social conventions and make people like her, and it had blown up in her face. She wasn't wasting her energy on that again.

"I'll see you at the meeting later?" said Brianna.

"Another residents' meeting?" said Chloe.

"No, Richard's going to outline the plan for everyone," said Brianna. "I gotta go."

"Of course, go ahead," said Chloe.

The plan. The residents' meeting last night after the disaster with Aaron had seemed like . . . just as much of a disaster. Half the residents wanted to run and the other half wanted to give in to Aaron, try to work with him. If one thing was certain, it was that working with Aaron was not an option. Xander needed to know that too. She headed straight to his quarters and knocked on his door before she could think too hard about it.

When Xander slid it open, he was perfectly put together, jacket and tie included.

"Would you like to come in?" he said. "I have"—he checked his watch—"five minutes until the meeting."

"Okay," said Chloe, stepped inside, and shut the door. "What's your plan against Aaron?" she said. "We can't let him get the City. He could use it to take over the towns here, yes, but he could take it to another region and control the towns there—"

"Chloe," said Richard. "The time to debate the merits of various approaches was yesterday at the residents' meeting, at which, I will remind you, you did not voice your opinion."

"Yes, but—"

"Brianna and I spent the better part of the night developing the plan that I will be outlining in . . . two minutes for everyone. The time for discussing it is over."

"Yes, *sir*," said Chloe, injecting every ounce of derision she could muster into the honorific.

"There now, that wasn't so hard," said Xander and tamped down his smile. "Would you accompany me to the lounge?"

Chloe sighed. She would gain nothing by throwing a tantrum and refusing to go.

"Fine," she said.

Richard waved her through the door and then followed her out.

***

Chloe and Richard arrived at the lounge together and every head in the room turned to them. Chloe froze, and Richard left her there and strode to the low platform at the front.

Chloe glanced around at the other residents covertly. Yes, a few of them were watching her none too kindly. They all looked away just before her gaze fell on them. It wasn't important. As soon as she found her family, she'd be out of here, back to living with them . . . wherever they were living now. Even if that meant living in Aaron's compound? They'd figure it out. This was a town. She wasn't staying here long term. Brianna and Richard had just reminded her of the reasons she and Vishesh had agreed they would never be town residents, reasons that still held true, even after a few years. She hadn't changed and neither had the towns.

Richard surveyed the residents, and they immediately quieted.

"Good morning, everyone. Thank you for attending this follow-up meeting. The deputy townrunner and I have gone over all of your input very carefully. As you know, there will be no discussion of the points I will lay out here today. The course of action I will outline momentarily has been decided upon. Please reserve your comments for the operation's post-mortem.

"The operation will consist of two distinct factions. The first will remain here in Town Kappa and coordinate with the settlements to provide what aid they can. The second will make their way to the City and wrest control from those who have forcibly taken it. I believe that most of you already have a preference as to which faction you wish to be a part of. Please inform Deputy Brianna of your preference, as she will be putting the personnel lists together for each part of the operation. As always, I cannot guarantee that your preference will be fulfilled, but we will do our utmost to ensure that the majority of residents are participating in the operation of their choice.

"Once control of the City has been reestablished, the situation will be triaged and a new interim ECM will be selected if necessary. Once again, I appreciate you all taking the time to attend the residents' meeting and share your thoughts with us, they were invaluable to the planning process. The post-mortem will be opened following the conclusion of the operation, as usual."

Richard didn't wait for the hubbub to start up again; he simply strode from the lounge, off down the hallway, and out of sight.

Attack the City head-on? How did Richard and Brianna get *that* from the meeting yesterday? Not that she was complaining. Getting the City back from Aaron was exactly what she wanted.

"Hey, new girl," someone called. The driver whose name she had never learned.

"Name's Chloe," she said.

"Whatever. I hope you're proud of yourself," he said, not even bothering to offer his name.

"Why would I be?"

"Got your way, didn't you?" he said.

"I didn't even speak at the meeting," said Chloe.

Other residents had stopped talking to listen to their conversation.

"That's exactly my point. Don't need to bother going through the proper channels when you can just make a deal with the townrunner behind closed doors."

Chloe glanced at Brianna, who was watching her intently. If Brianna cut in now, it would only make things worse. The driver kept on.

"If you hadn't messed around with your dark mode in the first place, gone to the City and got mixed up in their business, we wouldn't be in this mess."

Turns out even saying nothing was making things worse, so why restrain herself?

"I didn't *cause* Aaron's attacks," said Chloe.

"You sure seem to know *Aaron* well though, just saying," said the driver.

"I met him while I was looking for help for my farm—"

"And he offered help in exchange for undermining the whole region, did he?"

"That's enough." Brianna's voice was a whipcrack in the silence. Her stare drove Chloe back into the hallway and out of the lounge.

Chloe considered going after Xander, but if she followed him now, every single town resident would see her trailing after him like a lovesick puppy. *Lovesick?* Where had that analogy come from? No way. Not possible. But the clench in Chloe's gut said otherwise.

* * *

Without the skylight in his "quarters," Vishesh would have completely lost track of the hours he'd spent locked here. It was still daytime. He could tell because he could follow the tracks of the raindrops on the glass. The City would catch the rain, decontaminate it, and store it. Vishesh didn't even blink when the door opened. Aaron belatedly knocked on the door frame. The rain was getting heavier. The tracks wove together in a beautiful lacy pattern. Monty followed Aaron into Vishesh's room. He had to pull his arms into his body to keep his elbows from cracking the walls. Aaron was practically pressed against the far one. Monty slid the door shut behind them. Didn't they realize there was no need to put so much effort into convincing him anymore? He'd done what they wanted. He'd fixed the problem with the hover capacity. What else could they possibly need? The City itself was crawling slowly down Sussex Drive to King Edward Avenue and the only bridge large enough to handle the massive City. They already had everything they wanted. He would greatly appreciate being left alone to stew in his guilt.

"It seems you thought we wouldn't notice what you did," said Aaron.

Vishesh huffed. Yes, the rain was definitely getting heavier.

"How you could have thought we were stupid enough to miss it is beyond me," said Monty.

"You will be required to reverse it," said Aaron.

How long had it been since someone had evaluated the rainwater decontamination apparatus? Even tested the water supply for the City? He wouldn't put it past the ECM to let that fall by the wayside.

"Is it really necessary to waste our time?" said Aaron. "We all know that you will comply. Why not do it sooner rather than later?"

"If you need further motivation, we can arrange that," said Monty.

Vishesh blinked slowly and heaved a breath. He levered himself to sit on the edge of the bunk and stared at the floor.

"It didn't work anyway," he said.

"Why the fuck would we trust you on that?" said Monty.

"Whether it worked or not, you will be required to remove it," said Aaron.

"Why not get one of your many other minions to do it?" said Vishesh.

"Because you're the one who knows how, traitor," said Monty.

Vishesh slowly tilted his head back and looked out the skylight again. It would be nice to feel the rain on his face, even contaminated rain at this point. So many locked rooms and cars.

Aaron and Monty had a quick conversation, but Vishesh wasn't paying attention to their words. Unless they demanded something of him, it didn't concern him. The door slid open, and Monty stalked out. Aaron sat down beside Vishesh on his bunk.

"Is this about Chloe?" he said.

Chloe. He hadn't thought about Chloe in so long. Interesting. The surge of butterflies that would have filled his stomach at the mention of her name even just a week ago didn't come. He wouldn't put it past her to come up with some way to keep her town free.

"I'll give you my word that if we find her, she won't be harmed," said Aaron.

Meaning that as things stood, she would be harmed. Vishesh had to fight to keep his eyes open. He just wanted to curl up and go to sleep. Or what passed for sleep right now. Why did Aaron have to bother him all the time?

"Whether it works or not," said Aaron, "we need you to remove it."

Vishesh cleared his throat and worked his dry tongue loose. "How do you know I won't fix the switch instead of removing it?"

Aaron grasped his shoulder firmly. "I know it hasn't been easy for you, these past few days. I think, in time, you'll become accustomed to your position in the settlement. It's totally up to you how quickly you regain your privileges, you know. Monty might call you a traitor, but

I know that your heart was in the right place when you sent out that warning, and you're smart enough to see what we're doing, the bigger picture." Aaron let out a beleaguered sigh. "I can't make you do this the easy way, Vishesh. But I'd really like it if we could be on good terms again."

Again? Was he talking about when they'd first met and Vishesh was sure that he was a lying scumbag? Or was he talking about when Vishesh teamed up with other folks who hated his guts to undermine his masterplan? It didn't actually matter.

"But you make a good point. It would be prudent to get the City to its final destination before letting you mess with things again," said Aaron. "I'll be back when we've arrived, so be ready." He left.

Vishesh lay down on the bunk again and closed his eyes. The rumble beneath him morphed into the hover just coming to life. He was standing, once again, on the bridge and watching the folks in the tent city, some frozen in place, some popping out of their shelters, as they realized what was going on. Like an anthill sprayed with water, they poured from under the tarps. Vishesh smacked the kill switch he'd surreptitiously added to a gap where someone had ripped the GPS receiver out, but nothing happened. The City kept crawling forward, crushing and tearing at their homes, at anyone who couldn't move fast enough to stay ahead of it, grinding them into the dirt.

Chapter Eighteen

Log: Town Kappa, Richard A. Phillips, Townrunner, 24 May 20—

It appears the other towns have all been summoned by the City as well. The City's final destination remains unclear. I cannot and will not sit idly by as they are marshalled to Aaron's will. I take full responsibility for the operation I am about to undertake and let the record show that both my deputy and Chloe are blameless.

That last seems to be necessary since some Town Kappa residents are convinced that this operation was concocted by Chloe and not myself and Brianna. As much as I admire Chloe, she is neither townrunner nor deputy and thus has no influence over the operational decisions of Town Kappa.

C hloe would have turned around and left the bridge again, but the driver had already seen her. They were alone. He sat with his arms crossed over his chest, despite the fact that the town was driving, albeit slowly, down the highway they'd called the Queensway, into the old city.

"How are you doing that?" said Chloe. Making nice with the town residents could start with this guy.

"I'm not."

"Who is?"

"Your pal, Aaron."

"He's not my pal," said Chloe.

"Could've fooled me. Bet you're excited to see him crush us like bugs when his plan goes to hell."

Damn this jerk. *Don't rise to the bait. Fix this, for Xander and Brianna.* She crossed to her laptop and hunched over the little desk space.

"Why not switch on dark mode?" she said, conversationally. It's not as if he was busy.

"The townrunner ordered me not to. Unlike some people, I don't question my orders. I heard about you going behind the townrunner's back and answering that distress call. Wanted to get to the City pretty bad, eh? Couldn't go through the proper channels? Just like this plan of yours."

"It's not my plan," said Chloe, scowling. "Richard and Brianna—"

"We all saw you with the townrunner. I never liked Isabelle—ask anyone, but at least she never plotted around against her comrades."

Except about the Seed-verts. But saying that to this guy wouldn't help anything.

"Nothing to say for yourself?" he continued.

"Seems like you've already made up your mind . . . What can I say that would make you change it?"

The jerk *laughed* at her. "Nothing."

"See? Why waste my breath?" Chloe opened up her laptop and waited for it to boot. "I don't even care about myself that much," said Chloe. "Hate me if you want, but Richard and Brianna are doing their best for all of you. Don't take it out on them."

"See, that right there? Proves you have no idea how this works. There's a word for refusing to follow orders from your superiors. It's called mutiny, and it would take a lot more than an annoying dirt-folk to turn me mutineer."

"Reassuring," said Chloe. She opened up the water purification efficiency project she'd been working on. Except it wasn't there. Chloe scrolled through her file tree and scanned for it. Had she accidentally moved it?

"Lose something?" said the driver. He wasn't doing a very good job pretending to be concerned.

"You deleted my program?" said Chloe. Why would he do that? What purpose could it possibly serve? "That code was designed to help the settlements."

"Altruistic, was it?"

"Um, yes, actually, it was," said Chloe.

"I'd be a bit careful who you accuse of what. Isn't it possible you moved it and it got lost?"

Chloe fought down the urge to scream in this guy's face. She'd been working on that project for days, but it could be rebuilt. No, it was this guy's smug smile, trying to make her think his sabotage was her own fault, that was doing her in.

Richard's light tread and Brianna's stomp sounded on the steps, and Richard strode onto the bridge, followed closely by Brianna. Did they have some kind of townrunner sixth sense when residents were fighting?

"Any news from the City?" said Richard.

"No, sir," said the driver.

Richard's gaze flicked between them and landed on Chloe. "What are you working on?" he said.

"I'm getting started on increasing the efficiency of the on-board water purifiers," said Chloe.

"Getting started?" said Brianna. "I thought you were almost finished with that." She looked over Chloe's shoulder at her blank screen. "Where's your program?"

· Chloe sighed and tried not to glance at the driver, but she must have failed. Richard's townrunner mask settled over his face, his neutral expression and rigid bearing effectively hiding everything.

"Deputy Brianna, you saw this program?" he said.

"Yes, sir. This morning," said Brianna.

"And Chloe, where has your laptop been since then?"

"I brought it to the bridge to work just after the meeting this morning, and I left it here while I went to lunch," said Chloe.

"You were here the whole time and saw nothing?" said Richard to the driver.

"I stepped out," said the driver.

Chloe opened the change log for her program. Maybe she could get an accurate timestamp for the deletion.

"We don't know that it was on purpose," said Brianna. "Maybe it was just a glitch."

"It was on purpose," said Chloe.

In the change log, right before the entirety of her work was summarily deleted, it had been replaced with a message.

Go back to your dirt patch.

***

Chloe half wished she'd kept the deleted program to herself. The inquiry meeting had dragged on long past the end of her patience. A formal investigation was now in process, though with the operation to take back the City looming, there wouldn't be any work done on it today.

"Inform me of any developments," said Richard. "I will be in my quarters."

Chloe had the urge to follow him again, but she hung back as he passed. Xander paused and took in her hesitation without her saying a word.

"You have something to discuss with me?" said Xander.

"Yes," said Chloe and glanced at Brianna, who was pretending not to listen in on their conversation. "Privately?"

"My quarters will suffice," said Xander and motioned her to follow.

"You're not worried about the other residents?" said Chloe.

Xander shot her a quizzical look, shrugged, and beckoned her off the bridge. Chloe followed him up the steps to his quarters and slid the door shut behind them.

"Please, begin," said Xander. He took off his suit jacket and hung it up, then rolled up his sleeves. "I'm listening."

"Right, okay," said Chloe. "Brianna said the town residents don't like me."

"That seems to be the case, yes," said Xander. He leaned over the sink in the corner and turned the water on. "I'm still listening."

"And apparently, now they hate me enough to sabotage my work. So why start this investigation? Why invite me to your quarters? Don't you think that'll make it worse?"

Xander splashed water on his face and then buried it in a towel. He hung the towel back up. "Perhaps," he said. He crossed to one of the chairs near where Chloe was standing and dropped into it. "You're worried their sabotage will escalate?"

"Not exactly," said Chloe and deflated into the other chair. "Wouldn't it be better for you not to associate with me?"

"You think that, in order to maintain their goodwill, I should forgo an asset such as your knowledge to avoid associating with you," said Xander.

"Isn't that what you do? Calculate what's best for yourself and your people before you take action?" said Chloe and her face flushed. "That came out wrong."

Xander chuckled. "I don't think it came out wrong. You are exactly right. It is what I do. It does not, however, include acquiescing to public opinion at every turn. Granted, I take it into account when I make my decisions, but I value your insight as an outsider and your familiarity with the software running the City and towns."

"Brianna mentioned that I shouldn't talk to you anymore," said Chloe.

"Approaching me with a request to influence an operation is one thing, my inviting you back to my quarters is something else," said Xander. He cleared his throat. "Inviting you here for a *meeting*." Was he blushing? She must be imagining it. "Was that all you wanted to address? I'd like to get a bit of sleep before the confrontation with the City."

"You haven't slept?" said Chloe.

"Brianna and I were up most of the night reviewing the material from the residents' meeting yesterday," said Xander.

Chloe sprang from her chair. "Sorry, this really wasn't important enough to keep you up for."

"That won't be necessary, Chloe," said Xander. He stood as well. "I agreed to this impromptu conversation. You didn't press it on me."

"Somehow, I keep accidentally disturbing your sleep," said Chloe and turned to the door. "You need a Do Not Disturb sign for your door."

Xander laughed as he followed her to the door. "Would you pay any attention if I had one?" said Xander.

Chloe laughed as well. "Probably not, if I had something important to talk to you about. One time walking in on you with someone would cure me, though."

"You walked in on me with Brianna just yesterday," said Xander.

Chloe paused with her hand on the door handle and raised her eyebrows at Xander. "*With* someone," she said. He was definitely blushing this time.

"Alas, I shall have to endure your surprise visits for the foreseeable future, in that case. There's no one else that I would be *with* to walk in on."

No one *else*? Xander must have noticed the smile Chloe was trying to hide.

"Once we have a minute to catch our breath, maybe you and I can discuss the need for a Do Not Disturb sign at greater length," said Xander.

Chloe covered her smile with her hand. "It's a deal," she said.

"One would think you would be less inclined to make impulsive deals with me," said Xander. "I'll hold you to it."

"I hope you do," said Chloe and slid the door open. "Sweet dreams."

"Thank you," said Xander. He glanced up and down the hallway, then caught her hand and brought her knuckles to his lips. She must have looked as shocked as she felt, because he chuckled as he let her hand go, then slid the door shut.

Chloe went back to her own quarters, but she didn't plan to nap.

***

Vishesh scrambled up when the door to his quarters-turned-cell slid open.

"Come on," said the uniformed City resident.

This wasn't one of Aaron's people, but maybe all the City residents were his now.

"Come where?" he said.

"ECM's orders."

ECM. He'd heard that one before, in the early days of armageddon. Emergency City Manager, the person elected to manage the region's City and by extension the towns. Aaron had mentioned the Phillips family, Richard's parents. But weren't they supposed to be monsters? *Aaron* had said they were monsters. Vishesh followed the City resident out of his cell.

The resident led him down to a grubby hallway on the lowest level and into a surprisingly cozy, if windowless, lounge. A grey-haired woman stood when he came in, and the rest of the folks sitting with her filed out.

"Welcome, Vishesh. I'm glad you could join me," she said. She nodded to the resident who had escorted him here, and they stepped out and slid the door shut.

"And you are?" said Vishesh.

The woman smiled. "I used to be the ECM."

"The ECM? Aaron didn't lock you up?"

The woman laughed, dropping a decade off her face. "He tried." She took a step toward Vishesh, and he flinched away. "Where are my manners? I'm Isabelle." She stuck out her hand. A handshake. He'd startled from a handshake.

"You already know I'm Vishesh," he said. Shaking her hand felt strange, like a relic from another time, which it was for him. Maybe, with the life she led, it was normal for Isabelle to meet new people.

"Vishesh," Isabelle repeated thoughtfully.

"Never heard it before?" he said, trying to keep the biting tone out of his voice.

"On the contrary, I believe I heard it quite recently," said Isabelle. She rested a manicured finger on her cheek, pondering. "A programmer came to the City not too long ago to help us out. Chloe, I think her name was? She was from a town, and the townrunner demanded her return. Otherwise, she might have stayed." Isabelle shrugged. "I guess we'll never know."

"Chloe was here?" said Vishesh.

"Yes, she rescued us the first time Aaron tried to hijack the City. Ripped a piece right out of the dashboard," said Isabelle fondly.

"That sounds like Chloe," said Vishesh, and relief flooded his body. She'd been okay a few days ago. Sounded like Richard had taken her back again. She was still under his power. Maybe she was the one who needed rescuing?

"If only she was here now, I know she could find a way to beat Aaron for good," said Isabelle. "Any allies at all would be nice right about now. Is there anyone at the settlement who could help us?"

The hair at the back of Vishesh's neck prickled. "Even if there was, we have no way of contacting them," he said.

"I have my own communication methods. If I could get a message out, who would I send it to?" said Isabelle.

She was definitely pushing this for a reason. She wanted him to give up names. She was working with Aaron. That was the only explanation. She must have seen the suspicion on his face.

"You have absolutely no reason to trust me. I know that," said Isabelle. "I could be working for Aaron, for all you know, right?"

Vishesh nodded and crossed his arms. If she was expecting him to give up any information now, she would be sorely disappointed.

"Look at it this way," Isabelle continued. "What have you got to lose? You're under lock and key every minute, separated from your family. No resources, no allies. Wouldn't it be nice to have me in your corner?"

Vishesh just narrowed his eyes.

"I see that you're not going to share with me, and that's totally okay," said Isabelle. "But maybe we can find a way to get Chloe here, just us. The towns are already on their way to our location. Getting individuals off any given town won't be easy, but if we work together, we might be able to pull it off."

"Is that it?" said Vishesh. "If you don't have anything else to say to get me to trust you, you might as well take me back to my cell."

"Now that's a trifle dramatic, don't you think? I heard about that business with the big red button, and I just *had* to talk to you. I see that I'm not going to convince you with bribery. Let me be frank. I also have very few allies at this point. Yes, I want to get my City back. That's no secret, but I'd like to avoid ruffling too many feathers when I do it. What can I do to help you with your plan?"

"Plan?"

"The button, of course," said Isabelle.

Vishesh shook his head. "The button didn't work. I don't know why."

Isabelle's expression soured. "Perhaps you can still be useful to me."

The back of Vishesh's neck prickled. There was the real Isabelle. She stalked to the door and slid it open. The uniformed resident came back inside, but this time they grabbed Vishesh's arm and towed him along behind Isabelle as she marched up the corridor.

"Where are we going?" said Vishesh. He tried unsuccessfully to shake himself free.

Isabelle smiled thinly over her shoulder. "I think Aaron will want to know that you've escaped your cell, don't you?"

Chapter Nineteen

Log: Town Kappa, Richard A. Phillips, Townrunner, 24 May 20—

I have never launched an operation with so much uncertainty and so little planning. As it stands, there is no other option. We must apprehend the City before it reaches Aaron's settlement and ensure that its integrity is maintained in order to safeguard the network of towns necessary to sustain the surrounding settlements.

Aaron's ultimate plan remains obscured, his ultimate goal unclear. I have no doubt it is larger than simply taking the City and the towns to dismantle them and add the constituents, both personnel and technological, to his settlement. This course of action may fulfill that goal, but it seems . . . larger somehow.

Chloe sat on Kappa's bridge, her laptop open in front of her, but she was riveted by the scenery that floated by outside the windshield. She hadn't been downtown since armageddon, and the hulking vacant buildings that loomed over Town Kappa seemed somehow more awe-inspiring than they used to.

"We're almost at the City. I bet the second team could start toward them now," said Brianna.

Despite possibly being an accessory to sabotage, the jerky driver still piloted the town.

"Thank you for your assessment, deputy," said Richard. He had just come onto the bridge and was perfectly put together as usual, no sign that he'd just been napping. "Chloe, any progress on remotely accessing the City?"

"No," said Chloe and shut her mouth. She'd been about to say "No, sir." Brianna and Dorothy were bad influences.

"As expected," said Richard. "Send out the second team."

"Team Two is away," said the driver.

Town Kappa's job was to attract Aaron's attention, and they couldn't do that with dark mode engaged. Still, when Major's Hill Park came into view, Chloe had the urge to switch it on and run. A crater snaked its way down the hill, and dirt, plants, and debris littered the bare earth. What had once been a thriving, if grim, tent city was now a sea of collapsed tarps and tents that flapped in the light breath of wind under the gathering clouds.

A steady trickle of bedraggled folks crossed back and forth to the cathedral across the square and stopped to watch Town Kappa turn toward the Alexandra Bridge.

As they rounded the corner below the National Gallery, their view onto the bridge was unimpeded. No City.

"Town Kappa, Team Two. We have eyes on the City," said Dorothy's voice over the town's speakers. If only Chloe hadn't ripped out the City's GPS receiver, they'd be able to pinpoint its location without visual contact. "They're on the MacDonald-Cartier Bridge."

The City was taking one bridge and sending Town Kappa over another. Chloe rubbed her palms on her jeans. The Alexandra Bridge was too small for the City. That's all.

"Understood," said Richard. "Please call the City."

"Yes, sir," said the driver.

A ding was their only warning before Aaron's face filled the windshield. Chloe jerked back in her chair. Seeing him again, larger than life, had goosebumps crawling over her skin.

"Good evening, Town Kappa," said Aaron.

Richard stepped forward into the frame. "Good evening, Aaron. I would tell you how good it is to see you again, but why bother with pleasantries at this point?"

Aaron laughed. "Especially when I know you're the one who switched the other towns into dark mode. You certainly didn't hesitate to toss the other townrunners to the wolves. *You* were particularly outspoken, Chloe," he said.

"I'm sure you understand that Chloe was speaking in anger," said Richard. "She's been searching for her family ever since we returned to her farm and found it empty. You must understand her distress."

"I do indeed," said Aaron. "Rest assured that I've been taking good care of your family, Chloe. We're actually heading to my settlement right now, as I'm sure you've deduced."

"And when we get there, I can see them?" said Chloe.

"Of course you can! What a question. I thought you were more trusting than that. I guess spending so much time with Phillips over there would erode anyone's trust," said Aaron. "Just one problem. You've already admitted to being a traitor. I'm afraid I can't let you see your family until I'm sure that you're on my side."

"What evidence could possibly satisfy you that Chloe is loyal to you?" said Richard.

"Disable your little *dark mode* mod permanently. In all the towns. I'll wait," said Aaron, all hint of humour gone now.

"I will discuss the details with Chloe, but it should be manageable," said Richard. "Give us, say, thirty minutes to sort out the feasibility."

"Thirty minutes, eh?" said Aaron. His amusement sent a shiver up Chloe's spine. "That's a good timeline. It'll give your team just enough time to sneak in here and take me out."

***

How had Aaron discovered them so quickly? Dorothy must have just barely made it to the City. Unless someone tipped him off? Richard was busy trying to get in touch with Team Two and warn them, but there hadn't been a response.

"I'll ask you once more, Phillips," said Aaron. "Disable your silly dark mode, and then we'll talk. Take ten minutes if you feel it'll help." Aaron's face blinked out.

"He's bluffing," said Brianna. She was so pale when Chloe and Xander turned to look at her that Xander gently guided her to a seat.

"I'm sure Dorothy is fine," said Chloe, but even she could hear the doubt in her own voice.

Town Kappa reached the middle of the bridge and ground to a halt. The Ottawa River rushed by almost a hundred feet below them. If Aaron blocked them in here, there would be nowhere to run.

"So we deactivate dark mode," said Chloe. "It's pretty much out-lived its usefulness anyway."

Richard shook his head slowly. "Aaron is very unlikely to honour his bargain," he said.

"So what do we do?" said Chloe.

"This operation is going to get us all killed," muttered the driver.

Richard couldn't quite hide his flinch behind his stoic mask. What was there to do? Aaron had trapped them.

"Please engage dark mode and remove the town from this bridge at the very least," said Richard.

The windshield flickered, and Aaron's face appeared once more.

"I'm disappointed in you, Phillips," he said. "I thought for sure you would have a better plan than this."

How was Aaron blocking dark mode? If it had been activated, he wouldn't be able to contact them.

Chloe grabbed the driver's arm. "Activate dark mode, dammit!"

"I don't think so," said Aaron. He turned to his left out of frame. "Fire at will."

They barely had time to see the trail of the shell that rocked the bridge. The structure rumbled beneath them, and Chloe staggered toward Brianna. Chloe had barely reached her when another shell rocked the town and almost knocked it onto its side. The legs groaned and squealed, trying to keep it upright.

"City, hold your fire," said the driver. "We'll be taking the traitors into custody."

"Mutiny?" said Aaron. "Excellent choice."

The driver wasn't gloating now. He didn't spare any of them a glance. The doors on either side of the bridge slid open, and a host of town residents poured through one. Dorothy came through the other. She beckoned to Richard and Chloe and grabbed Brianna to help her through into the hallway. Chloe didn't stop to think, just pounded after Dorothy along the length of the town, up into the helicopter bay.

"We better hope their cannons can't hit the chopper," said Brianna.

"Yup," said Dorothy.

"My laptop—" said Chloe.

"No time," said Dorothy.

They scrambled into the helicopter, and Dorothy took off as they strapped themselves in. Brianna handed Chloe a headset and she shoved it over her head.

"Are they really mutinying?" she asked.

"Yes," said Dorothy.

"I thought they were loyal to Richard," said Chloe.

The silence that followed could have meant the others had thought so too, or it could have meant that they had been . . . until she came along and messed everything up.

***

Isabelle led Vishesh into the heart of the City. She banged on a thick door on the top level, and it slowly slid aside. The dark room within was lit only by the glow of several monitors and the resident holding Vishesh jerked him forward.

"I caught the traitor trying to escape," said Isabelle. "He foolishly thought to ask me for help. As you know, I wouldn't dream of working against Aaron."

"Of course not." The voice drifted into the hallway, but the speaker was invisible in the shadows. A familiar voice. "Leave him to me. Your loyalty has been noted."

Isabelle flashed Vishesh a predatory grin, and his captor pushed him into the dark room, right into a wide chest . . .

Vishesh blanched. He hadn't even known Neil was in the City. Though, of course the head of security would be here for this operation. The hand Neil rested on his shoulder was gentle and reassuring as opposed to intimidating. Isabelle and her retinue disappeared down the end of the hallway.

"Let's go," said Neil. He grabbed Vishesh's arm and marched him back out of the security room.

"We're just going to walk away?"

"Drive," said Neil. "The City isn't moving that fast. Should be a piece of cake."

They clattered down the steps into the deserted loading dock, and Neil unlocked the hatchback parked in a corner.

"How will we get the . . ." Vishesh trailed off as the loading ramp groaned and began to descend.

Neil saluted a figure in the control room and motioned Vishesh into the car. Vishesh climbed in, slammed the door, and clutched the handle until his knuckles were pale. Neil backed out of the corner and turned the car toward the partially descended ramp, and the City lurched and rattled into motion.

"Neil . . ." said Vishesh, every muscle in his body tensed.

"I got it," said Neil, and the car shot forward.

Vishesh couldn't even draw breath to scream. The ramp tilted as they crossed onto it, and then they flew off the end of it through the air. For a weightless moment that seemed like an eternity, the wheels left the ground, and then they landed, bounced, and drove along the bridge and onto a normal road as if nothing had happened. Neil glanced in his mirrors.

"Not worth coming after us," he muttered.

"Wait, what are we doing?" said Vishesh. Panic fluttered in his chest. "You can't go back now. What will the others do? You were in the perfect position—"

"They'll figure it out," said Neil. "I couldn't let Aaron keep doing that to you."

"Who says it was up to you? I knew what I was doing!"

"Vishesh," said Neil. He slowed down so he could look Vishesh in the face. "We're going to take Aaron out. Portia and I tried for years from inside and we got nowhere. Time to change up the strategy. We'll get it done. We'll get your family back. I promise."

Vishesh took a deep breath and tried to believe Neil. But they didn't even know where their next meal was coming from. Vishesh tilted his head back and closed his eyes.

"In four hundred metres, turn left," said the GPS, making Vishesh jump.

"Damn thing is trying to get us to go back home," said Neil.

"Where *do* we want to go?" said Vishesh.

"Not entirely sure," said Neil. "Away from the City to start with. Got any friends who could put us up for a while?"

"No, just Chloe, and I think she has her own problems right now. I don't even know where she's gone," he said.

"From Town Kappa?" said Neil. "They escaped."

"Escaped?"

"Aaron tried to . . . It's not important," said Neil and eyed him warily. "Where would Chloe go to hide?"

Where *would* Chloe go to hide? Hiding wasn't really her style. The woman who'd ripped the GPS receiver out of the City to keep Aaron at bay. All it had done was stop Aaron from controlling the City remotely and made him come hijack it in person

"In one hundred metres, turn left," said the GPS.

"The GPS," said Vishesh.

"Yeah, you can turn it off if it's bothering you," said Neil.

"Not that, the receiver Chloe took from the City," said Vishesh. "It's still coded to the City, I'll bet."

"What does that mean? They can find her?" said Neil.

"I guess they could if they knew what they were looking for. More importantly, *we* can find her," said Vishesh.

"We can?" said Neil doubtfully. "We don't have any fancy supplies or anything."

Vishesh patted the dashboard. "This is a City car, right?"

Chapter Twenty

Log: In transit, Richard A. Phillips, Fugitive, 24 May
20—

Town Kappa mutinied. Dorothy evacuated myself,
Brianna, and Chloe in the helicopter, but we have
limited fuel. Currently searching for a safe place to
land and regroup. Supplies are limited, but we can
survive for a short period safely.

C hloe stared out the window of the helicopter at the long shadows stretching across the ground below. They'd have more luck
finding somewhere to land before the sun set.

"Fuel is almost empty," said Dorothy. "Where should I set her
down, sir?"

"As far from the City as possible," said Brianna.

"More specifically," said Dorothy.

"I guess you don't have any allied settlements," said Chloe. "The
one I went to with Brianna, the inhabitants were less than friendly."

"Correct, the settlements are not our allies," said Richard.

"Is anyone?" said Chloe.

"Yes," said Brianna. "Cassandra."

"I would prefer to avoid—" said Richard.

"Assuming they really did get away from Town Lambda in time, she's out there somewhere," said Brianna.

"Assuming she's still alive. Besides, she's less than friendly to my family," said Richard.

"To Isabelle," said Brianna. "But you're not Isabelle, Xander."

Their gazes locked, and Brianna squeezed his arm.

"Dorothy, please take us to Town Lambda," said Richard. "From there, we will search for Cassandra and any other Town Lambda survivors."

"Yes, sir," said Dorothy.

They landed beside the husk of Town Lambda, under its hulking shadow.

"We'll spend the night here in the town," said Richard. "It will offer some protection, at least."

They ferried their supplies from the now-useless helicopter into the town. Dorothy insisted that Brianna stick to the lighter items.

"Joints that feel like jelly," said Brianna. "All part of the magic of pregnancy."

Chloe nodded, even though she had no idea what Brianna was talking about and never wanted to experience that particular magic.

"Do you two want the main cabin?" said Richard when the supplies were all gathered in the loading dock. "There are no appearances to keep up here."

"I won't say no to a bigger bunk," said Brianna. "Grab our stuff." She and Dorothy lugged their packs up the steps and out of sight.

Chloe and Richard hauled the supplies through into the corridor and dumped them in the lounge. The wind whistled eerily through the empty window frames, and Chloe pulled her collar more tightly around her neck.

"I can't believe Dorothy had all this ready," said Chloe.

"She knew the town residents were . . . volatile," said Richard. "I will admit I believed her to be overreacting."

"I'm sorry I went off on the other townrunners," said Chloe.

"That was days ago," said Richard. "What made it come to mind now?"

"I've been thinking about it a lot. Even Aaron brought it up," said Chloe. "If I'd kept my cool, maybe we would have been able to convince them all."

"Chabot was out of line," said Xander and shrugged.

Chloe shook her head. "I thought I was past reacting like that, but apparently it still gets under my skin."

"Still?" said Xander. He slung his pack on his back and picked up Chloe's computer parts—Dorothy had thought of everything—before she could. She didn't have the energy to fight about it.

"Getting an education in a male-dominated field leaves its mark," said Chloe. She swung her own pack up onto her shoulder and headed for the stairs.

"It seems incredible that he called you *miss*," said Xander. "He didn't even seem to be trying to bother you. He may have thought he was being polite, even."

"Well, he wasn't," Chloe snapped before she could stop herself.

"I am aware," said Xander.

Chloe paced down the hallway, past the cabin doors. She poked her head into each in turn, but they were empty, aside from a few knickknacks. She settled on the same one she'd occupied on Town Kappa. Xander ducked into the one next door. Chloe ditched her pack and popped into Xander's quarters to get her computer parts.

"Anything that will set *you* off I should know about?" she said.

"Being compared to my mother," said Xander, his gaze hard on hers.

"Makes sense," said Chloe. She snagged her pack of parts and laid it carefully in the back corner of in her quarters. The sun had dipped below the horizon while they were unpacking and it was almost full dark now. Chloe rubbed her hands on her thighs, not looking forward to lying awake for an hour in the dark. Xander popped his head around the doorframe.

"I suspect sleep will elude me tonight," he said. "Join me for a snack?"

"Sure," said Chloe, genuinely relieved.

Xander used his phone flashlight to light their way as she followed him down to the kitchen.

"How much battery do you have left?" said Chloe and stepped through the doorway after him.

"Enough for now," said Xander. He laid his phone on the counter on its face so the flashlight illuminated most of the room. "Let me find you that snack I promised."

Chloe's stomach fluttered. The first time the two of them had found themselves alone in a town kitchen, Xander had cooked for her. That might have been the first time he let his guard down with her. It was a wonder he'd ever done it again after she'd taken the information she'd learned and gone behind his back to contact the City.

"I think we're even," she said when Xander came back with a couple of wrapped bars.

"Pardon me?" said Xander. He turned and handed her a bar, presumably nonperishable food of some kind.

"You kidnapped me, and I goaded Brianna into going behind your back on that City distress call thing," said Chloe.

"That makes us even?" said Xander.

Chloe hopped onto the counter so her legs dangled and tore into the wrapper of the bar. "Don't you think so?"

"I certainly wouldn't count that way, no," said Xander. "You offered to help a stranger who then betrayed you, but you helped anyway. Then you helped the very people at the City who refused you when you were most in need, despite every obstacle in your way. Each time you have a chance to help, you take it."

"And look how that's turned out for me," said Chloe.

"It's not over yet," said Xander. "It could still turn out fine."

"What about you? You'd do anything for the Town Kappa residents, and they betrayed you without a second thought," said Chloe.

"As you said, I'm not doing it for the people, I'm doing it to consolidate power," said Xander.

"I said that?"

"You quite rightly established that I believe myself to be the arbiter of what's best for everyone else and bend them to my will no matter what they actually want."

"There's no way I said that," said Chloe.

"Perhaps not those exact words," said Xander. A smile softened his voice even though the flashlight was too dim for her to see it. "Unfortunately, I don't know any other way."

"So learn a new way," said Chloe.

"Are you offering to teach me?" said Xander. He stepped closer until she could feel the heat of his body next to her knees in the cold kitchen.

"Maybe if you keep me around long enough," said Chloe.

"It would be my pleasure to keep you around . . ." said Xander, all the playfulness gone from his voice now leaving only sincerity.

What had he been about to say? *Forever?* Butterflies threatened to overwhelm Chloe's stomach.

The crunch of gravel broke the tension building between them, and headlights flashed outside and then up the corridor. Someone had found the town.

***

Chloe poked her head out into the corridor. The hum of an EV cut out, but the headlights still lit the hallway.

"Who could be out there?" Chloe whispered.

Richard didn't answer. The two of them crept toward the loading dock. Shadows played over the hallway as a figure walked in front of the headlights. A car door popped open, and Chloe leaned forward so that she could see around the corner. A tall figure stepped forward, followed by another, only slightly shorter.

"They found us so fast," Chloe whispered. "What do we do?"

The two figures were backlit by the headlights, and their faces were too deep in shadow to make out. They spoke in low voices that still echoed out to where Chloe and Richard watched.

"They must have taken shelter here," said one.

"It doesn't have power," said the other. "They must have a better long-term plan."

"Let's hope they do," said the first one. "We sure don't."

Was that . . . Vishesh? It couldn't be, not here. What were the chances that he would stumble on her so far from Aaron's settlement?

"Hello?" called the figure who sounded like Vishesh.

"Seems like they're all asleep. We don't want to surprise them in the night. Let's just sleep in the car."

Chloe couldn't help herself. "Vishesh?"

"Chloe?"

She sprinted across the floor of the loading dock before she could give it a second thought. She threw her arms around Vishesh and he fiercely returned her hug.

Chloe wiped tears off her face and turned Vishesh so she could see him properly. She cupped his face and ran a thumb across his cheek. The dark circles around his eyes were apparent, even in the strange lighting. He had been through a lot since she'd last seen him, but now was not the time.

"Have you eaten?" she said.

"You have food?"

"Some," said Chloe. "Your friend can come, too." She nodded at the other man who had watched silently as they embraced.

"Neil," said Vishesh.

"Neil," said Chloe. "You're right. We don't have power. Got a flashlight?"

"I do," said Neil. He rummaged in the car, and a light clicked on. He turned the headlights off and handed the flashlight to Chloe.

She led Vishesh up to the kitchen, and Neil trailed them. Richard stalked behind, still silent. Chloe got the two newcomers food and focused on holding in all of her questions. Vishesh clearly didn't need an interrogation right now.

"How were you able to track us?" said Richard.

"The helicopter isn't exactly subtle," said Chloe.

Vishesh shook his head. "You have the City's GPS receiver on you still. The car we took is keyed to the City as its home point."

"Someone else could do the same?" said Richard.

"Yes, if they thought of it," said Vishesh.

"They'll think of it," said Neil. "Maybe not Aaron himself, but he has people. Unless we need the receiver for something else, I recommend we destroy it."

"You'll never get Chloe to destroy a piece of tech," said Vishesh.

"Unless our lives depend on it," said Chloe. "I'm guessing they do, if we're dealing with Aaron."

"No, he won't kill you," said Neil.

"But we still don't want to be found," said Vishesh. He shuddered and leaned closer to Neil.

"I'll get rid of it," said Chloe.

"Is there a plan?" said Neil.

"We can meet in the morning to discuss one," said Richard. "I'm sure you're exhausted."

"Once you're finished eating, choose a cabin—cabins for the night. All the quarters on the other side are empty," said Chloe. "We'll figure it out in the morning." She yawned and handed the flashlight to Vishesh. "It's good to see you again." So much more than good, but there were no words for it.

"You, too. No more disappearing on me," said Vishesh. He squeezed her hand, and guilt bubbled through Chloe. She hadn't been trying very hard to locate them the past few days.

"Don't worry. I can't escape this time. The helicopter is out of fuel," said Chloe, but no one laughed. So much for breaking the tension. "We're in this together this time. I promise."

***

Chloe and Richard retreated upstairs, leaving Vishesh and Neil alone in the kitchen. Vishesh leaned into Neil's body, rested his head against his strong chest, and wrapped his arms tightly around his waist. He and Neil rubbed his back, his other arm wrapped tightly around Vishesh in return.

"We made it," Neil whispered. "You're safe."

Vishesh tried to swallow the lump in his throat. "We're not safe yet. I still can't believe you put yourself on Aaron's hit list for me."

"It was only a matter of time," said Neil. "I could barely stand it, watching Aaron order you around like that. I can't believe it took me so long to get you out."

"But you did," said Vishesh. "And it gave me a chance to add that kill switch that ended up doing nothing. Maybe Chloe can tell me what I did wrong . . ."

"You check with her in the morning," said Neil. "Let's get some sleep."

"You can sleep," said Vishesh before he thought it all the way through.

"You can't?" said Neil.

"Not since . . . fixing the hover," said Vishesh. *And killing a bunch of innocent people.*

Neil's chest rumbled in a growl. "I'm so sorry."

"I made my choice," said Vishesh.

"A choice you should not have had to make, Vishesh," said Neil. "Don't take that on." Neil's hand still rubbed up and down his back, and he found himself relaxing into it. "Would it help if you"—Neil swallowed hard—"slept beside someone?"

Heat rushed through him, right to the tips of his fingers. "It might," he said breathlessly. "What about waiting until I can commit?"

"I'm talking about actual sleep, Vishesh," said Neil, but he was smiling. "I still want to wait until you're free to be all in."

Vishesh shivered and clung to Neil, who gave him one last squeeze and then held him at arms' length.

"We should get you to bed immediately," said Neil.

Vishesh nodded and followed Neil out of the kitchen to the end of the hallway and up a short flight of stairs. The town was similar to the City, but much smaller, more cozy.

"These are all quarters," said Neil as they made their way down the hallway. "Take your pick."

"You know the layout of towns, then?" said Vishesh. He rolled open one of the doors and stepped inside. It was eerily similar to the cabin he'd been assigned in the City, complete with a skylight on top. He took a deep breath.

"I used to be a town resident," said Neil. "I'll tell you about it sometime."

Vishesh hovered in the doorway, trying to fight down the panic that threatened to make him turn and run or collapse on the floor. His fingers tingled. *Panic attack.* His first one in years.

"Hey," said Neil. He didn't try to grab onto Vishesh, which was a good move. He just laid a hand firmly on his arm to ground him. Neil was a nurse, after all. Neil was there. He wasn't going to try to trap him. Vishesh kept taking deep breaths, trying to slow them down. "Good and slow. You've done this before?"

"Yeah," said Vishesh. He turned and leaned his forehead on Neil's shoulder. "I used to get them regularly, a few years ago." He didn't have to say *during armageddon.* They'd all lived through it. Neil would know what he meant.

"Do you want to leave the door open?" said Neil. "Or we could sleep in the lounge downstairs. Push some chairs together. It's more open down there."

"I'll be okay . . . You go in first. You don't mind leaving the door open?" Vishesh stepped aside.

"Not at all," said Neil. He stepped into the cabin and flopped down on the bunk, taking up pretty much the whole thing.

"I can sleep somewhere else . . ." said Vishesh.

Neil rolled onto his side and pressed his back against the wall. "Get over here."

Vishesh lay down next to him and then shyly snuggled in close, his arm still hanging off the side of the bunk. Nonetheless, he was already half-asleep, dreams poking through into his mind.

"Goodnight, Vishesh," said Neil. "I've got you."

***

Connor could see the City from his bedroom window. His heart leaped. That meant everyone would be home. Vishesh, Neil, Aaron, maybe even Chloe. Monty too, probably, but it would be worth it to have everyone else back.

It was already past nine. He'd slept through his alarm again, and Sheila didn't have the energy to get him out of bed anymore, not with the other kids to take care of. If he'd known the City was there, he would have dragged himself up earlier. He tore his eyes from the curved roof of the City he could just make out over the trees.

He pulled on jeans and a hoodie and slouched down the stairs.

"Connor, come have breakfast," Sheila called from the kitchen. A glance confirmed that no one else was there with her except the kids.

"I'm not hungry," mumbled Connor and kept walking. He crammed his feet into a pair of Vishesh's shoes; he'd grown out of his, and no one had bothered to find him new ones. He slammed the front door behind him.

His breath puffed out in a cloud, and he pulled his hood up over his head and crammed his hands in the hoodie's pocket. No one even glanced at him as he ambled toward the river along the well-used paths. Grinding and banging drifted over the ridge, breaking the usual calm atmosphere of the settlement. Connor crested a hill and paused.

Seven towns were parked neatly in the hydro cut, all of them clearly in the process of being ripped apart. He'd seen a town before—of course he had. When he was a kid, maybe ten. He remembered them as huge and awesome, but he would admit, at least to himself, that they were still huge and awesome. Not as huge and awesome as the City, though.

He stared at the ground as he trudged along the ridge past the towns toward the river and the City. Seemed like a lot of the folks working on the towns were in uniform. Town residents. Ripping apart their homes? Neil had told him that Aaron had plans for the City, plans for the towns, but he hadn't gone into it. Maybe he was trying to turn the settlement into one of those old cities with thousands of people. Connor left the cacophony of the town deconstruction behind for the rush of the river. He crossed through the trees, and there it was.

Connor craned his neck up, taking in the shining metal and photocell roof curving away, the rows of long windows staring down at him. If they were planning to rip the City apart, they hadn't started yet. It hovered mostly over the rushing water, with just the nose climbing the riverbank into the parking lot beside the hydro plant. The sharp front legs anchored it in place while the back ones dragged in the river, probably finding purchase in the riverbed. The forward loading dock was open, but no one crossed in or out.

Connor shivered at the reflective windows of the bridge and another row above those; anyone could be watching him from up there.
He hunched his shoulders and kept moving. He nearly pissed himself
when the intercom crackled.

"Hey, kid, what are you doing here?"

"You seen Neil around?" said Connor, glancing around for the
intercom person.

"Nope, Neil is gone," said the intercom again.

Connor spotted a window looking down over the dock, a figure
clearly watching him from above. He waved.

"Go on home, kid," said the intercom.

"What about Vishesh?" said Connor.

"Go home," said the figure, not unkindly.

Connor pushed the lump in his throat down. He didn't care if they
were here or not.

"Whatever," he said. Chloe said she'd be back, and she wasn't.
Vishesh screwed something up, and Neil had to go save him. What did
he care if they ever came back?

"Connor!" Aaron strode towards him, his arms flung wide.

"Hey," said Connor.

"Good to see you again," said Aaron and stuck out his hand for
Connor to shake. "If you're looking for any of your friends, I'm sorry
to say they've been delayed. We'll get them back here for you as soon
as possible. Don't worry."

"Whatever," said Connor. Aaron's assurances should have made
him feel better, but they didn't. Something about them seemed sinis-
ter, as if his family was running, but Aaron was closing in on them.

"Actually," said Aaron, and he pulled back as if something had just
occurred to him. "You might know where they are. Is there anywhere
they might have gone if they thought they were in trouble?"

Connor shrugged.

"We already checked your old settlement and came up empty," said Aaron. "They don't have any supplies, so it's best we track them down as soon as possible." Aaron stared into the middle distance and chewed his lip. Was he worried about them? "If you think of anything, let me know. But for now, you should head home. Take care of your family." Aaron strode away, leaving Connor alone again, just the intercom person still watching him from above.

If what Aaron said was true, and his family were okay for now but they had no supplies, coming back to Aaron's settlement would be best for them.

Don't confuse best for them and best for you. His mother's voice filled his head. He choked on a sob and then glanced around, hoping no one was watching him.

"Hey, Connor." It wasn't the intercom this time, it was Portia. Right behind him. "Let's get you home." Of all the people to see him break down, it had to be Neil's hot friend.

"I don't need an escort," said Connor.

"If I don't come with you, will you actually go home?"

"No," said Connor and shrugged again.

Portia sighed. "Fine, come with me. We won't head to your house." She sauntered down the loading ramp, then turned back when he didn't follow. "You coming or what?"

Whatever. Might as well go with her. It's not like there was anything for him here.

Chapter Twenty-One

Log: Town Lambda, Richard A. Phillips, Fugitive, 25
May 20—

We used all the remaining fuel in the helicopter to re-
locate to the remains of Town Lambda. Dorothy was
able to supply limited essentials, but we don't have
long. Chloe's compatriot and a defector from Aaron's
settlement arrived after dark last night, having tracked
our location using the City's GPS receiver that was
still in Chloe's possession. We have since deactivated
it. There is enough charge on the car they brought
to return to Aaron's settlement, but not enough seats
for all of us to do so simultaneously unless someone is
willing to ride in the trunk. We haven't ruled anything
out yet.

I'll admit that when Chloe and Vishesh were reunited,
their embrace triggered a wave of jealousy I was not
expecting. I understand that they are not and have
never been romantically involved, but I suppose my

feelings for Chloe have strengthened more than I realized. We agreed that we would wait until a more opportune time to discuss any romantic entanglement between us; perhaps today will be the most opportune moment for the foreseeable future.

Now that we have all had some much-needed sleep, the time for rapid consolidation of our ideas has arrived.

Chloe pulled her coat closer around her shoulders as she crept down to the kitchen. The glow of the sunrise had begun lighting the sky, but she couldn't get back to sleep. They'd already wasted enough time sleeping. The silence drew some of the tension from Chloe's body. Days of being aboard hulking machines with their constant motion and noise had eaten away at her more than she'd realized. She padded down the stairs to the lower hallway, and her stomach grumbled.

Vishesh was huddled in a chair he'd dragged over to the outer windows, a blanket from one of the beds wrapped around him.

"You look like shit," said Chloe.

"Thanks," said Vishesh. "You, too."

"Never should have left the farm and all that," said Chloe.

"Told you so," said Vishesh.

"Yup," said Chloe.

Vishesh stared out at the highway and the trees beyond. Chloe rooted through the kitchen for something resembling breakfast and pulled a chair up beside Vishesh's.

"How are the kids?" said Chloe.

"Last I saw them, they were fine," said Vishesh. "Sheila's got it covered."

"Last you saw them?"

Vishesh glanced at her, his face mostly blank but for a tightness around his eyes. She didn't pry any further. She was the one who had put him in whatever position he'd ended up in, so she had no right to force him to talk about it.

"What's the deal with Richard?" said Vishesh.

"He was the townrunner of Town Kappa," said Chloe.

"And he kidnapped you. I know that part," said Vishesh.

"I guess," said Chloe.

"He kidnaps you last week, and this week, it's no big deal? It was a big deal to me. And to Connor," said Vishesh.

"Low blow," said Chloe. But it wasn't really a low blow; she'd just kept herself from thinking of her family in any detail for a few days, kept herself from thinking of the promise she'd made to Connor. She'd told herself she was doing the best she could.

Vishesh sighed. "Maybe," he said, leaned back, and closed his eyes. "You think he made the right call, kidnapping you?"

Chloe quelled the knee-jerk impulse to defend Richard and made herself consider the question. If he hadn't done it, she would have tried to help them remotely. What would have happened when that inevitably failed? Would she have walked away, convinced herself that it wasn't her problem? Would she have gone with him willingly, trusting his promise to take her home when she was done? Either way, Aaron would have found their farm and taken everything from them.

"I don't know if there was a right call," said Chloe, finally.

Vishesh nodded. "Like when Aaron convinced Monty to join his settlement."

"You couldn't have stopped that, though," said Chloe. "Monty will always save his own skin if given the chance."

Vishesh's bright gaze riveted on her. "I had the swing vote. Sheila abstained."

"You couldn't have stayed at the farm," said Chloe. "We all knew that, deep down."

In an alternate timeline, one where Gloria had lived, one where Isabelle hadn't implemented range restrictions, maybe they could have stayed at the farm longer. But with Connor growing up so fast, it had been apparent to all of them that, eventually, they would have to leave their farm, or at least the kids would have to. There had been no real future for them in the tiny bubble of safety they'd carved out for themselves all those years ago.

"Monty's gone completely off the rails," said Vishesh. "He turned me in for a pat on the head."

What was there to say? Of course he'd grasp for power, but couldn't he at least use any power he gained to help their family?

"So priority one is getting the kids away from him, then," said Chloe.

"I don't think he has much interest in them anymore, thankfully," said Vishesh. "But Connor . . . He might get into trouble with no one to watch over him."

Footsteps sounded on the stairs as Vishesh was speaking, and Neil poked his head into the hallway.

"I hope I'm not interrupting?" he said.

Vishesh shook his head, and Neil leaned on the handrail under the windowsill next to them.

"I asked Portia to look out for Connor, if she can," said Neil. "No guarantees that she'll have the leeway to do it. Not to mention that he seems determined to get into trouble." Neil smiled affectionately at the memory of Chloe's little guy, and she tamped down the pang of jealousy that shot through her.

Neil dropped a kiss on the top of Vishesh's head, which made Vishesh glance sheepishly at Chloe. She pretended not to be watching, but she couldn't quite hide a hint of the smile she tried to suppress.

"You know Connor?" said Chloe.

"I was assigned to be his mentor," said Neil. He ducked into the kitchen.

"Aaron thought he would be a good role model," said Vishesh. "In the end, I did too, but not for the same reasons. Neil is a nurse, and he used to run youth first aid classes."

Chloe laughed. "No need to sound so defensive. If even you trust him, I know he's a good person." She sighed. "I'm jealous of anyone who gets to spend time with Connor."

Neil returned with rations and stood next to Vishesh.

Vishesh put a hand on her knee. "We'll get them out, Chloe. We'll find a way."

And just like that, Chloe's eyes were swimming, and she cleared her throat, but she couldn't get a word out. Of course, Xander chose that moment to saunter down from the bridge. He paused when he noticed she was on the verge of tears and positively glared at the other two men. She rolled her eyes and tried to explain, but the words still wouldn't come.

"We were discussing the kids," said Vishesh quietly.

Xander crossed to her in an instant, fell to his knees, and hugged her to his chest so she could cry on his shoulder again. But this time, there were witnesses. Chloe tried to pull herself together. Not easy.

When she finally succeeded, Vishesh was watching her quizzically.

"I know, he kidnapped me, how can I forgive him, yes, I remember," she said when she was finally able to clear the thickness in her throat.

Vishesh shrugged. "Sometimes there's no right call."

***

Chloe trailed Xander and Dorothy up the long driveway. This was an inhabited settlement, or so they'd told her. The driveway was clear enough that cars could have passed recently and they'd be none the wiser. That really meant, if Cassandra had been and gone, they'd have no way of knowing.

"Why are we bothering with this again? You two are obviously townies, no offence. They're never going to tell you anything," said Chloe.

"Word of our presence may reach Cassandra," said Xander.

"Then she'll come to us," said Dorothy.

"Why we need help from some townrunner with no town—"

"When you meet Cassandra, you'll get it," said Dorothy.

The farmhouse squatted behind a two-car garage. Solar panels glinted on the roof, and one dark row in their field had already been planted. Richard marched across the yard, right up to the front door, and rang the doorbell. Chloe and Dorothy remained a more respectful distance away, just at the bottom of the porch steps. Chloe was ready to run, just in case they pulled a shotgun like the settlement she'd visited with Brianna. Chloe shaded her eyes with her hand. Overhead, the blue sky was scattered with clouds, but at the horizon, they gathered grey and ominous.

The front door opened, and a rail-thin woman stared blankly through Xander.

"Good morning," said Richard. "We're looking for a former town-runner of Town Lambda, wrecked not too far from here. Her name is Cassandra. Has she or have any other town residents been by here recently?"

The woman's blank stare didn't waver. Chloe stepped onto the porch. She was going to regret getting involved.

"Have you seen any strangers recently? Before us, I mean," she said.

The woman frowned at her. Was she thinking over the question or trying to decide whether to run them off?

"We heard about Town Lambda," she finally said. No indication of who she meant by *we*.

"Any information you might have would be very much appreciated," said Richard, but she ignored him completely and jerked her chin at Chloe.

"You," she said. "You're not dressed like one of them. Why?"

"Up until a week ago, I lived at a settlement," said Chloe.

"Why'd you join up?"

Chloe couldn't help her glance at Xander. The woman gave him an appraising look.

"You could do worse," she said. "You know anything about solar panels?"

Chloe shrugged. "A little," she said. Vishesh would be the one to ask for something that needed fixing, but Chloe could take a crack at it.

"Come on in," said the woman and led the way into the house.

Should she go into a stranger's house? Dorothy shrugged at her, and Xander motioned her inside. The thin woman led Chloe down to the basement and gestured to a box on the wall.

"We had some flooding. Power went out, and now it won't come back," she said and gestured to the mess of wires leading to the breaker panel. They must have wired the solar panels in themselves after the grid went out. "This here is the control for the solar panels."

The box was flashing something on its tiny screen. Never a good sign.

"Give me a minute or two," said Chloe. "You wouldn't happen to have the instructions handy, would you?"

"Never had them, sorry to say," said the woman.

"That's okay," said Chloe. It almost looked like—yes, the front of the box opened, and error codes were printed inside. Talk about lucky.

Once she'd figured out how to turn it off and on again, everything was set to rights. The woman escorted them back to the front door to show them out. Her eyes darted between them and then to the floor.

"If you have any information about Cassandra's whereabouts—" Richard began, but Chloe cut him off.

"I didn't fix the solar panels in exchange for information," she said. "If you know of any Town Lambda residents, just do us the favour of letting them know we're looking for them. We're camped at Town Lambda for the time being."

"I'll do that," said the woman and gave Chloe a genuine smile.

"But if you'd like to tell us—" Richard tried again.

The woman's face fell, and Chloe grabbed Richard's arm and spun him around.

"Good luck with your panels!" she called over her shoulder. "Just let it be," she hissed at Richard.

"Is it possible we have stumbled on an arena in which you are more tactful than I am?" said Xander with a wry smile.

"Looks like it," said Dorothy.

"You're just too used to having power to swing around. Settlement folks help each other without expecting anything in return."

***

Vishesh and Neil took the car, and Brianna tagged along in the back seat.

"Where do we start looking?" said Brianna.

"You haven't been on a salvaging mission before, have you?" said Vishesh.

"Me, neither," said Neil. "Not something normally done in the towns."

"Aaron never sent you out to scavenge?" said Vishesh.

"He likes to pick off towns, not the bones of the old world," said Neil.

"Is that what we're calling it now?" said Brianna. "The old world? Seems dark."

"It's pretty dark out here, or haven't you noticed, living in a town?" said Neil.

"We're all on the same side now," said Vishesh. "Head for Canadian Tire. We can get everything we need there."

"Just tell me where to go," said Neil.

Vishesh took a chance and punched "Canadian Tire" into the map programmed into the car's GPS. Yup, it still had stores on it, and soon it was telling Neil where to turn to get to the nearest one.

"So you just take things from stores, do you?" said Brianna as they pulled into the parking lot. Neil avoided the bushes sprouting through cracks in the pavement and parked beside an overturned shopping cart.

"Why not?" said Vishesh.

"Ever heard of stealing?" said Brianna.

Vishesh just shrugged and resisted the urge to retort, *Ever heard of surviving?* If she had been stationed on a town since armageddon, she'd never had to worry about getting clean food, water, or supplies.

He led the way across the parking lot to the sidewalk in front of the smashed-in windows. It had been too much to hope that the place hadn't been raided at all, but with any luck, no one else had seen the value in a stationary bike. Any other supplies they stumbled on would be a nice perk, but they had what they needed to survive for the time being.

He gave his eyes a second to adjust as he ducked through a shattered front window. The turnstiles were intact, and the shelves inside reached up into the darkness.

"Flashlight?" said Vishesh to Neil. Hopefully, he'd remembered to put it back in the glove compartment of the car.

"Got it," said Brianna and doubled back for it. She clicked it on and shone it up the aisle. "Anyone remember the aisle number for workout gear?"

"Might as well browse while we're here," said Neil. "Let's look for more flashlights to start with. It'll be faster to split up."

Soon, Vishesh and Neil were outfitted with their very own flashlights, but who knew how much charge the batteries had. Vishesh stumbled into the auto parts section, mostly full of replacement oil filters and spark plugs, nothing they would need since they had no way of gassing up an internal combustion car. He passed the patio furniture section, mostly intact; no one wanted to sit outside since the ozone layer was no more, though the barbeques were all gone along with the implements. It had been easy enough to break open a propane tank cage at any gas station and grab a full tank, at least at first.

The others' footsteps echoed around the big space, the music long-since silenced along with the ventilation system. He passed garbage and recycling bins, pet supplies, garden tools, the paint kiosk, the mostly empty plumbing section, then headed into the back corner where the tiny bikes stood in a row, their training wheels keeping them upright. Just past a rack of hockey sticks sat a couple of treadmills, a rowing machine, and weight bench, collecting dust.

He paused, and footsteps announced Neil approaching as well.

"No bike," said Neil.

"There are regular bikes. Will those work?" said Brianna as she joined them from the same direction Vishesh had come from.

"Maybe," said Vishesh. "But this rowing machine will work much better. There should already be an electromagnet in there. Just need to harness the electricity from running the thing."

"And how will we do that?" said Neil, examining the machine to see how it folded up.

"Same principle as regenerative braking on the car," said Vishesh. "Pull the handle, turn a flywheel inside, and capture that energy as electricity."

"You can make that work?" said Brianna.

"I kept an entire house running on spare parts for five years, so yeah, I think I can get a simple electric generator working," said Vishesh. "I know you town residents don't think much of us dirt-folk, but give me a little credit, please."

"Chloe said you two turned down offers from towns," said Brianna.

"And that's your measure of a person's worth, is it?" said Neil. He bent to take one end of the collapsed rowing machine, and Vishesh grabbed the other. They lifted it, and the edges dug into Vishesh's fingers.

"I get it. You have problems with the towns," said Brianna. She followed in their wake as Vishesh and Neil staggered back to the entrance with the machine. "Anything else we should check for while we're here?"

"A radio or walkie-talkie," said Vishesh. "We'll also need leads and electrical tape."

Brianna scampered back into the aisles as he and Neil wrestled the rowing machine out through the gate in the turnstile and through the shattered window they had used as an entrance.

The wind had picked up, and it was spitting down rain as they lugged the machine across the parking lot. Vishesh had to peer around the thing to make sure he wasn't walking straight into a pothole, though Neil had it worse, walking backwards over the uneven ground.

"You have a problem with Brianna," said Vishesh.

"She has a problem with you," said Neil.

"Most town residents do," said Vishesh. "There's no call to defend me, you know."

"Sorry," said Neil. He propped his end on the bumper and popped the hatchback. "I can't stand how arrogant the town people are."

"That why you left?" said Vishesh.

Neil hefted his end again in one hand and pulled the back open and up. The two of them manoeuvred it into the little car, and Neil slammed the back shut.

"One of the reasons, yeah," said Neil, finally.

Vishesh ran a hand through his quickly dampening hair. "Is it going to be a problem?"

Neil sighed. "I don't know yet," he said.

Vishesh squeezed his shoulder. "You tell me if it is, Neil. We'll talk it through."

Neil's shoulder relaxed a fraction under Vishesh's fingers. "I will," he said.

"Got some!" called Brianna, waving a radio in the air as she emerged into the dull light outside, a coil of wire looped around her shoulder.

"Nice work," Vishesh called back. "Let's get out of the rain."

***

They ended up at the pub. Portia hadn't meant to take Connor there, but the kid was more convincing than she had expected. Empty glasses clinked as the bartender prepared for the afternoon, and a couple of weathered regulars played cards in a corner.

"Can I have a beer?" said Connor and glanced at the bottles lined up behind the bar.

Not one of their contents matched the label at this point. Still, they looked good. Comfortingly normal.

"Not a chance, kid," said Portia. "Get him water, the good stuff." She raised her eyebrows at the bartender. She had promised Neil she'd take care of the kid, and that included making sure he didn't drink contaminated water.

"Anything for you?" said the bartender.

"No, I'm good," said Portia.

Connor huffed and grabbed the water glass off the bar, then Portia led him to the back corner booth where they always held their meetings. It wouldn't be easy getting the word out about upcoming meetings without Neil. Portia slid into Neil's usual seat facing the door, and Connor took the bench across from her. He grabbed a coaster and put his water glass down on top of it. Why the hell had she brought him here?

"Is this where Neil recruited Vishesh?" said Connor.

A thrill of adrenalin shot through Portia's body. Her heart pounded, and she couldn't control the edge to her voice. "What are you talking about?" The bar was not nearly noisy enough for a conversation like this. Any of the folks nursing drinks could overhear their conversation easily. Especially at this volume. To his credit, Connor caught on quick.

"To be on the security team, to go with them to the City," he said.

"Yeah," said Portia. "I guess Neil told you all about it, eh?"

"He said I ask too many questions," said Connor.

"He's right," said Portia. She crossed her arms over her chest and leaned back into the seat. She had to stop this kid from getting into trouble. If she didn't give him something to do, he'd find something on his own, probably something way too dangerous. Trouble was, everything in the rebellion was dangerous, to some extent. He had an advantage because he was young and impressionable, so Aaron was likely to be more lenient with him. But he was young and impressionable, so Aaron was more likely to sway him to his side. That man was too convincing for comfort.

This kid was starving for guidance, and Aaron was an alluring role model. Damn Neil for leaving them like this to chase after his boyfriend. No relationship was worth abandoning your principles for.

"I need to take care of my family," said Connor, gaze fixed on the table in front of him. "I'm all they have left."

Dammit. This kid. Portia huffed.

"Okay, fine, you can run some messages for me," she said. They hadn't used the paper message system in years, since Neil had access to better ways of communicating. Without anyone in security to pass messages along now, they'd have to go old-school and revive the note-hiding tree they'd built before Neil earned Aaron's trust. Fingers crossed that the folks who remembered the codes were still alive.

A slow smile spread over Connor's face before he shut it down into his usual bored teenager look. "Cool," he said.

Yeah, *cool*. Neil would very coolly kick her ass if anything happened to this kid. But Neil wasn't here. Chances were he'd never come back anyway. Why would he? Why would anyone?

Chapter Twenty-Two

Log: Town Lambda, Richard A. Phillips, Fugitive, 25 May 20—

My search for Cassandra and the other former Town Lambda residents has been fruitless. The surrounding inhabited settlements denied all knowledge of Town Lambda, though I am fairly certain they were not as forthcoming as they might have been were I not Richard Phillips, former deputy ECM. To think I once valued my reputation.

Chloe is in the process of building her computer from the backpack full of parts she has been hoarding for who knows how long, and she said she's almost ready to test it; I don't pretend to understand the intricate details of Chloe's work. With any luck, she can use it to access the City's network. Once we activate the kill switch installed by Vishesh, we're off the clock, so to speak; Aaron will be unable to use the City to expand into the surrounding regions.

Vishesh seems to dislike me less than he has in the past, but his companion Neil is much less accepting. I can't deduce whether it is a personal dislike or a general mistrust of town residents that has him up in arms. The more carefully I attempt to tread in his presence, the more hostile he seems to become.

"Okay," said Chloe. "Time to plug this baby in."

For once, she wasn't talking to herself. Their entire crew was crammed onto the bridge of Town Lambda. Xander, Brianna, and Neil pressed their backs against the wall to stay out of the way. Vishesh bustled around the rowing machine and made the last few connections, and Dorothy stood by, ready to row.

It sucked not to have a proper case for her computer, but sometimes you had to make do. In this instance, components covered most of the floor on this side of the bridge, and cables snaked between them, hooking the components together into a functioning machine. Hopefully functioning. Dorothy mounted the rowing machine and hunched over on the seat, ready to spin it up.

"Just one more minute," said Vishesh. He wrapped another layer of electrical tape over a connection and tore it off with a snap. They didn't need to start a fire in here. Chloe ran the cable from the power supply across the bridge to Vishesh, and he stripped it and secured it with more tape.

"I'm ready when you are," said Chloe and picked her way back to the switch on the power supply.

Vishesh straightened and nodded to Dorothy. Chloe waited until she was rowing steadily, the whir of the flywheel in the machine consistent and unfaltering. She switched the power supply on and booted up her creation.

Chloe sat in the driver's seat to check out her handiwork. The monitor displayed the proper diagnostics. Now to connect to the network. It only took her a few minutes more to connect to the City. She reviewed the City's hardware list and found the switch Vishesh had added. Sure enough, it wasn't recognized by their computer. Easy enough to find the proper drivers on the City's server.

"Kill switch should be functional," said Chloe to no one in particular.

"Hit it, so I can stop," panted Dorothy.

"I can't hit it," said Chloe. "It's a physical switch. For the last time, this isn't magic."

"You can't?" said Brianna.

"No, someone has to press the button," said Chloe. Her heart sank. She'd been so focused on getting this janky setup running, she hadn't really thought past accessing the City network and fixing Vishesh's switch.

"Who's going to hit it?" said Brianna.

"We have no way to communicate with the rebels at the settlement," said Neil.

"If you're done, can I stop?" said Dorothy.

"Yes," said Chloe. "I've done all I can with this."

Dorothy sighed and slid the seat forward. The monitor flickered and went dark.

"We'll just have to head back to the settlement and do it ourselves," said Vishesh.

"Without getting caught?" said Brianna.

"Vishesh and I would be recognized, but the rest of you could probably sneak in," said Neil.

"Aaron's met all of us," said Chloe. They'd all been on Iota's bridge except Dorothy. "He only saw Dorothy from a distance."

Brianna and Dorothy locked eyes.

"Go," said Brianna softly.

Dorothy nodded. "I'll go," she said.

"Just like that?" said Chloe.

"Just like that," said Brianna. "That's my wife."

"You'll have to take the car," said Chloe.

"I'll go with her and bring it back," said Brianna.

Vishesh shook his head. "There's not enough battery to make the round trip."

"We don't have any way to charge it," said Chloe. "Unless you want to row for a month straight."

"We require the kill switch to be activated," said Richard. "Dorothy, you have the car. We can negotiate with a nearby settlement for transportation."

"Settlements don't generally have transportation," said Neil.

"Not generally," said Richard, mildly. "I suspect that the Town Lambda cars remain in the vicinity, however. I am confident that we can arrange transportation."

Neil shrugged. "It's on your head if we're stuck here forever."

"The walk would likely take no more than a day, if it comes to that," said Richard.

"Enough joking around," said Brianna. She wrapped her arms around Dorothy. "Go press that damn button. We'll meet you there."

***

Chloe surveyed the computer, still spread out on the floor. Time to start taking it apart. A shame really. The poor thing had lived all of a day. They didn't need it for anything else, though.

"It may be prudent to leave it for now, in case Dorothy encounters problems," said Richard from behind her.

"I can rebuild it," said Chloe. "Probably do better the next time too. Not sure I chose the right processor . . ." She'd had one that drew a little less power, at one point, but she'd rummaged through her stuff and come up empty.

"Chloe," said Xander.

His tone was so soft that Chloe glanced at him over her shoulder. He pushed his glasses higher on his nose and fidgeted with his phone in his pocket. Was Xander nervous?

"What's up?" said Chloe. She stood and put her hands in her pockets, trying to look nonthreatening.

"I'd like to discuss a possible romantic entanglement between us," said Xander.

Chloe couldn't keep in a snort. "Romantic entanglement?" she said. "Have you drawn up the paperwork?"

Xander's brow furrowed. "No, I—"

"I'm kidding," said Chloe. "My point was I think you could stand to relax about the whole thing."

"I'm taking it seriously because it is very important to me," said Xander.

"How important could it be? We've known each other a week," said Chloe, but her heart leaped at his admission.

"Precisely, Chloe. We have only known one another a week, and yet I find myself to be preoccupied with you quite often. With your well-being and . . . other things," said Xander. He glanced at the ground.

Chloe considered herself mildly prudish, but Xander was way more prudish than she was. She couldn't square it with his normal confidence. The second they started talking about physical intimacy, he seemed jumpy and uncertain. Getting to the bottom of his reaction while they had clear heads was essential.

"Should we go somewhere we won't be walked in on to have this conversation?" she said. Yes, there was no mistaking the wariness in his eyes when she made her unintentional innuendo. "I don't mean for intimacy, I mean for privacy. I'm going to need you to tell me about what's holding you back before we go any further."

Xander's shoulders relaxed, but his face looked as though he was being led to the gallows. Whatever he was going to tell her, he was obviously sure it would scare her off. They needed to get this out in the open before imagining what it could be really *did* scare her off.

With no power, the only closed rooms that wouldn't be pitch dark were the quarters, but that was a loaded suggestion.

"Come with me," said Xander and held out his hand. She should have known Xander would know of a better place.

Chloe took his hand, and Xander led her up the steps, past the row of cabin doors, all the way to the end of the hall. It was just a blank metal bulkhead with a small hatch that must lead somewhere right over the loading dock. Xander bent and opened it.

"You sure there's enough room in there?" said Chloe, as she watched his body disappear through the hatch.

"I'm sure," said Xander's voice, muffled by the bulkhead.

Chloe crouched and peered in. It wasn't actually that dark inside, and Xander was totally gone. Chloe took a breath and got on her hands and knees. She crawled into the hatch and left it open behind her. It wasn't a tunnel as she'd expected.

"I suspected they might have missed these window panes," said Xander. He sat with his back to a curving wall. The space wasn't big enough to stand in, but they could sit comfortably. The opposite wall was covered by a long narrow window, and as he'd said, the glass was intact. "The panels are so small, they'd hardly be worth taking, anyway. Gobi reps used to store their goods in here."

Chloe sat against the wall beside him, close enough that their shoulders brushed, and watched the sky through the window. It had clouded over, and even more rain was threatening. It was always rainy in spring, but it seemed like a particularly wet one.

"I'm asexual," said Xander. "Ace."

Chloe kept her mouth shut, trying to filter her immediate response. Xander felt vulnerable about sharing this information with her. Why else would he be more comfortable shutting them in a dim room to share it? She couldn't stay silent for too long, though.

"Okay," she said. "Good to know."

"That does not preclude wanting a relationship with you," said Xander quickly.

"I'm not asexual," said Chloe.

"I understand," said Xander. "There are several options worth exploring, if we do decide to move forward."

Chloe swallowed. Her turn to be vulnerable. "I'm really attracted to you, Xander," she said.

He flashed her a grin. "At least one of the options does involve sexual intimacy between us," he said. "I would very much enjoy giving you pleasure, in whatever way you desire."

"But you?"

"I what?"

"Don't get pleasure from . . . sexual intimacy?"

Xander took a moment to formulate his response. "I don't require a sexual component in my romantic relationships. I can derive pleasure from it, but my pleasure stems from my partner's more than any physical sensation of my own."

"Okay," said Chloe.

"Okay?"

"Okay. Let me make sure I fully absorb what you're saying, and we can talk about it more and come up with some boundaries," said Chloe. "I guess I should tell you that I never want to be pregnant." She'd tacked her admission on to the end of her thought before she could talk herself out of saying it.

"I understand," said Xander. "Anything else I should know up front?"

"I have an IUD that will last a few more years," said Chloe. "In case that ever comes up."

"Noted," said Xander.

Chloe expelled her breath. This was real. They were actually having the talk, trying to figure out if an actual relationship could work between them. The man who kidnapped her. Chloe's nerves spiked. The kidnapping was only part of it. If they were laying it all out on the table, now was the time to talk about this, too.

"No more overriding my wishes," she said.

"How so?" said Xander.

"The kidnapping? You knew I didn't want to come back to Town Kappa with you," said Chloe. She kept on before he could interrupt. "It's not just that. You have a habit of twisting peoples' words to suit your purposes. Don't get me wrong—I like it when you use it for good. But you can't do that in our relationship. I need to know you're acting in good faith."

Xander turned to her and took her hand. "I will not twist your words," he said. "I will do my utmost to act in good faith within our relationship."

"You're doing it already with your *within our relationship* bullshit," said Chloe.

"It's a difficult habit to break," said Xander. "It may take practice."

"That's all I can ask," said Chloe. They watched a dark-grey cloud zoom past the window.

"You like it when I use it for good?" said Xander, holding back a laugh.

"Yeah, when you help me get my way," said Chloe, and she laughed with him.

Xander took her hand, and Chloe squeezed his fingers back.

***

Vishesh and Neil caught Dorothy as she was getting the car ready to go. They hadn't gotten around to unpacking their things, and she'd pulled everything out and piled it neatly on the floor.

"Hey," said Vishesh. "Neil thought you might want more intel on Aaron's settlement."

Neil had his hands jammed in his pockets, and he was staring at the floor. Dorothy straightened and looked over the car at him. She didn't say anything.

"I used to be head of his security team," said Neil. "And I organized some rebel activities."

Dorothy raised her eyebrows.

"You thought I was just going along with Aaron's human rights abuses until Vishesh swept me off my feet?" said Neil.

"Never heard otherwise," said Dorothy.

Neil gave her the rundown on Aaron's security. Hopefully, she could slip in unnoticed, at least until she met someone from the towns who recognized her.

"Ditch the car far from the settlement. They have a bunch, but it would likely be recognized as the one I took," said Neil.

Dorothy nodded. "How do I contact the rebellion?"

"Contact them?" said Neil. "Why?"

"Once I'm done, I'll blend into the settlement. Might as well lend them a hand," said Dorothy.

"Look for Portia. Little white lady, like translucent white. Usually wears red lipstick. She'll be in the back corner of the pub, the good one," said Neil.

"What's the code phrase?" said Dorothy. At Neil's quizzical look, she continued. "How will she know I'm with you?"

"Tell her I sent you," said Neil.

"Why would she believe that?" said Dorothy.

"Tell her Neil and I sent you," said Vishesh. "Tell her thanks for looking out for Connor."

Dorothy nodded again.

Vishesh held up a walkie-talkie. "Take this with you as well. We're using channel three," he said.

"What's the range?" said Dorothy.

"We won't be able to talk from here," said Vishesh. "But we can tell you when we're getting close. We'll keep ours on, but turn yours off if there are other people around. Don't want to risk blowing your cover."

"I'll take care of it," said Dorothy and smiled wryly.

It was Neil's turn to nod. "Stay safe out there," he said.

Dorothy ducked into the car and then popped back up. "Keep an eye on Bri," she said. She was looking at Vishesh, but her glance took in Neil as well.

"We will," said Vishesh. "Not that she needs it."

Dorothy shrugged. "Not right now." She ducked back into the car and slammed the door. The car started with a hum, and she backed out of the loading dock. Vishesh rummaged through their pile of stuff and Dorothy's words finally sunk in.

"She thinks she won't come back?" said Vishesh.

"She might not," said Neil.

"Then why is she going?" said Vishesh. He opened his pack and found clothes and the Seed-verts jumbled together inside. Either Neil had been in a rush, or Connor had packed it.

"Why did you warn this town about Aaron's attack?" said Neil.

He had a point. Sometimes the consequences were worthwhile. Under no circumstances could they let Aaron take the City to a new region and grab all their towns as well. They had to disable it while they could.

***

Trudging through the mud in the rain to hide notes around the settlement wasn't exactly what Connor had thought being a rebel would look like. Neil had refused to tell him much about it, so really, this was his fault. The mud gave under his feet and made every step that much harder. His toes were starting to hurt. The only boots he'd been able to find were Chloe's and his feet were bigger than hers.

Portia hadn't even told him what was in the notes, just where to leave them. He wasn't even supposed to talk to anyone. Boring. Not to mention she'd refused to tell him when the meeting was that he was spreading the news about. She still thought he was too young to go.

Connor trudged the last few dark metres back to their new house. He couldn't even tell whether it was still daytime. On the porch, he threw off his hood and got cold water dripped down the back of his neck for his trouble. He wriggled out of the raincoat. Still too cold to stay on the porch long, even in his hoodie. He pulled up the hood and stepped inside.

Connor hung up his coat and paused. Snatches of a deep voice drifted from the kitchen. If it was Monty, he was going straight up to his room. The kids were chattering in the living room, though, so probably not Monty. Who could it be? He pried off Chloe's boots and slouched casually into the kitchen.

Aaron sat with his back to Connor at the kitchen table, across from Sheila. Her gaze flicked up to Connor in the doorway, and Aaron turned. He broke into a grin, and a warmth spread through Connor's middle in spite of himself. It had been so long since someone was glad just to see him walk into a room.

"Just the man I wanted to see," said Aaron and gestured Connor to a chair.

"Aaron, I said no," said Sheila.

Connor was startled enough to pause.

"Let's let him decide, shall we?" said Aaron, still beaming.

Sheila pushed back from the table, and her chair thumped against the wall. She ducked into the living room.

"It's hard for her to accept that you're growing up," said Aaron, staring after her into the living room.

"Did you find Neil and Vishesh?" said Connor. He didn't leave the doorway.

"Not yet," said Aaron. "I'm sure they'll be back soon. I came here to talk about you, Connor."

Maybe he should just leave. But he *was* more capable than anyone gave him credit for. Anyone except maybe Aaron. If he could make a real difference around here, not a messenger-level difference, he couldn't turn it down. Aaron seemed to take his silence as the go-ahead to keep talking.

"As you yourself mentioned, Neil is not with us for the time being," said Aaron. "I'm having a lot of trouble finding someone to take over for him."

"As head of security?" said Connor.

"Just so," said Aaron. "Only temporarily, you understand. Just until he comes back. And I thought, since you trained with him, shadowed with him, and it's only temporary, it would be good experience for you."

Connor's heart pounded. This was a real job, somewhere he could make a real difference.

"You're not busy these days, are you? Of course, I'll keep looking for a mentor for you if you want to continue with your studies. But then, when Neil comes back, you can keep on with him as well."

"Yeah," he said. "Sounds fine." Portia had been having so much trouble lately because she'd lost her in with security. With him taking on Neil's old role, maybe he could do what Neil had done as well, pass on information or whatever.

"Excellent! I knew you'd be the one for the job," said Aaron. "Would you like me to let Sheila know, or would you prefer to pass on the good news yourself? She should be proud of you."

Connor couldn't tell Sheila why he was taking the job; she'd run straight to Monty who would pass it along to Aaron. Connor would just have to deal with Sheila being disappointed in him or whatever. "I'll tell her."

"Excellent," said Aaron. "I have to run, but I'll see you tomorrow. Meet me at my office bright and early!"

"Yeah," said Connor.

Aaron shook his hand, called his goodbyes to the rest of the family, and strode out the front door. He turned up the collar of his coat and opened an umbrella as he stepped into the dark street.

Connor closed and locked the door behind Aaron. He took a tentative step toward the living room, but Sheila was already coming back into the kitchen. She dropped into the chair she'd vacated and rested her elbows on the table.

"You have something to tell me?" she said.

"Yeah," said Connor. "I told Aaron yes."

Sheila sighed. "Nothing I can say will change your mind, will it?"

Connor shrugged and stuffed his hands in his hoodie pocket.

"Gloria wanted more than anything for you to be a kid as long as possible," said Sheila.

As always, Connor's mom's name stabbed through him, and his throat closed.

"She was determined to give you as carefree a childhood as possible," Sheila continued. "Just know that your home is here for you to fall back on. Not that it's always been the most welcoming. We've lost a lot of folks recently. But I'm still here." Sheila didn't just look older; she looked *old*. Maybe it was the light, but the lines on her face never went away anymore and neither did the dark circles around her eyes.

"Yeah," said Connor. "I'll be in my room." The last thing he needed was Monty to come home and find out about this, or worse, congratulate him on it.

Chapter Twenty-Three

Log: Town Lambda, Richard A. Phillips, Fugitive, 26
May 20—

I was hesitant to send Dorothy into hostile territory
alone, but she will be safest without any of the rest
of us, for numerous reasons. I am confident she can
carry out her mission. We will organize some form of
support for her and back her up as soon as possible.

My attempts to contact Cassandra have at long last
been successful, as I have been told to expect her this
morning. Unless we can bolster our numbers, I see no
utility to approaching Aaron's stronghold.

C hloe took her breakfast rations to the window and breathed in
the crisp dawn breeze. The morning mist was slowly lifting,
but she could already make out three figures by the side of the road.
Was that Neil? Their voices barely reached her from here. She'd have to
join them. Chloe tried not to hurry too obviously as she hustled down
the ramp and across the pitted asphalt. She munched her rations and

waved at the two strangers, who looked none too happy. Neil crossed his arms and waited for her.

"What's up?" said Chloe.

"Nothing. They were just leaving," said Neil.

"Without talking to the rest of us>" said Chloe. She addressed the strangers. "Who are you?"

"Town Lambda residents," said one.

Chloe raised an eyebrow at Neil. The folks they'd been searching for for days, and Neil was trying to send them away in the wee hours?

"We don't need them," said Neil. "There's a settlement we can approach."

Cassandra or a random settlement, what did it matter? So what if they couldn't trust town folks? Didn't seem like anyone beyond their immediate circle could be trusted these days.

"Richard thinks Cassandra will help us," said Chloe.

"She will. We all will," said one of the Lambda residents.

"There's something about Cassandra that Richard isn't telling us," said Neil. "He's biased."

Biased. Just as he was back when he refused to answer the City's distress call, when she and Brianna had gone behind his back. And she'd discovered that Xander was absolutely justified in not trusting Isabelle. His trust in Cassandra was probably absolutely justified as well. Plus, with no power and dwindling food and water supplies, they had to do something, and soon.

"Come with me," she said to the Lambda folks, and strode back toward the wrecked town.

Neil grumbled something unintelligible, but he followed.

Everything came together shockingly fast once Xander had his hands on the coordinates of Cassandra's settlement. Neil glowered, but he didn't argue. Brianna scampered off to pack her things, and

Chloe and Vishesh headed for the bridge to take apart their contraption.

Vishesh seemed unusually quiet as he peeled the electrical tape off her power supply. Chloe wrapped her motherboard in an old shirt. This might be the only time alone the two of them had for a while.

"Something on your mind?" she said.

"I know we need help from this Cassandra person, and we don't have a lot of options. Townrunners just make me skittish, you know?" he said.

"I know. But it can't hurt to hear her out, right?" She put the wrapped motherboard carefully in her pack.

Vishesh nodded. "That's what I told Neil."

"We can always walk away if we don't like her conditions," said Chloe. "At least we'll have a real roof over our heads, eh?"

Vishesh grunted. He didn't seem entirely mollified.

***

Cassandra's settlement was painfully similar to Chloe's old farm. The farmhouse set back from the road down a long driveway, a greenhouse out back, the whole place surrounded by fields and meadows. Folks meandered between the greenhouse and the field; some pushed wheelbarrows; all seemed to be in no hurry. The seven of them trudged up the driveway, laden with their packs of supplies.

Cassandra met them on the porch. She wasn't what Chloe expected. A carbon copy of Isabelle, she was not. The townrunners she'd seen dressed like businesspeople from the before times; not so Cassandra. She wore a town resident uniform and a wide-brimmed hat, rubber boots on her feet.

"Hey, Phillips," Cassandra called, her sharp voice cutting through the quiet morning.

"Cassandra," said Xander with a nod.

"Heard you split with your mom," she said.

"That's correct."

"About time. Did Town Kappa run into the same kinda trouble as my Lambda?"

"Not exactly," said Xander. He shook his head.

"Might be better if we go inside to chat," said Cassandra. She put a hand on Xander's shoulder.

"Hey, Cassandra," said Brianna with a grin and went in for a hug.

"How've you been?" said Cassandra and held her at arms' length to look at her. "Where's Dorothy?"

Brianna's face fell. "On a mission."

"I'm sure Xander will tell me all about it," said Cassandra. "Come on in." She held the front door wide and stepped aside for them to pass her.

Chloe and Xander fell in behind the two of them, and the rest of the gang followed. There had to be a reason Cassandra used Xander's pet name, but it wasn't the time to ask. With a smile, his eyebrows raised, Xander offered his hand to Chloe. She smiled back and put her hand in his. His grip was strong and warm. How long had it been since she'd held hands with someone? Not counting the kids, of course. She swallowed and heaved a sigh, and Xander squeezed her hand. He was so sure it was all going to work out.

"You can sleep in the living room," said Cassandra. "Get yourselves settled, and we'll meet at the table to talk strategy."

Cassandra left them to get their things stowed, which they did in short order. Like Chloe, they all seemed anxious to make the plan

Cassandra had referred to. Neil hung back and Vishesh stayed with him.

"You go ahead," said Vishesh to Chloe.

Xander and Brianna had already settled at the dining room table when Chloe came in, and she quickly sat as well. Cassandra's people hovered in the hallway, and Cassandra got up and closed the door.

"I won't beat around the bush," said Cassandra. "The person you're dealing with has been on my radar for a while now."

"Understandable," said Xander. "He has been causing problems for the City for some time."

"Seems like we both want to bring this guy down," said Cassandra. "Where's your mother land on all this?"

"I haven't spoken with her. As far as I know, she remains on the City. Whether or not she is allied with Aaron remains to be seen," said Xander.

They all seemed to silently absorb the possibility of Aaron and Isabelle working together. Chloe shuddered.

"What's stopping you from taking Aaron down yourself?" said Brianna. "Isabelle can't forbid you from signing a corporate contract now, right?"

"Where do you think all this came from?" said Cassandra, gesturing around to the settlement. "I've got no leverage left after signing my life away to Gobi for this. You do."

"The corporations are not an option," said Xander.

"Suit yourself. If the towns really are all destroyed, we'll need to go crawling to the corporations eventually. Why not now?" said Cassandra.

"We won't need the towns if we distribute the Seed-verts we found," Chloe cut in.

Cassandra laughed. "And who do you think made the Seed-verts?" Cassandra had the same ability as Isabelle to totally throw her off, but in the complete opposite way. "I admire your idealism, but the corporations are the only way forward."

"There's got to be something we can do," said Chloe. "We already have the Seed-verts. All we have to do is grow them. Some of the settlements have already been decontaminated this spring. We can get through a couple more years until there are enough Seed-verts to go around."

"Could be," said Cassandra. "That still leaves the problem of this Aaron character. I'm betting he stole all the Seed-verts with the towns, eh?"

"That he did," said Xander.

"All this is just semantics. Here's my deal, plain and simple. You get corporate backing, me and mine will come with you to get rid of Aaron. Without backup, Lambda is out. I have no interest in being steamrolled by Aaron and his crew. That's all there is to it."

"What if we don't need you?" said Chloe. The way Cassandra pushed them around turned her stomach.

"Seems like you don't have many resources at your disposal. How's about you take some time to consider it," she said.

"Rest assured, we will consider your offer carefully," said Richard.

Cassandra glanced to the doorway behind Chloe, and a grin wrapped her face. "Well, fancy stumbling on you here," she said.

Neil hesitated in the doorway.

***

"Townrunner Cassandra," said Neil.

Vishesh couldn't see around the corner, and Neil was blocking the way.

"Come on in," said Cassandra. "We need to get caught up."

Vishesh gripped Neil's arm and turned him gently.

"Do we need to leave?" he said.

"I'm supposed to be your rock, not the other way around," said Neil.

"We can switch," said Vishesh wryly. They took two breaths together.

"I'm good," said Neil. "Just . . . don't judge me too harshly."

"Of course not," said Vishesh. He followed Neil through the doorway into the dining room.

Cassandra sat at the head of the table. Neil gripped the back of the chair at the foot and faced her squarely.

"Glad to see you alive and well," said Cassandra, and she sounded as if she meant it. Neil had said that he was once a town resident; maybe Cassandra knew him from those days.

"You too, townrunner," said Neil.

"Not really a townrunner anymore," said Cassandra and gestured to the field outside the window.

Neil shrugged.

"Where did you end up when you left us?" said Cassandra. "I'd prefer if you sat. My old neck doesn't crane up like it used to."

Neil took a breath and sat next to Brianna. Vishesh perched on the seat next to him and entwined their fingers under the table.

"Look at you and Xander with your bodyguards," said Cassandra.

Vishesh hadn't even taken in Chloe, who sat across from him, Richard's bastion as he was Neil's.

"If anyone's the bodyguard, it's me," said Neil.

"It wasn't a criticism, just an observation," said Cassandra. "I guess you're the ones who know all about Aaron's operation?"

"We have passing familiarity with it, yes," said Neil.

"You changed your mind, eh? Once you saw what he was up to, the towns didn't seem so bad after all, did we?" said Cassandra.

"Not all settlements are like his," said Neil.

"But you knew the settlement he was building wasn't like the others," said Cassandra, waving his protests away. "I'm glad you came to your senses."

That meant that Neil's town hadn't been hit. He'd made the choice to leave a town and join up with Aaron. Vishesh ripped his hand from Neil's, and Neil flinched and glanced at him warily.

"It took me some time to realize there was no point in staying there, yes," said Neil.

"Too late to come crawling back to the towns," said Cassandra. "You missed your chance there." Her smile was twisted. "Doesn't matter now. We're all in this together."

Vishesh's skin crawled. Neil had joined with Aaron to build his settlement, left a town behind to do it. He hadn't been coerced into joining it when his town was destroyed; Aaron had somehow convinced him to leave a safe town life to build the hellscape Aaron had made. And Neil had sat by and watched him do it. Fighting back how? His paltry little information network? Playing head of security, watching town after town be destroyed and doing nothing.

Vishesh's chair thumped on the wall, and he stumbled to the window. Neil was telling Cassandra about Aaron's settlement, but Vishesh couldn't absorb the words. Before he realized what was happening, Chloe had towed him into the kitchen and closed the door.

"What's up with you?" she said.

"Nothing," said Vishesh.

"Don't bullshit me," said Chloe.

"Neil helped Aaron *build* that place," said Vishesh.

"He didn't know what Aaron was going to do," said Chloe. "At least give him that much credit."

"But he participated. He lied to me," said Vishesh.

Chloe gave him a hard look. "Seems natural that he didn't want to tell you the extent of his involvement. I bet he was afraid you'd react like this." She gestured to him, and he took a look at himself.

His hands were planted on the island countertop and he leaned over it toward Chloe as if he were going to leap over and tackle her. His breathing was ragged, and he made an effort to smooth it out, slow it down.

"I can't believe I trusted him," said Vishesh.

"I really think you're overreacting," said Chloe.

"You're fine with it?" said Vishesh.

"Don't bring me into this. I barely know the guy," said Chloe and held up her hands. "But from what I do know of him, he's not the kind of person to go along with Aaron. Didn't you say he was part of a rebellion of some kind?"

"Yes," said Vishesh. "But they didn't do very much."

"And did we ever do much against Monty?" said Chloe.

Vishesh's thoughts screeched to a halt. No, they hadn't had a choice against Monty. He was integral to their survival. Just like Aaron had been for Neil. He sighed. "You have a point."

"That's what I thought," said Chloe. "Go easy on the guy. Cassandra practically ambushed him."

"That's true," said Vishesh. Neil had been working up to telling him the story of how he stopped being a town resident and joined Aaron's settlement. Between packing and the trip here, they hadn't found time to discuss it. This definitely wasn't the way Neil had wanted him to find out.

"Ready to go back in?" said Chloe.

"You go," said Vishesh.

The door opened, and Neil stood framed in the doorway, his normally calm expression frayed.

"Thank you, Chloe," said Vishesh.

She nodded and hurried toward the door, and Neil stepped aside to let her pass. He shut the door behind her.

"By the time I realized what was going on. The hierarchy was already embedded in the settlement," said Neil. He stared at the floor; his eyes unfocused. "He pretended it couldn't be helped, that we didn't have enough resources, but that he really wanted to save everyone. I—I know now that's just what I wanted to hear. I should have questioned it, questioned him, but I wanted a real home, to go back, I guess, to how things were before. Living in houses, with people." He took a shuddering breath.

"Chloe and I could have joined on as town residents," said Vishesh. "But that kind of life wasn't for us, either." He smiled. "Chloe reminded me that life with Monty wasn't exactly idyllic." Vishesh stepped around the island and took Neil's hands in his.

Neil finally dislodged his gaze from the kitchen tile, and their eyes met.

"We go forward from here," said Vishesh.

Neil's face fell. "Cassandra wants us to work with the corporations, and I . . ." He shook his head.

Vishesh went cold. "And Chloe? Richard?"

"They seem inclined to agree," said Neil. "I won't sit idly by and watch it happen again, Vishesh. I want to take Aaron out, but we'll do it the right way."

"So we propose another way," said Vishesh, but Neil shook his head again.

"I can't stay here and watch them do this," said Neil.

Vishesh's chest tightened. "Where will you go?" he croaked out.

"Back to Town Lambda for now. Coming here was a mistake," said Neil.

Vishesh was being torn in half. If what Neil said was true, Richard and Chloe would not be put off, which meant . . .

"Don't make me choose between you and Chloe," Vishesh whispered.

"It's not about you," said Neil, and the tightness in Vishesh's chest nearly stopped his breath. "I'll stay at Town Lambda tonight. You change your mind and want to come join me, I'll be there. In the morning, I'll head back toward Aaron's."

Back to Aaron's. Alone. Without support, what could they possibly hope to accomplish besides being thrown back in a cell?

Vishesh couldn't tear his gaze from the floor. Neil gently pulled his hands out of Vishesh's. Neil's feet turned and walked across the kitchen, then disappeared out the door, and his footfalls faded away.

***

Connor led the team from behind. He was technically in command, but he wasn't trained in combat as they were, and the other security guys knew what Aaron would do to them if he got hurt. He followed them up the ramp into the City's forward loading dock. They wound their way up to the bridge. Low voices drifted out to them and then quickly cut off.

Someone had entered the settlement and come here, to the bridge. He had to find out who it was and what they hoped to accomplish. By the time Connor stepped through the door, his guys were ranged around the bridge, their target hemmed in against the back of the console. Isabelle, the ECM, whatever that meant. She had been in charge before Aaron took over the City.

"Who were you talking to?" said Connor. As far as he knew, the ECM was allowed to be here. But then again, he didn't know very much. Everyone had been removed from the City, probably to keep something like this from happening. Keep people from sabotaging the thing. He didn't know exactly what Aaron's plans were, but keeping the City in good condition was part of them.

Isabelle glanced at him and raised an eyebrow, then turned to a security officer. "Just reminiscing about my old post," she said.

The security officer glanced at Connor.

"That wasn't my question," said Connor.

"She's stalling, sir. Should we go after her accomplice?" the security officer barked.

Saying *no* would be way too suspicious. "Yes, please do," said Connor.

The officer took a couple of guys, and they clattered down the stairs at a run.

"What was your question again?" said Isabelle. "Oh yes! Who was I talking to? You heard that, did you? How embarrassing for me. I was talking myself into . . ." She reached into a hole in the dashboard and jabbed at something. Two of Connor's men grabbed her arms, but they were too late. With a soft *click*, the City lurched. Connor staggered and landed on his hands and knees on the deck. The huge machine was dead silent.

"Evacuate!" shouted Connor. "Everyone off. Bring her."

Connor stumbled to his feet and reeled across the bridge. They hustled out the way they'd come. Once they were standing in the parking lot, it was clear why the City had moved. The legs had curled up into what was probably supposed to be a default position. *Oh, shit!* Since the City was half in water, the legs weren't touching the riverbed anymore, and the back ones dragged in the water instead, not deep enough to grab the bottom. The front legs on land creaked and scored the ground. *Please hold on!* The water rushing by pulled on the back two-thirds of the City, and the handful of front legs didn't have a chance. *Or maybe please don't hold on?* Connor's head was spinning. One by one, the legs dropped loose from the riverbank, pulling an avalanche of gravel into the water with them. Then, with barely a splash, the City was swept out of sight.

Connor stood, dumbfounded. Just the kind of sabotage Aaron had been trying to prevent. Connor had failed him. Which was probably good for the rebellion, right? Still, the thought of Aaron's pitying look when he found out about this . . .

Connor took stock of his people. Isabelle was in custody, already trying to sweet-talk her guard.

"Where's the accomplice?" said Connor.

"We were unable to apprehend them, sir."

Maybe taking this job had been a bad idea. Either way, he'd been bound to disappoint someone: Aaron since he'd failed; Portia and Neil if he'd succeeded.

Chapter Twenty-Four

Log: Settlement Lambda, Richard A. Phillips, —, 26 May 20—

I hate to admit that I see where my mother was coming from. After all this time. I don't mean to say that I agree with her; however, her integrity is undeniable. Refusing to be beholden to the corporations took gumption on her part, but at what cost? Presumably, many of the settlements we abandoned would have gladly given all they had to one of the corporations if it meant they could stay safely in their homes.

What Cassandra is offering, though, would start something in motion that I'm not altogether sure I can control. In fact, I'm fairly certain it would mean giving up my control entirely. Once again, however, I can't help but wonder what other options there are. If it's Gobi or Aaron . . .

C hloe jiggled her leg and waited for Richard's phone to ring through. Cassandra had hooked it into Gobi's satellite network and assured them that they would be able to make a good deal with these people. Good thing they had Richard on their side, master of making good deals. They still had a chance to back out of this, if the corporation tried to screw them over. *When* they tried to screw them over? She and Richard had been through this. They had no satisfactory options, including this one.

"Hello," said a warm voice over the phone speaker. "Cassandra let me know to expect your call. I'm Henry. Who am I speaking with today?"

"Richard Phillips, lately of Town Kappa," said Richard. "My deputy, Brianna Guigues."

"Hello," said Brianna.

"Chloe Michaels," said Chloe. She didn't offer anything more. She had technically been a town resident, but saying that would be disingenuous.

Vishesh remained silent, arms crossed over his chest. He'd insisted on being here, but he clearly didn't like anything about this idea. Being outvoted didn't sit well with him. Ever since this morning, when Neil had left, he'd been snippy.

"Cassandra's not there? Shoot, I was looking forward to talking to her," said Henry. "I'm sure I'll talk to her another time. How are you all?"

"We're well, thanks," said Richard. "Yourself?"

"I'm good! Very good, thanks for asking. The prospect of helping people out always puts me in a good mood. Now, what can I do for you?"

They'd talked about how to play this. Chloe had wanted to tell them about the towns being hit, appeal to their indignation over having their products destroyed, but Richard had laughed at her, called her naive. *If their towns are destroyed, they can try to sell us new ones.* Chloe had been soured on the whole concept of doing business with these people, but such was their position. *Beggars can't be choosers.*

"We need to take over ownership of a settlement, but we don't have the resources to complete the takeover ourselves," said Richard.

"I see," said Henry. "Sorry if I pause. I'm just taking some notes. And what resources exactly would you need for the takeover?"

"Transport for a large group of people, preferably by air," said Richard. "The means to overpower their security forces, and support while we triage the settlement with the option to extend our arrangement depending on the needs of the residents."

"Someone who knows what they want. I like it," said Henry. "Any idea what you'd expect to pay for that package?"

"We have a variety of skills, but a list of your priorities would speed up the negotiation process," said Richard.

"I'm sure it would," said Henry. "Maybe if I knew more about each of you, I could come up with a ranked list of most desirable skills."

"Of course, if that would help," said Richard. "However, I would be worried about leaving something off that you might find useful."

"Fair enough. Set your list up, and I'll set up mine. We can exchange," said Henry. "I'm sure you understand I would expect a long-term commitment from at least one of you for this kind of high-value support."

"I would expect nothing less from a high-profile corporation such as Gobi," said Richard.

"It's been a pleasure talking to you. I'll expect that list by end of day," said Henry.

"I will expect the same," said Richard. "Speak to you again soon." He tapped the Hang Up button and slumped back in his chair.

"Well, shit," said Brianna.

Chloe glanced between them. That Henry guy had been friendly and nice, and so had Richard. Where did *shit* come from?

"We'll make it work, Brianna," said Richard. "Are you up to putting a draft of that list together?"

"Yes, sir," said Brianna. "Don't worry, Vishesh. I won't mention you."

Vishesh nodded and strode from the lounge.

"I'm missing something," said Chloe.

"Good luck, sir," said Brianna and departed as well.

Xander leaned forward and rested his elbows on his knees. "We knew that the corporation wouldn't help us for nothing."

"I remember how they operate," said Chloe.

"When Henry said long-term commitment, he meant a multiyear indenture," said Xander.

"Is that legal?" said Chloe.

"Who's going to stop him? Even before armageddon, corporations got away with breaking the rules with impunity. I can't imagine anyone is in a better position to put a stop to it now," said Xander. "Besides, what else do we have to bargain with? If we can't enter into a contract, as they suggested, we have no payment options at all. We need their help. If we report their illegal activity, it is we who will suffer, not them. They don't have any other impetus to help us."

"Besides the fact that it's the right thing to do," said Chloe.

"We both know that. Someone like Henry might even know that on a personal level. But he's not being paid to do what's right. He's being paid to do whatever will make the corporation money. And right now, that's ensuring he gets as much work out of us in exchange for as little support as possible."

"And I thought the towns were bad," said Chloe. She dropped her head into her hands. Was beating Aaron really worth teaming up with a corporation?

"Indeed," said Xander. "Government officials like me with our weasel words are nothing compared to greedy corporate types."

"It'll be less funny once we're all working for the corporation for the next five years," said Chloe.

"I'll do my best to make sure that doesn't happen," said Xander. "I need to help Brianna with that list. I'll keep it to skills you are willing to use for them, have no doubt of that."

"So no sex acts, then," said Chloe and managed a wry smile.

Xander didn't smile back. "That's correct."

"This is the worst idea," said Chloe.

"Only hindsight will tell us," said Xander. The kiss he laid on her on his way out the door almost made her stop worrying what they were getting themselves into.

***

Henry was as good as his word. He sent over his list within a few hours. To Chloe's chagrin, there were a few sex acts on there, though she couldn't miss the note in bold at the bottom stating that all services contracted must be up to the professional level. A copy of the eventual contract was also attached for their perusal. Chloe munched on a ration bar while she read it over.

"What's this about public appearances?" she said.

Brianna glanced up from comparing their list with Henry's. "That's standard in these contracts. It means they can use your face in ads and get you to promote the corporation without asking your explicit permission," she said.

Like on that *Oasis Magazine* cover. "Gross," said Chloe. In the event of termination repayment clause, monetary value estimate table, non-disclosure clause . . . It had been a while since Chloe had read over an employment contract; had they always been filled with so many confusing legalese sections? Of course, this wasn't exactly an employment contract. It was an indenture agreement, or so it said on the first page. Chloe tossed it onto the table in front of her and rubbed her eyes.

Vishesh prowled into the room and glanced at it. His face twisted.

"You're not thinking of entering into one of those, are you?" he said.

"We haven't signed anything yet," said Chloe.

"I really hope you don't regret this, Chloe, since I know you have no idea what you're doing," said Vishesh. He sighed. "I understand that you forgive Richard over there and trust him, but even he can't control what a corporation does with a contract like this one."

"That is correct," said Xander. He watched them from across the room. "I have a legal background, and thus I can advise you, but ultimately, you must be comfortable with any agreement that bears your signature."

Chloe shook her head. "Connor needs us. The kids need us. Those people you told us about that Aaron is killing need us. He's not going to stop at just them. If I have to sign away a few years of my life and pander to a corporation for a little while, it's worth it," said Chloe. "I think we all know Aaron's plans are far from over."

"And we won't let him get away with whatever he's doing," said Vishesh. "I just . . . can't accept that this is the way."

"If you have an alternative to present, by all means, now is the time," said Xander.

"I don't," said Vishesh.

Xander nodded, as if the subject was closed, and went back to the lists.

"I won't ask you to sign anything," said Chloe.

"But *you're* going to sign something," said Vishesh.

"I am," said Chloe.

Vishesh's eyes shone with tears. "I can't stay and watch."

"What do you mean?" said Chloe. She was on her feet so fast, spots clouded her vision.

"I'm going after Neil," said Vishesh. "I know there's another way to bring Aaron down that doesn't involve your reckless self-sacrifice. I can't follow you over this cliff."

Chloe tried to swallow the lump in her throat, but she couldn't croak any words out. In the end, she just nodded, gave him a hug, and let Vishesh go.

***

The walk back to Town Lambda was too long and gave Vishesh's dread too much time to spiral out of control.

"At least it's not raining," said Brianna.

When she'd finished up with Richard, only to announce that she was coming with him, he had stood dumbfounded and watched her redistribute their packs so that she had all the pillows and sweaters and he had all the water and shoes. Finally, Dorothy's request that he and Neil watch out for her had swayed him to just accept it and let her come.

Vishesh shielded his eyes when the sun broke through the clouds as it dipped into the horizon. The pink and gold of the sunset threw into sharp relief the emptiness in Vishesh's gut. They'd have to spend the night at Town Lambda, whether Neil was there or not. The thought of spending it in the town without Neil made his fingers tingle and his breath come quicker. He didn't have to sleep in a cabin. He could sleep in the lounge. The feeling dissipated, and Vishesh kept on.

He and Brianna rounded the last corner, and Neil stood beside Town Lambda. He waved when he saw them.

"How did you know we were coming?" Brianna called.

Neil patted the walkie-talkie clipped to his belt.

"Chloe warned me," he said, but he didn't take his eyes from Vishesh.

Neil swept him into his arms before they'd even reached the loading dock. Vishesh sank into the embrace, let the tension flow from his body, and rested his head on Neil's shoulder.

"Let's get inside," said Neil. "It'll be dark soon."

Indeed, the breeze chilled Vishesh's face as they parted and turned toward the town. A light twinkled from one of the window casings, where Neil had hung a lantern. Maybe so Vishesh could find him in the darkness if they arrived late.

Vishesh tried to swallow the lump in his throat. "Thanks for waiting for me," he said.

"I would have waited much longer," said Neil.

Brianna immediately shut herself in a cabin, something about being on the verge of collapse.

Neil showed Vishesh into the larger cabin. He had been the only one there, so there had been no reason not to take it. The larger bunk along with a long row of windows at the top made it feel more open than the little cabins. They snuggled under the blankets in the bunk with a bit of food for dinner, and Vishesh sighed.

"They're really going through with the corporation thing," said Vishesh. "You were right. Gobi is bad news. They've got some indenture agreement thing going on." Vishesh shuddered, and Neil squeezed his knee.

"When Aaron first suggested that we get the corporations to help us be independent of the government—"

A chill crept up Vishesh's spine. "What?"

"I'm sorry. I know you don't want to talk about Aaron," said Neil.

Vishesh shook him off until they just had one arm wrapped around each other. "I don't, but it isn't that. Aaron suggested that you work with Gobi? What made him change his mind?"

"He didn't change his mind," said Neil. "Aaron's been working for the corporations for years."

Vishesh was not going to have a panic attack. He *wasn't*. He took smooth breaths and leaned into Neil again. "Why didn't you tell Chloe and Richard and Brianna that?"

"I thought you all knew that," said Neil. "How else could he have gotten all those resources? He destroys towns and provides corporate contracts with the people he collects in exchange for support and resources."

"Who knows about this?" said Vishesh.

Neil shrugged. "Not many people, I wouldn't think. Most of the ones who knew are dead. Some of the rebels know."

"Why keep it to yourself? Why not tell everyone?" said Vishesh.

"What does it matter? Trapped is trapped."

"Not if you trust Aaron and then find out he's got you bound to a contract you never signed up for," said Vishesh.

"I never thought of it that way," said Neil.

"Is there an agreement for me?" said Vishesh. He tried to swallow down the bile creeping up his throat. "For Connor?"

Neil was silent for too long. So that was a yes.

"I don't think they ever meant for Aaron to take *all* the towns," Neil said. "They had a pretty balanced system going where Aaron would take one every so often, just often enough that the government could afford to replace it."

"So now they want to get Richard and Chloe to take him down since he's causing them problems," said Vishesh. "Chloe is paying to do something that the corporation already wants them to do. We have to warn them."

"We can try," said Neil. "Do you think it'll change anything?"

"Of course I do," said Vishesh. "Do you still have that walkie-talkie?"

Neil handed over the walkie-talkie, and Vishesh drew out the antenna. He switched it to channel three.

"Chloe and Richard, this is Vishesh, over," said Vishesh. He stood the walkie-talkie on the table beside him and waited. The speaker crackled.

"Vishesh, this is Richard. What seems to be the problem? Over."

"I have some information for you, Richard. Is Chloe there? Over."

"She's already asleep. I will be sure to pass the information on to her. Over."

Vishesh's neck prickled, but he ignored it. Chloe trusted Richard, and Vishesh trusted Chloe. "Aaron seems to be working with the corporations, according to Neil," said Vishesh. "As far as we can tell, they are trying to rein him in at the moment. You and Chloe are planning exactly what they want you to do. Over."

The silence stretched so long that Vishesh was about to repeat himself.

"Understood, Vishesh. Thank you for the information. I will be sure to use it to my utmost ability," said Richard. "Over and out."

"Over and out," said Vishesh, but he left the walkie-talkie on. Gobi was somehow masterminding all of this: Aaron, the fight against Aaron . . . He wasn't the real enemy. He sure as hell wasn't in the right, but he was a parasite, exploiting the system for profit, nothing more than that.

"Let's get some sleep," said Neil.

"That's probably best," said Vishesh.

"We can worry in the morning."

"No," said Vishesh. "In the morning, we're going to get something done."

Chapter Twenty-Five

Log: Settlement Lambda, Richard A. Phillips, —, 26 May 20—

I have just concluded a call with Henry. I'm not certain who was more surprised to be negotiating my contract in the dead of night, me or him. His facade of generous understanding in the face of my attempt to reduce Chloe's term by extending my own gave me some measure of comfort.

Chloe won't forgive me for my actions tonight. That is, if she discovers what I've done. She was right when she said I was very specifically stipulating that I wouldn't manipulate her within the confines of our relationship. This does not fall under those confines. I don't believe that can be argued. Regardless, it would be best if she doesn't find out. Unfortunately, the success of this operation is more important than any interpersonal feelings I might have, no matter how strong they happen to be. My role is to protect those under my command from harm, and I will continue to do so. Chloe's year-long contract will secure us Gobi personnel; everything else we need falls under my contract. As it should.

C hloe and Richard had slept on the living room couches, which ended up being more comfortable than town bunks. When Chloe rolled over, Xander was staring at his phone, his brow furrowed. He looked up and gestured to the breakfast he'd made her, laid out on the coffee table. She pulled the covers around her as she sat up to eat.

"Vishesh contacted me last night, after you were asleep," said Xander.

"Did he make it to Town Lambda okay?" said Chloe between bites.

"Yes, and Neil informed him that Aaron is already working with Gobi," said Xander.

"Hm. So he's working with Gobi," said Chloe. "Why am I not surprised?"

"I agree, it is not entirely unexpected, but it does change things," said Xander.

"They're hiring us to hit Aaron when Aaron is also working for them?" said Chloe. "That makes no sense."

"The corporations have broad agendas," said Xander. "I'm certain it fits in with Gobi's overarching plans."

"So we figure this out without them," said Chloe. "We don't let them manipulate us."

"You have a strategy in mind?" said Xander.

"We call up Aaron, and we make a deal with him," said Chloe.

"It seems unlikely that Aaron will compromise with us. We don't pose a threat to him, not without Cassandra and her people," said Xander. "And without the contracts, no Cassandra."

"We have to try, though. Giving up years of our lives in exchange for support?" said Chloe. "Do you really want to work for a corporation for years? Because I don't."

Xander fixed her with a hard stare. Was he hiding something? No, he wouldn't. Not from her. He sighed and pulled his phone back out. He dialled, put the phone on speaker, and laid it on the table between them. It rang and rang. If Aaron didn't pick up, then they would still have their answer, in a way. Finally, the line clicked over.

"Hello?"

"Good morning. We're calling to speak with Aaron. Please put him on the line," said Xander.

"Who wants to speak with him?"

Chloe's stomach jolted. She would know that voice anywhere.

"Connor?"

"Chloe?" he said.

She rubbed her palms on her jeans. *Don't scare the kid away. Anything he's doing right now, it's not his fault.* "It's good to hear your voice," she said.

"Yeah," said Connor.

"Are you keeping busy?" said Chloe. She cleared her throat. It wouldn't do to have Aaron hear her crying.

"Yup," said Connor. He was likely still angry with her for breaking her promise. Had that really been only a couple of weeks ago?

"I'm sorry I didn't make it home for dinner," said Chloe. What else was there to say?

"That was my doing," Xander cut in. "Chloe had no choice in the matter."

"Yeah," said Connor. "Aaron said you were kidnapped."

"Aaron told you that?" said Chloe.

"Yeah."

Connecting with the kid was hard enough when he was in the same room. Over the phone? Chloe scrambled for something else to say, but Connor got there first.

"Here's Aaron," he said. "Bye, Chloe."

She wanted to scream, *Wait!* But Aaron was definitely on the line now, if he hadn't been the whole time.

"Bye, Connor," said Chloe. "I'll see you soon."

Xander glared at her sharply, and Chloe mentally kicked herself. Way to warn Aaron that they were planning to come knocking.

"Hi, again, Chloe, Phillips," said Aaron. "As you can tell, Connor is doing great, learning really fast and handling everything I can throw at him." What exactly had Aaron been throwing at him? A question for another time when they didn't have an agenda. This was important, and she needed to focus.

"Good morning, Aaron," said Xander. "It has come to our attention that you are currently working with Gobi, and we wanted to make you an offer directly instead of wading through all the bureaucracy that comes with those corporate contracts."

Aaron laughed out loud. "I love talking to you, Phillips! Always trying to pull one over on me. I'm glad you got in touch. This way I can make it absolutely perfectly plain that I will under no circumstances be negotiating with you. You want to get involved in my little setup, I will crush you. Get all the corporate backing you want. I don't give a shit."

Chloe recoiled. Aaron had flipped from affable and genial to deadly ultimatum in a nanosecond. Xander seemed completely unfazed.

"I appreciate your candour," he said. "I would urge you to at least consider our offer. Gobi will take their cut on either end. We could both benefit much more from dealing directly with one another."

"You don't need to school me in dealing with the corporations. If you think I've ever signed my own name on the dotted line when dealing with either of them, you've been underestimating me."

Either of them?

"You're dealing with more than one?" said Chloe.

"Yes, sweetness," said Aaron. "I'm dealing with more than one. Phillips over there might be good, but I'm better. I don't go up against the corporations. I don't pick fights I won't win."

"You play them against each other," said Chloe.

"I would never admit to such a thing where it could be recorded," said Aaron. "If we're done here, I have business that needs attending."

"If you'd just—" said Chloe, but Aaron cut her off.

"No, I don't think I'll *just* anything, Chloe," said Aaron. "*See you soon.*" He echoed Chloe's words to Connor back in her face. The line clicked and the blare of the dropped call tone filled the small room.

Xander prodded the Hang Up button.

"Gobi it is," said Chloe.

***

Chloe stabbed her trowel into the dark earth. She scooped out the bean seedling and added it to the wheelbarrow. She could almost calm her swirling thoughts with this familiar work. Almost. Connor, not just living under Aaron's rule but working for him? Vishesh hadn't mentioned that part. Maybe Connor had a good reason for it, just as she had a good reason for selling her soul to Gobi in exchange for their help.

The wheelbarrow was full. One of the folks who actually lived here grabbed it and trundled it away, leaving Chloe to stand by the bed of seedlings, her arms limp at her sides. What was she doing? She wanted to free her family, and she was going to tether herself to a corporation? Thinking that Gobi would just let her go when the indenture agreement ran out was naive. As both Xander and Isabelle had proven, her skill set was too valuable to be cast aside.

Chloe drew herself up and brushed off her hands. No, there was another way, and she would find it. First thing was to tell Xander that she was not going to sign anything, and then she'd radio Vishesh and see what they could coordinate. They were not going to be able to overthrow Aaron without Gobi and Cassandra's promised support, but they would get their family back.

Chloe found Xander in the living room, deep in conversation with Cassandra, but he stopped short when she knocked on the door jamb. On her way out, Cassandra gave Xander a look and then shut the door, leaving the two of them alone.

"What do you think of the agreement?" said Xander.

"I've made my decision," said Chloe. She dropped into the chair that Cassandra just vacated.

"I know it's not what any of us want, but it's the only way," said Xander.

Chloe shook her head. "I'm not signing, Xander. I can't set that kind of example for my kids. Hearing that Connor was working for Aaron, I realized that that's the example I set for him with Monty, deferring to an aggressive man to keep the peace. I never thought I'd let myself fall into that dynamic again, but I did. I thought I had no choice. Seems like there's always a choice, and this time I choose to say no."

"I thought you might," said Xander. "Perhaps *dreaded* would be more accurate."

"We'll just have to come up with another plan, convince Cassandra to help us some other way," said Chloe. "She has to see that now is the time to stand up to Aaron, before he integrates all the towns' resources into his settlement."

"That won't be necessary," said Xander.

Chloe's stomach dropped, and goosebumps prickled her arms. "What do you mean? Xander, what did you do?"

"Gobi and I have come to an agreement that does not necessitate your involvement. They will provide the resources we discussed," said Xander.

"When?" said Chloe, barely able to choke out even that one word. *Do my best to act in good faith within our relationship.* That was what Xander had promised her. This didn't count, apparently.

"Last night," said Xander. "After Vishesh contacted me to let me know that Aaron was already involved with the corporations. I had no expectation that he would agree to settle with us, but I had . . . hoped you could remain ignorant of the situation, of the exact details of my contract. As I said, there is no other option."

"What did you give them?" said Chloe. "You said it's just you. How many years of your *life* did you trade?"

"Seven," said Xander. He didn't even seem upset about it. It was merely the most advantageous transaction.

"And you didn't think I would mind my boyfriend being MIA for seven years?" said Chloe. How could she make him understand that his actions affected her as well?

"I wasn't sure that we would . . ." Xander cleared his throat. "They have assured me that I will be afforded some flexibility in terms of my work location."

"Assured you? It's in the contract?" said Chloe.

His silence was answer enough. They both knew that if it wasn't in the contract, there was no holding them to it.

Xander would, of course, value his big picture plans over their relationship; hell, they'd only known each other for a couple of weeks, but he should have at least had the guts to tell her about it instead of going behind her back.

She swallowed. "I don't think this is going to work," she said. The words seemed to float from her mouth as though she hadn't been the one to say them. She and Xander had been together a grand total of two days and already he'd done something to break her trust. This was never going to go the way she wanted. Had she expected that he would change for her?

"I understand why you feel that way," said Xander. "I knew there was a chance you wouldn't accept my decision." His voice caught. "Perhaps under different circumstances . . . but we are not under different circumstances, are we?"

"I guess we can try again in seven years," Chloe bit out.

Xander flinched. "I suppose I deserved that. I would still very much like your help with this operation, Chloe. Now that we have the details in place, we can proceed."

"Then let's proceed," said Chloe. There was no time for either of them to acknowledge that they were torn up inside, that they were both doing what they felt they needed to. As she herself had said, they needed to strike now before Aaron integrated all the extra resources he'd acquired from the towns.

***

The wind whipped straight down the river and ruffled Vishesh's hair. They'd agreed they would get across the Gatineau River and make camp for the night. There was just one problem. The bridge they'd planned to cross had crumpled into the water. Whitewater splashed around the base of the gap separating the two halves of the bridge, debris from the collapse scattered downstream. Vishesh shaded his eyes and peered northward toward the railway bridge. Maybe they could cross farther up. They would at least have to try. He squinted. It wasn't possible that the railway bridge had collapsed as well, was it?

"Something happened," said Neil.

"Yeah, something like a bridge collapsing," said Brianna.

"No, something destroyed it," said Neil.

Brianna brushed past Vishesh, farther out onto the crumbled bridge. Just watching her made every muscle in his body tense.

"You don't think Aaron did this on purpose, do you? What advantage could it possibly give him?" said Vishesh.

"I don't know. It cuts us off for one thing," said Neil.

"Face it, Aaron would never put this much effort into cutting us off. We're a buzzing fly to him. Very easy to swat." Vishesh shook his head.

"I think you're right. The railway bridge is down as well.," Brianna called back to them.

"Alonzo-Wright Bridge it is," said Neil.

"What?" said Brianna as she rejoined them.

"Can't cross here, and the railway bridge is down, so we keep going north. There's just one more option. Otherwise we hoof it all the way to Wakefield," said Neil.

"It would take us an entire day to walk to Wakefield," said Brianna.

"The Chelsea dam hasn't been passable in years. If all these bridges are out, there's no other way across," said Neil. "Not that I can see, anyway."

"Not unless you have a boat," said Vishesh.

"Nope," said Neil.

"Then let's get moving," said Vishesh, retreating off the crumbling structure. "If the Alonzo whatever bridge is out, we'll camp for the night and go to Wakefield tomorrow."

"Then make our way back down to Aaron's settlement the next day," said Neil.

Brianna groaned. "We'll do what we have to," she said. "But I don't have to like it. My feet are already killing me."

An hour later, they were examining the wreckage of the Alonzo-Wright Bridge. What have caused this destruction? They wouldn't be able to cross here; none of them needed to say it out loud. Vishesh sighed, and they turned back up the road.

"There's a neighbourhood up the way where we can bed down for the night," said Neil.

"Didn't Portia say something about a safe settlement on this side?" said Vishesh.

"*Safe* is a stretch," said Neil. "Taking you in is one thing. Sheltering us so we can attack Aaron is something else."

About fifteen minutes up the road, Neil led them across a ditch and over what had once been a lawn. They waded through the tall bracken, thankfully still not yet sprouted to become impassable.

"Take your pick," said Neil, gesturing to the big brick houses dotted along the small street.

Vishesh pointed vaguely to one of the houses, and they fought their way up the overgrown driveway to the front door. It had obviously already been cracked open once before. Splinters stuck out from the hinges on one side, and a wide crack ran up the frame from the dead-bolt on the other. They'd be unlikely to find any supplies inside, but at least it would keep them dry and give them shelter from the wind, which picked up as they stood on the porch.

Vishesh set his shoulder to the door, and it practically fell into the house. Brianna explored inside while he and Neil propped it back in the frame. Neil set up the lantern on the kitchen table while Vishesh flicked on the walkie-talkie. Might as well see whether they were in range of Dorothy. They couldn't be in range of Chloe anymore.

"Come in, Dorothy, over," said Vishesh. He would avoid identifying himself until he knew who was on the other end. If Dorothy had been caught, Aaron could very well have her walkie-talkie.

"Dorothy here," said Dorothy, right away.

Vishesh let out a breath.

"My mission is complete, but there were some unintended consequences," said Dorothy.

Neil cut in. "Are you in touch with your contact there?"

"Not yet," said Dorothy. "I've been lurking."

"They can help organize something," said Neil.

"It's a risk," said Dorothy.

"Yes," said Neil.

"Understood," said Dorothy.

"Over and out," said Vishesh, and Dorothy echoed it.

Brianna stood with her back pressed to the dark window and her arms wrapped around her body. She shrugged when she noticed Vishesh watching her. "Knowing I'm here will only make her worry."

Vishesh nodded. "Does Portia have access to boats?" he said to Neil.

"Not that I know of. On the other hand, there are a ton of vehicles at the settlement. If they can get their hands on those, it doesn't seem nearly so far up to Wakefield."

"If we can let Chloe and Richard know that the bridges are out, we should. They don't need to go through what we did when we got there," said Vishesh thoughtfully.

"Once they're close enough, we can radio them," said Neil.

"We have no way of knowing when that will be," said Vishesh.

"Guys," said Brianna and jerked her chin at the door. A silhouette clouded the frosted-glass sidelight.

The front door crashed open, and a figure loomed in the open doorway. The glint of metal in the lantern light had Vishesh raising his hands, and Neil and Brianna followed suit.

The figure stepped into the kitchen. "Who were you talking to? Aaron?" The woman's pale skin was reddened from the cold wind rattling the windows, a knife gripped tightly in her fist.

"No, we're not with Aaron," said Neil.

The woman narrowed her eyes. "You were trying to cross the bridge?"

Vishesh sighed. Might as well get right to it. "Aaron has my family. We want to get them back."

"And you were talking to who?"

"A friend of ours. She's trying to do the same," said Vishesh.

"Won't work," said the woman. "Folks go in there, they don't come out."

"Then there's no reason not to let all of us go in," said Neil.

The woman jerked her head at Neil. "You got family in there too?"

"No. Just interested in screwing over Aaron however I can," said Neil.

"Got a plan?"

"Not much of one," said Neil.

The woman glanced down and seemed to realize she was still brandishing a knife at them. She tucked it in her belt. "We saw your light, came to check it out. Thought maybe Aaron was thinking of expanding. We fought him off a time or two."

Vishesh glanced at Neil. The settlement he'd mentioned asking for help. He must have known about the previous skirmishes, that their settlement could hold their own against Aaron.

"Any interest in taking him down?" said Neil.

The woman grinned, but there was no humour in it. "Looking to recruit us to your doomed venture? Sounds like you have a vendetta. No, we're happy with what we've got. Don't need to get mixed up in Aaron's bullshit."

"Any chance you could help us get across the river? I'm sure your lives would be easier if Aaron was out of the picture. If we fail, it's no skin off your nose," said Brianna.

"Might have a boat you can use," said the woman. "Wouldn't chance it in this weather, with the river how it is."

"We'll wait for the weather to clear," said Vishesh. "Thank you."

"Come on back to our place. Don't have much, but more than this."

"Thank you," said Brianna.

Maybe others at the settlement would be more open to helping them. It was worth a shot; they wouldn't get far just the three of them.

***

The tall, serious woman walked right up and slid into the booth across from Portia as if they knew each other. Probably one of the new town or City residents. It was unlikely that they'd met before though. Portia sipped her beer and waited for the other woman to speak, but she just crossed her arms. Portia broke first.

"If you're planning to hurt Aaron by killing me or whatever, be aware that he doesn't give two shits about me," said Portia.

"Noted," said the woman. "I'm Dorothy, and I'm just checking in."

"That's a weird way to say you're hitting on me," said Portia.

"Neil seemed to think you're the one to talk to," said Dorothy. "He thought you could keep Connor safe, after all."

"His mistake," said Portia. "He of all people should know none of us are safe."

"He and Vishesh are now."

"Neil sent you?"

"Neil and a few others."

"Vishesh's people?"

"Some of them."

"Were you responsible for the City thing?"

"Indirectly," said Dorothy.

"And now you need me?"

"Neil and Vishesh do, yeah," said Dorothy. She slid a package across the table, and Portia moved it to the bench beside her.

"Mysterious," said Portia. "How do I get in touch with you?"

"Just act normal. I might come around again."

"Sounds good, now fuck off," said Portia, raising her voice at the end. She attracted a few glances, but it wasn't at all out of character for her to swear at someone hitting on her, and it would give Dorothy an excuse to immediately leave the pub.

Portia rested her hand on the package. She wanted to hightail it out of there and tear into the thing, but she had to give it a bit of time between the two of them leaving. Plus, she never left a drink half-finished, that in itself would raise eyebrows.

She clunked her empty glass on the table, tucked the package under her arm, and sauntered out of the pub into the cold evening air. The wind had really picked up since she'd gone inside, and she tucked her coat more tightly to her body. Portia didn't have anywhere safe per se to open the package, but out here in the dark was probably safest. She couldn't open it in the apartment she shared with Aaron. She tore into the package as she walked, glancing around at the loud ripping noise, but as usual, her route home was deserted.

She hefted the walkie-talkie she found inside. This would be impossible to explain to Aaron if he saw it. If she brought it home, he *would* find it. She sighed. Losing Neil had totally fucked her over. Men. Always thinking with their dicks.

True, Neil was gone, but there *was* someone she could pass this to. The thought made her sick. She hadn't wanted to pull the kid into this fight. He was totally innocent and naive, not to mention that she'd promised Neil that she would protect him. She was running out of options, and Aaron had forced her hand by giving him Neil's old position.

She'd find a way to get it to him tomorrow. She could keep it hidden from Aaron for one night. Hopefully.

Portia stepped in the door of their dark, silent apartment. The walkie-talkie was burning a hole in her coat pocket; the sooner she could hide it somewhere, the better. Aaron wasn't home now, but that just meant he could walk through the door any minute. She tried to act normal. She flicked on the light and hung up her coat. Aaron would have no reason to go through the pockets. Maybe the walkie-talkie would be safest right where it was.

Act normal! Portia busied herself getting ready for bed and nearly jumped out of her skin when the front door opened and then closed.

"Hey, baby, I'm home," Aaron called.

Portia plastered a smile on her face and stuck her head out the bathroom door.

"I'm just getting ready for bed."

His footsteps stalked down the hall. The door creaked wider behind Portia, and Aaron appeared in the mirror. "How was your day?" he said.

Her day? Her hand shook as she wiped off her lipstick to give herself a second. Aaron's smile in the mirror made her heart pound, fear and excitement twisted together. Asking how her day was and then waiting patiently for the answer while wearing that smile? *He knows.*

"Not very exciting," she said. "How was yours? I was thinking about you." She licked her lips and glanced down his body in the mirror.

Aaron stepped up behind her, wrapped his arms around her middle, and clasped his hand on his opposite wrist. Trapped. He leaned in, and his breath tickled the shell of her ear.

"Clumsy play, baby," he said.

Portia shuddered, whether with fear or desire was still up in the air.

"Should we see what was in that package you got handed in the bar? I'm so curious, I can barely contain myself." He ground his rapidly hardening cock against her ass. This time, her shiver was definitely desire. He chuckled in her ear. "Looking forward to your punishment, I see. I must say, after all these years, I didn't think you had it in you to do something so . . . brazen.

"Go get it, and bring it back to me," said Aaron and let her loose.

Resisting now wouldn't do any good. Portia stumbled down the hall to her coat and pulled out the walkie-talkie. Aaron met her in the living room.

"What's this?" he said. His smile still made it perfectly clear that he already had a good idea what it was. He wanted to watch her scramble for an answer. See what she came up with.

"It's a walkie-talkie," she said.

"I can see that," said Aaron. "And who will I find on the other end?"

"I don't know," said Portia. The truth.

"Let's try something easier. Where did you get it?"

"You know I got it from the bar," said Portia.

Aaron held out his hand, and Portia put the walkie-talkie into it.

"And the one who gave it to you? A townie, wasn't she?"

"Yes, I think so," said Portia. Like a bolt from the blue, she had it. "Connor left it behind. You know how he likes to hang out at the towns."

"Mmm," said Aaron. "Go on."

"I was going to give it back to him tomorrow."

"How kind of you," said Aaron. Then his smile widened, and he snapped his fingers. "I have an idea! I'll take it back to him. I'll see him anyway, and it'll save you the trip. I know you don't care for my nerve centre."

Fuck. She didn't bother to keep playing along.

"Now that that's decided," said Aaron. He crossed to his safe and blocked the keypad from view as he opened it. He slid the walkie-talkie inside and shut the door with a thunk. The grinding of the lock sliding home was almost drowned out by Portia's pounding pulse as Aaron turned his attention back to her and said, "What do you think your punishment should be for trying to keep things from me?"

Chapter Twenty-Six

Log: Settlement Lambda, Richard A. Phillips, 28 May 20—

Having expected that Chloe would distance herself from me because of my recent actions has not made it any easier to be apart from her. On a certain level, I'm glad that she is free from corporate contracts, despite the personnel we could have procured in exchange. We'll simply have to recruit the townrunners to our cause when we arrive.

Strangely, it's my mother's ethos that drove me to do what I did: it is a leader's responsibility to shoulder the burdens, to shelter their people from the worst consequences and pay the price to keep them safe. One would think that fact would have been a deterrent, but in some ways it's freeing. I find myself avoiding ruminating on that. Did I simply fall back on platitudes that were driven into me from childhood as an excuse

to sacrifice myself so that I could keep those I love safe
in the only way that was available to me?

A t least the corporation had come through with the transport
they had promised. Three vans showed up just after lunch,
enough to take the ten Lambda residents who wanted to go, Cassandra, Richard, and Chloe. The drivers took Richard's signature, left the
keys, and immediately disappeared. Apparently, he hadn't negotiated
for any drivers or backup.

Their plan was to get close enough to be in range of the
walkie-talkies the other members of their party had taken and get a
status update. Hopefully, they could all be ready to move together and
spook Aaron into running for the hills. His regime would fall apart as
soon as he disappeared. They were counting on that. First things first.

"Ride with me," said Cassandra as she passed the living room door..

"Is Xander riding with you, too?" said Chloe.

"Sure isn't," said Cassandra. "We need to talk about him. No point
if he's there."

When Chloe got outside, Richard opened the driver's-side door of
one of the vans and motioned for Chloe to get in the passenger seat,
but she shook her head and got in with Cassandra instead.

Once they were on the road, Cassandra had her people shut the
partition between the front seats and the back of the van. *Crap.* She
wanted to *talk*.

"Noticed you helping in the greenhouse. There's no call to break
your back for my settlement," said Cassandra.

"You can never have too much help with planting," said Chloe.
"Besides, I like to keep my hands busy."

"Otherwise they'll ring your boyfriend's neck, eh?"

"He's not my boyfriend," said Chloe. Ominous clouds gathered at the horizon.

"Bullshit," said Cassandra. "He's always been a bit of a martyr. Don't you think?"

Chloe sighed. "You won't like what I have to say about it."

"More than likely," said Cassandra. "Go ahead."

They'd gotten on the road just in time. Rain pattered on the windshield, and the wipers turned on automatically. Chloe shivered. Hopefully Vishesh and Neil had found somewhere cozy to hole up.

"Gonna let me have it or what?" said Cassandra.

"I should," said Chloe. "It's your fault. You forced Xander's hand. He knew we wouldn't have your support without Gobi's backing."

"How far do you think you would have gotten without corporation support?" said Cassandra. Chloe didn't have an answer. "Let me put it this way. How far did Isabelle get? Didn't even put up a fight, right? Unlike most of those useless townrunners, I was made a townrunner to get me out of Isabelle's hair. I was on her to take corporation assistance, use it to her advantage. She couldn't put up with my nagging anymore and tossed me onto Town Lambda, framing it as a promotion. Xander knew that when he agreed to come find me. My demands were no surprise to him."

"You don't think Aaron being in league with the corporations changes things?"

"He made a deal with them, same as everyone does. I'd hardly call that being in league," said Cassandra.

"That's how you knew they'd be willing to stab him in the back," said Chloe.

Cassandra shook her head slowly. "Seems to me you're misinterpreting what a corporation is. They have no loyalty to betray. A corporation is not a person—it's a money-making machine. If humans get in its way, they get chewed up."

"And Xander is the one getting chewed up for all of us," said Chloe.

She stared out the rain-obscured windshield, the silence punctuated by waves of raindrops spattering against it.

"Xander is good at pretending he doesn't need anyone," said Cassandra, her voice soft, for once.

"I know," said Chloe. "I'm just so damn mad at him."

"Be mad at him," said Cassandra. "Just don't abandon him. He needs us, no matter what he says."

***

They installed themselves in a big house just south of the Alonzo-Wright Bridge, the bridge they would hopefully be able to take to Aaron's settlement, once they coordinated with the others. As they finished bringing supplies in from the car, thunder cracked, and a deluge of rain frothed the Gatineau River out the big back windows. Chloe clicked on the walkie-talkie and stood it on the kitchen counter. She double-checked that it was on channel three and turned up the volume. She didn't want to miss any messages now that they were in range.

The walkie-talkie crackled, and Chloe's stomach turned to ice as Aaron's voice filled the kitchen.

"Aaron speaking," he said. "Good news, everyone! We're moving up our timeline. Be ready to evacuate the kids tomorrow at the usual time." Faint voices came through in the background, and then Aaron laughed and the walkie-talkie went silent.

Evacuate the kids. Tomorrow at the usual time. Aaron had a walkie-talkie. Most likely Dorothy's, but there was no way to know.

"So much for contacting the others," said Chloe under her breath.

Xander leaned against the wall next to the kitchen. "It's a tight timeframe. We'll have to do some level of recon, but we should be able to make it before dawn tomorrow."

"You think he's serious about the kids?" said Chloe.

"Are you willing to risk the eventuality that he is?" said Xander.

"You're right," said Chloe. "We have no choice. Get your recon done. I want to be ready."

Xander nodded and went to arrange whatever his recon was. Chloe would have packed up right then and stormed the place on her own, so it was a good thing Xander was more deliberate in his preparations; his recon uncovered that the bridges across the Gatineau from Wakefield all the way down to the Ottawa River had been destroyed.

"And the vans are low on charge," said Cassandra when they met back in the kitchen to plan their dawn attack.

"How low?" said Chloe.

"If they make it up to Wakefield at all, they sure as hell won't make it back south again," said Cassandra.

"Gobi knew," said Xander.

Chloe shot him a quizzical look, and he continued.

"Gobi knew the bridges were out. They orchestrated this so that the vans wouldn't get us all the way to the settlement."

"The trip will take at least a day," said Cassandra.

"A day we don't have, unless we want Aaron to take the kids and disappear tomorrow," said Chloe. She caught Xander's eye. "Call Henry."

"What are you proposing?" said Xander.

"Call Henry," said Chloe. "Get us better transport. A helicopter or something. We need to get to that settlement."

"And what do I offer in exchange?" said Xander.

"You'll have to offer me," said Chloe.

"Chloe, I refuse to—"

She raised her eyebrows at him and he fell silent.

"We're playing into their hands," said Xander.

"I know," said Chloe.

"You're sure?"

"Just tell me where to sign."

***

Their dance hall had been a barn, once. Huge and red with a tin roof. The few little drops of rain already ticked a merry tattoo to accompany the fiddler in the corner. The dance floor overflowed with merrymakers.

When Vishesh got their family out, he would bring them here. Still, he had to get them out first. And to do that, it would be nice to have some allies. At Brianna's urging, they had decided to sacrifice a day to attend this dance, where they really hoped to gain some allies. But the folks that Vishesh talked to brushed him off, and he gave up and collapsed into a chair next to Neil.

"Any luck?" he said.

"Nope," said Neil.

They both watched Brianna. She burst out laughing at something a resident had said, then seemed to make her farewells, and moved on to the next group. Whatever she did worked. Their scowls and glares soon softened to smiles and banter.

"How does she do that?" said Vishesh, shaking his head.

"Beats me," said Neil. "Stands to reason that she and Richard worked well together."

Rain drummed on the roof and almost drowned out the fiddle. Vishesh turned up the volume on the walkie-talkie. If Portia finally contacted them, he wanted to be able to hear it. Brianna made her way back to them.

"Looks like you made some friends," said Neil.

"Only time will tell," said Brianna and grinned.

Vishesh smiled back at her. Someone tapped him on the shoulder, and he turned and looked up at the person.

"You folks have been raising a lot of chatter," said the tall, swarthy tapper. A few other residents stood behind him.

"Have we?" said Vishesh.

The tapper jerked his chin at Brianna. "You're pregnant?"

"Sure am," said Brianna.

"Is that true, or you just trying to get us interested?"

"Why would her being pregnant interest you?" said Neil.

"Do you see any kids?" The tapper waved around the room. "We don't have tests for our water, our soil. We've done our best, but . . ." He shrugged.

"I don't know if we can help you," said Vishesh.

"I hear you're talking about getting rid of Aaron for good."

Vishesh surveyed the handful of curious onlookers, who shuffled and fidgeted and wouldn't make eye contact.

"That's right," said Neil. "If we do, I'll make sure we run a hydro line across to your settlement here."

The tapper shrugged. "We get by without power."

"What about food?" said Vishesh.

"We don't want Aaron's radioactive crap."

Vishesh shook his head. "I have a new type of seeds, and Aaron has more. Seed-verts. They counteract contaminated soil."

The onlookers muttered at that. He'd caught their interest this time.

Vishesh's walkie-talkie crackled and he fumbled for it and turned the volume up even higher.

"Aaron speaking." Aaron's voice echoed through the dancehall. The fiddle stopped abruptly, and the chatter died away. "Good news, everyone! We're moving up our timeline. Be ready to evacuate the kids tomorrow at the usual time."

As soon as the echoes died away, dozens of voices filled the hall. The tapper and their onlookers retreated, tossing a few choice curses at Vishesh, Neil, and Brianna.

"No," whispered Vishesh. He shook the walkie-talkie, as if he could make it take the words back.

"Wait!" said Brianna, but no one was listening anymore.

The woman who had brought them here stumped over, scowling.

"You can still stay here, but be gone in the morning. Back to Aaron with you." She stumped away. All the other residents seemed to retreat after that as well, leaving Vishesh, Brianna, and Neil alone in their corner.

"What happens now?" said Brianna.

"We get Vishesh's family out," said Neil.

"And let Aaron be?" said Vishesh.

Neil shrugged. "What can we do with just the three of us?" He downed his drink. "I'm tired of being glared at. You coming?"

There was nothing for it. They dashed through the rain to the little cabin they had been assigned for the night. Even next to Neil, Vishesh couldn't sleep. After tossing and turning for an hour, he gave up.

Vishesh pulled out his pack and leafed through the Seed-vert packets. These folks could use them. He sorted out two-thirds of the packets, pulled on his coat, tucked the packets inside, and dashed back to the hall. The rain still drumming on the roof was the only noise filling the hall now, and only one knot of folks sat bunched around a table. They looked over when he came in, but once he took off his hood and they realized it was him, they ignored him.

The seed packets were only very slightly damp when he pulled them out of his coat. He laid them on the table nearest the door.

"Take good care of these," he called. "I hope they help."

They eyed him suspiciously, and Vishesh left the little envelopes on the table. He'd done his good deed, now maybe he'd be able to sleep.

***

Just before the end of the day, Aaron called Connor into his office. A deluge of raindrops pattered against the big window. *Crap.* Connor hadn't brought his coat. He'd have to run home, and he'd still be soaked through.

"Shut the door, please, Connor," said Aaron.

Connor complied and dropped into the chair across Aaron's desk from him. Aaron pulled out a little box with a speaker and an antenna on it.

"Portia found this," said Aaron.

"Yeah?" said Connor. What was he supposed to say?

"Don't you recognize it?" said Aaron. He raised his eyebrows and smiled.

Oh shit. Portia had fed Aaron a story about him.

"Yeah, of course I do," said Connor.

Aaron slid it across his desk, and Connor reached for it, but Aaron stopped short, the box just out of Connor's reach.

"You didn't tell me you implemented a new communication system," said Aaron. Why did his smile creep Connor out so much?

"Oh," said Connor. "Well, I did."

"And do all the security officers have access to this channel?"

"Of course they do," said Connor.

"We'll save ourselves some time, then," said Aaron. He put the thing up to his mouth, pressed the button on the side, and spoke into it. "Aaron speaking," he said. "Good news, everyone! We're moving up our timeline. Be ready to evacuate the kids tomorrow at the usual time."

"Evacuate the kids?" said Connor. "Shouldn't your head of security know what's going on?"

Aaron laughed and tossed him the communicator. Connor caught it.

"You and Portia. Determined to make my life interesting these days. I think I'll keep you two."

"Keep us?"

"Indeed. Now run along. I have a busy evening ahead of me."

Chapter Twenty-Seven

Log: Riverside residence, Richard A. Phillips, 28 May
20—

I am not at all in agreement with this course of action
Let the record show that, at the very least. I have made
every attempt to divert Chloe, and she will not be
deterred. The irony might be amusing if the consequences were not so dire. I suppose now I understand
how she felt about me doing the same. Perhaps that is
why she feels justified.

T he rain pelted down so hard that the opposite bank of the river
was invisible. The dampers on the hood fan in the kitchen
rattled with each gust of wind. Gobi had promised them a helicopter,
but they would have to wait for the weather to clear before it could
come for them. And it turned out staring at the rain and willing it to
let up didn't work very well.

The lanterns scattered through the house created welcome pools of
light. Xander stood at the window next to Chloe.

"Would you rather I leave?" he said.

"No," said Chloe.

"Do you understand now why I had to sign the agreement?" said Xander.

"No."

"Do you at least forgive me for going behind your back?"

"Nope."

Xander huffed out a breath and turned to leave.

"Wait," said Chloe and grabbed his arm..

Xander stopped.

"I want to forgive you," said Chloe. "I still think we could have found another way."

"Perhaps," said Xander.

"I guess it doesn't matter now, does it?"

"Not particularly."

"So we start from where we are," said Chloe.

"We?"

Chloe sighed. "After everything, I shouldn't still want you. I shouldn't trust you," she said. The rain showed no signs of letting up any time soon. "But I do. Xander, I want to be with you. Do you want to be with me?"

"I would very much like to, yes," said Xander.

"Want to sleep next to me?"

"Are you referring to actual sleep?"

"I haven't decided yet," said Chloe. She pressed her lips together to keep from grinning.

"I would like that very much," said Xander and smiled back.

Lying cuddled up together in bed, the decision was easy. Xander lay on his back, and Chloe snuggled up next to him with her head pillowed on his shoulder. She threw one knee over his body, and a stab of desire jolted through her.

"So do you want to sleep?" said Xander.

"Not even a little bit," said Chloe. She chewed her lip. Did Xander think sex was the price of admission for a relationship with her? "But I don't want to take advantage of you."

Xander's chuckle rumbled through his chest. "Trust me, you are not taking advantage."

He slid his thigh between hers and palmed her ass to get her to rock her hips against it. She ground on him, and it wasn't long until Chloe bit her lip and tried not to make too much noise as she came.

Xander kissed her with a satisfied smile. Apparently, he wasn't lying about enjoying this. "Just one orgasm sufficient?" he said. His smug smile and dancing eyes said he was far from done.

"You're up for more?" said Chloe.

"Seems a shame to squander the capacity for multiple orgasms, don't you think?" He flashed her a grin. "Just give me a number."

"I get it," said Chloe and rolled her eyes. "It's a game to you. If you make me come, you win."

"I'm fairly certain that when I make you come, we both win."

Chloe couldn't argue with that.

***

Chloe woke up with a warm weight over her waist and rolled onto her back. Xander stirred and snuggled her closer. Had she ever woken up feeling so secure? Not in recent memory, at least. Xander's phone rang, and Chloe startled. He gasped and sat up while she fumbled with it.

"Hello?" she ground out.

"Your transport will be arriving within the hour," said Henry.

"In the middle of the night?" said Chloe. She tried to clear the sleep from her brain.

"It'll be dawn by the time it gets there," said Henry. "I thought you were in a rush."

The kids! "I am," said Chloe. "We are."

"Then be ready," said Henry. The line went dead.

"Was it him?" said Xander.

"Yes," said Chloe and stifled a yawn. "We have about an hour to get ready. I can't believe it's finally time."

Xander rubbed her back. "Your family is our first priority. If we can scare Aaron off, we will, but we *will* get the kids back."

"Yeah, I know," said Chloe. The thought of seeing their little faces again . . . How angry would they all be that she'd left them? Would she really be able to just waltz back into their lives like nothing had happened? Pluck them from what might be a stable home for all she knew? She shook her head. Time enough to worry once they were safe.

They gathered outside and listened for the sound of rotors in the quickly dissipating darkness. The rush of the river and the quiet murmur of the Town Lambda residents' voices were the only breaks in the silence. Birdsong trilled through the still air.

Finally, a distant whir made Chloe scan the sky, and soon enough the chopper was setting down in an empty lot a block away from where they had left the vans. A stream of black-clad folks hopped out of the chopper and made their way over to Cassandra and Chloe.

"Chloe Michaels?" said one of them.

"Where do I sign?" she said.

She took one copy of the contract, and Xander took the other. He finished reading first and nodded. The contract reflected what they'd agreed to. When she turned to the last page, one of the Gobi folks handed her a pen, and she signed both copies. She handed one back with the pen and crammed the other in her pack.

"The vans?" said the Gobi rep.

"Down the street," said Chloe.

"Nice doing business with you," he said and gestured his folks to follow him to the vans. Were they contractually obligated to say that on behalf of the corporation? It wouldn't be surprising.

Thankfully, Xander had thought to add a pilot into the bargain for the helicopter, though it was probably in the best interests of the corporation to control who flew the thing; they wanted to get their helicopter back in one piece, after all.

Who would have thought the post-apocalypse would involve so much helicopter flight? Not that she'd spent a lot of time pondering it before armageddon. The helicopter could only seat eight people, and Cassandra conversed quietly with the Lambda squad. Some of them would have to be left behind.

Even from the air, it was obvious that the bridge they had planned to take was smashed all to hell, and a boat would have been a risky proposition on this section of the river with the water this high. Yeah, this was the only option, as painful as it was to admit.

The pilot set down the helicopter in a nearby baseball diamond—something about too many power lines closer in—and gave them just enough time to gather their things and hop out before taking off again. Aaron had seen their approach; they could count on that.

They couldn't wait around. They needed to find the other townrunners, gather support, find Chloe's family, and find Aaron. He was probably in the nerve center Neil had mentioned, filled with his crew, and likely to already be locked down tight. Hence the other townrunners.

They hustled down a residential street and crossed through a yard toward the power lines that peeked over the low houses. All the towns lay before them, parked in a row in the hydro cut. A few residents stirred, including a skinny one in a hoodie with dark brown skin . . .

"Connor!" called Chloe, and he lifted his head. She stumbled across the rough ground to where he stood frozen, and she pulled him into a hug. He was really here, alive and well. Had he grown in, like, the week they'd been apart? "Take me to the family. We're getting you out." She would never let him go again.

Connor shook his head and glanced behind her. Everyone was probably watching them, but that didn't matter. Her baby was safe.

"Where are the others?" said Chloe. They were here somewhere, maybe just over the hill. As soon as Connor pointed her toward them, she'd be unleashed.

Connor's bored teenager face firmly shuttered his thoughts. He'd clearly been practising it. "I can't go yet," he said.

Everything in Chloe wanted to grab him and drag him away with her, maybe lecture him on not arguing, but she mentally counted to ten and listened to him.

"I have to go," he said and gestured with his head to a couple of warehouses behind her.

"To Aaron?" said Chloe, and her stomach clenched. He wanted to stay with Aaron instead of going with her?

But he shook his head. "I have access to the security system. I'll let you into the nerve centre. But I gotta go now."

A thirteen-year-old kid had access to the security system? She would rip Aaron limb from limb when she got her hands on him. But she would only get her hands on him if she let Connor go unlock the door for them. She took a deep breath.

"Okay," she said. "Go. Clear the way, and we'll come for you." Chloe swallowed hard. Connor could definitely see the tears swimming in her eyes, but she couldn't hold them back. "Be safe." She gave him one last bone-crushing hug and let him go.

***

Vishesh, Neil, and Brianna had enough light to keep their footing on the riverbank down to the boats, but that was it. The river lapped at the grassy bank, but the section they'd chosen was calm enough at the moment.

Neil grabbed the stern of the boat they'd been offered, and Vishesh took the bow. The tiny dinghy would serve them fine. They slid it into the water, and Vishesh hooked the painter around a tree and straightened.

Neil and Brianna already stared at the handful of folks from the settlement who stood silently watching them.

"Making sure we're really going?" said Neil.

The tapper from last night stepped forward. "Got your seeds," he said.

Vishesh nodded. "They should help you reduce your radiation doses."

"If we have power, we could reduce them more," said the tapper. He spoke to Neil. "You really gonna do that?"

"If Aaron is out of the picture, absolutely," said Neil.

"Okay, then," said the tapper, "we'll follow you," and the folks at his back dispersed and headed to the other boats lined up along the river.

Vishesh nodded to him, and then the three of them scrambled into their dinghy, Vishesh at the bow watching for rocks, Neil on the oars, and Brianna in the stern.

"I'll take a turn rowing if you want," said Vishesh when they reached halfway across the river.

"Nope, I'm good," said Neil.

The river upstream of the hydro dam was surprisingly calm; even so, the current carried them a good distance downstream. The string of little boats was spread diagonally out across the river now, the splash of oars and quiet voices shockingly loud in the chill morning air. Vishesh blew on his hands, but his breath misted and didn't make much difference to their temperature; it just made them clammy.

Neil ran their dinghy aground on the opposite bank, and Vishesh hopped out and dragged the boat onto the grassy shore.

They led the others toward Aaron's nerve centre, prepared to storm the place. Vishesh wanted to unseat Aaron; he really did, but all he could think about was that he needed to make sure his family was safe, make sure they weren't being taken.

"I'll head for the kids," said Vishesh.

"I have to take these people to the nerve centre," said Neil.

"I know," said Vishesh. He held Neil's gaze. "I'll meet you after."

Neil leaned in and kissed him, stealing Vishesh's breath. "To tide you over," said Neil when they broke apart.

Vishesh gave him a curt nod, very much incapable of speaking, and turned up the path to their little townhouse.

***

Aaron was still asleep when Portia woke up. She pulled on clothes, and the first rays of the morning sun at least let her see what she was putting on. She turned back to the bed as she headed for the door, and Aaron's phone caught her eye. If she was really going to do this, she might as well go all the way. She sidled up Aaron's side of the bed and unplugged the phone. She slipped it into the pocket of her cardigan, and as she turned to creep back toward the door, Aaron's eyes fluttered open. They blinked at each other.

"Hey, baby," Aaron whispered. "You better run if you want a head start."

A jolt of adrenalin coursed through her and she was out the bedroom door before she could stop to think. She snatched her coat and tore out of the apartment, despite the fact that she hadn't heard Aaron so much as get out of bed. The chill morning air soothed her pounding heart as she hustled to the pub. Everyone fell silent as she entered. The bartender bobbed his head at her.

Dorothy sat in Portia's usual booth, and Portia paused to greet knots of folks at the other tables as she made her way there. She gripped Aaron's phone in her pocket. Once he noticed it was gone, there would be no fun "punishment" for her. She'd be tossed in the gutter and forgotten.

Portia climbed onto the single step up to the booth and cleared her throat. The packed pub fell silent.

"Thanks for coming on such short notice," she said. "We don't usually meet in the morning, for obvious reasons." She gestured to the silent space. "Today is the day, folks." A babble broke out, but she talked over it. "We've all been waiting a long time for this moment."

"Those of us who've lived long enough."

"What's the plan?"

"What happens if they catch us?"

"They kill us," said a rail-thin woman. She glared at Portia. "Well, most of us."

"You really believe that Aaron would forgive me?" said Portia. She clenched her hand around Aaron's phone in her pocket.

"His little fuck-toy? Um, yes?"

"This is just one of your twisted games with him."

"Why should we risk our lives?"

Portia held out the phone in a white-knuckled grip. "This isn't a game to me. Want to know what this is? It's Aaron's lifeline. He calls the corporations on this, and they come bail him out. He doesn't have it, no bail out."

"You're serious," said the rail-thin woman.

"I'm dead serious," said Portia. "This is our shot, and it might be our only one."

Chapter Twenty-Eight

Log: Aaron's encampment, Richard A. Phillips, 29
May 20—

The culmination of our plans is at hand, but I find
myself pondering what future Chloe and I might
have, both tied to the whim of Gobi going forward.
No sense in dwelling on it. Remaining alert and fo-
cussed is essential.

T he townrunners had consented to meet with them, but Chloe
hung back near the corridor. No need to remind them of her
little outburst. They were all gathered in the lounge of one of the
towns; the towns remained impossible to tell apart. So far, the townrunners had shown no sign of being on board with their cause.

"If we go against Aaron, we stand to lose everything," said Eloise.
"We don't all have settlements to fall back on like you do, Cassandra."

"We don't have time for this bickering," said Chloe to Xander,
under her breath.

"Isabelle would want this," said Cassandra. "And with her apprehended, I'm the most senior townrunner, and this—"

"I think you'll find Richard is still technically Deputy ECM," said Sigma.

They all looked to Richard.

"So I suppose you say the word, and we all jump? I've no doubt what you want us to do," said Chabot.

Richard steepled his fingers and glanced at Chloe, then at each townrunner in turn. "I don't feel that ordering you or your residents into a dangerous situation like this one against your convictions is . . . the right way forward," he said. "Even though I could do so, and perhaps it would be in my best interests."

"How magnanimous," said Greene dryly.

"What a time to grow a conscience," said Cassandra, under her breath, but still clearly audible. It drew a chuckle from the townrunners, and Richard smiled and squeezed Chloe's hand. All the townrunners looked at her. The last time she'd spoken to these folks, she'd been less than polite.

"We don't have time for this," she said and lurched to her feet.

Xander still held her hand and followed close behind her down the corridor. "What's your strategy?"

Chloe froze in the doorway to the loading dock. At least a hundred residents stared right at her. The Town Lambda residents stood at the back, almost on the ramp. Good. They could follow her out easily.

"You want these people's help? Here they are," said Xander. He squeezed her hand again.

They had the five Town Lambda residents, by Cassandra's orders, but they really needed more people to make a statement to Aaron that his time was up. The Town Kappa residents lounged against a wall, and the jerky driver mouthed the word *dirt*. Why did he hate her so much?

Chloe turned to Xander. "You can't do it?" she whispered.

"I could order them, as I said."

"No . . ." Chloe took a deep breath. The jerky driver made a rude gesture. She took another breath and closed her eyes. *Just lay out the facts and they'll get it.* She pitched her voice to carry. "Aaron mistreats his residents. Today we have a chance to put an end to it. We can give the people of this settlement access to clean water and food. I've been developing a water decontamination device that we can distribute, and we have all the Seed-verts from your towns. I know that together we can turn this settlement around, but first, we need to get out from under Aaron's control."

A hundred pairs of eyes stared at her. "And who the heck are you?" said someone, and it triggered a tumult of grumbling that would surely drown out anything else she tried to say. She was wasting her time. The handful of Town Lambda residents would have to be enough. Chloe clenched her fists at her sides and elbowed her way through the crowd towards the ramp.

Jerky driver stepped into her path.

"Where do you think you're going?" he said. The grumbling dissipated so they could watch this pointless drama play out.

"My son is going to give me a chance to get at Aaron. Probably my only chance. I said I would be there when he does, and I'll be there. I already broke one promise to him, and I won't do it a second time."

"That boy you were hugging before?"

"Yes, that's him. A thirteen-year-old kid with more integrity than the lot of you put together. Now get the fuck out of my way."

"*You'll* be running the place when Aaron's gone?" said jerky driver.

"No," said Chloe. "Not in a million years."

Jerky driver nodded and almost smiled. "I'll hold you to that." He thrust Chloe's laptop bag into her arms. "Town Kappa is in."

***

Chloe tucked her walkie-talkie into the laptop bag and settled it across her body. The comforting weight on her shoulder let her breathe a little easier. She stepped out of the town, Xander on her heels, the Town Lambda and Kappa residents in her wake. As they drew closer to the warehouses, chanting drifted through the morning air.

Hey hey, ho ho, Aaron's crew has got to go! Hey hey, ho ho, Aaron's crew has got to go!

The crowd almost completely surrounded Aaron's "nerve centre." Chloe's uniformed residents joined them to finish the job. If Aaron hadn't gotten the message that he was being overthrown, he would soon. His crew was vastly outnumbered, and it looked as if the rebels had barricaded the road so he couldn't take the kids anywhere, even if that had been his genuine plan.

Chloe worked her way between the warehouses to the front of the nerve centre. Neil stood in the parking lot with a small white woman. He waved Chloe over when he caught sight of her, the trail of uniformed town residents evidently having caught his eye.

"Where's Vishesh?" said Chloe.

"He went to their house for the kids," said Neil. "We didn't think we'd have enough folks to drive Aaron away but . . ." He gestured to the sea of chanting rebels. "Connor is still inside. With Aaron."

Chloe nodded. Vishesh could take care of the kids and Monty. Chloe had promised she would be here for Connor, and she would be.

"Why are we standing around?" said Chloe.

"The doors are still locked," said Neil.

"Connor said he was going to open them," said Chloe. She rubbed her palms on her thighs.

"He knows how," said Neil.

"Got any bricks?" said Chloe and eyed the big windows on the front of the warehouse.

"See? You're outvoted, Neil," said the small woman.

"No," said Neil. "We don't want to trigger a cascade of violence. They have weapons in there. Any excuse to use them, and Aaron will give the order. We can't give him an excuse."

"I agree," said Richard.

"Point me toward another way in then," said Chloe. The flat roof probably had some kind of access. "The roof?"

"There's a ladder around the back, but—" said Neil.

"No buts," said Chloe. "I'm going to get my kid."

Neil pointed the way, and Chloe rounded the back of the building toward the ladder. Xander stayed with her as she dodged through the crowd. Of course, the ladder didn't come close to reaching the ground.

"Shit," said Chloe.

"No problem." Dorothy had appeared at her elbow and nodded at Xander. They clasped their arms together into a platform, as though they'd practised it before.

"You go first. We'll follow you," said Brianna, somehow materializing out of the crowd next to her.

Chloe handed Brianna her laptop bag, and Dorothy and Xander boosted her to the bottom rung of the ladder. Flakes of rust on the rungs stung her hands, and the creaks and groans of the worn metal gave way to a crunch as she climbed quickly to the roof. Her final hop over the low wall was too much for the rusted-out ladder, and it crashed heavily to the ground. So no backup, then. She was on her own.

***

Vishesh crept up the quiet street. The row of houses was so familiar, it almost felt like home. Almost. He paused at the door to their little town house. Monty had caught him out like this once before. There was no helping it. He opened the door and slipped inside.

Sure enough, from the shadows, "Get out, or I do something you won't like," said Monty.

"And what's that?" said Vishesh. A little cry had Vishesh's skin crawling, and he flicked on the light.

Monty had Flora's upper arm in a viselike grip. He shook her and she whimpered again.

"What's the plan, Monty?" said Vishesh.

Monty growled something unintelligible.

"No plan, scaring a little kid half to death," said Vishesh.

"Scaring?" said Monty. "She's not scared of me. She knows I'd never hurt her." He shook her again. "She's just being dramatic."

"Then let her go," said Vishesh.

"And lose my only leverage? I don't think so," said Monty. "I'm taking her with me."

"Over my dead body," said Sheila from the stairs.

"Get the fuck back upstairs, woman," said Monty.

Sheila continued down the stairs, silently, her arms crossed across her bathrobe. "Get your hands off her and get out of my house," she said.

Monty's eyes narrowed dangerously, and despite himself, Vishesh flinched away. Sheila did not. She brushed past Vishesh, opened the front door, and pointed, glaring at Monty all the while.

"You can't kick me out of my own house!" he blustered.

"And if you stay?" said Sheila quietly. "Once Aaron is gone, you think anyone who's left is going to have patience for you? I'm giving you a chance to save your own skin, dear. Take it."

Monty snarled and wrenched Flora's arm. She cried out, and then her tiny teeth sank into Monty's hand, and he yelled and pushed her to the ground. He grabbed his injured hand and looked from Sheila's cold stare to Vishesh. The rage building in Vishesh's chest must have shown on his face because Monty stomped out the door and slammed it behind him.

Vishesh's rage cleared in an instant at Flora's wail. He crouched and gathered the sobbing kid to him while Sheila collapsed on the couch and buried her face in her hands.

"I never thought he'd really put hands on them," she said. "He was always saying—but I thought—"

***

Connor was locked in the nerve centre with Aaron and his people. Maybe he'd made a mistake coming here. But it was done now. He was the only one in here that could work against Aaron, and he would.

The security system was in Aaron's office. Connor knocked on the door, and Aaron called him inside.

"Do you hear that?" said Aaron.

Connor cocked his head, and sure enough, the shouts of the crowd gathered outside showed no sign of abating.

"*That* is not worth fighting. We could never win against it," said Aaron. "You're here to deactivate security, I imagine?"

Connor nodded, numb.

"Would you care to join me on the roof instead?" said Aaron.

"The roof?" said Connor.

"LunaCorp will come for me. If you'd like to get out of here, just say the word. There won't be anything left for you here once I'm gone.

This settlement will fall apart without me to hold it together. It'll be like armageddon all over again. With no towns in the region, how long do you think these people will last?" said Aaron.

They'd been fine at their farm with no towns. For a while. Even Chloe had admitted they needed the towns. *Chloe.*

"I'm not abandoning my family," said Connor.

"Of course you're not! I wouldn't dream of it! You'll be in a position to *save* your family if you come with me to LunaCorp. Just think of how happy Chloe will be when she realizes you've secured a place for you and your family, a safe place away from here where you don't have to worry about contaminated food or water. You and your siblings could go to a real school!"

A real school where he could learn whatever he wanted? Safe from the looming threat of contamination? Wasn't that what Chloe had been trying to do all along? Chloe couldn't be mad at him for doing exactly what she'd done in the same situation, right?

Unbidden, his mom's words popped into his head. *Don't confuse best for them and best for you.* She was right. He was justifying his own desires by saying his family would choose this. But he didn't actually know what they wanted without asking them.

"No," he said.

"That's a real shame," said Aaron.

Connor pounced on the security keypad and tapped in the code Neil had drilled into him.

"I'm off," said Aaron from behind him. "If you survive, I'll see you later. You still have to fulfill your contract with Gobi, after all." Aaron's grin turned Connor's stomach.

"My contract?" he said.

"Don't worry about it, kid," said Aaron. "I'm sure Phillips will get you out of it. Or he'll try, anyway." A distant rhythmic thump had Aaron cocking his head, and then he was gone.

Chapter Twenty-Nine

Log: Aaron's settlement, Richard A. Phillips, 29 May
20—

The doors to Aaron's nerve centre, as he calls it, have
been unlocked, but they are barricaded from within.
A helicopter landed on the roof not long after Chloe
ascended. Unfortunately, the ladder she used is completely destroyed and there seem to be no alternative
access points.

We *will* penetrate the nerve centre. We *will* get Chloe
and Connor to safety.

C hloe and the helicopter pilot stared at each other. She had
dashed off the helipad as the helicopter landed, but the rotor
still turned overhead. The access door swung open, and Aaron himself
stepped lightly through to the roof. He did a double-take when he
caught sight of Chloe and laughed out loud.

"Look at you, Chloe! You've always been resourceful," he called over the thump of the rotor. "Though maybe not resourceful enough. I hear Gobi got you."

"Where's Connor?" Chloe snapped.

"He was safe when I left him," said Aaron and gestured toward the access door. "Downstairs. But do you really want that, Chloe?"

"Want what?" Why was she letting herself be sucked into this conversation?

"To be crammed back into the 'mom' box? There's space in the helicopter for you, you know. I'm sure LunaCorp could find something interesting and groundbreaking for you to work on. They could probably get you out of that shitty Gobi contract, too."

Get her out of her contract? Maybe give her the resources to work on a real water purification device? No. Not *give*. The corporations didn't *give* anything. Chloe shook her head.

"I'm not going to be crammed anywhere. There's interesting and groundbreaking work to be done right here, work I don't have to abandon my family to do. You were too fixated on your own advancement to see it, but I'm not," Chloe shouted. "*I* care about someone other than myself."

Aaron shrugged. "Okay, if you're sure." He climbed into the helicopter and waved.

Chloe lunged for the access door. The helicopter was already spinning up as she wrenched it open and leaped down the stairs.

She burst through the doors at the bottom and elbowed her way past the big men standing behind it and scanned the room for Connor. He hunched in the doorway to what looked like an office, hands jammed in his pockets. Chloe had him squeezed tight in her arms without knowing how she made it across the room. He buried his face in her shoulder, despite being *taller* than her now, and his shoulders shook.

Chloe welled up. "I missed you," she said. "I'm so glad you're okay." She wiped her own tears and then brushed Connor's off his cheeks, too. None of it even began to express how she felt, but she let the platitudes fall from her lips and hoped Connor understood what she was trying to tell him.

Connor pulled back and stared at something over her shoulder. The security guys. Chloe kept her arm wrapped tightly around Connor as she turned.

"Aaron's gone," she said. She gestured to the barricaded doors. "You might as well open up. We're all on the same side now."

None of them made any move to obey.

"Connor, can you go into Aaron's office and find the corporate contracts on these guys?" she said.

Connor didn't move —he must know something Chloe didn't—but the security guys looked startled, angry, suspicious . . . She'd gotten to them.

"Corporate contracts?" said one.

"Yup," said Chloe. "Aaron signed away your lives in return for resources from the corporations. Neil told me himself." Just a white lie. "If you don't believe me, ask him. He's right outside."

"Neil is a traitor."

"Aaron was the traitor," said Connor. "He said he had a contract for me. I'm thirteen."

Chloe squeezed him into her side.

"You can talk about contracts all day long, prove it."

"Think about it," said Chloe. "What kind of despot would do that? What kind would feed their own people contaminated food? Get a bunch of thugs to keep the populace in line." *Oops.* She'd just called them thugs, and they'd definitely caught that. *Okay, new tactic.* "You all knew he was taking the kids away today, right? Were none of you prepared to stand up to him?"

"Are we really going to stand here and let her insult us?"

"I sure as hell won't."

Chloe's ears rang as a low pop echoed in the small space, and she stumbled back against the wall.

"Shit," Connor mumbled and slapped a hand to her shoulder, which blossomed in pain. "Come on," he said, and dragged her back into Aaron's office. He was right. Far too many guns and knives suddenly flashed out there in the open space. Connor slammed the office door and locked it. Of course Aaron had a deadbolt on his office. "Sit," said Connor, and she sat in Aaron' chair. "Put your hand here." The spot on her shoulder was warm and wet and gross. Why did she have to have to her hand there? Connor rummaged in a white box, and his hands shook as he bandaged her arm.

"I was shot wasn't I?" said Chloe, her own voice a million miles away.

"Yup," said Connor.

"And you're fixing me up," said Chloe and giggled.

"Neil taught me first aid. There are first aid kits every two feet in this place. He took it really seriously."

"The guys out there?" said Chloe, her head clearing a little now that she couldn't see the blood flowing from her wound.

"I locked the door, but . . ." he said and shrugged.

"They want proof," said Chloe. "Do you think that'll make a difference?"

"They're just people," said Connor. "Most of them didn't want to be on Aaron's crew in the first place." Talking to Connor like an adult was surreal, but he really seemed to know his stuff, and they needed to work together to get out of this before anyone else got shot.

"Okay, where do we find the contracts?" said Chloe. She glanced around the barren office: just a computer on a desk plus a couple of chairs.

"Aaron doesn't have a filing cabinet or anything," said Connor. "Just a computer."

Chloe went for her laptop bag, but it wasn't there. Damn. She'd taken it off to climb onto the roof. Maybe with her laptop, she could get into electronic contract files, but without it, what could she do? Guessing Aaron's password would potentially take years, maybe decades.

"Shit, my walkie-talkie was in the damn laptop bag," said Chloe, pawing at her belt where she'd been sure it hung.

"Like this thing?" said Connor and held out a walkie-talkie.

"Aaron gave it to you?" said Chloe. "Okay, let's see if we can get some remote tech support going."

Chloe radioed Xander and let him know the problem.

"You've been shot?" Xander ground out. "We're breaking down the doors."

"No!" said Chloe. "I can win these guys over. I know my track record is spotty, but I can do it. Just get me those contracts."

She swivelled in her chair and peered through the blinds at Portia, Richard, Brianna, and Dorothy, all huddled together trying to figure out her laptop. She gave them her password and waited for the machine to boot up.

Neil held the walkie-talkie and he watched the big office window. "Connor, sounds like you've got her stable," said Neil. "Good work."

Connor beamed.

Once she got confirmation that her laptop was running, Chloe paused. Her head was fuzzy, true, but even so. Her laptop wasn't connected to any kind of network, nor could they hook it into Aaron's computer directly without smashing the window and passing it in to her.

Chloe blew out a breath. This was never going to work. She opened a guest profile on Aaron's computer. Maybe she could somehow get in on her own?

Chloe jumped as a bang sounded on the door. Connor hopped to his feet, and dragged a heavy chair across to reinforce it.

"I got it," he said.

They didn't have time for this. They didn't have time for anything. The guest profile was a dead end. Nothing was signed in, nothing was connected. It might as well be her own laptop, but without all her useful programs.

The walkie-talkie crackled. "Hey, Chloe," said a new voice.

"Portia, right?" said Chloe.

"That's me. I have Aaron's phone. Is that useful at all?"

"Network access?"

"How the hell should I know if—"

They established that Portia could access copies of at least some contracts stored on the network. Lucky for them, Aaron was not a cyber-security buff. Neil's voice in the background grumbled about being a nurse, not a hacker. Connor dragged the other chair over to block the door as the thumping continued. Chloe connected her guest profile to the network using the passkey Portia read off for her and created a shared folder they could both access.

"Okay, just copy a few files over to the shared folder I made. It's called bring-Aaron-down," said Chloe, her heart pounding. Damn, this might actually work.

"Neil, whose contracts should I get?" said Portia.

A splintering sounded from the door, and Chloe rubbed her sweaty palms on her jeans and grimaced at the bloody streak left behind. *Come on!* Files popped into existence in the folder on Aaron's computer. She opened it and yelled over the cracks from the door.

"I have a contract for Gary Firth! For five years, in exchange for dividers for the office."

Another two files had downloaded, and Chloe opened those and read them out as well: Harold Munsen, five years, for a new phone; Mohammad Al-Habir, five years, a designer suit. The thumping had stopped.

"Show us the contracts."

She spun the monitor around as Aaron's crew filed into the little office. They silently perused the contracts, which kept popping into existence in the shared folder. Chloe leaned back in the chair and closed her eyes. Her arm throbbed, and she just wanted to pass out.

Two security guys went to clear the doors and nobody stopped them. Soon, the nerve centre filled with chattering people.

She barely heard Isabelle take over the intercom and start making a speech that echoed through the building and across the entire settlement. Someone must have freed her.

"Who's that?" said Connor.

Chloe opened her eyes. Xander strode towards them, Neil close behind. Neil didn't say anything, just brought a big medical bag into Aaron's office and plunked it on the floor beside Chloe.

"This is Richard," said Chloe. "Richard, this is Connor."

"You can call me Xander. Chloe has spoken about you at great length."

"I heard about you too," said Connor. "You kidnapped Chloe."

Chloe's and Xander's eyes met, and Chloe shook her head. Xander would have to work hard to win her family over, but he'd made the choice to kidnap her, and now he'd have to deal with the fallout. Neil finished up dressing Chloe's wound, gave Chloe some painkillers, and cleared her to leave, as long as Xander came with her. Obviously, he knew he wasn't going to stop her going home to her kids.

"It's not too far, but if you feel faint, let Richard catch you," said Neil sternly.

"Are you okay with Xander coming with us to find the rest of the family?" said Chloe to Connor.

He narrowed his eyes but nodded. "I bet they're at home," he said.

Chloe tensed but made herself relax before Connor took notice. He'd called their place here at the settlement *home* so casually. They'd been here less than a month, and already they'd settled in?

"Lead the way," said Chloe.

***

The little neighbourhood Connor led them to looked . . . normal. A series of row houses, complete with gardens and flanked by streetlights, seemed well maintained under the last vestiges of snow that hadn't quite melted yet.

The porch light welcomed Chloe to the house Connor indicated. Chloe took a deep breath and climbed the front steps slowly. Facing Monty and Sheila would not be pleasant, but this was what she'd been fighting for for weeks. She knocked on the door.

Footsteps padded inside, and then the door was flung wide. Vishesh smiled at her, then frowned as he took in her arm and bloody jeans. He glanced behind her to where Connor and Xander stood, awkwardly silent.

"Come in," said Vishesh.

Terry and Flo snuggled on either side of Sheila on the couch. She looked up from the book she was reading them when Chloe came through the doorway. The kids looked up too, and after a moment of frozen disbelief, they tumbled off the couch and scrambled towards her.

Chloe crouched down and let them bowl her over. They both chattered at once, totally unintelligible, but she got the gist that they were happy to see her. She hugged them one at a time, savouring the feel of their little arms holding her tight. Over Flora's shoulder, Sheila's face was impassive. Where was Monty? No sense in ruining the moment by asking about him. If he was around, she would deal with him.

Connor and Xander took the little ones out to the backyard so that the family adults could have a few minutes to catch up. Chloe, Sheila, and Vishesh retreated to the kitchen, and Vishesh busied himself making tea for them all.

"Connor's grown up so fast," said Chloe.

"Too fast," said Sheila, and Vishesh nodded.

Vishesh plunked a mug of his herbal tea in front of each of them and took a seat as well. Chloe had never considered herself a big fan of the stuff, but having been without it for weeks, it smelled like home. The tension gradually left her shoulders as she breathed in the steam, even in this strange house.

"Too fast," Chloe repeated. She bit back an apology. Not everything that had happened had been her fault. "Monty?" she said instead.

"Gone," said Vishesh.

"And if he comes back?" said Chloe and glanced at Sheila.

"He won't," she said, her face stony.

Chloe hesitated. She and Sheila had never been close, exactly, but maybe they could be now? "Are you okay?" she said.

"I will be," said Sheila, and Chloe nodded. The feeling was familiar to her as well. "Are *you* okay?" Sheila nodded to her arm.

"Yeah, Neil already looked at it for me," said Chloe. "You—both—should know that I'm not exactly free."

"Free how?" said Sheila.

"I signed a contract with Gobi," said Chloe. "I had to, to get us here." She shrugged, as if it were no big deal.

"Aaron implied that he'd signed agreements for several people here in the settlement as well," said Vishesh.

"Yeah, I know. Is that . . . legal?" said Chloe.

"He seemed to think it was," said Vishesh. "Even if not, challenging it will be a pain."

"We'll do what we need to do," said Chloe. "The family is staying together from now on."

"Where?" said Sheila.

Chloe watched Connor chase the kids around the backyard and then pretend to get dizzy and fall down, at which point they mobbed him and pounced.

"We can try to make a life here," said Chloe. "Seems like you have a stable power grid and some kind of food supply?"

Vishesh heaved a sigh. "It won't be a smooth transition. The way Aaron had things set up . . . We can't continue that way."

"I have no love for Isabelle in any way shape or form, but I do trust her to do right by the people here," said Chloe.

"There are other kids around here too, if they decide to stay," said Sheila. "They could all use a real school." She had a far-off look in her eye. She'd been a teacher once upon a time. With Monty out of the picture, maybe it was time for her to do something for herself.

"I'm sure they'd all love that," said Chloe.

***

Vishesh had been taken aback by the rush of relief that had surged through his body when Chloe suggested they stay in the settlement. It would be a lot of work to get things sorted out, but they had lots of good folks, and they would get there.

He sat by himself in the blessed silence on the edge of the porch and tried to catch his breath from the suddenly energized kids. Neil came around the corner of their street, and Vishesh waved at him and clambered to his feet.

"How's Chloe?" said Neil.

"She's good. Asleep, I think," said Vishesh.

"Might as well let her sleep. It's all up to her body at this point anyway," said Neil. "I'll come by tomorrow to clean her shoulder and change the dressing. Want to go to the pub?" said Neil.

"Are you asking me out?" said Vishesh, not even trying to hide his grin.

"Definitely," said Neil. "Need to get your coat?"

"Nope, I'm good. If I go in the house, I'll be bombarded with questions I have no intention of answering. Sheila can be nosy as hell," said Vishesh.

"She's talking to you again?" Neil took his hand. "I'm pretty sure she already knows we're an item," he said.

They strolled out of the neighbourhood toward the centre of the settlement.

"So where are we on that feelings stuff?" said Neil.

The question was expected, but it still gave Vishesh pause. He hadn't stopped to think about feelings in days. He was over Chloe. It had snuck up on him, but seeing her with Richard had given him nothing but honest joy.

"Much less complicated than the last time you asked me," said Vishesh.

"That's a step in the right direction," said Neil.

"We have a lot of work ahead of us to make this place livable," said Vishesh.

"I was thinking we could do it together," said Neil. "The work, I mean."

At the thought of the two of them planning and building a community together, a bubble of excitement swelled in Vishesh's chest. Just one more thing nagged at him.

"What about the kids?" said Vishesh.

"What about them?"

"They're practically my own kids. I'm not going to leave them," said Vishesh.

Neil stopped and gripped his shoulders. He looked Vishesh in the face seriously. "I would never ask you to leave your children, Vishesh. I have some idea what they mean to you, and I would never come between you and your family."

For once, Vishesh didn't try to tamp down the joy that came bubbling up through his middle, and the peace that flowed through his body, though unfamiliar, was nonetheless welcome.

***

Portia wandered through the apartment she and Aaron had shared. She couldn't—wouldn't—stay here, so she had two duffle bags packed with her things by the door. They'd give away the rest of Aaron's stuff. She jumped when her phone rang. Not exactly her phone. The phone she'd appropriated from Aaron. She swiped to pick up.

"Hello?" she said.

"Hey, baby," said Aaron. "Glad to hear you found my phone."

"Finders keepers," said Portia. "How did you call that chopper without it?"

Aaron just laughed. "I have a new one anyway, so call it a gift."

"I'll call it mine," said Portia. No credit to him for giving her something she'd very rightfully stolen for herself.

"Whatever you want to tell yourself, baby," said Aaron. "Just calling to check up on you. I'll be sending someone to pick you up. I think you'll like it here. It's nicer than that dump of a settlement." Did he really think she would just go with him? That she would even want to?

"Yeah, in your dreams, Aaron," she said.

"What happened to *Sir*?" he growled.

In spite of herself, Portia's pulse pounded in her ears. What if she needed this in her life? She'd never had . . . conventional tastes in the bedroom. What if being with Aaron, and hating herself for it, was the only way she could get off? He seemed to read her mind.

"It's cute how you're trying to resist me," said Aaron. "We both know you can't. The longer you hold out, the worse your punishment will be. Not that I'm complaining, mind you."

Fuck. Her whole body flash-boiled with need. *No.* No, it wasn't worth it. She mentally punched the part of her that wanted to give in to him and shoved it in a box. This was her chance to be free, and she was going to grab it with both hands.

"Goodbye, Aaron," said Portia. "If you send someone for me, I can't guarantee their safety. Folks around here don't like the corporations much." She hung up on him and blocked the number.

She stuffed the phone in her purse with a shaking hand and hefted her bags onto her back, then walked out the door without a backward glance.

***

Thanks so much for reading *Dread Spring*! If you liked it, please leave a review on your platform of choice. Even a line or two is very helpful for other readers!

If you want to be the first to hear about new releases, consider joining my newsletter at join.elizabethshearly.ca.

Dear Lovely Reader

When I came up with the idea for Dread Spring, I wanted to take a crack at a post-apocalyptic kidnapping romance where the kidnapping felt earned. I'll leave it up to you whether or not I succeeded, but from this seed (that was supposed to be a short novel or novella) grew *Dread Spring*, my longest published work so far!

On my blog, I have a post complete with street views that will take you through all the locations mentioned in the book, but the one that inspired me the most is on Highway 7, which runs between Ottawa and Toronto in Ontario. An abandoned farmhouse, windows gone, weeds and trees growing out of it, is splashed with brightly coloured spray paint. That farmhouse inspired me to set *Dread Spring* in the Ottawa Valley instead of in a fictional world, which is my usual go-to.

I planned out Chloe and Richard's romance, and I knew Vishesh was going to be a secondary protagonist (I had no idea he was going to get a love interest until Neil popped into Aaron's office and Vishesh swooned). But my biggest surprise by far was Portia. She was a side character at most, someone to exist in Aaron's settlement, make it feel lived in, and be under his thrall, but when she popped onto the page and dove right into a totally toxic relationship with Aaron that brought out a completely different side of his character, she fought her way into a secondary character role. (Don't tell anyone, but when I wrote Portia and Aaron's first steamy scene together, I told myself

I was just writing it to get a handle on their relationship and I could totally cut it out of the finished manuscript. Turns out, my muse already knew it was important to the story.)

Over in the real world, when I was writing *Dread Spring*, I had just published *Endless Sea of Stars* to Amazon and confronted their terms of service for the first time. I think I was working through a lot of feelings about big corporations who have a stranglehold on the market, leaving us normal folks to accept or fend for ourselves; there's no negotiation, no wiggle room. The terms are set and you can either take them or leave them. Considering that Amazon is by far the largest bookstore in the world, opting out of their terms has real consequences for anyone who wants to get their work out there, just as opting out of using corporation infrastructure has real consequences in the Radioactive Rain universe. (I don't like the "my book is my child" parallel, but I think my muse ran with it on this one. While I was writing *Dread Spring*, *Endless Sea* was effectively held hostage in KU like Chloe's family.)

And, of course, in 2022, my family was emerging from our COVID bubble. Just as Chloe realizes her family can no longer survive isolated on their little farm, I was realizing that I couldn't keep hiding from COVID. It was dangerous out there beyond our safe walls, but staying inside wasn't going to be an option forever.

If *Dread Spring* means something to you, as it does to me, that's all I can hope for as a writer. I'm so glad we could share these pages together. <3

Looking forward to our next adventure,

E. F. Shearly

Elizabeth F. Shearly

Land Acknowledgement

I set *Dread Spring* where I live: on the unceded land of the Omàmìwininìwag (Algonquin), Anishinabewaki ◁σ∫ὰ∨·◁ᑭ, and Kanien'kehá:ka (Mohawk).

I am a settler on this land. I grew up in Ottawa, and spent my childhood roaming the Gatineau Hills, hiking, and swimming. The closest I ever got to learning about the Indigenous peoples who were driven from this area was a historical project that made Indigenous peoples seem like an artifact, disconnected from the present. That could not be further from the truth.

This is unceded land, which means that the land rights of the Algonquin people were never signed away. The Crawford Purchase covers most of the land that appears in the book, but there were no Algonquin signatories to that agreement. For centuries, the Algonquin have been petitioning the government to assert their rights, so far unsuccessfully.

I am a settler on this land. My ancestor, Philomen Wright, settled here in 1800 and began to destroy the local ecosystems to make a fortune in the lumber trade, a trade that quickly took over and destroyed the wildlife of the Ottawa Valley. You'll recognize the name "Wright" from the Alonzo-Wright Bridge, featured in *Dread Spring*, as Alonzo was Philomen's grandson; the original colonizers' legacy continues to be unjustly honoured and upheld even now as an ongoing act of colonization. No rights agreement was signed, either at that time or at any point since, between any of the settlers or their governments and the Algonquin people. Though members of the Algonquin Nation at the time attempted to warn the government about the absolute decimation of the environment and disappearance of the local wildlife due to the lumber industry, the government ignored them.

In 1853, the Algonquin inhabitants were forcibly removed to Kitigan Zibi, so that settlers could colonize the fertile lands of the Ottawa Valley. The reserve lies in an area in the Gatineau Hills that would have historically been an occasional hunting ground for the Algonquin, not a permanent home; as stated in *Dread Spring*, the arable land up there is limited. For a century, Kitigan Zibi inhabitants were forbidden by the colonial government from hunting, cutting wood, and voting, and the school on the reserve was a federally run day-school. In the past few decades, the members of the Algonquin First Nation who live at Kitigan Zibi have transformed the reserve into a vibrant community, having gained hard-won control over their own health, education, and police services after decades of effort.

Throughout *Dread Spring*, I used the colonial place names for the Kichesippi and Tenagatino Zibi (now called the Ottawa and Gatineau rivers). During a fruitless search for the Algonquin name for Farmer's Rapids, all I found was an itemized list of everything the titular Farmer brought with him from England (apparently that knowledge is deemed valuable through the lens of colonization).

I would encourage anyone who enjoyed *Dread Spring* to read books by Indigenous authors as well! In the genre of post-apocalyptic science fiction and from my area (Ontario), I can recommend a few to get you started.

Moon of the Crusted Snow by Waubgeshig Rice. The book takes place as the apocalypse is unfolding. We're in agreement that taking care of little kids during the apocalypse wouldn't be much different than taking care of them now.

Take Us To Your Chief and Other Stories by Drew Hayden Taylor, particularly *A Culturally Inappropriate Armageddon*, the most apocalyptic of the stories. The collection is so wide-ranging, it somehow covered all of sci fi, thoughtfully and playfully.

The Marrow Thieves by Cherie Dimaline. This one is set a little further out from the apocalyptic event, and I found it to be a little darker in tone. The ensemble cast has a delightful range of distinct characters and personalities, set against a stark dystopian world.

To Break A Dragon Bond

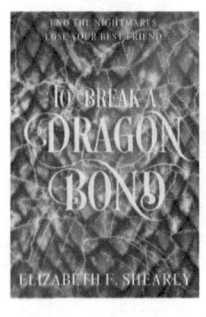

Kraisa ignores the other passengers staring at her as she steps onto the rickety ferry. They think what everyone will think: that her dragon is dead. But Kalanthi is alive. Kraisa brushes her hand over the emerald scales at her hairline, in stark relief against her bright red mop of hair. The image of a staring corpse blazes into her mind. She can't shut it out so near the Roost, so near Kal. The only way to make the gruesome thoughts stop is to get far, far away from her dragon.

The Roost disappears into the distance, dragons swooping into their dens, riders clinging to their necks. She'll never ride Kalanthi again. She'll never see Kalanthi again. If only she'd been assigned to another task, any other task. But she'd been thrilled with her first assignment. How could she have known that it would end like this?

To Break a Dragon Bond is an epic fantasy dragonrider novelette. It's part of the *Second Acts of Weary Warrior Women* collection.

Also By Elizabeth F. Shearly

Endless Sea Of Stars
Dread Spring
Keep the Good Parts

Second Acts of Weary Warrior Women

The Swordswoman and the Vampire
To Break A Dragon Bond
A Pentagram Of Candles and Spectres
Her Castle, Her Howl, Her Pack
The King's Pixie Seer

About The Author

Elizabeth F. Shearly writes science fiction and fantasy tales, from flash fiction to novels and everything in between. She holds a B.Sc. in physics, and you'll find plenty of science in her science fiction, though the fiction always takes precedence. No matter what she writes about—spaceships or magic, walking cities or medieval castles—romance always finds a way to blossom, whether as the main plot or as a background story.

When she's not watching characters play-act in her head, you can find her relaxing on the couch with her two cats, playing a video game or knitting a sweater.

instagram.com/stitchnscribble/

bookbub.com/authors/elizabeth-f-shearly

facebook.com/ElizabethFShearly/

goodreads.com/elizabethfshearly